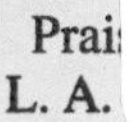

Prai
L. A.

The Crimson Moon series

BITE THE BULLET

"The second book of Banks's electrifying werewolf saga [is] part special ops thriller, part supernatural adventure...Utilizing her storytelling flair, Banks imbues her characters with both nobility and kick-ass attitude. It doesn't get much better than this!"

—*Romantic Times BOOKreviews* (4½ stars)

"Tension, lots of action, and a current of sensuality...a novel that will provide hours of electric entertainment."

—Singletitles.com

"Filled with action, this fast-moving read is as powerful as the first, and will keep fans coming back for more."

—*Darque Reviews*

BAD BLOOD

"Super-talented Banks launches the complex and darkly thrilling new Crimson Moon series, which bursts with treachery and supernatural chills. The plot intricacies are carefully woven throughout, but Banks piles on the danger, making this one exciting thrill ride!"

—*Romantic Times BOOKreviews* (4½ stars)

"Banks takes on werewolves and makes them her own...A blast to read."

—Kelley Armstrong

"Shadowy, sexy, intense."

—Cheyenne McCray

MORE...

"An action-packed thrill ride!"
—#1 *New York Times* bestselling author Sherrilyn Kenyon

The Vampire Huntress Legend™ series

THE CURSED

"A wild amalgam of Christianity, vampire lore, world myth, functional morality, street philosophy, and hot sex…fans couldn't ask for more." —*Publishers Weekly*

THE WICKED

"A complex world of Good vs. Evil…The story is so compelling, the whole series must be read."
—*Birmingham Times*

THE FORSAKEN

"Readers already enthralled with this sizzling series can look forward to major plot payoffs." —*Publishers Weekly*

"In the seventh book in her incredibly successful series… Banks presents interesting myths—both biblical and mythological…with prose that's difficult to match—and most certainly just as difficult to put down."
—*Romantic Times BOOKreviews* (4½ stars)

THE DAMNED

"All hell breaks loose—literally—in the complex sixth installment….stunning." —*Publishers Weekly*

"In [*The Damned*], relationships are defined, while a dark energy threatens to destroy the entire squad. Banks's method of bringing Damali and Carlos back together is done with utmost sincerity and integrity. They have a love that can weather any storm, even when dire circumstances seem utterly overwhelming. Fans of this series will love *The Damned* and, no doubt, will eagerly await the next book." —*Romantic Times BOOKreviews*

FORBIDDEN

"Passion, mythology, war and love that lasts till the grave—and beyond....fans should relish this new chapter in a promising series." —*Publishers Weekly*

"Superior vampire fiction." —*Booklist*

THE BITTEN

"Seductive...mixing religion with erotic horror dosed with a funky African-American beat, Banks blithely piles on layer after layer of densely detailed plot...will delight established fans. Banks creates smokin' sex scenes that easily outvamp Laurell K. Hamilton's." —*Publishers Weekly*

"The stakes have never been higher, and the excitement and tension are palpable in this installment of Banks's complex, sexy series." —*Booklist*

"Duties, pain, responsibilities—what this duo does in the name of love is amazing." —*Romantic Times BOOKreviews*

THE HUNTED

"A terrifying roller-coaster ride of a book."

—Charlaine Harris

"Hip, fresh, and fantastic."

—Sherrilyn Kenyon, *New York Times* bestselling author of *Dark Side of the Moon*

THE AWAKENING

"An intriguing portrait of vampiric society, reminiscent of Anne Rice and Laurell K. Hamilton." —*Library Journal*

"Again, Banks brilliantly combines spirituality, vampires, and demons (and hip hop music) into a fast-paced tale that is sure to leave fans of her first novel, *Minion*, panting for more, but nothing seems quite as hot as the steamy, often tense relationship between Damali and Carlos...a newcomer to the vampire genre...[Banks] lends a fresh and contemporary voice." —*Columbus Dispatch*

MINION

"[*Minion*] literally rocks the reader into the action-packed underworld power struggle between vampire rivals with a little demon juice thrown in. Nothing less than the future state of the universe lies in the balance...Cutting-edge wit and plenty of urban heat flies from the pages of this quick read." —*Philadelphia Sunday Sun*

"[A] tough, sexy new vampire huntress challenges the dominance of Anita Blake and Buffy...Damali is an appealing heroine, the concept is intriguing, and the series promising." —Amazon.com

St. Martin's Paperbacks Titles by

L.A. BANKS

The Crimson Moon Novels

Cursed to Death
Undead on Arrival
Bite the Bullet
Bad Blood

The Vampire Huntress Legend™ Novels

The Thirteenth
The Shadows
The Darkness
The Cursed
The Wicked
The Forsaken
The Damned
The Forbidden
The Bitten
The Hunted
The Awakening
Minion

Anthologies

Stroke of Midnight
Love at First Bite

Cursed To Death

A Crimson Moon Novel

L. A. BANKS

This is a work of fiction. All of the characters, organizations, and events portrayed in this novel are either products of the author's imagination or are used fictitiously.

CURSED TO DEATH

For information address St. Martin's Press, 175 Fifth Avenue, New York, NY 10010.

ISBN: 978-0-312-94299-1

Printed in the United States of America

St. Martin's Paperbacks edition / October 2009

St. Martin's Paperbacks are published by St. Martin's Press, 175 Fifth Avenue, New York, NY 10010.

10 9 8 7 6 5 4 3 2 1

PROLOGUE

New Orleans... French Quarter

Sir Rodney took a sip of Fae ale, feeling the buzz of the lager hit his bloodstream. The thick malt caused a pleasant hum that finally began to lift his spirits. Under the circumstances, it was good to see Ethan McGregor's establishment filled with happy patrons. The Fair Lady was a good place for his constituents to see their king out and about enjoying life as though he hadn't a care in the world . . . as though nothing was amiss.

It was important to keep up appearances even as darkness crept upon them. In the three hundred years he'd ruled, he'd never seen anything as devastating. Fae magick was under attack and not even his top advisors could stop it. Even his most trusted investigator had come up empty-handed. But it had to be dealt with and eradicated before the Midsummer Night's Ball a few evenings hence. It had to be or everything would fall to ruin.

His personal bodyguard, MacDougall, inclined his head closer, pulling him from his thoughts.

"Milord," the bodyguard murmured in a discreet tone. "The young lady is trying to get your attention."

"Indeed," Sir Rodney said quietly as he made eye contact with the gorgeous redhead across the room. Clearly she was performing tonight; her low-cut semi-sheer red costume told him that. He watched her saunter over, her large breasts swaying with each step. Despite her delicate bone structure, her body was lush in all the right places. Red stilettos made her long legs seem to go on forever and a flicker of flame haunted her pretty green eyes. Something settled into place within him. This was what he needed. To lose himself, to completely drown himself in the fire and passion of a lovely Phoenix.

"Desidera," he said with a gallant smile as he stood when she arrived at his table. Rich, dark hair spilled over his broad shoulders as he leaned forward to kiss her gently at the corner of her mouth.

He frowned and MacDougall gave him a sidelong glance. Something was wrong.

"Sir Rodney," she said calmly, but he could hear the agitation beneath it, "please sit down or you'll cause a stir."

If anyone was causing a stir it was she, but he could see that Desidera was in no mood to tease.

"Desi, what—"

She looked him right in the eye and said, "Foul magick is afoot, is it not?"

Sir Rodney froze and his bodyguard went on full alert. He felt his best man step forward, but Sir Rodney made a slight gesture with his hand telling his guard to stand down.

"What are you talking about?" he said, his face giving nothing away.

"Please, Your Highness," she said softly and she touched his arm gently. "Sit." Her eyes held fear; this was no game.

This time he slowly complied, folding his athletic build back into his chair. She slid into the seat opposite him.

Desidera glanced nervously around the crowded room before leaning forward and speaking to him in a private murmur. "Rodney, I must talk to you in secret tonight. It is of the utmost importance."

"Tell me now," he said, his voice soft but dangerous.

She shook her head. "Too many eyes and too many

ears . . . What I have to say is crucial, but it cannot be done here out in the open."

His gaze was hard as he stared at her. "Tell me where and when I can meet you, then."

"At my apartment," she said.

"No, if it is a matter of such urgency," Sir Rodney said, "then I will have one of my guards relay a message to Ethan McGregor that I needed to *meet* with you. It will be a king's request for his—"

"No, Rodney, please. I have to dance tonight. Everything has to appear as it always has been. But bring a guard with you when you come . . . I don't know if I've been discovered, and if anything happens to you—"

He reached out and took her hand, suddenly seeing how distressed she was. "I'll meet you at the end of your shift and we will escort you home. You can tell me then." He squeezed her fingers. "It will be fine."

Desidera nodded as two large tears rose in her glittering green eyes before she blinked them away. She stood with great flourish, gathering the brightly colored plumes of her dancing costume about her. She leaned down, placing a hand on his shoulder, and brought her lips close to his ear. It looked like an intimate exchange between lovers. "I have hidden it in the wine cellar," she murmured. "I'll collect it then will meet you in the dressing room." She squeezed his shoulder, then leaned back and smiled at him. "And I appreciate the escort."

Sir Rodney looked up at her, his expression serious. "Desi, you're in danger. I can take you back to the Sidhe immediately. Know that you have amnesty at the castle. As a matter of fact, tell me why I shouldn't do it right now?"

She gave him her first true smile. "Relax, Your Highness. I'll be fine on stage. I already feel better that you're here."

"You trust me?"

"Without fail," she said, then leaned down again and this time kissed him for real. It was a passionate kiss, just like the woman, but over all too quickly.

Sir Rodney licked his lips. He could taste her fear. "Desi—"

"Later," she said, caressing his cheek. Then she turned with a flourish and walked away.

Sir Rodney watched her go. He clenched his fist on the table before forcing his hand to relax. Only his bodyguard noticed the slight trembling in his fingers.

CHAPTER 1

Sasha stooped down and kept her fingers just above the ashes at her feet. Still warm. The acrid scent of burned Phoenix flesh stung her nose as she surveyed the charred remains.

This was so not how she wanted to return to New Orleans, but she'd do anything to help Sir Rodney the way he'd helped their Wolf Clans. And as tragic as it was, what had happened in Ethan's wine cellar gave her a cover for the nervous energy she'd been feeling ever since the invitation came. Shogun would also be here for the annual Midsummer Night's Ball, and her jumpiness wasn't appreciated by Hunter. It had taken everything within her to hide her excitement, as well as the guilt that went along with it. However, this new situation made all that go away.

Without her having to evade his razor senses, Hunter now assumed her previous nervousness had to do with somehow picking up on what lay at her feet. Which sucked, on a variety of levels.

A twinge of guilt twisted in her side as Sasha looked up at Ethan McGregor. "Who found the body?"

"Sir Rodney and his best man," Ethan McGregor said quietly.

"We're going to need to talk to them more thoroughly," Hunter said in a low rumble. "Where is Sir Rodney?"

"In my office . . . after he witnessed this, we necessarily removed our monarch from this . . . this awful sight. He is up there with his bodyguard."

Sasha gave Hunter a glance. "Did she say anything about why she was down here? Is there anyone you know of who might have wanted to hurt her?"

The establishment owner shook his head and let out a weary sigh. "I don't know why she came down here, but I do know that she wouldn't hurt a fly, and everyone loved Desi. She was well liked by everyone here at The Fair Lady. Everyone. Desi had been working for me for over ten years . . . I've never seen anyone who got on so well with others. That was Desi. She and Penelope, my other Phoenix dancer, came to town together and are from the same rookery. They were like sisters. I don't even know how to begin to tell Penelope."

Sasha listened as she stared at the body, going over each detail of the intact ash, and then an eerie symbol on the victim's body drew her attention. Was it a tattoo or some other strange marking on Desidera's belly that, for some reason, hadn't burned?

Moving carefully so as not to disturb the ashes, Sasha pulled out a small notepad from her jeans' back pocket and extracted the small pen that had been wedged in the spiral at the top of it. She sketched the symbol quickly and then placed her hand inches above the symbol, trying to feel any vibrations that might have been coming off of it. But just as suddenly as she'd reached out to cover it, the symbol collapsed in on itself, making her jerk back her palm.

"Where's Penelope?" Sasha said, glancing up at Ethan.

"Every other night she works at the teahouse. It closed at ten."

"So she's probably home in bed," Sasha said, now glancing at Hunter. She returned her gaze to Ethan. "So nobody called her yet to tell her what happened?"

"No. I wanted to wait until you had a chance to . . ." Ethan motioned to where Desidera's body lay on the floor and then brought his fist to his mouth for a moment. "I wanted to see if there was anything I could tell Penelope that would make sense of this."

"You're sure no one else went by there or spoke to her? They were coworkers," Hunter said flatly, crossing his arms over his stone-cut chest. "You said Desidera was well liked, others would know Penelope would be—"

"No. We're the only ones, save the king and his best man, that know. We didn't want to start a panic . . . Rumors would fly, and if there is a killer in our midst, we need him to be comfortable, not go into hiding." Ethan said quickly, "I've been sworn by oath before the king not to divulge any of this to a soul . . . as it could hamper the investigation. But eventually it will leak out. I must tell Penelope, as well as the rest of the staff here, and Sir Rodney understands the need for this."

"All right," Sasha said. "I understand, but I'd like to talk to Penelope first thing in the morning, if not tonight."

"Of course," Ethan said, nodding.

Sasha let out a hard breath and stood, stretching her cramping legs and back. "Then was she dating anyone? Any current or ex-boyfriends?"

"No . . . not really," Ethan replied carefully. "She hadn't been dating anyone for some time . . . However, she and Sir Rodney sometimes got together."

Again, Sasha shared a glance with Hunter. That was the last thing she'd expected Ethan to tell her. But now it made sense why the Seelie monarch was so upset.

"Was it serious?" Sasha asked, pushing for details.

"Oh, no," Ethan said quickly, seeming more uncomfortable by the moment. "Desidera knew that she was one of many he cared for. She was very sophisticated about the whole thing, which is probably why Sir Rodney liked her so much."

"So they were hooking up tonight," Hunter said in a deadpan tone.

Ethan shrugged. "I would have to assume so." Ethan's

gaze held Sasha's for a moment and then went to Hunter's before seeking a far-off point in the small, dank cellar. "It is my understanding that they were to meet at her apartment after her show. That was all Sir Rodney said on the matter."

"Okay, then . . . like I said, we're gonna need a list of people she might have talked to—a friend, coworker, anyone she could have confided in." Sasha looked at Ethan, studying him hard and guessing that Desidera's boss, whom she worked with daily, would probably know more than the kingly lover who only visited her for trysts.

"Penelope would be the best start," Ethan said quickly, blotting the tears from his face. "Our Phoenixes are rare, and she and Penelope are from the same rookery, like I told you. If there was any girl talk or shared secrets, Penelope would have been her most likely confidante."

"Thanks, Ethan," Sasha said absently, returning her gaze to the ashes.

If she didn't catch Penelope at home, she was going to have to go hunt her down at the teahouse and *the last* place she ever wanted to revisit was the teahouse . . . the place where an indiscretion had happened that almost made two alpha wolves go to war over her. *Two brothers.* It didn't matter that meddling garden Fairies and outraged Pixies had been the culprits; the event was still a sore spot—one that neither she nor Hunter ever discussed. Damn, this was *so not* how she'd envisioned returning to New Orleans with Hunter for Sir Rodney's annual Fae Midsummer Night's Ball. In her mind's eye she'd envisioned having the time of her life for her twenty-fifth birthday, a milestone that Doc had assured the general would pass without incident.

She caught Hunter's expression with a sidelong glance, but said nothing. The muscle in his jaw pulsed a steady beat. He'd obviously come to the same conclusion about the possibility of having to go to the teahouse. Okay . . . so investigating at the tea house was going to be fun. Sasha let out a soft sigh.

"I trust that you understand the delicate nature of this

investigation," Ethan said, clasping his hands behind his back, his gaze sweeping between Sasha and Hunter. "I have spoken at length to Sir Rodney, as I am sure you will . . . and he'll tell you that this situation must be handled with the utmost discretion . . . News of this event, just before the ball, could cause undue panic, rumors . . . It is not a shallow matter of a social event coming before the death of a beautiful young woman—the death of anyone would be and is considered tragic, but . . ."

"But this has to be handled diplomatically," Hunter said, finishing Ethan's statement. "As clan leaders, we understand. Some things are not meant for public consumption until all the facts can be coherently presented."

Hunter gave Sasha the eye, which she immediately read as his unspoken reference to the teahouse incident.

"Precisely," Ethan said, oblivious to the couple's undercurrent, and then closed his eyes, releasing a long breath and turning away from the charred body at Sasha's feet. "Thank you."

Quiet surrounded them and in those few awkward moments, Sasha's thoughts strayed, wishing that just once there'd be no drama . . . that New Orleans would be a vacation destination, instead of a hotbed of paranormal intrigue. That was such an awesome fantasy. A grand fête, a sexy escort—Hunter—an enchanted village, her best friends . . . what was not to love? It would have been perfect. But Sir Rodney was a friend. A dear friend. And if something had happened to someone close to him, in Ethan's bar—another dear friend—then it was like somebody messing with her family.

And, yeah, she knew the brass would want to monitor her, so between her and Doc's fabrications and assurances that "going live" in a known paranormal zone was the best test that she wouldn't flip out and turn into a demon-infected werewolf, it had still taken every theatrical ploy she'd known to get them to allow her and her team to return to the Big Easy so soon. Now this?

"She was such a dearheart," Ethan said softly, walking away to catch his weight against the wall. "How could something like this happen in The Fair Lady?"

"We'll solve this," Sasha said, trying to offer some comfort. "You keep your head, man, all right."

Ethan nodded, but the gesture was unsure.

All of this had to be smoothed out and kept below the military radar, while they were probably doing everything in their power to track her.

"You're sure your human superiors will remain uninvolved?" Ethan asked, his question loaded with concern.

"Yeah," Sasha replied, holding his gaze for a moment. No one in the room, except her, had to deal with the human population; she was the only one straddling the fence by dealing with the brass and having a human team of paranormal investigators—which had remained a sore point between her and Hunter from the beginning. "I have it under control," she finally muttered, giving Hunter a quick, sharp glance.

Okay, she admitted it; to make everything work out she'd stretched the truth back at the base. Had to throw the brass a bone. Said there was still some suspicious activity in the area that she and her squad needed to do reconnaissance on. She'd told that whopper well before Sir Rodney had sent a self-destructing Fae missive that he needed help with a delicate job. So, maybe it was a good thing after all, or even a little precognition, that she'd told the brass back at the base that New Orleans was a way station for black market supernatural activities. That was no news flash.

But it had put her in the right place at the right time to be here just before the ball, and just before this tragedy. Maybe she and Hunter could get this problem addressed before her human crew or any of Hunter's men arrived. That was the hopeful thought.

Sasha rubbed the tension from her neck as she tried to glean clues from the site. Since war had already broken out on the streets in the paranormal community, she'd been able to convince her superior officers that it was advisable to keep a Paranormal Containment Unit peacekeeping presence here . . . just in case. Especially around Midsummer events. All that was true, just slightly exaggerated, so she thought.

Sheesh. Liar, liar pants on fire—now the BS she'd trumped up to get her and her team a little R&R had come to pass.

Sasha let out a quiet sigh heavily weighted with frustration. Who knew that Sir Rodney's invitation to an over-the-top Fae bash was going to turn out to really be a work detail, a possible murder investigation at that? Clarissa and the guys were gonna have a cow. Hunter was already snarling. For that matter, so was she. Not because of doing a favor for Sir Rodney, he was a doll, but because someone had dared hurt a friend of her friend. It was like going against the pack; whoever did this would pay. Both she and Hunter were so pissed, the hair was standing up on the backs of their necks. She could only hope that was why they were quietly sniping at each other. But right now, none of that mattered. She had to focus.

The only saving grace was the fact that the poor girl had torched in her Phoenix form rather than her human form—which only made it a little less horrible. However, had it been the other way around, Sasha was sure that she might not have been able to look at the remains with investigative dispassion.

"I don't understand," Ethan finally said, beginning to pace. It was clear that the quiet tension was closing in on him and he needed the chatter for comfort, even though she and Hunter needed the quiet to think in order to piece together sketchy clues.

Ethan balled his small chubby fists at his sides while walking to and fro. "She never came back from the flames. The poor girl . . . it was awful!" He heaved in a shuddering sob and pressed a fist to his plump mouth. "She was so pretty . . . a redheaded beauty, that she was. My best waitress, a fantastic showgirl, my good friend—I just don't understand."

For a moment, Sasha couldn't reply. Ethan was so upset that his Fae glamour was fading right before her. The tips of his ears were becoming more pointed and less human and his eyes had lost their warm brown hue, giving way to the multicolored Elfin irises she'd always found so fascinating. Even his frame was changing to the slighter Elf build, causing his pants and shirt to begin to sag.

"She was a lovely young woman, no one disliked her. Not even the Vampires found fault with her," Ethan said with a thick swallow.

Sasha glanced up at Ethan, the word "Vampires" sticking in her mind and her craw. Hunter caught it, too, but said nothing. She moved toward Ethan with her sketch pad. Maybe he'd be able to tell her about any tattoos or strange body markings.

"Sasha," Hunter called out from deeper in the cellar. "I've got something."

Hustling over to where Hunter stood, Sasha crouched down and sniffed. It was feral and female, but nothing like she'd ever smelled before. "What is that?" she asked frowning. "It smells like Were, but not any kind of wolf, Shadow, or demon." She shook her head. "I've never smelled this kind of Were before."

Hunter's eyes narrowed. "Neither have I." Hunter scented the air again. "And there's something more down here. Blood."

Sasha watched intently as Hunter cocked his head, seeming to listen to the sudden stillness as though he could hear the past. It was always an amazing thing to witness, seeing his wolf senses awaken, seeing Hunter's primal instincts ignite to scour the environment for clues. The Native American warrior battled with the Shadow Wolf Clan warrior just under the surface of Hunter's skin. It was sexy as hell, that pivotal moment when his internal tracker flipped on with a subtle snap.

Sasha kept her eyes on Hunter, watching his line of vision spend itself around the tavern wine cellar. Six-foot-five inches of pure muscle packaged in a 220-pound ebony-hued human frame was ready to slip into a shadow and emerge pure wolf. The hair stood up on the back of his neck and ever so slightly his dark ponytail lengthened.

"What's going on, Sasha?" Ethan said nervously, starting to come closer.

But Sasha held up her hand. "Just give us a moment, Ethan . . . keep your scent back and let Hunter work."

After a moment, Hunter returned to her side. "There's blood down here, but every time I think I'm closing in on it, the scent just dances away."

"Does it belong to Desidera or to the Were we're smelling?" Sasha replied with a frown.

Hunter shrugged, now seeming edgy. "I don't know. I can't get a lock on the scent in order to tell."

Sasha rubbed the nape of her neck. They had a dead Phoenix, some type of female Were scent, and blood that may or may not belong to either one. Sasha turned and looked at the body again. It was possible that Desidera was attacked by a Were and, rather than going out by teeth, she decided to go out by flames. But that didn't explain the symbol she'd found on the body or the lack of signs of a struggle. If a Were had come down here to attack, then there should have been scuff marks on the floor, things turned over. But the scene looked like Desidera simply lay down quietly on the floor and calmly turned to ash. She'd think suicide if all the other pieces weren't getting in the way—namely, no note, an agreement to meet a lover after work, a feral female Were scent, and the elusive scent of blood far away from the body, even though there were no signs of struggle. Personally, she was leaning toward murder, although the why wasn't making any sense and the who was completely unknown at this point.

Walking back over to Ethan, Sasha spoke in a gentle but

firm tone. "Ethan, are there any Weres in the area that aren't Wolves?"

Ethan's gaze shot between Sasha and Hunter. "Why? What did you see down here?" When they didn't answer, he mopped his damp brow with the back of his forearm. "Only the Serpentines and Reptilians," he said quickly. "The Serpentines are primarily over at the Blood Oasis . . . those with alligator abilities stay deep within the swamplands."

Hunter shook his head. "It wasn't reptile. What I picked up on was mammal—warm-blooded."

Ethan slumped with relief so fast that Sasha almost reached out to catch him, but Ethan caught his weight on the banister instead.

"You okay?" she asked, now holding him beneath his elbow. It wasn't necessary, but her touch conveyed comfort to her distraught friend. She waited for Ethan to nod and then tried another line of questioning, just to be sure to rule out all possibilities. "Do Phoenixes ever have a type of contagion that makes it hard for them to transition from one form to the next?" Sasha briefly looked at Hunter, remembering all too well how that had happened to him.

"Not that I know of," Ethan said in a solemn voice, staring at the ashes across the room. He shook his head and briefly closed his eyes. "She was such a nice person, truly a gem. This shouldn't have happened to her."

"No, you're right. Something like this shouldn't happen to anyone," Sasha said quietly, looking at Ethan's stricken expression.

Ethan ran a trembling palm over his partially balding scalp. His shoulders slumped; fatigue and grief were making his stout little frame seem to be that of a bewildered child. He looked from Sasha to Hunter, his gaze begging for answers.

Hunter raked his fingers through his hair and stared at

the grisly remains. "And you're sure Desidera didn't have any run-ins with anyone, a Were, for example?"

Ethan stared up at him, looking confused. "I guess anything is possible, but I honestly never heard about anything so serious that someone would want to kill her over it. And when it's all said and done, the supernatural community in New Orleans is a small one compared with the humans. Most likely we would have heard about such bad blood between a Phoenix and a Were. Why are you asking?"

"We picked up a feral Were scent," Sasha said as calmly as possible. "Possibly female."

The color drained from Ethan's face. "I don't know why you would smell a Were down here."

"Did she have a changing room or an employee locker?" Sasha rubbed her temples. There had to be more to this than a dead Phoenix.

"Yes. Certainly," Ethan said in a tense, clipped voice. "This way."

Ethan moved up the steps as though someone were chasing him. Sasha and Hunter loped behind him, taking the narrow cellar stairs two at a time. But once they all exited, Ethan locked the door and tried to appear calm before his kitchen staff as he showed Sasha and Hunter to the employees-only section of the establishment.

"I have a changing room for them in here," Ethan said in a private murmur to keep others from hearing, sounding more and more distraught as he spoke. "It's all pink and white tiles, pretty with mirrors and vanity lights and marble benches with a private shower, so my girls can fully transform in comfort. That's why Sir Rodney and I called you. Something just isn't right about this. My Phoenixes have never had a problem like this . . . and I didn't want to alert my other employees for fear of starting a panic in the Fae community just before all the galas. You now bring up the possibility that it could be some virus . . . I pray what she had isn't contagious. Me own wife, Margaret, isn't sure—and she's an empath . . . a healer and she cannot make heads or tails of this."

"No, no, no—I just had to ask that question," Sasha said, holding him by both arms.

She waited until he calmed and then they entered the changing room. Now she wasn't sure which was worse—murder or contagion? Guilt threaded its way around Sasha's conscience and choked it. This was indeed a person, someone who was loved and cared for by others in the supernatural community. The last thing she should have been thinking of was a silly party or her birthday, or any issues between her and Hunter . . . it was just that work was always the focus and she'd been hoping for a break in the action for only a little while. Then again, she reasoned, she was blessed. At least she wasn't charred ash, which certainly could have been the case when dealing with pissed off Vampires.

But that was then and this was now, besides, this girl didn't have any direct enemies, a crazy boyfriend, or any of the makings of domestic troubles. A brief prayer crossed Sasha's mind: *Please God, don't let it be some serial killer whack job, though.*

Looking up at Ethan and then glancing at Hunter, she made sure her voice was gentle. "I guess I was just trying to rule out anything medical before we started down that path," Sasha offered, hoping that it really was something benign that didn't involve foul play.

Ethan nodded and released a sad sigh. "Here's her locker." He motioned toward it and then shrugged. "But I don't have a key or the combination."

Hunter reached out and yanked the door off. "No problem."

"All right," Ethan stammered. "Then . . . I should go to my office to report what we've learned thus far to Sir Rodney. Once you look through, please come up. I know he's pacing the floors in need of answers."

"We won't be long," Sasha said, beginning to go

through Desidera's personal effects. She glanced at Hunter. "And we'll try to put the door back so the other employees don't immediately see a busted locker."

"Thank you," Ethan said quickly and then slipped out of the door.

Hunter moved in close behind Sasha, his presence like a warm, stone wall of silence behind her.

"You're crowding me," she said with an arched eyebrow, glancing at him over her shoulder.

"Just trying to pick up a scent," he muttered and then backed off.

"Mostly pretty standard stuff," she called out, looking at a lightweight pink sweater, an extra pair of flat shoes, jeans, a tank top, and a purse. "She had a change of clothes in here . . . makeup." Sasha let out a hard breath and began going through Desidera's purse.

Holding up her driver's license, the photo of a stunning woman stared back at her. No wonder Sir Rodney was so taken. Tissues, lipstick, a compact . . . nothing was out of the ordinary. But there was a roll of smaller bills held in a rubber band—no doubt dancer's tip money. The contents of her wallet were also fairly standard: credit cards, several twenty-dollar bills. Then a small carnival strip photo fell into her hands. It had been held between two credit cards and showed two smiling girlfriends laughing and hugging each other. One redhead, one blond.

"This must be Penelope," Sasha said, handing the photo strip to Hunter.

He took it, glanced at it, and handed it back to Sasha. "Looks fairly recent, judging from the same hairstyle in the driver's license."

Sasha nodded. "Good call." But then, in a small slit inside the well-worn leather, her fingers hit pay dirt. "A Blood Oasis member card?" She handed off the card to Hunter, who raised a brow as he accepted it. "What's she doing with one of these?"

"My question exactly. Vampires do not hand these out

on the street. This is a donor card, not a member card." Hunter handed Sasha back the card, which she stashed in her jeans' pocket.

"Looks like we're going to have to stop by the Blood Oasis," she said, staring at him.

"Can't wait," Hunter muttered sarcastically.

A sudden presence made them both turn quickly. Upper and lower canines had ripped through Hunter's gums. Sir Rodney's bodyguard held up both hands in front of his chest, which eased the pair of wolves.

"Milord has been called back to Sidhe, and he would like a word with you in Ethan's office before he leaves." The bodyguard glanced at Sasha's shoulder holster and weapon and then at Hunter's slowly retracting canines. "Tensions are high . . . but know that our monarch is also extremely upset. To see a display of aggression—"

"Yeah, yeah, we get it," Sasha said as Hunter rolled his shoulders. "We're just a little jumpy after what we've seen in the basement."

The guard glanced at the broken locker door and then turned without comment. "This way, please."

The threesome headed down the backroom corridors, meeting Ethan along the way.

"I've tried to call Penelope," Ethan said, catching up to their pace, "but she didn't answer. I know it sounds silly, but if you're going to ask her questions tonight, will you call me? I wanted her to hear it all from me first, but I have to close down the bar and Mike left his shift early." Ethan let out an exasperated breath. "Having employees is sometimes like having children. My bartender is known for taking off before his shift ends, and he did it again. I need to deal with him, and I don't want anyone else closing for me tonight, given the circumstances."

"We'll call you, for sure," Sasha said. "But you make sure you have someone you can trust stay in here with you while you close. Promise me that."

Ethan nodded as the king's best man turned and also

nodded. "Milord has sent for Fae archers to reinforce me. I will be fine. Just check on Penelope . . . and let her know I wasn't being callous to have strangers contact her before I'd had a chance. Make her know—"

"Ethan . . ." Sasha said, stopping before his office door and hugging him. "We've got your back. We'll explain to her that you by rights couldn't leave here and she was unreachable by telephone. Just make sure you give us her address before we leave."

Ethan's body relaxed against hers and they parted after a moment. "Thank you, Sasha. Thank you both," Ethan said with a sniff and then walked down the hall in the opposite direction.

The guard opened the door and stood aside before entering behind Sasha and Hunter and closing it behind them. They found Sir Rodney pacing with his hands behind his back. Sir Rodney walked a hot path between Ethan's desk and the bank of file cabinets against the far wall, dragging his fingers through his thicket of dark brown tresses. His handsome face was near ashen with grief, but his jewel-blue eyes glittered with unspent rage. "I want whoever attacked this girl found and dismembered," he said in a low, threatening tone.

"Not a problem," Hunter replied, anger beginning to make his wolf canines crest. "It is the way of the wolf—however, we must be sure of who the assailant was, beyond all doubt, before we act in such resolute terms."

"Thank you," Sir Rodney said, rage glittering in his eyes. "Then I appreciate your allegiance on such short notice."

"We are one," Hunter said, offering the monarch an Old World handshake, by clasping each other's forearms.

Sasha nodded. "Did she say anything about why she was down there in the wine cellar? Is there *anything* you can tell us that might shed light on the tragedy?"

Sir Rodney's gaze held Sasha's for a moment and then went to Hunter's before seeking a far-off point in the office.

"No. I was to meet her at her apartment. That was all she said."

Brief silence created a new level of tension in the room as Sir Rodney leaned an outstretched arm against the file cabinet. He allowed his head to drop forward and he spoke to Sasha and Hunter with his eyes closed. "I cared for her," Sir Rodney finally said in a gravelly tone. "Many of us did. Find her killer . . . this wasn't an accident. We need a neutral party—someone who can look into a Phoenix death without the Fae being directly involved . . . or it could cause diplomatic complications and raise questions we are not prepared to answer at present."

"We'll do our best." Sasha held the distressed monarch's gaze and then she looked away. It was time to get out of here. But she had to show Sir Rodney what she had found. Extracting the card from her wallet, she held it out to him. "She was a blood donor for the Vampires . . . Were you aware of that?"

Sir Rodney straightened and snatched the card from Sasha and then flung it down on Ethan's desk. "I knew she'd danced for them once or twice, but I d'not know she was a damned donor."

Sasha glanced at Hunter. Sir Rodney's Fae brogue had become thick, his rage allowing his dialect to surface as swiftly as the color that had risen to his face.

"In that case," Hunter said evenly, "we'll approach the death as highly suspicious."

"It *is* highly suspicious," Sir Rodney said flatly. "The timing of this, just as I was to collect her after her work shift and the way she approached me in the bar . . . no, this wasn't some Phoenix transition gone wrong." He looked at Sasha and Hunter. "You can rule out some crazy concept of contagion. Ethan told me the theories. And what of this Were scent you picked up?"

Sir Rodney's voice had escalated on every word. Sasha gave Hunter a look to allow her to speak in a more calming female voice to the upset monarch. Hunter inclined his head slightly, agreeing without words.

"It was female and feral, but none like we've ever encountered in this region. That's two potential leads . . . the only clan of local Weres we know of that has any feral females is the old Buchanan clan. This card," she said, walking over to the desk to pick it up and stash it back in her pocket, "means, of course, we have to stop by the baron's establishment just to rattle his cage for grins." Oh, yeah, she and Vampire Baron Geoff Montague had history, the rat bastard.

"If you need anything—men, artillery, whatever you require, say it, and it is done."

"Thank you, Sir Rodney . . . we'll be sure to do that. But first we need to do the groundwork before we go to war."

Hunter held his gaze. "We want to be sure to seek redress from the right culprit."

"Yes, yes, you're right," Sir Rodney said, blotting the sweat from his brow. "Just keep me advised."

"We will," Sasha said, glancing at the air conditioner's thermostat. She felt like she was burning up, yet it was only on sixty-seven degrees and blowing full blast.

A trickle of sweat ran down Sasha's neck and almost made her jump out of her skin. The cellar with a body in it was giving her the heebie-jeebies. For reasons she couldn't explain if her life depended on it, her senses were more than keen—there was a level of skittishness haunting her now that was normally not a part of her makeup as a soldier.

Hunter caught her start, his gaze steady but questioning. There was also something too tense in it that she wasn't ready to cope with right now.

Regaining her concentration, Sasha sought Sir Rodney's sad expression as a focal point. "If someone was chasing her, there would have been Phoenix plumes all around, and it doesn't look like there was a struggle. No crates are crushed, the shelves are intact, there are no scuff marks on the floor or evidence of an accelerant, if someone came in and set her on fire or anything. No sulfur residue, so I'm not so sure it was a Vamp attack . . . a Black Death charge leaves a really distinctive odor. But having a card from their club means something—I can feel it."

Charred remains still stung her nose, even though they were well away from the immediate site, and the general-regulation damp cellar scent added to it, making Sasha slightly queasy. But there was nothing abnormal for her to latch on to . . . except a feral animal odor that she couldn't define—and blood. She looked at Hunter for a moment, frustrated by the lack of evidence. "If it was wolves that went after her, well . . . they generally don't go in for barbecuing their victims first."

As soon as she'd said it, she regretted the last part of her statement when Sir Rodney blanched and looked away. "I'm sorry, you know what I mean. Wolves eat raw, the attack is immediate, and Desidera's remains weren't disturbed as though a wolf had gone after her and left her dismembered before she flamed."

"It's all right," Sir Rodney said, turning away. "I know you're just trying to make sense of this the best way you can . . . and your assessment matches mine. That's why I just don't understand how something like this could happen. She wasn't suicidal. She was happy!"

Sir Rodney's gaze was fixed on a point on the wall and he slowly nodded. "Save for her unusually nervous behavior tonight, she was happy." He briefly closed his eyes again as he released a long sigh. "The damnable part of this is, it all happened in a crowded establishment. There could have been hidden Vampires here, sorcerers, witches—covens even, Werewolves from the outlawed Louisiana Buchanan clan. How would we even know where to begin? But she got on with everyone . . . didn't have an enemy in sight."

Sasha and Hunter exchanged a glance.

"Before you arrived, we searched the entire cellar, even turning over dusty bottles and looking within and beneath every crate down there," Sir Rodney said, his voice tight with emotion as he pushed off the banister. "There's nothing there but her remains. As you said, no sign of a struggle, no Vampire sulfur residue, and no evidence of a Werewolf attack. It makes no sense."

"That's just the thing," the bodyguard said, his gaze traveling to each face before him, "Ethan McGregor told us that his girls have no reason to be down there. His bartender might go for a restock of private label—should they have Vampire guests . . . but ever since that disastrous row with them a few months ago, they wouldn't put out a shilling much less pay US currency to support his establishment. McGregor claimed that he hadn't had to break a blood-tainted case of Marsecco in months. So, if milady ventured down here, for what reason could it have been?"

"Rest assured, man," Sir Rodney said, glaring at his best man before returning his angry gaze to Sasha and Hunter, "this was no accident, nor is it contagion, and it has nothing to do with her wanting privacy to flame. Someone was responsible and I want that person found!"

Sasha reached into her back pocket and held out her notebook to Sir Rodney, flipping to the page that she'd sketched the symbol on. "No offense . . . but you knew her body nude, I'm assuming. Did she have this mark on her before she died?"

Sir Rodney snatched the book and quickly handed it back to Sasha. "No!"

"What is it?" Sasha said in a soft voice as Sir Rodney turned away.

"Sorcery at its worst."

CHAPTER 2

Hunter pulled the jeep into the driveway and cut the ignition. As expected, all the lights were off in Penelope's small trailer, but the outside light at the front door drew a flutter of moths. Sasha dabbed her temples and neck. Sticky June humidity made her clothes cling and a visible line of moisture was beginning to form on her tank top around her gun harness.

But the moment they got out of the car, both she and Hunter froze. The scent of charred flesh hung in the air as though an afterthought. Hunter approached a front window and forced it up an inch as Sasha covered him. He didn't need to nod to tell her that her sense had been right; it smelled just like the crime scene they'd just left.

"Shit." Hunter's gaze narrowed as he headed for the front door with Sasha on his heels.

He opened the screen door and then pushed the front door open with ease. Sasha gave him a look; it wasn't locked. The air conditioner was on full blast, circulating the putrid air within Penelope's trailer. It was the same. Charred Phoenix mixed with something feral. But this time, no blood. Sasha's wolf senses were keen in the darkness. She could see Hunter's deep amber irises glow as he stalked through the small living space, and then suddenly, he stopped.

Sasha lowered her weapon for a moment as she looked down at the body at her feet. What did these two women do that got them murdered? Her mind was on fire and her grip tightened on the semiautomatic. If whatever did this was still here, she had a full clip of silver slugs for it.

"Stay with the body," Hunter said in a low rumble, casing the rest of the trailer.

When he returned and clicked on the living room light, Sasha stooped down to fully examine the remains.

"Just like the other one," Sasha said, standing after a moment to look around the cozy, well-kept trailer. "Nothing in the room to signify a struggle, no evidence of sulfur, just these strange symbols burned into the Phoenix's belly. That's all there is."

"You and I both know there is no such thing as coincidence," Hunter grumbled, staring down. "But, coincidentally, this Mythic being was the next one on our list to question . . . a close friend of the redhead. Add that," Hunter said as he rolled his shoulders, "this charring is still fresh. We're being stalked. I can feel it in my soul. Something is coming behind us, around us, herding us." He sniffed the air and frowned.

"Yeah, I picked that up, too, when we were in the cellar. I've definitely never smelled it before."

Hunter shook his head and stooped down to get a closer look. "At first I thought that it could have been the scent of fear coming from the Phoenix before she flamed . . . has a musty undertone to it. Feral, but not Werewolf or Vampire—just like at Ethan's. This kicks my ass that I can't place it."

"Also not human . . . or any Fae scents I've come to learn."

"Either it is owned by the killer or related to the aftermath of the burning." Hunter studied the ashes and then stood.

"You might be right," Sasha said, nodding. "I need to find out more about this symbol . . . if Sir Rodney hadn't outright said sorcery, I would have thought that maybe it could have been something that showed up once a Phoenix flames for the last time. But the Fae know their magick, and if the man said sorcery was involved, I'll take him at his word."

"It could be a warning, a marker—something that says 'keep out,'" Hunter said in a low, even rumble. "Tribesmen of all cultures mark territory with fearsome symbols."

"Yeah . . ." Sasha said in a faraway voice. "But there's a link we're missing between these Phoenix deaths. Why go after the Phoenixes? They played no major role at the trials. I don't get it. Who would want them dead? Why would Vamps have an axe to grind with them? Even though I can't stand the rat bastards, it doesn't completely add up."

"Fresh air, distance, meditation—we must add this to our arsenal, Sasha," Hunter said, placing a flat palm on her back. "Let us talk with Ethan and Sir Rodney. Maybe they can shed a little more light on this."

She nodded and whipped out her cell phone, then cursed. "Damn . . . can't get Sir Rod, he's in the Sidhe. Cell phones don't work there." She let out a breath and placed the next call to Ethan. The conversation was brief—it was best to deliver bad news that way, since there was no delicate explanation available. Penelope was dead.

Hunter had already left her side to begin looking for anything they could go on. The living room offered no hints, nor did the small dinette area. Sasha found him going through the cutlery on the counter, sniffing the butcher's block of knives.

"I don't think she'd fight whatever was after her," Sasha said with a half smile. "At least not in hand-to-hand combat. She wouldn't defend herself like one of us would. We've gotta think like a Phoenix, not a Wolf."

He nodded and raked his hair with his fingers, then stepped away from the counter, clearly frustrated. "Truth."

Sasha sent her gaze around the tight confines and her line of vision landed on the refrigerator door. It held a small drugstore calendar under several fruit-inspired magnets. Quickly going to it, she read the neat shorthand: *BO 12-5.*

Digging in her pocket, Sasha produced the card she'd gotten from Desidera's wallet. "How much you wanna bet BO twelve to five is her shift at the Blood Oasis from midnight to five AM, prime Vamp time?"

Hunter took the calendar off the refrigerator and flipped through it. "The entries go back several months. If you're right, she was working there three to four nights a week."

Sasha nodded, heading toward the bedroom, and then stopped at the dresser. She glanced at Hunter over her shoulder, motioning toward a jewelry tray. "Seems Penelope had some really nice admirers, either that or she made a fantastic salary at the Blood Oasis. This is the real stuff, not cubic zirconia."

"She also had a Pixie friend," Hunter said, lifting a small oval frame off the nightstand. He offered it to Sasha's inspection as she walked over to take a closer look.

"Desidera, Penelope, and maybe a coworker?" Sasha studied the photo harder. "This is in the gardens at Chaya."

"Then I guess the teahouse is definitely on the agenda to visit."

Sasha and Hunter shared a look, and then she averted her gaze, trying to focus on getting the small picture out of the frame and into her pocket. It was obvious that neither of them wanted to discuss the teahouse, much less go there.

But the sound of a vehicle and quick footsteps put them on guard, evaporating any issues between them. By the time Ethan came through the front door, Hunter was in the living room and had taken a stance, and Sasha's arms were outstretched, one palm under the gun butt, the other ready to pull the trigger.

"Sheesh, Ethan! You know better than to roll up on a couple of wolves in hunt mode! Damn! You could have gotten yourself hurt."

Sasha uncocked her weapon and Hunter rolled his neck

from side to side, clearly fighting adrenaline. When Ethan's wife came to the screen door, Sasha blew a damp curl up from her forehead.

"Let's go outside," Hunter said in a low rumble when Margaret gasped.

"Good idea." Sasha crossed the room and held open the door for Ethan, and Hunter closed it behind everyone.

The Elfin couple stood on the front steps of the double-wide trailer wringing their hands. Margaret's face was puffy and red, the result of unrelenting tears, as she twisted a tissue into confetti.

"This is so horrible," she whispered. "I knew both of them for years . . . each girl was just a doll. This isn't any kind of contagion I've ever seen in that community."

Sasha and Hunter just stared at each other for a moment.

"That's why I insisted Margaret come with me," Ethan said. "Two girls? *Two girls?* We had to be sure it wasn't a plague, and my wife is the only supernatural medical person I knew of who would keep this discreet, as Sir Rodney instructed."

"It's not a plague," Sasha said flatly.

Hunter nodded and wiped a thick layer of perspiration off his brow with the back of his forearm. "Both were in the same condition—undisturbed, no signs of a struggle. But two deaths in the same night rules out coincidence. This was definitely foul play."

"Foul play . . . as in murder?" Margaret said with a quiet gasp.

"You have to get word to Sir Rodney," Sasha said, glancing around at the group. "I can't reach him by cell phone, so you'll have to do your Fae missive thing."

"His guards thought it best that he retire to the castle, given the circumstances. As our monarch, with a possible killer on the loose . . . or a possible disease afoot, his advisors felt it prudent that he remain in the fortress until further notice," Ethan said. "I will get him word of this immediately." Glancing around nervously, Ethan held the group enthralled. "Behind the castle walls, human technology doesn't work . . . The glamour affects the transmission of cell phones and radios—but with the heightened security, he wouldn't want a message of this nature being broadcast over the airwaves where it could be intercepted. So, yes, yes, it will have to be sent by way of a Fae missive."

"Makes sense," Hunter muttered, walking around the side of the building. "But let's get one thing straight—you can drop the ruse about it being some sort of contagion. Your monarch said it was sorcery of the worst kind."

Ethan opened his mouth and then closed it as his wife covered her mouth with her hand.

"Your glamour is also gone," Sasha said gently, looking at Ethan. "Something is so not right about any of this."

"Well, given the circumstances," Ethan said, swallowing hard and lifting his chin, mustering indignation. "That is the least of my concerns."

Ethan and Margaret shared a look.

"Listen, you both have a *lot* of seriously old Vampires really pissed off at you. That's point number one. They can't afford to openly come at you—but who knows what twisted way they did, though. Sorcery isn't out of the question, nor is it out of their league. They have all kinds of alliances with dark covens, so hey." Sasha shrugged and lifted her damp hair off the nape of her neck, holstering her weapon. "When I was driving over here with Hunter, I was thinking about Dugan. Anybody who stood to inherit his once substantial estate wouldn't be too thrilled about the way things went down, either. You got everything that Dugan once owned as a result of your testimony." Sasha paused, allowing the potential consequences of what might be happening to sink into Ethan's brain.

"Maybe this has nothing to do with the Phoenixes and more to do with who employed them—you?" Hunter glanced at Sasha and then turned his steady, intense gaze on Ethan.

"Perish the thought," Margaret whispered, drawing closer to her husband.

Sasha ruffled her hair up off the nape of her neck again in frustration. They'd hit a brick wall and she was temporarily out of answers until she could get to anyone who might talk at the Blood Oasis, or maybe somebody over at Chaya—the teahouse where Penelope had also worked.

Coming closer to Ethan, Sasha looked at him hard. "Okay . . . you mentioned that, quote, 'even the Vampires liked her,' when speaking of Desidera. What was that about?"

Margaret hugged Ethan and hid her face in the cleft of his shoulder. "I knew we should have stayed out of all of this. We have children!"

"No, no, don't fret," Ethan said, petting his wife's back. "We will take this new information to Sir Rodney and he will hear our petition for protective custody."

"That's practically living like we're banished. Our children will have to be pulled out of their schools here and we'll have to live at Seelie Court!" A panic-stricken sob cut off Margaret's argument.

"Maybe just for a little while," Sasha said quietly, going over to also hug the small, distraught Elf. This broke her heart; Margaret was a gem, as was Ethan. "We'll do everything we can to protect your family and see that you can return to your normal lives as soon as possible . . . but one thing I know for sure, Sir Rodney will have your backs."

"You never answered the question about Desidera's relationship to the Vampires," Hunter said, waiting.

Ethan lowered his gaze. "Phoenixes are rare . . . and are an exotic temptation—before the dispute, Desidera and Penelope were regularly welcomed at their blood clubs."

"And after?" Hunter folded his arms over his chest.

"They may have gone there a few times, on their own, to earn money or personal favors . . . I cannot know for sure," Ethan admitted quietly.

Digging into her pocket, Sasha showed the couple the photo that had been in the small, oval, silver frame on Penelope's nightstand. "Do you know this Pixie? Is she an employee of yours?"

"No," Ethan said, his tone confused and earnest. "Maybe she's an employee at Chaya?"

Sasha put the photo back in her pocket and gave Hunter a look as she pulled away from the distraught couple. She then found the small pad in her back pocket and held it out for Ethan to see.

"Ethan, Margaret, I need to ask you something . . . When a Phoenix takes his or her last flame, does this show up on the belly?"

Margaret gasped and turned away as Ethan hugged her.

"Destroy it, cover it up!" Ethan shouted, making Sasha hurriedly comply. She thrust the pad into the back pocket of her jeans and looked at Ethan and Margaret as though they'd lost their minds.

"Okay, that got a reaction," Hunter said, walking closer to the couple. "What was it?"

Sasha joined the huddle as Ethan waved his hands about as though to signal for them to say nothing.

"Tell me this wasn't in my cellar?" Ethan gasped.

"It was on Desidera's body, hard to see because the ash had started to fall in on itself by the time we got there, I suppose . . . but the one we just saw on Penelope was fresher." Sasha glanced at Hunter from the corner of her eye.

"That wasn't there when Sir Rodney and I found her body—we would have immediately noticed something so horrific." Ethan gathered his wife tighter in his hold, pressing his face against her hair. "Or . . . maybe it could have been there—frankly, when I saw her dead I didn't stoop over her to observe. It was just too terrible."

"*What* was it?" Hunter said in a deep voice reminiscent of thunder.

"It was a sigil," Ethan whispered, sweating profusely.

Sasha and Hunter gave each other another look.

"It is a sign of pure evil," Ethan croaked. "That is as much as I know."

Sasha looked at her watch and then at Hunter. "We've got a few hours before daylight. You thinking what I'm thinking?"

Hunter nodded. "We ride."

"The little guy was thoroughly shaken," Hunter said as he maneuvered the jeep into the parking lot of the Blood Oasis.

"You think?" Sasha said, not waiting for him to come to a complete stop before hopping out of the vehicle.

Hunter turned off the ignition and quickly caught up to her, grabbing her arm to stop her. "What's with the sudden attitude?"

She shrugged out of his hold. "I don't have an attitude. What's your problem?"

"My problem is we're about to go into a blood club, asking questions, putting ourselves in mortal danger, and we aren't a team."

For a moment Sasha just stared at him, trying to get the adrenaline rush that gripped her to slowly ebb. Eventually she nodded. He was right. It didn't make sense to go barging into a Vampire entertainment den filled with very hungry Vamps and their loyal human donors unless they were a united front.

Sasha eased the tension out of her neck. "We've been off since we were in Ethan's cellar."

"We didn't arrive in New Orleans battling," he said quietly, staring at her.

"No, we didn't." Sasha glanced around the parking lot, aware that the lack of bodyguards didn't mean they weren't being watched. Vampires always had lookouts. There were always bodyguards for the elite who might be passing through and to keep lower-level vamps that might be semi–blood crazed in line. With the high tensions between the wolves and the recent war, there should have been more obvious security. Then again, Vampires didn't do obvious.

"Do you wanna go through the bouncers, or simply show up at the bar?" Hunter reached out and pushed a stray wisp of her hair behind her ear.

"Let's just do the in-and-out thing," she murmured.

Hunter nodded and pulled her into a nearby shadow.

"Johnny Walker Black, straight up," Sasha told the startled bartender as she stepped out of a shadow in the corner. She slid onto an open seat and Hunter took the one beside her.

Pulsing techno-fusion music thrummed, the steady rhythm reminiscent of a rapid heartbeat. The sound vibrated through the floor, through the black marble bar, and through the chair she sat on. Sasha gazed around the black and red light–washed area, watching exotic Serpentine dancers cling to the poles, baring fangs, while a mobbed dance floor pulsed with eager Goth-clad bodies.

"We don't serve your kind in here anymore," the bartender said, presenting full fangs.

"Oh, my bad," Sasha said with a hard smile. "Then I guess I'll have to take my complaint up with the owner."

Hunter spun and swung as a burly bouncer materialized out of thin air, dropping him to the floor. Sasha whipped out her semiautomatic from her shoulder holster, leveling the weapon point-blank at the bartender's forehead.

"Don't be foolish," she said in a near snarl. "You can smell the silver. We just want a civil conversation with Geoff."

The slightly dazed bouncer spit out blood on the floor and picked up his chipped fang, hissing at Hunter while patrons gawked and other bouncers moved in slowly.

"A civil conversation is always welcomed," Baron Montague said in an even tone, parting the crowd. "What brings you to my establishment under such foolishly hostile circumstances?"

He held Sasha's gaze for a moment, a pair of hardened blue eyes slowly turning black as he studied her. Geoff tossed a long spill of dark brown hair over his shoulder with a nod as Sasha's gaze narrowed on his aristocratic features. He wore a midnight blue velvet jacket and his white ruffled shirt was slightly askew at the neck and stained by the slightest hint of blood. It was clear that he'd been enjoying some feeding companions when he'd been interrupted. Screw him. A hard smile found its way to Sasha's lips.

"A word . . . in private?" Sasha said, lowering her weapon.

"As the lady wishes," the baron said, inclining his head toward an empty VIP table behind the casino area.

Sasha kept an eye out for any twitchy Vampires as they followed the baron. She knew that they wouldn't attack on their own with Geoff right there. But that didn't mean Geoff wouldn't tell them to attack. She knew Hunter, who was bringing up the rear, was on alert as well.

When they reached the table, Sasha declined to sit when he swept his hand before them in a gallant gesture.

"This won't take long," Sasha said. "I'm sure by now you've guessed this isn't a social call."

"I'm shocked," the baron said in a sarcastic tone, placing a graceful hand over his heart. But then his tone took a sinister dip as he stared at Sasha, then Hunter. "So to what do I owe the pleasure of your intrusion here at my place of business?"

"Do you know of the Phoenixes Desidera and Penelope?" Sasha folded her arms over her chest.

"Of course," the Baron said coolly, taking a seat and snapping his fingers. A blood goblet appeared at his table and he took a sip from it. "We value diversity here at the Blood Oasis."

"Did they work here?" Sasha said with a low growl beginning to form in her throat. She hated these game-playing bastards.

"Now why would you think they do anything at all here, other than enjoy the—"

Sasha whipped out the card and flung it down in front of the baron, cutting his denial short. "This was in Desidera's purse. Penelope's calendar had *BO twelve to five* written in it at least three days a week for months."

"The card is a member's card," the baron said evenly with a deadly smile. "Penelope is one of my dancers. When she gets Desidera to dance regularly, there may be a bonus in it for her."

Sasha glanced at Hunter and then returned her gaze to Geoff. "So, they danced for you, at least one did regularly, and the other came on occasion to see if she wanted in?"

"They are the best exotic dancers around . . . McGregor cannot nearly begin to pay what we are willing to pay. Therefore, the girls are torn—loyalty versus commerce. It is always the conundrum, *oui*?"

"Now was that so hard? Why did you keep it a secret?" Sasha demanded, losing patience by the second.

"We're not exactly popular with the other paranormals right now, are we?" The baron glared at her and pursed his lips for a moment before he went on. "I don't think they want anyone to know. I don't hold it against them . . . we all have our secrets and we honor that in our realm, unlike others. They are magnificent performers. Extremely popular."

"Did they let anyone feed off them?" Indignation crawled through her, just thinking about the possibility.

"No," the baron said, his fangs beginning to crest. "They aren't on the menu. I make sure that is very clear to anyone who set foot in here. I do look after my own employees. Now that I have answered a flurry of your questions, I have some of my own. For starters, why are you in here asking about these two lovely ladies and sounding like you're accusing me of something?"

"They're dead," Sasha said, watching him closely as he

calmly took a sip from his goblet. "Killed sometime in the last four hours, I believe."

Hunter folded his arms over his chest, keeping his back toward the wall.

"And you think I had something to do with their deaths?"

"I think a lot of things, Baron, but I know we have two dead girls and that they both worked for you. That's enough for me to become a major pain in your ass while I find out who killed them."

"And where did you find their bodies?" The baron leaned forward with his elbows on the table, making a tent in front of his mouth with his long, graceful fingers as he stared up at Sasha.

"Desidera was found in the basement of The Fair Lady and Penelope was found in her home."

The baron sat back, one eyebrow raised, and he picked up his goblet again. "Your requirement for guilt is that they both worked for me and yet they also both worked for Ethan McGregor . . . and you actually found one of them in his basement. Seems to me that you should stop looking into coffins and pay attention to those in your little alliance."

Hunter pushed off the wall with a warning growl so quickly that security instantly materialized around them. "How about if we look into coffins during the day?"

"I suggest you keep your guard dog on a short choker chain in here, Sasha," the baron warned. "Unprovoked violence could be misconstrued as a reason to go to war."

"Going to war is the way of the wolf, when a principle is involved," Hunter said in a low rumble, sizing up the potential combatants.

The baron took a sip from his goblet. "When there is no evidence that we've been involved in any wrongdoing, going to war against us is both illegal and unjustified—*wolf*." He then brought his goblet away from his mouth slowly and set it down on the table before him with precision. "That, like the loss of those two beautiful Phoenixes, would be a waste of resources—a terrible waste of resources." Turning his attention away from Hunter in a cool snub, he stared at Sasha. "How did it happen?"

"We were hoping you could tell us," Sasha said, her gaze narrowing.

"When you find out, you will advise us?" the baron asked evenly, picking up his goblet again.

Sasha pulled out her notebook and flipped to the page with the symbol on it. "This was on the bodies. What is it?"

The baron shrugged. "I haven't a clue."

"Know that we're watching you," she said, leaning down to place both hands on either side of the table.

"Fair exchange is no robbery, she-wolf," the baron murmured. "Know that we have never stopped monitoring you."

The hair on the back of Hunter's neck was standing up by the time they got back into their jeep. As he pulled off, she watched him maneuver the vehicle in the wrong direction from the bed-and-breakfast.

"Where to?" she said, trying to break through his wall of fury.

"The teahouse. If Penelope worked there tonight, we should be able to pick up her fresh scent, and if a Were followed her from there home, there should still be a scent lingering there."

Sasha leaned back against the seat and simply closed her eyes to endure the ride. The last place she wanted to be was back at Chaya. Hunter didn't say two words while driving over to the now infamous tea salon, and he dismounted from the jeep with his gaze straight ahead. She couldn't blame him; what had transpired here between her and Shogun was scandalous—albeit Faerie spell induced.

"Ethan said it closed at ten, so nobody will be there to question . . . But we could go through the gardens, and if our murderer is a Were, maybe it was lurking for her out there, stalking her," Sasha said, keeping the conversation directed toward the investigation.

Hunter just nodded.

New Orleans heat, even at night, was kicking her ass. The humidity made her jeans and tank top cling to her like a second skin. It also didn't help the irritability factor, which was now on full blast for some odd reason. She'd felt that way ever since she'd left Ethan McGregor's cellar. Dealing with the baron definitely didn't help.

"You know . . . thinking back on it, was it my imagination, or did Sir Rodney seem overly tense?" She stared at Hunter, waiting, watching his gaze rove past the bamboo blind.

"The man just lost a lover. His cause for tension was justified."

Sasha let out a quiet sigh. Okay, so this was going to be a long night.

Ignoring the subtle dig, she easily propelled her body over the wrought-iron gate, needing the physical exertion. Hunter simply slipped into a shadow and came out on the other side of the barrier. Now inside with closer access to the main building, it was clear that the establishment was locked up tight. Breaking in was possible, but there'd be no way to do it without leaving evidence of intrusion; wolf scent would linger and could confuse the issues for Fae investigation.

"Pixies and Faeries to ask as possible witnesses won't be out this late—not with angry Vampires in the area," Sasha remarked casually, walking through the gardens. "We'll have to come back at dawn when they normally begin collecting the dew."

She glanced around at the level of disrepair that confronted her. Once immaculately sheared dwarf azaleas and bonsais were ragged. The giant yew trees in huge Japanese ceramic pots on the porch seemed wilted, some owning yellowed leaves. Crabgrass and dandelions were prolific, littering the layered look of the small stone walls on the lawn and taking up residence between carefully placed Himalayan boulders. It even threatened the once clean spaces near the granite Yukimi lanterns, and algae drifted lazily on the surface of the oval pond above the slow-moving giant carp, blanketing the green paddle stones.

The only flora that appeared to be holding its own were the weeping cherry trees, Japanese wisteria, and graceful roseas. Anything that needed careful cultivation was a mess. This was not the pristine garden she'd known, but she kept that sad observation to herself. Unfortunately, the economic downturn had even reached the Fae community, it seemed.

Sasha turned away and placed her hands on her hips to stare at Hunter. "I'm not getting anything."

"Then why are we still here?" Hunter muttered without looking at her.

"Okay . . . we have got to get this out and dealt with once and for all," Sasha said, now folding her arms over her chest.

"Now is not the time." Hunter began to walk, seeking a shadow.

"Maybe not, but it's going to be real hard working as a team to investigate a situation with you having an attitude."

Hunter spun and stared at her. "I do not have an attitude."

"Really? Could have fooled me."

He didn't respond, but simply inclined his head toward the jeep. "Let us focus on the task at hand."

Now he was really pissing her off.

But as she began to head back to the jeep, choosing the path near the small gazebo, the fleeting scent stung her nose. Hunter stopped walking and turned. He'd obviously picked it up, too. Running toward the scent that had been downwind from them, they both stopped at the gazebo prepared to instantly shift into their wolf forms.

Yet the abandoned seating area left them disappointed.

"Whatever it is was here," Hunter muttered.

"I know . . . I just wish I knew what the hell it was." Sasha turned around in a wide circle and then let out her breath in defeat.

CHAPTER 3

Sasha had never been so glad to see a place to lay her head in all her life. Just walking up the front steps of what used to be Dugan's Bed & Breakfast nearly brought tears to her eyes. She was so exhausted that every step felt like she was lifting an anvil instead of a boot. By the time they got to their room, she had to lean against the wall to simply fill Ethan in by cell phone. As soon as the call disconnected, she was so tempted to just walk across the room and flop down on the bed, but she knew Sir Rodney would be calling back any moment.

Hunter stood quietly inside the door, his expression stoic as she waited. Her phone sounded. Then it was just a matter of allowing Sir Rodney to vent about the baron trying to lure beautiful Phoenixes away from Ethan's establishment. She was beginning to feel too tired to care, but checked her responses when she replied to the Seelie king's rapid-fire questions.

"I'll keep you posted as we get more intel," she promised him, staring at Hunter. She waited until Sir Rodney disconnected the call and then closed her eyes, ready to fall asleep standing up.

A pair of warm, muscular arms enfolded her. She hadn't even heard Hunter cross the room. His presence, the feel of him, was like a drug and she laid her head against his shoulder, finally giving in to a yawn.

"Let's go to bed," he murmured.

She just nodded, already drowsy enough to practically sleepwalk. It wasn't necessary to open her eyes as she pulled off her weapon harness and handed it to Hunter, then kicked out of her boots and stripped off her jeans. What she was feeling was an unnatural kind of exhaustion, the bone weariness that she rarely felt as a wolf. She could tell it was beating Hunter down, too. It seemed like he could barely raise his arm to place her gun on the dresser. The moment they climbed into bed, he just pulled her into a spoon and seconds later was snoring in her ear. She wasn't far behind him as a deep dark sleep consumed her.

The pillow against her cheek might as well have been anesthesia. First there was darkness and then, slowly, red glowing symbols haunted her sleep. Strange images burned and charred beneath her fluttering lids. She could see her wolf running through the shadow lands, mist obstructing her view of the hooded figure holding a brand. Then, with a yelp, she was naked and cold, her spirit rising as the stench of burning flesh, hers, filled her nostrils. Pain gripped her abdomen and as she looked down, her belly was raw, newly branded by the eerie sigil she'd seen.

Then suddenly she was jerked awake by Hunter's lips on hers and the sound of wild barking in her ears—or was it in her head? Sasha yanked up her tank top and stared at her stomach and then relaxed. *Great—this case is already starting to show up in my dreams.*

Releasing a soft groan of annoyance, she pushed her tousled damp hair away from her face, realizing that Hunter had never moved in his sleep. Then who kissed her? Had to be part of the dream, just like the barking. She looked at him for a moment and then caressed his cheek. He was sleeping peacefully and dreaming. The sight of his easy exhalations and inhalations made her smile softly, kiss him, and then fall back to sleep.

* * *

Dawn came with a vengeance. Fatigue clawed at Sasha, but the couple of hours of shut-eye that she and Hunter had been able to catch at the old Dugan B&B was simply going to have to do. She could tell he was also feeling it by the way he dug his fingers into his mass of onyx hair and hung his head as though merely contemplating getting out of bed was more than his mind or body could deal with.

"I feel like I have a hangover," Sasha muttered, slowly heading for the bathroom.

"You're telling me," Hunter said in a hoarse murmur. "This isn't normal, Sasha. I feel like hell warmed over."

"Probably a parting gift from the baron."

"Remind me to kick his ass the next time I see him," Hunter said, closing his eyes and breathing slowly through his nose.

Sasha's cell phone went off, making them both cringe. "Jesus H. Christ," she muttered and hurried to get to it just to stop the awful sound. "What's up, 'Rissa?"

"You okay?" Clarissa asked. "Your voice came out as a growl."

"Sorry. Late night," Sasha muttered. She hadn't meant to snap at her teammate, but it was an ungodly hour in the morning.

"No apology needed . . . I guess I really owe you one, looking at the clock," Clarissa said gently. "But you know I wouldn't have called unless it was important."

"I know, I know," Sasha croaked and swung her legs over the side of the bed, knowing full well that Clarissa was the sensible one on the team. She wasn't given to sudden histrionics. As their resident psychic, Clarissa wouldn't have called unless there was a good reason. Sasha fought the haze in her brain and tried to focus. "Talk to me."

"I've got a bad feeling, Captain. Like, there's this serious dark energy vibe all around you . . . and I was worried."

"Have you told Doc or the fellas?"

"No," Clarissa said quickly. "But I told them they need to hurry up and get down there, just to have your back, just in case. This is New Orleans, you know."

"Okay," Sasha said, realizing how complicated this was becoming. "Here's the thing . . . I'm looking into something for Sir Rodney that has to stay off the radar for now. I can't go into it, but Hunter and I are fine."

"Do you need any help? What do you need us to do?"

"It's cool. We're good. Just come down as planned and be ready to hang out at the Fae ball—it should be a blast."

A moment of silence was Clarissa's initial response. Sasha flopped back against the pillows when Hunter gave her the eye. It made sense that Clarissa picked up dark energy. Hell . . . the baron was pissed off, something Were was lurking, there was a killer on the loose, and two Phoenix chicks had torched.

"Just be careful, Sasha," Clarissa said, strain evident in her tone.

"We will," Sasha replied, trying to make her voice sound upbeat. But when she clicked off the phone, she just closed her eyes. How did you fake it with a psychic?

One thing was for sure, when Desidera was killed, there was a feral scent and the smell of blood in the basement. If Vampires were involved in it somehow, then it was also possible that Weres were involved—specifically the Werewolves of the remaining Buchanan Broussard clan. Old Buchanan had tried to pull a coup and get his daughter, Dana, to marry Shogun—then send the Werewolves to war against the Shadow Wolves, all the while having a dirty backroom deal going with Shogun's sister Lei. Not to mention their demon-infected mother. With old man Buchanan, his daughter Dana, plus Shogun's sister and his traitorous mother all killed in the post-courtroom battle, the Buchanan clan was very likely suspect, to her way of thinking.

Plus, with sorcery and Vampires somehow involved, that would be an interesting alliance. Sasha opened her eyes and stared at the ceiling for a moment, clutching her cell phone in her hand. Yeah . . . What if they could have found a way to mask their scent? She wondered if a nasty coven spell might be able to make a Werewolf smell like something else . . . and if so, why not make the scent elusive, untraceable, exotic? "Hmmm . . ."

"You're going to give yourself a headache this morning," Hunter said, standing.

"Too late. Already got one," Sasha said, swinging her legs over the side of the bed and then pushing off it to grab her jeans.

She opened her pocket, found the spiral pad in it, and looked at the sigil again. If she hadn't promised Sir Rodney she wouldn't get her team involved unless absolutely necessary, she would have Bradley run a check on this. She'd have to loop back with Ethan about it, even though he and Margaret had completely freaked out about it last night. Regardless, there were questions she needed to ask . . . namely, what specifically did the symbol do?

Sasha glanced at the clock—the digital display said 6:12. Staff wouldn't be at Ethan's until ten. That was a lot of time to kill. Sasha looked up when she heard Hunter's stomach growl all the way across the room.

"Let's go get some grub . . . then try to find a Pixie."

It was no wonder the Pixies and garden Faeries didn't greet them when they entered the gardens at Chaya. Sasha took one look at Hunter's five o'clock shadow and surly mood, and if she were one of the wee folk, she would have avoided him, too. But she wasn't much better—two Shadow Wolves that looked like they'd seen the worst side of the moon.

Sasha trudged forward, undaunted, keeping her voice low and calling out gently. If Penelope worked at the tea salon, then the Pixie staff or garden Faeries would know whoever else she worked with, so they could track that person down. They'd also know who the Pixie was in the photo. Somebody had to know something. But after a moment, Sasha stopped walking.

"I know Pixies and Faeries are unusually shy, but it's just way too quiet out here."

Hunter nodded and glanced around. "We have done them no harm and have helped them in the past—why would they hide from us?"

"Listen . . . nothing," Sasha said, standing very, very still. "Not even crickets or morning birds."

On guard, both Shadow Wolves moved slowly toward the small mansion that had been turned into a delicately ornamented teahouse. Sasha motioned with her chin toward a long shadow cast by a weeping cherry tree. At this point, they couldn't worry about the Fae investigators. There was probable cause to enter Chaya via break-in. Within moments, she and Hunter had entered the shadow, coming out of it inside the shadows within the abandoned salon.

A thin film of dust covered the surfaces of once gleaming wood furniture and privacy screens. The gorgeous hardwood floors had lost their luster and dust sat in the crevices of intricately carved panels. Sasha and Hunter shared a look.

"This place looks like somebody got out of Dodge in a hurry. I don't get it."

A small *pssst* sound gave them a start, causing both wolves to spin in its direction only to spy a small, frightened Pixie. She stood in a tiny pool of light that was coming in around the shuttered windows, and she hugged her fragile arms to her body, her large brown eyes changing colors rapidly as she spoke.

"I heard the news," she squeaked. "That is the only reason I am coming forward—you Shadows helped us before, but this is so tragic, just so very wrong!" The Pixie glanced around again. "I'm not even supposed to be here, but I heard you'd come to this place last night . . . I hoped you'd come here in the early morning."

Sasha gave Hunter a glance that told him to stay back. The small Pixie was beginning to turn blue-green, her glamour totally faded, which could only mean that she was scared half to death. Large tears slid down her cheeks and Sasha immediately knew this was the Pixie in the photo.

"We'll help you," Sasha said in a gentle voice. "But we have to know what's going on." She squatted down to bring her gaze more level to that of the small person before her. "What's your name?"

"Pixie Gretchen," she said, as two more large, opalescent tears rolled down the bridge of her button nose. She tossed her strawberry-blond curls away from her face and lifted her chin, obviously trying to be strong. "They killed her."

"Who?" Sasha said carefully.

"Poor Desidera," the Pixie whispered and then covered her face.

Sasha glanced at Hunter, who remained stoic. "I meant, who killed Desidera?"

"The spell-casters." Gretchen lowered her palms away from her face.

This time Sasha didn't just glance at Hunter, she held his gaze for a moment before returning her line of vision to the Pixie. "You mean the Vampires?"

The mention of Vampires made the Pixie dash back and forth within the pool of light for a few seconds.

"They must be the ones stealing our magick—but who knows how they've cast such a spell? Our magick has been waning for months. That's why we've been in hiding. Desidera learned something by consorting with them . . . Penelope said she wasn't herself since the night before last, and I've been waiting here for word . . . we all have. Then the night moths told the Faeries about Desidera's flaming . . . oooohhhh . . . so horrible!"

Hunter cast a sidelong glance at Sasha.

"When was the last time you spoke to Penelope?" Sasha chose her words carefully, beginning to add up facts in her head as she spoke.

"Yesterday, when she got off from work in the afternoon . . . She works for Ethan McGregor, you know."

Gretchen looked between Sasha and Hunter. "What have you not told me?"

"When Penelope gets off work at Ethan's, she comes directly here to work?" Hunter addressed the Pixie in a low, calm rumble, trying to keep his voice modulated.

"She used to . . . when we were open," Gretchen said, now beginning to wring her hands. "But now she just comes by regularly to bring us honey and other supplies we need, as a friend. We, the Fae, are very private, and leaning on charity from those outside our community is very difficult indeed. That's the only reason she started adding full shifts at that *other* place."

"The Blood Oasis?" Hunter asked as gently as possible.

"Ohhh, that evil, evil place—yes!" The Pixie grabbed her hair with both hands and shook her head. "Penelope was going there too much and Desidera was worried about her, rightfully so. Penelope wanted Desi to dance there with her and I guess she finally gave in . . . and because the Vampires wanted her to join the club so badly, I think they let her in deeper than they even let Penelope. After that, Desi just wasn't the same. She told us not to worry; she'd heard something that she had to tell Sir Rodney." Gretchen bit her lip. "She was trying to help us, trying to be sure our magick would return. It had all come down!"

Sasha hugged herself, new worry roiling in her mind. So, Rodney was also playing games—he wasn't just going to hook up with a lover; he was there to learn what Desidera had found out. For a moment, Sasha's heart froze. *Please, God, Sir Rodney couldn't have killed that girl . . .* But she shook the thought. It didn't make sense. If Desidera was going to tell him something about those committing sorcery against his kingdom, killing Desidera would be the last thing he'd do. Besides, why would he have called her in to investigate the crime? It would have been easy for him to simply sweep the matter under the rug. A dead Phoenix in the paranormal community wouldn't have shown up on her personal radar. And, if Desidera didn't tell Penelope, then why did she end up dead? One thing was for sure, she needed to make a visit to Sidhe to get in the Seelie king's face about withholding intel.

"Did Desidera tell you what she learned?" Sasha finally asked, bracing herself to deliver the bad news about Penelope.

"No. She wouldn't tell us because she wanted to keep us out of it, wanted to protect us. She said it was too dangerous," Gretchen replied, stifling a sob. "Not even Penelope could pry it out of her, and now Desidera is dead."

"That's not your fault," Sasha said as she stared down at the distraught little being. "Did the night moths tell you anything else?" She glanced at Hunter and then back at Gretchen.

"No. I went into hiding as soon as I heard about Desidera. I should really go back to our secret mound," Gretchen said, glancing around nervously. "I've been gone too long already."

"But why wouldn't you just have other Fae help you, then, instead of the Phoenixes?" Sasha said, trying to stay the Pixie's leave.

"Sir Rodney said that for security reasons we should keep our fading-magick problem to ourselves until he could investigate," Gretchen said in a bitter tone. "But Penelope saw our condition with her own eyes as we closed the tea salon temporarily . . . That is not common knowledge; I don't believe McGregor even knows. Everything has been going fallow and so hard to cultivate the more our magick wanes. We've told Sir Rodney all of this, but his investigation is moving slowly—Thompson Loughlin hasn't made a dent in things and we're left at the mercy of fate! We had to eat."

"Can you tell me what supplies Penelope used to bring?" Sasha asked gently.

"Yes . . . but why?" Gretchen looked from Sasha to Hunter.

"We'll make sure you have supplies while all of this is

being sorted out," Sasha said, trying to soothe the Pixie while attempting to find a way to deliver the awful news.

"No, that will only draw attention. Upon the king's orders, this condition we face is to remain a secret . . . and we are protected from the spell-casters behind the wrought-iron gate. Dark magick cannot penetrate iron, which is why it surrounds the garden . . . far enough away from us not to leach our power, and a barrier to anyone sending ill will."

"Then how do you account for the fact that, iron gate or not, your powers are gone?"

The Pixie looked from Sasha to Hunter and back again, clearly perplexed.

"Either something got inside your gate that is impervious to iron or—"

"No, no, no!" the Pixie shrieked, covering her ears with her hands. "Then that means the monster who laid it here cannot be Fae, only we are allergic to the iron!"

Using her pointer finger, Sasha began drawing the sigil she'd seen in the dust on the floor. "Have you ever seen one of these? Do you know what it means?"

Gretchen threw her hands in the air and began screaming, running around in a circle. "Erase it, erase it!" she shrieked and then held her hands over her heart.

Sasha quickly wiped away the dust-drawn image and watched as the Pixie fell over, nearly faint.

Lifting herself to stare at Sasha, Gretchen's bottom lip quivered as she spoke. "Where did you see such a horrible thing?"

"On Desidera's and Penelope's bodies," Sasha replied as gently as possible.

"Penelope's?" Gretchen whispered. Her lip quivered and more tears rose to her eyes. "You are sure?"

"It was not your fault," Sasha said quietly. "But we'll help you. I promise."

Gretchen hugged herself, her tiny shoulders shaking as she finally gave way to a good hard cry. "Thank you," she finally murmured, not bothering to wipe her face.

"If you need me," Sasha said, writing her number in the dust on the floor, "here's my cell number . . . or you can send me a Fae missive."

Gretchen simply closed her eyes and nodded.

"I think it's time to have a conversation with Sir Rodney," Hunter muttered as he slammed the jeep door and pulled away from the curb.

"Ya think?" Sasha said, completely irate.

Before long they were back at Dugan's Bed & Breakfast. She waited for Hunter to find a parking spot in the back lot, fuming. Critical information had been left out of the equation. Ethan might have even been aware of some of it—and that damned Fae code of secrecy had her and Hunter out all night and at dawn on a wild goose chase! There was no discussion necessary as she and Hunter jumped out of the jeep and headed for the closest shadow.

CHAPTER 4

They came out in the middle of the bayou and the first thing Sasha did was begin yelling Sir Rodney's name. Within seconds, Fae archers appeared in the trees calling out their customary greeting.

"Friend or foe?"

"Very pissed-off friend at the moment," Sasha said. "But harmless to your king."

"And you?" another archer shouted down at Hunter.

"I'm unarmed and just along for the ride."

The archers looked at one another, and then their captain called down again. "We'll have to get you clearance, wolves."

"You do that," Sasha said. "Tell Sir Rodney I bring him some news that just can't wait."

It didn't take long for the relay to occur, and soon they were marching toward the hidden castle with a retinue of palace guards. Annoyed didn't begin to describe how she felt. Sasha bit her lip to keep from shouting obscenities as they trudged forward. Her team and Doc were due in this afternoon, all hell was breaking loose—hell that had nothing to do with them—and her nerves were shot.

The moment the gates appeared from behind the Fae glamour, it was all she could do to go through the pomp and circumstance of gaining proper palace entry. Hunter looked like he was ready to spit nails. She could definitely understand it. How were they supposed to investigate and help if they didn't have all the facts?

Sir Rodney's personal valet greeted them at the drawbridge. "I'll take it from here," he said in a calm tone. "Milady, milord," he added, ushering them forward with a genteel sweep of his hand.

Neither Sasha nor Hunter responded verbally. Instead, they just kept walking in the direction they were being led, through the unusually quiet streets of the small town beyond the gates, and through the main square to the palace.

Stoic palace guards never blinked as they passed, climbed the immense stone steps, and went through the huge barricade of doors. But the longer she walked, the longer she followed the security escort, the angrier she became. This was all such bullshit.

At a large double door, the valet stopped and gave a nod to Sir Rodney's personal bodyguard, who then ushered them in to see the king.

"Your guests, milord," the bodyguard said as he opened the door to what looked like a war room. He shut it gently and stood just inside the room, armed, with his back against the door.

"Yes, do come in," Sir Rodney said, seeming distracted and agitated.

Sasha's gaze quickly assessed her surroundings within the large stone room capped by a high, vaulted ceiling. Sir Rodney paced before a massive, round table that had high-back, hand-carved chairs. He kept his palms clasped behind him, occasionally raking his disheveled hair. It looked like he also hadn't slept last night, which was the only small consolation that Sasha would secretly allow herself at the moment.

Five dour-looking Gnomes in monk's habits, their age evident in their deeply lined faces and the frail wisps of white hair that pocked their bald scalps, looked on, seeming dispassionate. But their eyes held smoldering rage, just like their ancient hands and wands could conjure extreme magick when called upon.

"You didn't tell us the whole story!" Sasha blurted out, unable to deal with the tension of protocol.

"It was complicated," Sir Rodney said, his gaze now locked with hers and Hunter's.

"It always is, but we're either in it with you as full partners that you trust, or not," Sasha said, so angry that she was now talking with her hands.

"Trust," Hunter said evenly, "is the way of the wolf when we bond . . . Without it, friendship is in jeopardy."

"If we tripped over a critical fact, unwittingly, we could have gotten killed." Sasha got up in Sir Rodney's face. "From now on, either you tell us what's happening or we're out. If you need us, we're with you, but only as though we're pack. Real family, all right?"

Sir Rodney watched his lead advisor slowly reach inside his robe sleeve to begin fingering his wand. But the monarch held up his hand as his personal guard tensed, ready to draw arms in case one of the wolves decided to lunge.

"You're right," Sir Rodney finally said, releasing a hard exhalation. "But it is not the way of the Fae to disclose sensitive information outside of our community."

"When did you realize your magick was fading?" Sasha asked more calmly. "Or better yet, why did I have to finally go to starving Pixies to find out just how bad it had gotten?"

"That is a security breach, if it were to be common knowledge." Sir Rodney said, lifting his chin.

Sasha looked at the five o'clock shadow that covered the Fae monarch's normally clean-shaven jaw. "Although you were calm enough when I showed it to you, that sigil we found truly freaked out Ethan and nearly sent a Pixie into apoplexy," she said carefully. "So you want to start at the beginning so we can investigate this thoroughly on your behalf?"

Sir Rodney let out a long, weary sigh. “A few months ago, the Will-o’-Wisps and the Pixies of the Small Court began to see their magick wane. Their glamour was sporadic, causing them to have to take extra measures to hide themselves from humankind, lest they be discovered. The Faeries in the teahouse gardens were also affected. Now a small section of the outer garrison wall can be seen by the naked human eye, if we don’t redouble our efforts daily to cover it—which is no trivial feat. It has been like a creeping death.”

“Sorcery, Vampires, the sigil is black magick, right?” Sasha looked around the room. “There’s an iron fence around the teahouse, so someone sending in bad vibes should have literally been stopped at the gate, right?”

No one answered and quiet strangled the room.

“Ethan’s wife Margaret didn’t come with him to check on a possible plague; she came as a medical and spell professional . . . to examine Penelope’s body for the same sigil that had been on Desidera’s—tell me I am wrong,” Hunter said, folding his arms over his chest.

“Yes. And I want to know who is responsible for this dark malfeasance!” Sir Rodney spun on his advisors, his gaze hot with unspent fury as he waited for answers. “The mark was on both girls, and still we have no answers? Desidera tells me that she is hiding something in the cellar, and then that is where we find her dead?”

“That information would have been helpful to know while we were down there,” Sasha said as calmly as possible.

“It might have saved us twenty-four hours of blind searching,” Hunter said through his teeth.

Sir Rodney looked away. “It was a Fae matter.”

“And now it’s not?” Sasha said, challenging him.

“Have you any idea what would happen to the Sidhe if rumors of a loss of power were to get out?” Sir Rodney paced away from Sasha and spoke with his hands behind his back as he walked the perimeter of the room. “You have no insight into Fae culture or you would be aware of just how dangerous any perception of a loss of power could be." He stopped walking and stared at both Sasha and Hunter. "A weak monarch is a failed monarch. If he or she cannot keep the magick strong in the community, then he or she is destined to be overthrown—*that's* why it was a matter of Fae national security."

Sasha relaxed slightly and turned to Hunter. "No less than a weak alpha at the helm of the Wolf Federations . . . Someone would be bound to call a challenge match."

Hunter nodded and relaxed. "We gave you our word, and our word is our bond—to help you. That pledge will not change."

"Thank you," Sir Rodney said.

"But you need to tell us about the blood scent as well as the sigil," Sasha amended.

Sir Rodney dragged his fingers through his hair. "That is complicated."

The eldest advisor stepped forward, speaking slowly as dictated by his advanced years, but that in no way was an indicator of his keen mind. "Milord, as you know, Thompson Loughlin . . . one of our shrewdest Fae investigators, has a lead."

"Good man, Loughlin," Sir Rodney said, nodding, and ignoring the advisor's overt hint that they had their own man working on the case—therefore there was no reason to involve Sasha and Hunter. "Finest nose for discreet investigations . . . I believe his mother served in a high post in my mother's court years ago. His father was a digger Gnome in the Netherlands—a unique blend that makes him the best at unearthing hidden treasures and hidden truths. Yes, I am pleased that he is involved . . . Go on."

Okay, now she knew something was being held back. Sir Rodney had just gone into a politician's stiff spiel in front of his advisors, and he'd completely evaded her question about the blood. She'd wait for them to go through the motions, but not for long.

Glancing around the room when only silence greeted

him, Sir Rodney reassured his skeptical staff. "These are unusual circumstances where we would break from tradition to speak freely before outsiders. But I trust the Shadow Wolves with my very life." He looked at Sasha and then Hunter. "We may speak freely before trusted friends."

Both Sasha and Hunter gave Sir Rodney a nod that contained unspoken thanks as their bodies visibly relaxed.

The elderly advisor drew a weary breath and extracted a wand from his billowing robe sleeve. Tapping on the round war table, he waited as a small, spherical miasma formed, creating a ball of mist that soon cleared as though a snow globe had settled. All eyes stared at the grisly scene of a scorched bird carcass still smoldering.

"We have seen the sigil . . . but it is not one we are familiar with. It will take some time to decode it, even though we know it is a brand of chaos magick. Some of the markings are taking us an inordinate amount of time to decode. But the basic feel to it is darkness." The ancient advisor calmly returned his wand to his sleeve, causing the miasma to dissipate.

"This is an outrage; we will call for a Vampire inquisition. She could have been assaulted by a Vampire's Black Death charge or their sorcery, if the markings of the sigil are impossible to read! It must be in their guttural language. How do we know for sure that's not what it is?" Sir Rodney slammed his fist against the table and then walked away. "This is war."

"Inadvisable, milord," his second advisor warned, stepping forward with the others in a subtle display of solidarity.

"If you bring an inquisition on such speculative evidence as a Blood Oasis membership card and a few calendar markings, with only partial hearsay testimony that something was wrong from a dead Phoenix girl and your own special investigator, and we later learn it is not the bloodsuckers who are at fault . . . then we have not only presented a weak case that will come to nothing at the

United Council of Entities, but we will have also alerted our archenemy that our defenses are weak, that our magick is fading . . ."

"Penelope gave us nothing through the Pixie," Sasha added, siding with Sir Rodney's advisors. "Gretchen was waiting for her and she never showed—they never talked. That's a dead end."

"I have been king of the Seelie Court for more than three hundred years. Never," Sir Rodney said through his teeth, "has my court ever experienced such an insidious attack. Who else but Vampires would do this?" He spun on his advisors. "No . . . the better question is, who beside the Vampires would be strong enough or brazen enough that they could do this?"

"Need I remind you of your ex-wife, sir?" The eldest advisor just stared at him.

Sir Rodney waved him off and walked away. "After all these years, with her territories solvent, there is no reason to provoke war between us. We've already been down that path—she took her lot and I have taken mine here in New Orleans. There's no motive."

"Unless your powers were waning and your borders were weak. She is an excellent strategist and a very patient sort."

For a moment, no one in the room spoke as Sir Rodney stared at his top advisor. Sasha and Hunter shared a discreet look.

"This is why I caution you to employ temperance until we learn more, milord," his eldest advisor pressed on, his monotone voice slowly stating the facts. "There are those who would dare not challenge you while strong, but if there is any indication that there was an erosion of your power, you would have to fight off enemies as though a swarm of locusts."

The other advisors nodded.

Now Sasha really understood the dilemma marrow-deep. Both wolves caught each other's meaningful glances within their peripheral vision, both fully cognizant of what was at stake for Sir Rodney. The tension in the room was palpable as Sasha's previous rage dissipated.

Sir Rodney slowly returned to the table to lean against it with both hands. He closed his eyes and allowed his head to drop forward in frustration.

"Milord," a third and very shy advisor murmured, speaking so softly that Sir Rodney lifted his head just to hear him. "The situation, as you have guessed, is worsening."

Sir Rodney didn't respond to his advisor, but stared at Sasha and Hunter. "Now do you understand why we could not send Thompson on an errand to directly investigate this Phoenix death? It wasn't a matter of trust, but that of national security. Had we done so, it would have appeared odd . . . that the Fae would be delving into Mythic Parliament affairs. Once that became gossip . . . word of our involvement would surely travel. That could tip off our unknown enemies that something is amiss in our own yard. We must preserve the appearance of strength at all costs."

"Aye," a fourth advisor confirmed and then looked at the fifth advisor to his left.

Clearing his throat, the fifth advisor glanced at the others before he addressed the king, and then looked at Sasha and Hunter. "That is why we needed a friend outside of the Fae to repay a favor once given with a favor now needed and duly earned."

"Those who do not lie, whose silver auras speak of their sterling reputation for loyalty and honor . . . as is the way of the wolf," the fifth advisor said quietly. "We must have your word as your bond that you never speak of our waning powers beyond yourselves."

"My word given," Hunter said, lifting his chin.

"And mine," Sasha said.

The fifth advisor looked around at the group and the other advisors nodded, clearly having discussed this amongst themselves already.

"We should be sure that all our allies are at the Midsummer Night's Ball three nights hence . . . They must be in New Orleans during this time when the moon is full," his eldest advisor said, beginning to slowly stroll past each of the younger Gnomes as he spoke. "If there is foul play, our effectiveness could be strained. It would be prudent to have strong battalions of our friends at the ready . . . those who owe us, and who also know that once you owe the Fae, to renege is tantamount to treason."

Sir Rodney straightened, but his gaze was open as it went toward Sasha and Hunter. "I would never want to put any of the wolf packs at risk . . ."

"Indeed . . . but they are also excellent warriors unknown to your ex-wife and no stranger to battles with the undead. Vampires walk a wary path around them, sire, and it would not seem odd that they would be looking into matters that could potentially effect their packs or humans," his eldest advisor said calmly, going to the king to stand before him. His ancient gaze held the king's. "This happened in a Fae bar that humans frequent. That would give them both cover and cause."

"They cannot be harmed or placed in harm's way," Sir Rodney said in a rush, dragging his fingers through his hair as he now specifically stared at Sasha.

Hunter nodded with appreciation. "You had our backs, now we have yours. I am sure my brother Shogun will feel the same way."

"We stand with you at the ready, Sir Rodney," Sasha said. "Count on that." But as she held Sir Rodney's gaze, wolf instinct kicked in. "You never answered my question. What was the blood?"

"You also never fully disclosed your investigator's lead," Hunter said in a casual tone, but his expression was anything but that.

"Follow me," Sir Rodney said, ignoring his advisors' startled eyes.

"Milord," his eldest advisor said after a moment, stepping before Sir Rodney and withdrawing his wand. "I beg you to caution. Just as your comment to go to war with Vampires came out of passion . . . might this also be—"

"Do not forget your place, Bardis. We are old friends yet there are still parameters."

"And there is dark magick afoot . . . so serious that at times it has held His Majesty's judgment in question," Bardis said in a tight murmur meant only for Sir Rodney's ears.

"Not this time. If we are to ask for our allies' assistance, then we must trust them. That is common sense, old friend."

Although the senior advisor clearly didn't like it, he put his wand away and stood aside. Sasha and Hunter waited until Sir Rodney motioned for them to follow him, and he led the way through a door on the far side of the room that gave way to spiral stone stairs so narrow that one had to touch the wall to keep from feeling vertigo.

The moment they were at the bottom, Hunter glanced at Sasha and nodded. "It is the scent."

"Quite so," Sir Rodney said, still walking. He stopped at a huge wooden locked door.

To Sasha's surprise, the advisor named Bardis and the others who'd been in the war room opened the door for their king. Again, all she could do was glance at Hunter; Fae magick was deep.

But the body draped with a sheet on the granite slab before them nearly made her gasp out loud. The scent was cloying. And it was definitely the same blood trace they'd picked up in Ethan's wine cellar.

"Who is it?" Sasha asked as they neared the table and Sir Rodney flung off the sheet.

"Ethan's bartender, Mike," Sir Rodney said.

"The one who supposedly went home early?" Hunter said with sarcasm lacing his tone.

"Well, scratch his name off the whodunnit list," Sasha said with a scowl.

"This was the lead," Bardis said, ignoring the tension, and pointed at the lacerations on the nude man's chest. "His heart is gone, torn from the anchors so quickly it must have still been beating in the murderer's hand. There is only one entity we know of that can move that swiftly in a surgical strike."

Sasha and Hunter stepped closer. She gazed down into the stunned expression. The poor man's mouth was open in a frozen scream, his eyes wide and glassy. Too bad the dead couldn't talk. She traced the gashes left just outside the gaping hole in his chest and then looked at Hunter.

"Could have been a Vamp heart snatch. Usually a wolf attack isn't quite so clean—isn't directed at one organ."

"Wolves generally go for the throat or the gut, leaving viscera everywhere." Hunter leaned into the body and sniffed. "But there is most assuredly a trace of Were here as well." Hunter stood and stared at Sir Rodney. "And you didn't think this might have been useful information?"

Sasha folded her arms over her chest. "So, you guys found him and Desidera, removed his body and glamoured the cellar so we wouldn't see any trace of this body hitting the dirt, and then cleaned up the blood? Why?"

"We had to know beyond a shadow of a doubt," Sir Rodney said, lifting his chin, "that if it was a wolf, you would still stand with us."

"Now I really am offended, even if I understand your twisted logic," Sasha said and then walked away.

CHAPTER 5

Shogun doubled over, clutching his stomach, the moment he exited the plane.

"Sir, are you all right?" a member of the flight crew asked as he slowly straightened.

"Just fatigue from the long flight," Shogun's lieutenant muttered, helping him forward. Seung Kwon gave both Chin-Hwa and Dak-Ho a warning look to watch their backs as he ushered Shogun forward.

The two muscular enforcers bringing up the rear exchanged sidelong glances as they cleared the Jetway. None of the tense, silent exchanges were lost on Shogun. Pure humiliation burned his face. He should have passed on Sir Rodney's kind invitation. Were it not for the insistence of his half brother, Hunter, he surely would have. It had been bad enough that his need for Sasha was a private matter known and acknowledged only by him, but now, once again on North American soil, the desire to be with her had become excruciating.

Shogun wiped the sheen of sweat beading his brow, sipping in shallow inhalations. Her scent littered the air. She was already in New Orleans. To covet another man's wife was dishonorable; to covet one's brother's wife was tragic.

Seung Kwon's steady hand landed on his shoulder. "Cousin, are you still not well?" He stared into Shogun's eyes, his voice low and private and laden with concern. "The long flight, the lack of raw food so close to the moon shift . . . or maybe some human contagion is simply passing through your system as you purge it. They are germ conveyors—sickly beasts—and we've been in recycled air so long . . . unnatural for wolves."

Watching his cousin try to understand what he could never impart twisted Shogun's conscience. The only response he could give right now was a curt nod. He had to remember that above all else, he was a head of state. Deep within his core he sought that element of strength that made him the alpha clan leader of the Southeast Asian Werewolf Federation. The fact that Seung was also searching for something plausible, something that would allow him to save face, only seemed to make the humiliation more profound. How could one explain that losing Sasha was like losing a limb . . . or that the other women he'd burned his way through once home in Korea were merely prosthetic devices—temporary, clumsy by comparison, without warmth and fluidity and offering only dulled sensation, even though they were necessary, aesthetically appealing alternatives. But they would never be Sasha.

Damn what his aunt and her elderly advisors had to say about the appearance of grieving for the Shadow female. His mother's sister sounded like his dead sister Lei. Lady Jung Suk's name fit her well: chaste rock.

What would a Were Snow Leopard know of wolf causes or passions? Just because his mother, father, and sister were now deceased didn't give his aunt any familial rights of inheritance or a place in his den of government. So who was Lady Jung Suk to attempt to now interject herself into the running of a Werewolf Federation?

The Snows never mated with the ferocity of the wolf or stayed in a familial pack, never bonded for generation upon generation . . . They were loners who lived in the barren, icy mountains of Tibet and only came together to procreate once a season. And now his aunt would attempt to counsel him about appearances?

Shogun almost spat but refrained. She needed to be more concerned about how her dead sister and dead niece had committed treason, rather than trying to pretend that him marrying a nice Korean female Were and bearing an heir would wipe away the sins of the past . . . or allow her into his advisors' council.

How could anyone understand how the phantom pangs of holding Sasha near, his fingers playing against her supple skin, tasting her mouth, now haunted him? Even though their intimate union had never been fully consummated and had occurred long before he'd known that Hunter was his half brother, the memory of his sensual shadow dance with her refused to leave him.

It was so much worse now that he was back in New Orleans. He could almost feel her in the air and he tightened his grip on his carry-on duffel bag to keep from howling. Clan leaders could not go to war over a woman . . . Brothers could not go to war over a woman. Any hint of impropriety for such dubious reasons would make both men lose face. Hunter had saved his life; he had saved Hunter's life. Shogun repeated each fact to himself, making each one a silent mantra. A fragile peace between the once rival Werewolf and Shadow Wolf Federations had been forged, had followed the prophecy of a reign of peace ushered in by an amazing female of their kind . . . yet she also held the keys to more than mere peace; she owned both the keys and a lock on two men's hearts.

Tears of regret filled his eyes and quickly burned away as his cousin lowered his gaze, seeming confused and ashamed for him, but clearly not sure why. Shogun let out a slow and quiet breath to steady himself. The humor of fate was cruel. What the hell was wrong with him? This sentimental weakness was not the way of the wolf!

A few moments of reflection disappeared behind Shogun's normally controlled façade. He squared his shoulders and glanced around at his men. He refused to allow them to witness any distress that he owned. His wolf struggled for freedom but was trapped inside his skin waiting on the full moon, waiting on her. That was a private pain that he'd take to his grave, if necessary.

"I'll be fine," Shogun finally said as he briefly closed his eyes, again recalling Sasha's heated touch during their shadow dance in the teahouse, reliving it in his mind as he'd done a thousand times. "It will pass."

The figure moved out of the shadows and stood by the tree line near the Bayou House. Within moments, Buchanan clan sentries had picked up the scent, and Butch strolled over with a smile.

"It is in place. Make sure you do your part when the time comes."

Butch smiled, his gold-covered teeth gleaming. "Don't worry, we will. The heads of the Wolf Federation will fall."

"Excellent."

Before the wolves could howl their agreement, the shadowed figure was gone.

This was absolutely insane. Returning to Ethan's bar had resulted in nothing after an hour of talking to distraught employees. Hunter looked like he was ready to climb out of his own skin. But Sasha had to talk to Claudia, the waitress that was usually on Desidera's shift.

"Are you sure that she didn't have any beef with anybody around town?" Sasha said, willing her voice to remain calm.

Claudia shook her head. "Only a little fracas with Mike, but that was stupid."

"Mike the bartender?" Sasha said, now looking at Hunter.

"Yeah," the young woman said, her nervous gaze going between Hunter and Sasha. "He's due in at four."

"Uh-huh," Hunter muttered and then fell silent when Sasha shot him a look.

"So what was this little argument about?"

The young woman glanced around and then smoothed her auburn hair away from her round face. "Okay, this was not the kind of thing I want to see a guy thrown in the dungeon about, all right?"

"That's not what we're here for," Sasha said calmly. She ignored Hunter's raised eyebrow.

"Okay," Claudia said quickly, glancing around again. "He liked Desi, but she was *way* out of his league. So after he tried for who knows how long to get her to go out with him, she finally brushed him off, hard."

"When was that?" Sasha stared into the frightened woman's eyes. "Believe me, we are not going to be locking him up."

"It was the day before everything happened." Claudia let out a hard breath. "He got mad at her and said that she was the kind who would only lay down with rich kings that paid for it. But whatever she told him, he never said a mean word to her again."

Sasha didn't blink. "I already know about the Blood Oasis, so spill it."

"Okay, okay, she told Mike to fuck off because she was an employee over there and when he didn't believe her, she flashed her card. The guy went white, apologized, and left her alone, okay? Mike is a really decent guy. He's not a . . . you know." Claudia looked around quickly again and lowered her voice. "He's not a murderer."

Hunter wiped his palms down his face and pushed off the ladies' changing-room wall. "Yeah, we gathered. C'mon Sasha, everything here's a dead end."

Hunter was right. Ethan's place was making her skin crawl, and her nerves were so shot she could scream. Whoever killed Desidera had obviously found and removed what the poor girl had tried to stash for Sir Rodney, leaving them at yet another stupid dead end. Ethan had been virtually no help, either, not having a clue as to what it could have been—for all his Fae knowledge.

Sasha's cell phone buzzed and it gave her such a start that her hand flew to her chest as Hunter whirled at the sound.

"Yeah!" she said without formality. "What?"

"Uhmmm . . . we're outside?" Clarissa said, measuring her response.

"Be right out," Sasha muttered and clicked off the phone. What the hell was wrong with her?

"But what if we've missed something in here," Hunter suddenly said, beginning to walk down the hall, his gaze sweeping.

When he spotted the back staircase, he headed up, taking three steps at a time. Sasha was on his heels, but there was nothing to be found except storage space, a spare office, excess furniture, and old files. Above that was the attic, and Hunter stood in the middle of the floor staring up at the ceiling, sweat pouring off him.

Right now it felt like the walls of Ethan's Fair Lady were closing in on her and she could tell Hunter also felt it—but male pride refused to let it best him. Heat in the building had risen to the upper floors that lacked the benefit of air-conditioning. To make matters worse, now she had to deal with the fact that her human crew, along with Hunter's men, had tracked them down and were waiting outside, and still Hunter refused to relent.

"This is not going anywhere," Sasha finally said, throwing up her hands. "Give it up, dude. Whatever was here is gone. We've asked everybody we can ask. Look around—there are no hair fibers, not even any Were scent or blood scent up here . . . can we go?"

Hunter looked at her and growled. She pushed past him and headed for the stairs. The close confines and the heat were wearing her down, grinding her nerves to a fine dust.

By the time they'd reached the sidewalk, Hunter was almost panting and she could barely catch her breath. The interior air was damp but not as oppressive as the June humidity and midday heat on the streets of New Orleans. Looking at her bored, uncomfortable squad, she felt bad that she'd had to leave the rest of their team outside—but Ethan had insisted. It was also what Sir Rodney had requested, to keep as much of this as possible on a need-to-know basis only. Both Ethan and Sir Rodney wanted only her and Hunter to witness what had happened and she'd given her word.

Good thing they hadn't needed to stay inside The Fair Lady for too much longer, because she and Hunter might have come to blows. But as the thought crossed her mind, Sasha became still . . . Why was she thinking of doing battle with Hunter? They'd been getting on each other's nerves ever since they found the Phoenix, but prior to that they'd been making love and going at it like a couple of college kids. She glanced at him from the corner of her eye, noting how distressed his entire vibration seemed to be. What the hell . . .

Sweat had created a deep V on Hunter's army green t-shirt, starting at his heavy silver and amber amulet, and her tank top and jeans clung to her like she'd been poured into them. The thick silver chain around her neck with the etched amber piece dangling from it now felt like it weighed a ton. They'd only been inside about an hour and their guys that had been waiting double-parked in open jeeps looked like they'd been drenched in a sudden downpour.

Clarissa's plump face was red and damp, and her blond hair was practically plastered to her scalp. Woods, who was behind the wheel of the second vehicle, had a steady stream of sweat rolling down his temples, matting down his normally immaculate brunet hair, while poor Bradley, the eldest on the team and in his forties, had his head back with his eyes closed, apparently deciding to tough out the heat by going semiconscious. Right behind them in another haphazardly parked jeep, Fisher bopped to the radio like a lanky golden retriever that enjoyed the wetness—simply having the time of his life because it involved another adventure. Seeing him in the backseat joking with the baby of the group, Mark Winters, brought a smile to her face despite the circumstances or uncomfortable heat.

However, Hunter's main enforcer Bear Shadow, a three-hundred-pound Native-American double for an NFL line-backer, as well as Sasha's half brother Crow Shadow, a shorter, more sinewy, defensive tight-end version of "the Bear," seemed anything but relaxed and jovial. Sasha held her brother's gaze for a moment. Looking into Crow Shadow's face was like looking into a darker version of her own. His expression was tense but unreadable and only offered her a reflection of his exotic biracial elements of Native-American and African-American ancestry.

Still, there was a level of quiet anxiety in both Hunter's men's eyes that concerned her. Those two were normally laid back; they didn't do high anxiety unless something serious had raised their DEFCON levels. What had the two male Shadow Wolves locked in on that she hadn't seen or that her human squad hadn't detected?

Clarissa should have picked up something psychically wrong now, just like her Shadow Wolf familiars, Woods and Fisher, should have instinctively detected if something wasn't right. Their entire system was designed to preempt a threat. Plus, Bradley, their dark arts specialist, was always on guard, just like Winters's techno-gadgets should have sounded if there was something dangerous closing in on them. But everybody in the Paranormal Containment Unit squad seemed okay and only heat fatigued, except the Shadows . . .

She glanced at Hunter and then watched him take two more steps toward their vehicle, weave, and then catch his balance by grabbing on to a lamppost. Then he slowly turned around, his gaze pure wolf.

"You okay?" she asked, ruffling her hair up off her neck, seeking a breeze from any direction in the still air.

Hunter shook his head slowly. "No. Not at all."

For a moment she held his gaze and then looked around, stepping in closer. "What's wrong? What did you see in there that I didn't?"

Hunter's hands covered her bare arms, sending searing heat into her flesh. Confusion tore at her mind; was what he had to say so awful that he had to steady her with a touch?

When he angled his face and moved in, the strange action startled her and she pulled back, eyes wide. A kiss? Out in public? In front of their squad? *Hunter?*

Oh yeah, something was definitely wrong. They didn't do public displays of affection—ever.

"You okay?" she whispered, staring at him and then nervously glancing at her squad from the corner of her eye.

"I told you before. No," he said between his teeth, his canines beginning to crest.

"Then *what's* the matter?" She'd asked the question without blinking, almost without breathing.

"You." His grip tightened on her arms. "I can't explain it . . . but do I need to right now?"

"Yeah . . . *Hello* . . . We are out on the sidewalk and people are staring at us and a you're acting weird—"

The kiss was so sudden and feral that it knocked the wind out of her. One moment there was at least a half a foot between them, and the next she was wrapped in a vise-like grip, her body crushed against Hunter's stone-cut chest. Her amulet was pressing into her breasts from the force of its collision with the heavy amber and silver piece he wore. Winters's joking comments about them getting a room sounded so far away as Hunter's fingers threaded through her hair and within seconds splayed across her back. She swallowed Hunter's moan while trying to wrest herself from his grasp, but her legs were becoming rubbery as he devoured her mouth. The second he broke the kiss to gasp in a breath, she pushed his chest with both hands.

"Yo! Time out!" Sasha tried to step back as she wiped her palms down her face. "What just happened in there?"

Woods started up the motor of his jeep. "We'll catch you guys later tonight," he called out and put the vehicle in reverse.

Bear Shadow nodded and started his engine.

Fisher jumped out of the backseat of the third jeep and headed toward the jeep Hunter had been driving. "I've got you covered, man. Leave it here and you'll get towed for sure. Throw me your keys."

Hunter never answered, just dug in his pocket and threw his keys in the direction of Fisher's voice.

"No, no, no!" Sasha yelled, pure humiliation burning her cheeks. "This isn't what it looks like!"

Hunter stared at her. "*Yes,* it is."

It all happened so quickly that it seemed like a blur. One moment Hunter was staring at her, his eyes transformed to betray his inner wolf, the next second he'd spied the shadow cast by the lamppost, pulling them both into it to tumble into the shadow lands.

He'd landed them in the twilight place, the shadow lands where spirits walked and Shadow Wolves traveled, but that fact seemed completely lost on Hunter. Wide, hot palms covered her backside, pulling her in close as he aggressively sought her mouth with a moan. No matter how fantastic what he was doing felt, his entire demeanor was incongruent with what was going on. Two women had died, they had just been standing over the first victim's body . . . and that turned him on? Not a good sign.

"Stop!" Sasha said with a snarl and yanked away from Hunter's grasp. She lowered her head in wolf attack mode, feeling her ears begin to flatten against her skull. "It's dangerous in the shadow lands to be caught unaware. You of all people know that. How many battles have we fought in here? How many predators have we run from, coming through the zones? Once you start making love, you won't hear a thing. Never that in here."

She watched him back up and begin to rub the nape of his neck as though blood flow was returning to the thinking part of his body. Pointing toward the mist in a hard snap, she leveled her gaze at Hunter. "Two women just died, we just examined the bodies . . . now I want you to tell me real slowly and clearly why that just sent you into a mating frenzy."

"I haven't a fucking clue," Hunter said quietly in a far-off voice. His tone was bewildered, as though he'd come out of a bad dream. There was no anger or judgment in his response, only what seemed like pure disbelief. He looked down at his hands, studying them intently as they trembled, and then finally looked up at Sasha. "If one of my own men had gotten out of the jeep, I would have battled him for being too close to my mate while in season . . . but you're not."

"No . . . I'm not," Sasha said more softly, glad that the old Hunter she knew was beginning to return.

"I don't understand . . . I thought my system had beaten the contagion."

They stared at each other for what felt like a long time.

"This can't be the contagion," she finally said, now wrapping her arms around herself. "You beat it; Doc said you beat it—Silver Hawk saw you beat it in a vision."

"Then what was this!" Hunter began to walk in a circle, dragging his fingers through his disheveled hair, tearing the leather thong away from his ponytail to fling it on the mist-covered cavern floor. "It's come back before, lain dormant in my system for years, then erupted . . . I'm going back to our pack's north territory in the Uncompahgre. I need to be as far away from New Orleans as possible. Right now I can't risk an outbreak that could jeopardize you, my pack brothers, your human team, or even my blood brother Shogun again. He is on his way here; Sir Rodney is counting on us, and I'm unstable?"

He turned to leave and she caught his arm.

"We beat it before down here at Tulane Hospital . . . me, you, Doc, and Silver Hawk. The PCU's top biochemical expert, 'Rissa, is here—and she and Doc make a solid team. The core clan leadership is here in New Orleans. No one is back home, Max."

She hated that her voice had become so panicked, but if Hunter left, anything could go wrong, and that simply wasn't an option.

"Ethan's wife Margaret even helped sway the critical human physicians that we needed on our side at Tulane." Sasha bodily blocked Hunter as he shrugged out of her hold. "Max Hunter, listen to me for two seconds—you owe me that much. Think about it. If you've got the virus spiking in your system, all of your best enforcers are here—which means innocent women and children from the pack will be at your mercy up north. Do you honestly want that on your conscience? You could spread it up there, where no contagion currently exists, if that's what it even is. Plus, you've also got me and your brother down here, along with Bear and Crow. Alone up there, who can hunt you but us, if you have to be put down?"

It was insane logic, but her argument was what he'd needed to hear. She could feel it as his body relaxed and his eyes held uncertainty. Every fiber of her being knew the last thing that Hunter would be willing to risk would be an outbreak among the innocent, practically defenseless, members of the remaining Shadow Wolf pack.

"And what happens a few nights from now, when the moon waxes full . . . and it's your birthday, and we're out at Sir Rodney's ball? What happens if we are called upon for battle, and I may be an enemy within that you hadn't anticipated?" Hunter chuckled sadly and stalked away from her. "When are you going to just give up on me, Sasha, and finally put that silver bullet in my temple?"

"No time soon," she said, folding her arms over her chest and willing the quaver out of her voice. "Answer me this . . . When did you start feeling like you were losing it?"

Hunter let out a long, frustrated breath, keeping his back toward Sasha, and then jammed his hands into his fatigue pants' pockets. "I don't know. It just hit me all of a sudden."

"Think, man! Tell me when you felt the shift!"

"When we went back to Ethan's, all right!" He spun on her, eyes beginning to glow amber around the edges of his irises.

"Good. Now we're getting somewhere." She walked closer to Hunter, holding his gaze. When Hunter shut his eyes and swallowed hard, she stopped speaking.

"I never heard a word the staff was saying this second time we went in there—all I saw was you."

She hugged herself and turned away. This was definitely worse than she'd thought.

"Couldn't take my eyes off of you," he admitted in a deep rasp. "I could only focus on the way each pore leaked the smallest bead of perspiration . . . until your shirt clung . . . every shallow breath you took, trying not to breathe, but your breasts rose and fell. I had to walk away . . . had to go deeper into the room you interviewed them in to find a cool, dark place to stand, away from you. Every now and then the conversations you were having would fade . . . I'd simply hear the tone of your voice, Ethan's voice—the way a wolf would . . . without understanding the words, simply relying on the tone, then speech would return to me. At points I felt like I was blacking out. Then the pain came."

"Pain?" Sasha murmured, going to him.

Hunter nodded. "I've wanted you before, but never like I felt in there—no offense, just truth. I told you before I was no liar. But standing apart from you felt like an ache that twisted my gut into knots as a blade stabbed . . . Suffice to say, it hurt."

"It wasn't like that when you had the demon-infected Werewolf virus . . . was it?"

"No," Hunter said in a quiet rumble. "There was rage, there was hunt hunger, there was the painful transition and the increased desire, but wanting you was never a physical ache that hurt worse than a gunshot wound."

"A Phoenix flamed in that cellar in a totally weird way. Ethan can't hold his Fae glamour, albeit he was terribly upset . . . but still. Then you—and you weren't all right until we got outside of the normal dimension. Even outside on the street—"

"I was losing my mind." He looked at her without an apology in his eyes. "Truth."

"Yeah . . . you were," she said with a slight half smile.

"It's still there, you know," he said without a trace of humor in his expression. "Just not as acute, and requiring a great deal of concentration to keep it at bay."

"Oh . . . I'm sorry, I just thought . . . Never mind."

Hunter nodded. "But that does make me feel better, just knowing that in the shadow lands I have some measure of restraint. The more I think about it, before, when the contagion hit, shifting through the borders of dimensions made the virus spike in my system, so perhaps this is something else."

"In here," she admitted, "I'm not as angry . . ." Sasha lifted her hair up off her neck. "Did you notice last night, every time we went into the shadows, we might have been fighting, but we seemed to get clear once we came out?"

Hunter just nodded and stared at her.

CHAPTER 6

Clarissa held her cell phone away from her ear as the others in their ragtag, human-wolf combo squad watched her try to calm Ethan down.

"Ethan, Ethan," Clarissa soothed, "they are investigating, and uh, they will be back soon—you know Sasha and Hunter are on top of it."

Woods almost spit out his coffee as Bradley slapped his forehead. Winters snickered and just shook his head while both Shadow Wolves sat stone-faced, drinking their coffee and staring out the window. Clarissa gave the guys who were smirking the evil eye, telling them with colorful hand signals to knock it off.

"Why don't you tell ol' Ethan the truth, 'Rissa," Fisher said, shoveling eggs into his mouth with a wide grin. "The big guy got horn—"

Bear Shadow's grip on the front of Fisher's t-shirt stopped his comedic banter.

"That's my sister," Crow Shadow warned with a growl. "Be cool up in this diner, and any family business stays family business—understood, familiar?"

"You didn't have to get personal and call me a familiar, man. I was just joking around." Fisher yanked out of Bear Shadow's hold and stuffed a piece of bacon into his mouth. "Could everybody just chill out and eat? My bad, all right?" he said, chewing, which made both wolves visibly relax.

Bradley leaned forward, lowering his voice, glancing around the table while Clarissa continued to try to appease Ethan on the phone. "But don't you think all of this is a little strange?"

"What's strange?" Bear Shadow said with a low growl. "Ardent affection toward one's mate in season is natural." He shoveled a large forkful of sausage into his mouth, followed by a healthy hunk of pancakes. "It is the way of the wolf, human. You wouldn't understand."

Ignoring the affront to his human heritage, Bradley pressed on. "You two have not been able to normalize your eyes since Hunter came out of The Fair Lady. That's not normal. Ethan's glamour was completely gone when I went back in to get directions to this diner." Bradley stopped speaking as the waitress came over to refresh everyone's coffee.

"Pardon me, but can I ask y'all a question?" their waitress said with a bright smile. She tossed her loose blond curls over her shoulder, openly flirting with Woods.

Woods smiled, as did every male at the table. "Shoot . . . but only with a very small-caliber weapon."

The young woman giggled and poured coffee all around. "I was wondering if there was one of those conventions in town, you know those science fiction kinds of things where people dress up? I know we get all kinds for Mardi Gras . . . but you fellas have the wolf-eyes contact lenses in, and a little earlier there were some real handsome gentlemen with long hair and bows and arrows and multicolored contact lenses in . . . but I never knew you could get the kind that changed colors depending on how the light hit—and they had the ears, too," she said laughing, gesturing to her own to describe how the ones she'd seen had been pointed. "I've always wanted to go to one of the cons, I guess they're called . . . Are they fun?"

Stunned silent for an awkward few moments, no one spoke. Finally Bradley piped up to cover for the group. "It's actually being held in Houston and all of us are just passing through . . . but they are fun. If they have one here next year, you should go."

"I think I will," she said brightly. "Thanks, guys!"

Fisher and Crow Shadow got up from the table.

"Reconnaissance," Fisher said. "Gotta get a visual."

Crow Shadow nodded. "Definitely."

Clarissa covered the receiver with her hand, and then quickly got off her cell phone with Ethan. "Call you back."

No one spoke until the two soldiers returned, shaking their heads.

"Dudes were probably long gone," Fisher said, sliding into his seat.

Crow Shadow confirmed Fisher's assessment. "No fresh scent of Fae."

"But did you hear that?" Bradley hissed in an urgent whisper, looking around five ways.

"The Fae glamour isn't holding in the streets—normal humans like me and Winters, and, and that waitress saw *Fae archers*?" Bradley took an agitated slurp of his coffee as Bear Shadow and Crow Shadow leaned in closer. "Now tell me that's the way of the wolf. Something really freaky is going on and I don't think we've been fully briefed."

"I thought it was just me, just second sight kicking in stronger this time for some reason," Clarissa said as she glanced around the table. "But Ethan is also wigging out and won't say what he needs to speak to Sasha and Hunter about."

Woods's line of vision was still on the retreating waitress's butt, however. "She sure is a pretty young thing, though."

Bear and Crow pounded each other's fists as Fisher nodded and released a low whistle of appreciation.

"Is it just me, or do you guys with a little canine in you seem to be inordinately preoccupied with tail?" Bradley folded his arms over his chest, drawing snarls. "Seriously. Plus, we're told to sit outside of The Fair Lady for over an hour with no explanation. Something went down. It's clear from the little bit of Clarissa's conversation I could hear that something else happened at Ethan's establishment—something he's not willing to discuss with us, and our fearless leaders are AWOL. All of this is just a little coincidental for my liking."

"Dudes," Winters said, his gaze ricocheting around the group, "not being judgmental but, you all have been a little *extra* . . . just a tad over the top. Like, on edge."

Clarissa nodded and then closed her eyes. "Winters is Winters, Bradley is Bradley . . . I'm all right." She opened her eyes. "But anyone with some paranormal in their DNA just feels a little off center, energy wise. I can't explain it."

"Do you think that's what hit our alpha, some funky mojo?" Fisher said, wiping egg yolk off his plate with his toast and then stuffing it into his mouth. He held up his hands when Crow Shadow snarled at him. "Hey, hey, hey, I'm trying to be sure that everything is cool. I admit, I wasn't feeling altogether a-okay when the big guy came out of the bar."

"Honesty will keep us all alive if something untoward is happening all around us," Clarissa said, giving Fisher a high five. "Talk to me. When Hunter exited The Fair Lady, what did you notice?"

"Aw, man, it's personal," Fisher said, taking a big slurp of coffee. "Let's just say I was really hungry and cannot wait for this party in a few nights."

"Woods?" She stared at him, but his gaze was still fixated on the blond's backside.

"Yeah. Me, too," Woods muttered, not looking at Clarissa as he spoke. "I definitely need to walk the dog tonight. I won't last three days."

"Ooookay, that was TMI, but appreciated data. Bradley?" Clarissa folded her arms over her ample breasts, clearly becoming perturbed.

Bradley held up both hands in front of his chest. "Don't look at me; I'm cool as a cucumber."

"Winters?"

"I'm good. No issues here, just looking forward to the party like any good soldier would, but I'm cool."

"Bear?" Clarissa said with less attitude in her tone as the huge enforcer's gaze locked in on hers.

"I need to hunt." Without further comment, Bear Shadow stood, slapped a twenty-dollar bill down on the table, and walked out of the diner.

All eyes went to Crow Shadow.

"I respect you as my half-sister's closest female companion . . . as her team's third eye," Crow Shadow said in a low, sensual rumble. "I think you know the answer to the question. None of the wolves in this pack are settled this morning. And the longer I am in your presence, dear lady, the more unsettled I become." He stood slowly, still holding Clarissa's stunned gaze, dropped cash on the table and then left in a graceful, fluid, wolf move.

"Okay," she said, releasing a shallow breath with her eyes on Crow Shadow's retreating, athletic form. She tried to stop looking at his fantastically tight ass as he walked away, but miserably lost that battle.

"That clinches it. There's something floating in the air that's affecting some of the supernaturals." She fanned her face and looked around at her teammates. "Okay, so maybe we humans are a little affected too."

Sasha looked down at her cell phone the moment she and Hunter came out of the shadow lands. It was vibrating so insistently once a signal had been restored that it was practically making her teeth chatter. Eight missed calls from Ethan and Clarissa combined, and they'd only been gone at most forty minutes. Not wanting to waste time, she began reading text messages from her cell phone out loud to Hunter as he loped by her side.

"Ethan just said to get in touch—repeatedly said that. Fisher left our ride in the back."

Hunter didn't comment. His gaze was straight ahead on their parked jeep that was sitting just where Fisher said it would be.

She glimpsed Hunter from a sidelong glance as they entered the parking lot of what used to be Elf Dugan's Bed & Breakfast. Her entire team was put up there, along with Hunter's men. Thankfully, Doc and Silver Hawk would be coming in soon, too. It would be good to have everyone with a concentrated set of skills in close proximity, given the strange circumstances. Dugan had to be spinning in his grave. She was just glad that the little rat bastard's estate had lost his establishment to Ethan for siding with Vampires in the double cross against the wolf packs.

Seemed a fitting punishment—Dugan had done a foul deed and would have been banished from New Orleans under Sir Rodney's Fae martial law, had the baron not blown the greedy black heart out of his little weasel chest in open court. Vampires hated being snitched on. But since Dugan had acquired his B&B via Vampire blood money, literally, it was seized by Fae Parliament and awarded to the one who'd turned state's evidence—Ethan.

Poor old Dugan had also lost Finnegan's Wake, his prized bar across the street. When the sentence was levied, she could only guess that he'd probably put up a pitiful fuss from Hell. Taking material goods from Dugan was worse than having him drawn and quartered. Same held true of Baron Geoff Montague, Vampire extraordinaire. Word on the streets was that he'd paid a hefty tax for his troubles, enough to almost cost him a premier blood club.

Satisfied that justice had prevailed, Sasha jumped into the jeep, curious that Hunter had yielded the driver's side. "So, where to first?" she said with a smile. "The diner to catch up with the team, or Ethan's . . . although I seriously don't want to talk to Ethan until he calms down and we have more answers for him."

"Would you listen to yourself?" Hunter said, closing his eyes and rubbing his temples. "Your mood . . . is . . . odd."

Sasha sat back in her seat, fighting not to pout. She kept her hands on the wheel and then fished under the visor for the keys. "Odd."

"Your voice is . . . singsong, happy. You just heard that our allies are panicked, your squad is trying to locate you . . . and you act like we haven't a care in the world. Odd." Hunter turned and stared at her. "You almost sound like you're high, or something . . . but I was with you the entire time and know you didn't ingest anything that could have been spiked."

"Whoa . . ." Sasha sat back quickly and then leaned forward so fast that she almost bumped her nose on the rearview mirror as she tried to study her own gaze in it. "You're right. My mind has been jumping all over the place . . . I feel almost giddy, you're right . . . like I haven't a care in the world."

Hunter rubbed his palms down his face and then banged his head on the dashboard. "You do not want to know what I feel."

"Oh, shit."

He released a long, weary breath. "Yes. Precisely."

"Then why don't I feel that way if you feel that way?" She looked at him squarely and shrugged.

"To make me crazy," he said flatly.

"Are you serious?"

Hunter closed his eyes and leaned his head back on the headrest. "Sasha . . . believe me, it's working."

"Okay, I'm sorry. I just feel like I've gotta be on the move, gotta go hang out . . . do something other than be cooped up inside. It's so nice out here, man . . . It's summer!"

"You are not yourself . . . I am not myself. Two Phoenixes are dead from the same establishment that turned state's evidence at the United Council of Entities trials. Sir Rodney confirmed there is dark magick afoot—it is in the sigils they cannot decipher. We are out of our depth, if we are so affected that we cannot even focus on following a warm lead."

"Wow . . . yeah . . . you have a point," she said, turning on the ignition. "But, hey, why didn't you wanna drive?"

Hunter looked away, sending his gaze toward the Spanish moss–laden trees. "I can't," he admitted quietly.

Sasha cocked her head to the side and stared at him, her brows knit. Then slowly but surely she understood, covering her mouth with her hand. "Going from the gas to the brake would hurt that bad?" she asked in a shocked murmur.

He abruptly turned to stare at her, fury in his gaze. "Just shoot me."

"Okay, guys, it's on us this go-round," Clarissa said, marshaling the team that was left around the diner table, and then setting down her cell phone very carefully, "Sasha won't exactly tell me what's going on with Ethan, or her, for that matter, but she admits that her mood and focus is all jacked up—Hunter is messed up, just like the two Shadows that left us to go God knows where. And, since it would be a death sentence to go busting into Vamp lairs looking for clues, despite the daylight factor . . . I say we start with the local scuttlebutt we can get from area covens, Voodoo practitioners, snake charmers, Tarot experts, and the like. If Fae archers are being sighted in frickin' diners, then somebody has heard something. They always do, and if, by logical deduction, we all know that from our last trip down here, Vampires have the biggest axe to grind, we're gonna need evidence—as well as a way to reverse whatever they've probably done to out the Fae."

"I'm with you, 'Rissa," Bradley said, folding his hands around his lukewarm cup of coffee. "But I think we need to let Sir Rodney know that his Fae community is in full view of the general human population."

"True, but that's really Sasha's call, not ours. Either that, or we might have to leave that up to Ethan, because I haven't the foggiest idea how to find Sir Rodney or the beginning of his yellow brick road, so to speak, that's in the swamps." Clarissa looked around the table, keeping her voice low and private. "We don't even know how long we'll be able to function until what's affecting the supernaturals hits us."

Fisher bumped Clarissa's fist. "I, for one, am not voting for us going into the swamps without a full and stable Shadow Wolf escort. Who knows what the hell is out there this time?"

"Last time, something came through the demon doors and opened up a can of whoop ass on alpha-class wolf fighters—and they had the advantage of a full shape-shift. An M-16 is a good piece of artillery, but I'm with Fisher—it ain't worth jack shit if your arm isn't attached to your body."

"So we take the nerd approach," Winters said, smiling. "Go to the places where the worst that can happen is you get zapped by some bad juju, or maybe zombified . . . but I'd prefer that to a quick and painful death by dismemberment."

"I hear you," Woods said, knocking his coffee mug against Winters's. "So let's fan out—two-by-two detail. Put our ears to the ground and see what we come up with before the sun drops. Winters, you come with me and Fish."

CHAPTER 7

Sasha held the cell phone tightly in her grip, listening to Clarissa's urgent tone of voice. Hunter had been right—she was off her game, seriously so. But as her squad member thrust hard-to-ignore facts into her ear, Sasha felt her reasoning return.

"Have you told Ethan?" Sasha asked quickly, the moment Clarissa drew a breath. She waited, hearing what she already knew to be true—Clarissa hadn't contacted him. Sasha pushed the mute button for a second and turned to Hunter, watching him draw in slow breaths. "Ten dollars says that's why Ethan was blowing up my phone. He's in town and had to see the glamour fading all around him."

Hunter just nodded as she took the remainder of the information from Clarissa and then ended the call. Without waiting, she speed-dialed Ethan, and just listened, after announcing herself, while he filled her in through hysterical bursts.

"You're going to have to tell your constituents something," Sasha said. "There's no other way. So get a missive to Sir Rodney that he, or one of his top advisors, or captain of the guards, or whoever, is gonna have to come tell these folks something." She pulled the phone away from her ear when Ethan's voice hit a decibel that made the hair on her arms stand up.

When the call ended, Sasha simply stared at the telephone for a moment. "That went well," she said sarcastically.

Hunter had not said a word since they'd pulled over and parked. He was reclined in the seat, eyes closed, with his head leaning against the headrest.

"This thing is messing with my mind," Sasha said, staring across the green field.

"Tell me about it," Hunter muttered.

She shook her head, allowing the irritable comment to pass. Whatever was going on with them personally wasn't of paramount concern. The facts surrounding the deaths were worrying her mind like a dog worries a bone. Fact one—sorcery of some sort was involved . . . but probably not Fae, because of the iron gate thing the Pixie explained. Fact two—both Phoenixes had been in the company of Vampires, which had access to covens that could have been involved, and the Vamps certainly had enough of a motive. It was their style, and Desidera had mentioned them in passing to Sir Rodney.

Next fact that needed more exploration was the feral scent at each site . . . If working with Vamps to deliver bad juju, Weres could certainly pass through iron; they wouldn't have a sulfur trail like a Vamp, but they might have been able to get some magick razzle-dazzle dropped on them to throw any wolves off the trail. Buchanan Broussard's people, the Louisiana clan—or what was left of it—certainly had an axe to grind with Hunter and Shogun . . . more so than the Fae. But an unholy alliance between the Vampires and what was left of a rogue wolf clan wouldn't be a first. At this point, all their enemies would be scrambling to create hemorrhages in the strong three-way alliance among the North American Shadow Wolves, Southeast Asian Werewolves, and the Fae. Then, there was also this Unseelie queen, an ex-wife for God's sake. Sasha flopped back against the seat.

"You know what—"

Hunter held up his hand. "Before you launch into a full-blown mental download, give me a minute. All right?"

Sasha blew out a breath, forcing a damp curl off her forehead. The shade from the tree gave a little respite, but not much. Her mind raced ahead of Hunter's, unable to get the gears to slow down. She looked at the telephone, wishing that a signal could go through to Sir Rodney's castle. Talking by cell phone by day didn't worry her in this remote, sunny location; if it was Vamps, the only way they could intercept her call was at night or through human helpers.

Impatient, she dialed Ethan again, this time speaking to him more calmly as she let him know her list of suspects, which was pretty much every enemy they had in New Orleans. Although she talked on the phone to Ethan, she faced Hunter as she spoke. The message was really for him. He had to get this mental download; he had to help her figure out how many hands were in the pie at one time. More importantly, they had to figure out how to reverse the bad spell.

"They will not force my hand!" Sir Rodney shouted.

"But milord, we must employ patience," Thompson Loughlin warned. He rubbed a meaty palm over his salt-and-pepper thicket of hair, adjusting his uncomfortable human businessman's attire. "I have been to town; the humans are still unaware."

Sir Rodney's gaze narrowed. "Patience, you say? You heard what Ethan McGregor said that Sasha told him. Her humans saw the absence of a glamour on *Fae archers* at *a diner!* Ethan's missive was fraught with histrionics! He had to shutter his doors at The Fair Lady to human patrons in the French Quarter, because none of his glamour is holding. Human workers are managing Finnegan's Wake, and the bed-and-breakfast has been turned over to Sasha's and Hunter's squads to fend for themselves, man, because the Fae workers cannot be seen behind the counter. In the last twenty-four hours, something has happened, something insidious to speed up this dark magick, and we're still chasing theories and ghosts!

"If the Seelie glamour is fading in the human streets, we must warn our people," Sir Rodney said, pounding his fist in his hand. "Also, Sasha Trudeau's list of suspects is formidable. At this point, who has done this is not as much a priority as how we can stop it."

"Sire, we must find the culprits; they cannot go without redress," his top advisor warned.

"But knowing how to stop it has everything to do with who cast this madness against us!" Sir Rodney shouted, totally contradicting himself. "How can you possibly come up with an antidote if you cannot even break the code on the sigil? If we know who our enemy is, then we know the extent of their capabilities . . . It's as though they are one step ahead of us at every turn, as though they are reading our minds!"

"Indeed, sire," his advisor said calmly.

The two men stared at each other in the king's private chamber.

"Milord, as you are aware, this could cause an uprising amongst the citizenry, if they felt your power was fading, thus affecting theirs, and they were not duly warned. Two rare Phoenixes are dead, but that is not our fault, as tragic as that may be. No one could have foretold those events any more than humans could have stopped Jack the Ripper. But if our Fae community were to learn that you had foreknowledge of our weakening powers and did nothing to alert them so that they could seek shelter and safe haven, that would be grounds for impeachment, sire."

When the king only looked at him, the elder advisor pressed on. "It is our primary responsibility to make sure that our constituents are safe from outside harm . . . That the wolves uncovered a sigil means that this is worse than we'd originally concluded. If those outside of the Fae community found a sigil, you know what that means . . . the perpetrators are baiting us, mocking us."

"But who would be so bold . . ." Sir Rodney walked over to the high, leaded, beveled glass windows of his chamber. "Chaos magick is not just the province of the Unseelie Fae, but could be employed by strong covens, Vampires, any dark sorcerers. This is outright terrorism!"

"Milord . . . as we investigate, our first order of business is to protect our citizenry."

A paranormal community emergency call had gone out to all the allies, and the result filled The Fair Lady with multiple Parliaments of varied entities. Time was too short to get everyone quickly to the Sidhe; Ethan's place, reinforced by readied soldiers, was the best they could do with short notice.

Fae archers; burly Order of the Dragon riders and their colorful, silk ribbon–sleek mates; Pixies; Brownies; Gnomes—every ethnicity of Elves was present. All except the members of the shy, forest-dwelling Mythics, like Unicorns and Yeti, were in attendance—but even they sent proxy representatives by way of nature Sprites and Wiccan Whitelighters.

Phantoms moaned and hid within earshot inside the walls, while tiny Faeries danced gray plumes of fear amid the bar lights. There were so many paranormal leaders crowded into the main hall that there was now standing room only.

The establishment drew its shades to the human public as the afternoon sun cast golden prisms against the immaculate blond wood floors. A discreet sign was hung outside—PRIVATE PARTY—so as to not offend the limited human clientele or law enforcement. No Vampires would have been allowed, however, under the given suspicions. But that point was moot, since the meeting was strategically being held during the day. Only allied wolf packs were given admittance.

Sasha looked around the room, knowing that Sir Rodney's worst nightmare had come true. The secret was out amongst the allies; it had gotten so bad that an executive decision had to be made—for the safety of his people and those who clung to his protection, there had to be some disclosure. Pure defeat filled her; she and Hunter had failed.

Ethan cleared his throat and tapped the stage microphone, trying to wrest order from the nervous patrons, while his bartenders passed out free drinks and overflowing steins of Fae ale to quell unrest and to make his message easier to absorb. The steely-eyed captain of the Fae guard awaited a proper introduction as Ethan tried to bring order. Then the door opened one last time and she saw him.

The sun framed Shogun with his retinue not far behind. His gaze hunted for her, found her, and locked on her with breathtaking intensity. Golden bronze, clean shaven, his hair an onyx spill down his back in sharp contrast with the white linen shirt and pants he wore. She couldn't take her eyes off of him and her libido came to life with a vengeance though Hunter stood right next to her. Yet she couldn't look away.

How could this be; why was this happening? Sasha felt like she was suddenly drowning in a well of emotions that made no sense.

This is insane, she thought to herself, casting her gaze to the floor while she struggled to breathe. *Get it together, Trudeau.*

Hunter's attention had snapped to the bar's entrance and now he tilted his head, narrowing his gaze. The two brothers nodded in strained recognition. Heaven help her—her inner wolf was clawing at her insides. Whatever had affected Hunter earlier in the day, she now had a full appreciation of his agony. Her breasts had become heavy and tender in a matter of seconds, the tips of them stinging pebbles that ached so badly she had to ball her fists at her sides to endure. Sasha briefly shut her eyes. She craved touch; wetness betrayed her, engorged her till she bit her bottom lip.

Eyes forward on Ethan, ever the soldier, she stood at

attention, watching the proceedings and hearing nothing. Her goal was singular—to get through the meeting without starting a Wolf war.

"Now that most of the leadership is assembled, we must make you aware of some strange goings-on that have some of us deeply concerned," Ethan said, hedging. He waited until the crowd settled down more and shouts and calls asking what the gathering was all about subsided. "My two lovely Phoenix waitress showgirls were recently found flamed . . . without the normal transition back to their gorgeous human bodies."

An audible gasp ripped through the bar and then entities began calling out questions all at once.

"Please, please, this is difficult enough to convey without a lack of order. I first wanted to address the rumors of the deaths of our most cherished employees and friends before launching into even worse matters at hand . . . if one can even compare. All of your questions will be answered. This is why Sir Rodney has sent his captain of the Fae guard—Captain McIntyre—to go over everything in greater detail. But as I said, our Phoenixes were the first to be so horribly—"

"Well, is it contagious?" a huge Dragon rider shouted out from the back. "If so, what the hell is wrong with you, man, bringing us all in here to catch the rot?"

Jeers met Ethan and he held up his hands and shouted above the din to be heard. "No, it's not contagious in that way," Ethan said quickly as the crowd erupted again into disgruntled murmurs.

Captain McIntyre stepped forward, causing a respectful hush to momentarily befall the crowd. "What is of foremost concern now is it seems the humans can see through our Fae glamour . . . It's not working . . . nor are any of the other races' illusion castings able to protect them from the naked human eye, for some reason. At least that is what is happening in New Orleans; we're not sure if it extends beyond this region."

"What?" a Fae archer called out. "Man, have you gone daft? Do you know what ye are saying?"

"We'll all have to hide, go deep into the woodlands as though in exile," another shouted, pointing at Ethan and ignoring the captain. "This is dark magick afoot, if ever I've seen such! You've brought this on our heads from the Vampires, Ethan!"

Hunter looked at Sasha. "Are you going to help the man out, or what?"

She nodded, but her voice wouldn't work on demand. She stared up at Hunter, mesmerized by his mouth as a shudder of violent need passed through her womb. A quiet gasp is all that came out instead of protest, but the recognizable sound drew Hunter closer. Common sense clicked in as she saw Shogun working his way through the crowd to get to her.

"Don't kiss me—not here. Please, I'm begging you," she said in a tense whisper, and then propelled herself forward toward the stage.

"My human squad witnessed what Ethan and Captain McIntyre told you—what they say is true," Sasha shouted and Ethan hurriedly dropped the mic down to her so she could be heard. The captain stretched out his hand to help her up, but in one fluid move Sasha jumped up, caught the microphone, and landed on the stage without assistance. She saw Shogun stop advancing. Hunter closed his eyes in a slow blink. She had to get them all to understand quickly and then get out. "This isn't Ethan's doing! And don't shoot the messenger," she said, motioning toward Captain McIntyre. "The same forces that tried to separate us before are no doubt trying to be sure that we do not stand united now!"

"Those are pretty serious charges," a Brownie called out nervously. "How do we know who's behind anything? It could be a new virus or Fae sickness."

"There's never been a sickness that steals glamour," Ethan yelled without the aid of the mic. "When in our history have innocent Phoenixes ever burned and not come back? This is foul play, I tell you. Open your eyes!"

"Ethan is right," Sasha said, each breath labored. "Something is wrong. It's not normal that Fae glamour is permeable to human awareness. It's not normal that Phoenixes can't transition properly, or that wolves are having primal transformation spikes before the full moon even rises. What's more important is we all know that after the trial, the Vampire Cartel, in collusion with a treasonous Fae, Dugan, and double-dealing area Werewolves, had an axe to grind. We can't prove they are the source, and to say so is libel and slander, which I'm sure they'd seek redress for—so I'm not saying they did anything without proof. But we've got two dead girls from an establishment that turned state's evidence against them. Where I come from, murder is a capital offense worth investigating."

Fearful murmurs broke out, creating a low din. Sasha closed her eyes and wiped the sweat from her brow.

"I hate to break it to everyone, especially before Sir Rodney's fabulous gala," Captain McIntyre said, standing firm and speaking in a loud, clear voice, "but it is advisable to watch your backs and to stay out of human sight. We don't want to cause a panic amongst the locals or human law enforcement."

"When did Sir Rodney learn about this?" an angry patron yelled out. "We need to find out if his Sidhe is still a safe haven, or maybe we should just go home this year. I didn't come all the way from the Bonnie Isles to have me last days end in a swamp in New Orleans! We could attend the fêtes in Scotland, Wales, Ireland, for that matter . . . even London—but we came at the invitation of the Seelie Court king."

A rousing aye rang out, and Sasha knew that she and Ethan were losing ground fast. The only thing to do at this point was appeal to the sense of righteous indignation that all worthy Fae owned when they thought they were being run off.

"When Sir Rodney learned of this is of no import! He is our sovereign and some things are not meant for public consumption! I have convened this meeting on the orders of our king, and his Sidhe is refuge," Captain McIntyre shouted above the din, but was promptly ignored.

Pandemonium had replaced order and there was only one thing to do—appeal to the primal instinct within the crowd.

"So, that's it?" Sasha shouted into the mic. Dead silence greeted her. "You're going to fold your tents and allow a group of dark forces terrorists to just run you off your land? You're going to allow them to best your magick, make you turn away from your Seelie king, put your tail between your legs, and hide? I don't know what this is, but I'm not running from it! I'm staying until we hunt the bastards down—staying until the last wolf stands!"

She looked at the strongest group in the room, the Order of the Dragon, feeling their indignation palpably rising as the spiked-armored bikers glanced at one another with angry glares, snorting fire. Fae archers lifted their chins, seeming resolute now that their honor had been called into question. Pixies and Faeries began emitting dark plumes of furious black dust, while the Brownies and Gnomes were finger-sparking mad. Even the Phantoms came out of the walls, hurling glasses in peak poltergeist form, clearly ready for war. This is what was needed—unity. Division would cripple them.

Fired up, Sasha walked across the stage and then looked at the Wolf Clan factions in the room. Perspiration rolled down her back, down her cleavage, her entire body was soaked with an adrenaline rush. She was so close to a wolf transition that her voice bottomed out on a low female alto and the hand that gripped the mic shook as her nails lengthened.

"Gentlemen, ladies . . . standing your ground and defending your territory, as well as your right to exist in pure freedom, may not be the way of the Fae, but turning tail and running is *not* the way of the wolf!" She released the howl that had been pent up inside her, and simultaneously all the wolves in the room joined in, sending chills down her spine.

"There is an allied team finding out who did this, and the moment we are sure, we hunt!" she shouted.

A loud aye went up as a singular roar. Fire blasts and released arrows hit the ceiling. Feet stomped the floor in a unified thud.

"As one!" a lead Fae archer yelled out.

"As one!" the leader of the Order of the Dragon confirmed.

A miasma of colored Faerie lights zinged around the room as Gnomes and Brownies chanted, "As one, as one, as one!"

But the voice that cut through the din stole her focus. It was a deep baritone from the middle of the crowd that made her insides tremble.

"As one!" Shogun shouted and simply nodded toward her—the private meaning implicit in his gaze.

Hunter spun, staring at his brother for a moment, and then released his assent in a deeper baritone that was just above a snarl. "As one, *brother*." He turned back to face the stage slowly, his expression unreadable as he stared at her.

The sight of two alphas so near to mortal combat spiked insanity within her. Sasha dabbed the perspiration from her throat with the back of her wrist. It was a slow, sensual invitation to claim her vulnerable kill zone and she couldn't have stopped herself if she'd wanted to. Her body was on autopilot, her human losing ground quickly to her inner wolf. The more the alphas prepared for a lunge, the more they turned her on. Potential combat crackled in the air; the Fae were oblivious, but the wolf packs stood at the ready for a bloody brawl—waiting to see if instinct or alliances would win the silent struggle.

Breathing deeply, watching every positioning move of the dominant males in the room, she wet her lips with the tip of her tongue. Hunter squared his shoulders as Shogun tilted his head. She could see thick ropes of muscles coiling tighter beneath bronze skin, beneath dark walnut skin . . . They smelled fantastic, canines cresting, battle imminent. They were magnificent. The air suddenly became still and there was no sound, only her heartbeat, their heartbeats.

The human part of her brain tried to wrestle with reason, tried to tell her primal instinct that this had to be part of the bad juju that was affecting the area. She had to get out of Ethan's bar. The energy here was dangerous for her, Hunter, most likely Shogun, too. But her wolf was hearing none of it. She studied both mating candidates carefully, the she-wolf within loyal only to natural law now—which one would be the dominant male . . . which one would produce the strongest heirs . . . which one would survive the vicious battle . . . which male would she mate for life. They seemed to know her questions, too; their understanding reflected back at her from the wolves in their eyes.

Ethan grabbing the microphone gave her a start and temporarily broke the spell. She watched Hunter's shoulders relax as Shogun pulled back closer to his men. Sasha dragged her fingers through her hair and let out a quiet breath. Her body ached, but a sudden death match had been averted.

"We have a Shadow Wolf envoy going with me and my wife to get word of the outcome of this meeting to Sir Rodney," Ethan said, seeming much more confident now that Sasha had swayed the crowd. "They will bring you return word about the state of his fortress. But we felt it would be completely irresponsible to leave, not inform all of you, and then come back to who knows what."

Whatever was happening to her was kicking her ass, big time. The adrenaline jolt, quickly followed by a fast diffusing of the wolf brawl, was sending her through changes that had her reeling. Sasha bent and placed her hands on her knees, gasping.

"You all right, lassie?" a huge Gnome in the front asked.

Sasha looked up and snarled. "No. Not at all."

The crone sat back in her chair, staring at Bradley and Clarissa, and laughed. "You two can't pay me enough to do a divination on that subject. Seeing Faeries and Elves, ha!" She shook her elderly head, causing the huge golden earrings in her sagging earlobes to bounce. "Leave it be; let it rest. It's an old fight. Sometimes you got to let sleeping dogs lie."

Clarissa stared at the drawn, paper-thin skin of the reader's face, studying each line in what used to be a tea-in-milk Creole complexion. Wisps of white hair escaped her lavender kerchief, making Madame Cottrell seem like a shrunken head wearing a wig. Giving up, however, was out of the question. Her second sight was waning fast and they needed answers.

Madame Cottrell smiled as Clarissa drew a breath to speak. "You're a seer. So why you got to come to me and try and drag me into it?"

"Because, for some reason, my sight has been off ever since I got here . . . except for very surface matters." Clarissa gave Bradley a look and he only nodded.

"Mayhap that's 'cause there's some things you ain't supposed to see."

"Maybe," Clarissa said, baiting the elderly woman into a game of indirect revelation.

"What you know about the history of these parts?" Madame Cottrell asked with a toothless grin.

"That's a broad question, ma'am," Bradley replied with a droll smile. "We could get into the founding of the city, the Louisiana Purchase, the Civil War . . . or we could talk Vamp—"

"No!" Madame Cottrell said, slapping down her bony palm on the small oval table that divided them and making the candle on it wobble. "We cannot talk about them in here, ever."

"All right," Clarissa said, eyeing Bradley. She toyed with the crocheted tablecloth. "We could talk about the history of magick spells in the area."

Madame Cottrell sat back, jingling her change purse. "That's always been an interesting subject, especially during hard economic times."

Clarissa nodded to Bradley, who immediately reached into his shirt pocket to produce a thousand dollars in ten crisp one-hundred-dollar bills. He fanned them on the table before the old Tarot reader like a card spread. The reader chuckled.

"That's just about enough to give you a history lesson that will take you to a coupla months ago, but won't give you much insight." Madame Cottrell picked up the bills and neatly folded them away into her sagging bosom. "Now, let me see . . . how can I put this delicately?" She clucked her tongue and looked off into the distance as she picked up her cards. "Lotta years ago there was a struggle between the wee folks . . . didn't start this side of the water."

"The Fae?" Bradley said, glancing at Clarissa.

"Mmm-hmm." Carefully shuffling the deck, Madame Cottrell took her time placing cards down in a Celtic cross spread. "Good ones and bad ones, just like people—good and bad."

"Seelie versus Unseelie," Bradley said, nodding.

"Oh, I see we've got us a resident expert, huh," the old woman said sarcastically. "You ain't as blind and dumb as you tried to make me think." Madame Cottrell narrowed her gaze on Bradley and then smiled. "All the better. Saves me having to explain what I really shouldn't be explaining, no way. But, yeah . . . the Seelie be the good ones, the Unseelie be the bad ones. Even the worst covens don't mess with Fae dark magick—that's why all of Louisiana decided to stay out of this recent row."

Clarissa stared down at the cards and placed her fingertips on the edge of the card containing a burning tower.

"It's all coming down, isn't it? The fortress . . . and old alliances. Just like in the cards . . . that's what it means, right?"

"Ain't nothin' in stone. Can't never be sure what people gonna do—but there's three men about to act a pure fool," Madame Cottrell said, pointing out cards with a hanged man, a knight surrounded by bundles of twigs, and a court jester. She then laid her finger on a card with a blindfolded woman who sat with two swords in her hand. "She's gotta make a choice, hold her ground. Seems she got blades that can cut deep no matter which way she swings 'em."

Both Clarissa and Bradley stared at each other.

"Something is driving the allies toward war," Clarissa said. "And they are using a female as bait."

"You said it, I didn't . . . You're the seer, child. I just read the cards," Madame Cottrell said smiling. "Sometimes men lose their natural mind over a pretty woman. Sometimes a pretty woman gets a kick out of watching them scrap like dogs just for her. Then, once everybody done got cut up and kilt up and the cops come, she cries. That's the sick part. Happens every day in the bars. Ain't so uncommon. I ain't tellin' tales outta school," she added, looking around nervously as though some unseen force might be eavesdropping. "Everybody's got a weak spot."

"Just like the Fae's weak spot is staying undisclosed to human view through a glamour . . . and Phoenixes must be able to transition from flames, and Yeti and Unicorns rely on being elusive, and Dragons count on brute strength that might fail in a firefight," Clarissa said softly, her voice gaining a far-off tone. "If all that changes . . ."

"Bingo," Madame Cottrell said with a triumphant smile. "Pixies and Faeries got to be sure their dust works, too . . . even they can get thrown off. But you didn't hear that from me."

"And wolf packs have to observe serious territorial protocols between clans . . . between brothers." Clarissa closed her eyes. "This could get really, really bad, if Hunter perceives a threat, and Sasha, under the influence of dark magick, stokes that in him . . . or a rival. It could tear the Wolf Federations apart. We've got to get back, Bradley. We need to let Silver Hawk and Doc know, stat."

"So you're saying dark magick is at the root of it? Then how do we counteract what's been done?" Anxious, Bradley leaned forward, but Madame Cottrell sat back and placed a gnarled finger to her lips for a moment.

"I ain't saying nothing." Madame Cottrell folded her arms over her bony chest. "Common sense be your guide, not me. Just stands to reason that when folks tend to make a really ugly spell, they generally seal it with a backlash. I ain't fittin' to be backlashed. This reading is over."

Bradley looked from Madame Cottrell to Clarissa as the old woman began collecting her cards. "This thing has what amounts to a dead man's switch. That's why none of our usual contacts will talk to us."

Madame Cottrell just nodded with a sad smile. "You folks have a blessed day."

CHAPTER 8

She'd transitioned so quickly that for a moment all Hunter could do was stare at the majestic silver wolf that graced the stage. Her clothes floated down to pool at her paws. Quiet murmurs of awe wafted through the room and in the next second she was one with a shadow and gone.

The righteous fury that he felt fled him the instant she disappeared. He felt his brother lunge forward in wolf form too late. Sasha had chosen the shadows—a place that Werewolves couldn't navigate. The choice, therefore, in his mind, was clear. She'd chosen him over a rival.

He wouldn't turn around to witness Shogun's distress, would allow his rival to save face, and wouldn't acknowledge that his endurance had shattered . . . That might start a war—and they were still brothers, after all.

Without turning, Hunter leaped up onto the stage in two easy bounds, swept up Sasha's clothes, and found her shadow haven.

The moment he saw her, saliva burned away from his mouth. She was sitting in the shadow land mist with her arms wrapped around her knees, shivering violently in her human form . . . beautiful eyes closed. There were a hundred points he needed to make, a thousand injustices to correct. The way she'd treated him had been outrageous;

she could have started something no life mate should have to endure—a dominance battle for the affection of one's chosen.

He dropped her clothes at his feet to make her aware that he was there, fury on a collision course with desire. Then she opened her gorgeous gray eyes and held his complaints for ransom.

"Why?" His voice came out sounding gentler than he intended. He hadn't wanted her to hear the hurt within it. Any other questions he'd had got trapped behind his Adam's apple when she stood in one graceful move, nude.

"It will never happen again," she said quietly, walking toward him.

"It can never happen again," he shouted. "Not like that! Not with him! Not with any fucking body, Sasha!"

He hated that she hadn't even flinched and that her eyes held no remorse, only desire. He hated that his will was in shambles as she sauntered closer . . . hated that he couldn't take his eyes off her exquisite nakedness. But more than anything, he hated that until his brother entered the bar, sex had been the last thought on her mind.

"Get dressed." His directive sounded hollow even to him; he hadn't moved, hadn't looked away. She owned him and she knew it. "This doesn't change anything, Sasha."

Her warm palm slid against his cheek. "I was so hoping that it would."

"You truly wanted us to kill each other—is that it? Is that what turned you on!" He still couldn't look away or back away as she closed the space between them and her body molded to his.

"What do you want me to tell you?" she whispered, tilting her head to the side as she studied him. "Some things are inherently female. You know the way of the wolf."

He wanted to slap her, needed to push her away. That was *not* what he wanted to hear. She seemed to understand that, too; her slight smile told him so.

"I love you. If anything happened to you, I'd die—and you know that."

"I'm done, Sasha." Dead serious, no nonsense in his tone, he would walk. On principle, he would!

"Actions speak louder than words. I came to where there could be no battle, knowing how badly I needed to mate . . . Despite the dark energy, my choice was clear." She took his mouth and stole all future protests with it. "If you're still angry, I can understand . . . but why don't you punish me now and we can discuss it later."

He'd slowly fisted her hair as she'd spoken; her murmur offering redemption, her plump mouth an intoxicant. This woman, bad spell or not, was incorrigible. There was no apology even in her tone, just an outrageous statement of fact. What she'd said was the bitter truth. It was an argument he would have used under similar circumstances.

Still, he wanted her contrition for the suffering she'd caused. Maybe even wanted her to walk a mile in his shoes—when he was so close to begging that he'd had tears in his eyes. All day long he'd wanted her like this and then to almost have to fight to be with her was more than he could tolerate.

She leaned in to kiss him again, and this time he lifted his chin, intent on telling her no. He would not be played like this, no matter what. It was in that moment that he knew something was wrong with him, with her, with them. If there was dark magick afoot, then clearly they'd been influenced.

But she stripped his resistance when she stripped his t-shirt over his head, then unbuttoned and unzipped his fly. There were things he needed to say, there was bullshit they needed to get straight, and she needed to know that . . . but damn.

Skin to skin, he was wide open. Sweat-slicked fire, she climbed up his body like a hungry flame and brought him to his knees, all offenses torched.

"Take me somewhere safe."

It wasn't a request but a throaty demand. He remembered her edict. *Never here.* She was right; there'd be no way to stop. He'd heard her in his soul, not with his ears. Right now he was deaf. Instinct kicked in as he kicked out of his boots, shed his fatigues, and dropped her in a hard roll in a wildflower field—the Uncompahgre was his territory, his home hunting ground. North country. Great Spirit deliver him, he'd die in her arms.

Sasha's fire burned away principle, scorched will, wiped the slate clean. There'd be no argument left once she got done.

Her hands traced heat-seeking shudders down his back and over his ass. Butter-soft skin fused to his, her tongue untangling sanity from his mind. Without warning, she pulled him inside a liquid inferno; pain, pleasure, a near loss of consciousness, all so fast and hard his voice rent the air.

Birds took flight from the field. Grass and flowers became one with her hair. She-wolf consumed him, ate him alive, her skin igniting crazed thrusts as he looked into her eyes. The bend of his elbow found the bend in her knee; he had to go deeper. Had to find that spot of contrition, that place that made her holler and beg his goddamned pardon.

Warm summer air licked his back, stroked his shoulders, and pelted his arms. His thrusts became a demand for redress. But she wasn't backing down; her alto moans simply begged him for more.

Gasping, sweat pooled in the small of his back, slid down his thighs. Hell yeah he knew the way of the wolf. Her hands threaded through his hair, her breasts a lifted offering he could not deny, the taste of her salt-stained sweetness. He found anchor on her smooth waist, the curve of her hip, then a tight lobe that made her whimper.

Skin slapping skin, making the sound of hot summer love . . . Yes, this was north territory, his territory, marked by the way of the wolf. Punishment for offenses exacted, alpha style. Yeah, they'd discuss it later. Apology in a pound of flesh accepted. The scent of her and broken grass, rich earth—summer madness. Sasha's voice bottomed out in his sac, her arches calling his wolf, driving him harder. Heaven help him. Let it rain. His body smoldered till he could feel sweat sizzle.

Her hard convulsion embedded his name in a sob. All movement stuttered. Blinding pleasure choked his groin, seized his heart, and emptied his lungs. He couldn't catch his breath as the climax tore through him. Staccato chants of ecstasy stilled wildlife. Eyes shut tightly, head thrown back, he was deaf to all sound but her and his howl.

After what seemed like a long time, he could finally roll over. Sound slowly returned, but the late afternoon sun was still too bright to open his eyes. Warm, soft skin coated his side and his fingers made a lazy figure eight in the small of her back.

"You still want to talk . . . you still angry at me?"

He didn't move, couldn't even open his eyes. "No."

Her mouth brushed his and he pulled her against him in a tender but possessive embrace. If she'd let him, he'd keep her here until moonrise . . . here in this very natural, uncomplicated place where next time he could love her slow and true.

But that was doubtful, and knowing that made him sad. He could feel her smile against his chest. The she-wolf had bested him. If he'd had the energy he might have laughed. The entire thing, in hindsight, was so ridiculous—yet he doubted that she would have given him the same pass were the shoe on the other foot. There was no equity; that he was sure of. Female justice was slanted. Any male with common sense knew that the female of the species was brutal . . . never as pliant or as easily satisfied as the male. Women also held a mean grudge. After a beer, he and Shogun would be cool. That was the way of men. Period. Hunter sighed.

"You're sure you're all right?" she asked quietly, seeming intent on destroying his peace.

"Yeah . . ." he said beginning to doze. "Consider yourself punished once I get my second wind."

Silver Hawk sat in a chair facing Doc, both men listening intently to Clarissa's and Bradley's report. The old shaman remained silent, his silver braids slowly rising and falling with each quiet breath as he looked at his friend of many years—the doctor who'd helped him save his grandson, Hunter. Two old men of many wars: Doc had fought within the military to keep his daughter Sasha's Shadow Wolf heritage a secret, while he'd fought within the Shadow Wolf Clan to keep his grandson Hunter alive. Silver Hawk stared at Doc, seeing how time had created a road map across his friend's weathered brown face and stolen a good portion of his gray hair, knowing that they were mirrors of each other. It was in his friend's eyes, and he could only assume that the bond was reflected within his own, too.

Occasionally they would glimpse each other, or look over to monitor Winters, Fisher, and Woods. The suite they'd congregated in at the bed-and-breakfast was crowded. Voices were low murmurs of halting facts. Winters's fingers were a blur on his keyboard as he accessed the PCU encrypted site, searching for data on the Unseelie-Seelie wars from Bradley's extensive files on all matters related to dark arts.

"The seer we went to, Madame Cottrell, got off on a tangent and started talking about ancient Seelie and Unseelie history. Now, I can't say for sure, but sometimes these old ladies encode their readings . . . so if I go back and assume she wasn't just sending us on a wild goose chase, hundreds of years ago," Bradley said, glancing among all parties in the room, "there was a major civil war between the Seelie, good Fae, and the Unseelie, bad Fae. Happened over in Europe and the human populations got caught in some of the crossfire. The conflict lasted for years. Their life spans are different than ours so their wars go on for decades, sometimes centuries."

Clarissa nodded. "You gentlemen may remember the Great Potato Famine, the Black Death . . . need I go on? When the Fae go to war and start slinging magick, it's no less than dropping bombs over Baghdad—the innocent are not spared. Whoever is in the kill zone gets hit right along with intended targets. These guys play for keeps."

"This is why, after truces and treaties, a contingent of the Seelie Court came to the Americas," Bradley pressed on, ruffling his hair as he paced. "There's been peace amongst the Fae for a very long time. Everybody sort of stays in their lane and there're no issues. But there's also no love lost between factions. It's rumored that some of New Orleans's worst plagues and outbreaks during that era were due to Fae-against-Fae terrorists attacks . . . yellow fever, scarlet fever, I don't have to go into some of the events that had the local human citizenry bringing out the dead."

"Then why would they act against wolves?" Silver Hawk said, studying Clarissa and Bradley with ancient eyes. He sat very, very still; his long, snow-white braids resting on his shoulders and his weathered, brown hands resting on his knees. "We have done the Unseelie no harm. This could be the work of Vampires attempting to start a war within the ranks of the Fae . . . just as they attempted to break our ranks. This is in their nature."

"A wrongfully placed allegation could cause severe collateral damage to human populations," Dr. Xavier Holland said, folding his arms over his chest. "We need to be very sure there was Unseelie or Vampire involvement before we make any sort of claim to that effect."

"Doc," Clarissa said quietly, staring at her mentor's elderly, walnut-hued face, and seeming to reference every line of wisdom in it before speaking. "That's just it, none of this makes sense. The wolves don't have beef with the Unseelie Fae—they've never even met them. The only logical agent of destruction keeps coming back to the Vamps."

"But," Bradley said carefully, "the level of sophistication of this spell set is beyond Vampire capability. I have nothing to go on, except the very strong hints an old seer gave us. To cast bad magick on the Seelie Fae is not in the province of Vampire skills, and to put dead man's switches in it . . . no. This is why they never get in an outright magick duel with strong members of the Seelie Court. Vampires use mind possession while in one's presence. They can send a dark energy zap to fry your heart or commit some other act of immediate violence, or even influence a human to do you some ill will. But once they leave the scene of the crime, generally their power doesn't hold. That's also why they have covens do their bidding. There have been no Vampires present when these strange occurrences have gone down."

"You said they get covens to do their bidding . . ." Doc Holland stood and walked to the window to stare out of it to think. "What if it's a strong coven?"

"I'd say yes, if they hadn't messed with the Seelie Fae . . . but no human witch or warlock in his or her right mind would attack a well-favored Fae community at the height of their power manifestation time during Midsummer. That would be a death sentence, even if the Vampires did pay a king's ransom or promise everlasting life. The Fae have a wicked sense of humor and would allow that person who was outted to live forever as the Vamps promised, but as a tadpole with fangs or something equally as heinous."

"Besides," Clarissa added, lifting her hair off her neck. "You can always get human spell-casters to go against one another, as long as a strong supernatural strike team will back them up."

"'Rissa is right," Bradley said, glancing around the room. "If the Vamps were backing dark covens, we should have been able to get the Whitelighters to go up against them, if they knew the Wolf Clans and the entire Seelie Fae Parliament had their backs. The fact that everyone is running scared from this thing tells me it's much larger than coven versus coven. It's who *won't* get involved that gives us the biggest clue to who *is* involved—like reverse engineering."

"Definitely," Woods said, pushing off the dresser. "They saw the wolves win the last battle, so why wouldn't the good coven community do something to gain more favor with their strong allies?"

"Right," Fisher said, nodding. "Like, why would the Whitelighters be scared, especially if the good Fae folk were also on their side for helping to out some black magick that had been used against them? That would make them golden in the Fae community—might even earn brownie points."

"That is *such* a bad pun, dude," Winters said, shaking his head. "Seriously."

"Okay, okay, but you know what I mean . . . and I wasn't trying to go for laughs." Fisher gave the group a sheepish grin. "It just came out like that."

"That's why this thing really troubles me," Bradley said, now staring at Silver Hawk and Doc, and visibly ignoring Fisher's shenanigans. "Even though I can't prove it, this smacks of powerful Unseelie magick—because of who doesn't want to get involved. None of the strong local covens want to touch it, Vampires can't be directly linked to it, and we don't have a reason why." He let out a hard breath and folded his arms. "All I've got is speculation."

"You are right," Silver Hawk said, choosing his words with care as he glanced at Doc Holland. "We cannot base our claims on speculation. But to understand the enemy and the nature of the attack, one must understand how the enemy thinks . . . One must understand how they feel wronged, and why. This will tell us their passion or not for the battle they have waged, and might tell us the weakness in their defenses."

The only way to get Hunter to stop was to finally flee his hold by playfully giving in to her wolf. He was still insatiable, not that she'd minded at all. But they had to get back to New Orleans well before moonrise; there was work to do.

In a flip roll, she kissed him hard and broke free. Up and gone, she turned back once, laughing as he scrambled to his feet. Running away from him, she had a twenty-five-yard lead when she slipped into her wolf to bound toward his hideaway cabin deep within north Shadow Wolf Clan country.

It was impossible not to turn for a quick glimpse over her shoulder. His wolf was pure majesty . . . a midnight-black coat that nearly glistened blue. Graceful bounds over logs and bramble, his massive form moving like liquid night through the dense stand of trees—how could she not look? Then his shadow play became an intense aphrodisiac, slowing her retreat as she watched him go in and out of shadows, becoming a blur of motion strategically advancing on her, wearing only the large amulet dangling by thick silver.

She almost forgot she was supposed to be escaping to a shower, finding clothes in their cabin, and getting back on mission. Hunger tore at her insides, as did renewed desire.

Sasha hit the porch on all fours and then transformed, laughing. Bare human feet collided with smooth pine planks the moment her back hit the front door. A huge black wolf landed right in front of her on the top step, baring fangs, head lowered in mock attack readiness, stalking her until she laughed and turned away, pressing the front of her body to the door. A loud growl made her release a playful scream as she hid her face against her forearms. Immediately, hot human skin covered her back, pressing against her butt.

Two strong arms gathered around her as Hunter's warm breath pelted her neck just before he nipped it.

"I need a shower and I need to eat, man, get off me," she said, laughing harder as he nuzzled her and began moving against her exposed backside. "No!"

"So, let's get in the shower and, yeah, I'd love to eat—"

"No," she said, squirming in his hold. He was making her laugh, was making her hot, but they had to get back before it got dark. "If the moon rises—"

"It's all over," he said, losing some of the playfulness in his tone.

"I know," she murmured, arching despite her protests. "But it'll be dark and we'll have allies vulnerable to Vampires while they've been weakened . . . we've gotta get back."

Hunter dropped his forehead against her shoulder and let out a hard breath. "Must you always be so practical?"

"I wasn't earlier." She smiled as her voice remained easy.

He kissed the nape of her neck. "I am profoundly grateful for that."

Slowly extricating herself from his fantastically warm embrace, she turned around so that his body could mold to hers. "I'm grateful that you forgave me," she said quietly, staring up into his intense gaze. "That wasn't me."

"It is forgotten . . . We don't have to discuss it," he said, taking her mouth.

"We should," she murmured when he broke their kiss. "Think about it for a moment, Hunter. We were all affected at what felt like ground zero—at Ethan's place. But once you and I went through the shadow lands and came out on the other side, we were okay . . . we weren't giving in to really bad wolf behavior."

A sly smile crept onto one half of his face. "We weren't altogether cured for a couple of hours, though."

Sasha chuckled. "True . . . but for me to bait a dominance battle between you and Shogun . . . c'mon, Hunter. I think you know me better than that."

He nodded and kissed her forehead, sobered by her admission. "And let me be honest," Hunter added, closing his eyes and resting his forehead against hers before continuing. "I was ready to go to war . . . ready to kill blood, family.

That didn't make sense . . . and he was ready to challenge me outright. Mortal combat."

"That's what I'm saying," Sasha murmured, placing a hand over Hunter's heart. "Not after what all three of us have been through."

"No," Hunter said, shaking his head, now staring into her eyes. "Shogun is above a mate challenge; he has more honor than that. My brother is clearly not himself, nor am I . . . or you. We have to get to the bottom of this to avert a possible tragedy."

"And I'm worried that as the moon rises and gets closer to full, the worse it will get for all of us." She touched Hunter's face, allowing her fingers to trace the strong line of his jaw, and he covered her hand with his own.

"It will get worse, Sasha. My brother transformed into his wolf before the moon was full. It was midafternoon . . . and as a Werewolf, he's not supposed to be able to do that."

"What?" A horrified whisper came out on a quick exhale as though Hunter had punched her.

Hunter simply nodded. "Your transition spiked desire in him so out of control that his wolf came immediately. I heard it, the snapping of bones and the tearing of ligaments . . . it was a hard transition and probably the only thing that held my honor intact to not turn around and kill him where he stood. He was vulnerable for several moments, but I opted to find you in the shadows and deliver your clothes."

"Oh, my God . . ." Sasha covered her mouth with her hand as Hunter's hands found her hair and he pulled her into a slow hug.

"We must find the source and eradicate it, Sasha. Under the influence of the full moon, who knows what any of us will be capable of with dark magick as a catalyst? And we may not have the shadow lands as an option to protect us all."

"Shogun can't go into the shadows . . . he will never

have a rest from this thing, no time to purge it or detox from whatever the hell this is."

"Nor will our men," Hunter said flatly, staring into her eyes. "My men are supernaturals, just like us. Your familiars are more human than not, but they still may be affected. Woods and Fisher cannot go through the shadow paths without injury to their bodies, just like my brother cannot."

"But Bear and Crow . . ."

"Only with one of us, or they can lose their way and wind up behind a demon door." Hunter closed his eyes. "Who knows what weakness within them this thing is preying on or using to make them break ranks, break alliances . . . If a lower-ranking male in our clan were to challenge me—an out of control alpha . . . I could murder my own man. And that's what it would be, Sasha, murder—not a righteous kill—that would haunt me forever."

"Or, I," Sasha whispered, finally understanding the strategic horror of what they were up against, "could attack my human brass, could rip the face off a general, go after a fellow soldier or civilian, or, while in a false heat, draw clans into full-scale war."

"We have to get back before it gets dark," Hunter said, nodding. "You were right. I just wish we knew where to begin. Dealing with the unseen is such a dishonorable, cowardly act. That is never the way of the wolf!" He stepped away from her and slammed his fist against the cabin wall with a snarl. "We of the Wolf Clans challenge an enemy to their face, we speak of our discontent openly, and we battle outright . . . We do not slide around back alleys and cast innuendo and disappear into the mist. We do not leave booby traps for the unaware to stumble over and detonate. If you are our enemy, you are well aware of the fact and you well know why . . . And we do not put innocents in harm's way."

"We'll find who's at the bottom of this," Sasha said, with a low growl in her throat. "We know we've got three factions truly pissed at us. Vampires, that goes without saying. Any leftover members from that double-crossing Louisiana Buchanan Broussard faction are also on my potential target list. Plus any Fae that thought they were gonna get paid by ol' Dugan . . . Could be relatives that were in line for his estate, or any closet Fae traitors—who knows. But one thing for sure, they're coming at everyone through their weak spots. Phoenixes flame when excited or frightened—and both of Ethan's girls bought it. Wolves go primal when totally aroused . . . and will fight till the last wolf stands. Fae need their glamour to stay concealed, and when threatened will sling magick—"

"That could backfire if it's booby-trapped," Hunter said, stepping even further away from Sasha, finally grasping the urgency of going back.

"Yeah," Sasha said, opening the door to the cabin. "You know . . . this isn't something that local human covens would get involved with. I don't care how much the Vampires paid a human sorcerer, all of the Seelie Fae as a united front, plus Wolf Clans, Whitelighters, and white witches, could mitigate the spell." Sasha shook her head. "Sigils that had Ethan and Margaret ready to faint dead away—unh-unh. That's Unseelie kinda stuff."

"We definitely need to get back," Hunter said in a faraway tone, thinking.

Sasha nodded. "Gut hunch . . . How much you wanna bet this is a progressive thing that gets worse each day and night the closer we get to Sir Rodney's big bash, where all of us who are left standing will be there to flip out on each other?"

CHAPTER 9

Clarissa sat in the jeep with Bradley and Winters while Bear Shadow and Crow Shadow dismounted with Ethan and his family. Fisher helped the timid Faes unload their suitcases, and Woods got out and took over the vehicle Bear Shadow and Crow Shadow had abandoned. They'd driven the jeeps in as far as they could; any further and the vehicles would get stuck in Louisiana bayou mud. The plan seemed reasonable enough—two Shadow Wolves would maintain forest patrol and would make sure the family was safe behind Sir Rodney's walls, and then would return to the team on foot. They'd report their findings about Sir Rodney's fortress to the rest of the paranormal community when they got back. If there were rogue Werewolves in the area, Bear and Crow would be the family's best defense. Maybe their only defense.

Quiet tension lingered in the air. Everyone was afraid; everyone was on edge. Ethan's toddler kept his tiny face buried in the crook of his father's neck. All anyone got to see of the small elf was a profusion of blond curls as he clung to his dad.

Ethan and Margaret's older ones clasped their parents' hands, eyes wide with fear and filled with unshed tears. Their glistening, luminescent eyes rapidly changed colors, giving Clarissa kaleidoscope stares that matched their quickening heartbeats.

Her soul ached as she stared at the little girl who couldn't have been more than six or seven. The child's forlorn expression made her want to just reach out and hug her. If Clarissa could have, she would have pressed the child's red ringlets against her breasts and told her it would be all right. However, that would have been an outright lie. Who knew how any of this would turn out?

The little girl's taller, knobby-kneed brother seemed to be trying his best to keep a stiff upper lip. But the nine-year-old intuitively sensed the danger. Clarissa could feel it deep inside her core. The poor boy's face was nearly ashen with fear, looking even paler against his dark brown hair and Elfin ears. Clarissa swallowed hard to keep from crying. There was nothing to do but watch a nice family become refugees in their own town all because they'd done the right thing, namely testified against some really bad entities. Where was true justice, she wondered.

Sweating profusely, Ethan urged his family forward into the dense stand of trees. Shadow Wolves hauled luggage while the McGregors toted children. Pure terror gripped Margaret, and Clarissa's heart shattered as she watched Ethan's wife move in short bursts of rapid steps, stopping every few feet to glance around like a nervous doe. Her jerky motions only spooked the wolves that flanked them. Every time Margaret stopped, Bear Shadow would tilt his head, his gaze rapidly scanning the terrain as Crow Shadow pivoted and scented the air on alert—which would set off Woods and Fisher in a hunter's domino effect.

Fear was more than palpable; it was an entity now. Soon it would be dark, and only God knew what would happen then. Perhaps more than anything, it broke her heart to see Ethan gather his family up under duress and have to literally flee into the swamplands with Bear Shadow and Crow Shadow as shaky escorts. But it was the only way.

Clarissa blinked back the renewed moisture in her eyes. Who could do something as horrible as targeting a family that had little kids? Doc and Silver Hawk were right; Ethan had to get out of town before sundown, Old West style. It was clear that he was the epicenter of the spiritual hit. Everything had spun out of control, starting at his establishment.

"I need my cell phone," Sasha said quietly. "It's in the pile of clothes we left in the mist."

Hunter nodded. "But that means we'll come out of the shadows in Ethan's bar; in the shadow you found on the stage."

"Just as well," Sasha said with a sigh. "If they're still in there debating, at least we'll come out dressed and showered and in human form."

"The better hope," Hunter said smiling, "is that the meeting was summarily adjourned and they've all gone home."

"Wishful thinking."

Sasha kept a sprinter's pace beside Hunter, letting him lead as they dodged corridors, homing in on the scent of her sweat-damp clothes. The shadow lands were always tricky to negotiate. How he did it with such grace and ease always blew her mind. One had to rely on superior tracking skills and attention to the slightest nuances within the practically nonexistent landscape in order to wend one's way back to a specific point. She was still learning; Hunter had grown up all his life being mentored by his grandfather, Silver Hawk, aka Silver Shadow.

"Here," Hunter said with a quick sweep into the mist, coming up with a handful of jeans.

"Thanks, but *how* do you do that?" Sasha accepted the discarded jeans, fishing in the pockets for her cell phone.

"Your scent was in the clothes," he said with a half smile. "I'd be able to follow that from here to Colorado and back, no problem."

She smiled but didn't respond. They were not going to start that kind of conversation when there was so much else that they needed to focus on, and they had to keep their heads on straight.

"Okay," she said. "Remember the plan. If you feel shaky, go into a shadow to purge it. If you see me get shaky, order me into a shadow or drag me into one kicking and screaming—and I'll do the same for you."

"Done. My only concern is encountering one of my men who may have been compromised . . . They may not go as easily or willingly, and if they spike fight adrenaline in me, I might not be of the mind-set to drag them into a shadow alive."

"I know." Sasha raked her fingers through her hair. It was a sobering reality. "I've thought about that. You might have to let me take them in . . . I'm female; hate to say it, but beta males will follow me to the end of the earth, if they think there's a chance."

"Which, under dark magick, will make me flip." Hunter closed his eyes and rubbed the tension away from his neck.

"Then let's function with a code word—so that you know what I'm doing . . . like a mental trigger." She stared at him. "We have to have a way to break the spell trance long enough to give the other party pause and recovery time."

He nodded. " 'Safe haven.' You say that and I'll know."

"All right," she said quietly, stashing her dead cell phone in her back jeans' pocket. "Let's just hope that we both remember when we have to."

"Stop! Who goes there?"

Ethan looked up at the castle gates and then around at the forest floor, confused. "It is Ethan McGregor of Meadhan Lodainn and me family seeking asylum from Sir Rodney—escorted by two Shadow Wolf allies."

Fae archers lowered their weapons and smiled.

"Ah, good laddie!" a captain called out. "Lower the drawbridge! Ye may enter!"

But Ethan and Margaret didn't move. Bear Shadow and Crow Shadow exchanged nervous glances.

"Where is your glamour, man?" Ethan shouted. He gave his son to his wife to hold and then opened his arms and began to frantically motion about. "The entire fortress is exposed, is out in the open! You can see the golden pathway right from the forest floor and the trees are neon coming through the normal human foliage!"

"What, are you daft, man?" the captain said laughing.

Margaret neared her husband and dropped her voice to an urgent whisper. "If I didn't know better, I'd swear that man had been in his cups."

"You're saying this guy is high?" Crow Shadow muttered, shaking his head.

"Watch your mouth, wolf," an archer said, weaving. "D'not cast aspersions—nothing wrong with a wee pinch of Faerie dust to make a long post go faster."

"How much dust have you 'ad, man?" Margaret called out, pressing her toddler's head against her shoulder. "The dust is tainted!" She spun on her husband, her voice tight, gaze panicked. "Ethan, if the Fae's Royal Highland Fusiliers have been compromised, by nightfall there's no protection!"

"Aye, the bonnie lass wants to know details of our revelry—"

"She's a nurse, a healer, and me wife!" Ethan shouted. "And it doesn't change the fact that your fortress walls are exposed to human view—which means your castle can be easily found. In fact, without the glamour, Vampires or rogue Werewolves can find and decimate the village! Where is Sir Rodney?"

They came out of the shadows and onto the stage at The Fair Lady. But it only took a few seconds to process the threat that greeted them. Three huge Werewolf lieutenants rushed them in human form, eyes blazing wolf, canines ripping through their gum lines.

Sasha ducked, pivoted, and flipped off the stage. Hunter went into a low roll as two attackers sailed over him. One crashed into the bar and the other hit the wall, as a third snarled and circled Sasha, sending Hunter into a death stalk behind him.

"No, wait," she shouted. "Seung Kwon, we can help Shogun. We didn't come to attack him!"

Sasha's words gave Hunter pause as he looked to the far side of the stage.

"Shogun!"

Seung Kwon left the floor, hit the stage, and barreled toward Hunter. In an evasive shake-and-bake move, Hunter flipped out of the way of a claw swipe and landed on his feet beside Sasha while three slow-moving, snarling Werewolf lieutenants circled their leader—his brother.

"You think we are foolish and that our eyes are blind?" Seung Kwon shouted. "Your bitch baits my cousin, the co-leader of the Wolf Federations, into an early transformation, which you both know will leave him vulnerable—and then you both return to finish him off so you can lead alone!"

"No!" Hunter shouted. "I came to help him. He'll die like this!"

"We have medicine—Hunter has had this happen to him before!" Sasha stared in horror at Shogun's shuddering frame. "Let us help, and if it doesn't work, *then* try to kill us."

Shogun lay on the floor in so much agony that all he could do was moan. His legs were twisted in mid-transformation, cramped in the position of backward-bent hindquarter limbs. His thumb was distended to where his dewclaw would have been, partly up his forearm, and his jaw was distended into a wolf's snout, but his forehead, back, and torso were still human.

"Kill them," Dak-Ho yelled, glancing at his brothers. "These are tricks to take full control of the Southeast Asia Werewolf Federation. Shogun's dead sister Lei Ho was right!"

"Wait," Chin-Hwa urged. "The she-Shadow claims she has medicine. They did not kill Shogun before when he had the sickness. If they were going to do it, that would have been the opportune time."

Seung Kwon walked away, circled Shogun, and pointed at him with tears in his eyes. "You fix this! He transformed only to dominance-battle for you! How could this be possible? The moon hasn't risen yet. No Werewolf can turn before the moon takes her due—only Shadows can do that. What has your mate's bite infected him with? That contagion still lingers! It can be the only true explanation!"

"It's not Hunter's bite. It's the dark magick in this region." Sasha tentatively jumped up on stage. "You have to get him out of here . . . This is where the epicenter of the spell happened, we think."

"You lured him here!" Seung Kwon yelled, his voice breaking. "He couldn't follow you into the shadows and you knew it! He tried to change back to save face and then . . . You fix this, bitch!"

Hunter was on the stage within seconds, snarling. "Beta, if you address her out of turn once more . . ."

"Safe haven!" Sasha shouted, spinning on Hunter. She lowered her voice. "Safe haven. They don't understand." She turned to Seung Kwon, her eyes appealing to any compassion he owned. Guilt and heartbreak ripped her insides. "Shogun has been like this for hours—suffering. Can't you see the man's in pure agony? We can't just sit around battling or debating this! You can't wait on the moon several hours from now, that's not going to make it better. He won't last till then."

Hunter lolled his neck and focused on Shogun. "When my system was rejecting the demon-infected virus, my transformations were hard like his. Brutal. They have antitoxin at Tulane . . . a small stash from just after the war here. It was an emergency supply my grandfather insisted be left here, just in case."

"It was based on the same meds they used to shoot PCU

human soldiers up with—the ones that got bitten." Sasha began to pace, talking with her hands. "But they've perfected it with Shadow Wolf blood in the serum. The demon-infected Werewolf blood isn't in it any longer. It's the only chance to get Shogun out of this aborted transformation."

"This is bullshit! You lie!" Seung Kwon shouted. "How do we know the truth from your lies?"

"Shadow Wolves do not lie," Hunter said in a slow rumble, walking forward, ready to attack. "That's why we can wear silver. Scent it in my aura. Truth smells like sterling. Do I look like I'm lying when I tell you that I'll kill you if you let my brother die, punk?"

A pained gasp followed by a long, agonized moan stilled the group. The sounds of bones snapping caused them all to cringe.

"He's transitioning back to human form too slowly!" Sasha shouted. "What about this don't you understand?"

"That's my brother you are dooming to a suffering death that lacks honor or dignity. I will not allow you to do that just so that you can be his successor." Hunter's voice was low and steady as he continued stalking forward. "If you don't allow us to take this man to the only source of transformation meds we know of, he will go into shock and die."

"We're not allowing you to take him anywhere while he's vulnerable to an assassination." Seung took a fighter's stance in front of Shogun's body, gaze hardened for war.

"Fine, die your way," Hunter said, preparing to lunge. "It's either that, or be merciful and shoot him."

Clarissa stared at her cell phone the moment the call disconnected. Bradley and Winters didn't say a word; their expressions spoke volumes.

"It was Doc," she said in a far-off tone. "He just left Tulane with Silver Hawk . . . headed toward The Fair Lady with antitoxin. Woods and Fisher have gotta bring artillery backup. This is not a drill."

"What *the fuck* is going on, guys?" Winters dropped back against the seat, demoralized. "Oh, shit. You mean Hunter came out of the shadows full blown again?"

"No," she said quietly, as Bradley stepped down harder on the gas. "It's not for Hunter, it's for Shogun."

CHAPTER 10

Pounding on the front door of The Fair Lady drew snarls from everyone, including Hunter. Sasha rushed forward, seeing the flashing red lights through the glass panels, her feminine intuition kicking in. She knew how Doc functioned; the males with her didn't. If Doc had gone to Tulane to get the meds while they all stood around and argued about how to move Shogun, Doc would have commandeered an ambulance, calling in his military markers.

"Stand down," Sasha shouted as she crossed the wide floor. "It's Doc and Silver Hawk with meds. All of our jeeps are in the bayou, en route. You guys didn't have a vehicle and wouldn't let me and Hunter try to shadow jump with him, so they brought an ambulance, okay?"

Muscles relaxed, hackles lowered, but still Shogun's men didn't move from their protective stances in front of him as she opened the door. But the moment she did, she froze.

Doc stood beside Silver Hawk, his troubled gaze locked onto hers. Silver Hawk had a shotgun, cocked and loaded with silver shells. Low warning growls were behind her, a clearly compromised Shadow Wolf elder stood before her. The dance would be delicate.

"We are no longer at war with the Werewolf Clans," Sasha said calmly, staring into Shadow Hawk's eyes. "Shogun is Hunter's half-brother. You know this . . . Grandfather, you are being affected by dark magick."

"His people killed my daughter," Silver Hawk said flatly, looking over Sasha's shoulder toward the stage.

"His father tried to save your daughter," Sasha said softly. "He died for her, fought and bled for her. Now we must return the favor and try to heal his son."

Gently and slowly, she reached out and lowered the gun barrel and then watched Silver Hawk release the hammer so that it was no longer cocked. She and Doc shared a look.

"Tensions are running high," Doc said quietly.

Sasha nodded.

"How are you and Hunter feeling?"

She looked at Doc, not blinking. "Better now that we've been to the shadow lands to purge."

Doc nodded. That's all that she needed to know; he'd gotten her unspoken message.

"Maybe later Hunter can go with you on a spirit walk," Sasha said, now looking at their clan elder.

"Yes . . ." Silver Hawk said in a faraway voice. "I am a man of reason and of peace." He thrust the gun at her, presenting it in a lateral move. "Take this. I don't know what has come over me."

Sasha immediately took the gun and turned to face Shogun's wary lieutenants. "Meds have arrived with an armed escort to be sure they weren't hijacked. We've experienced that before."

She waited and watched the Werewolves try to decipher the truth from the bit of yeast she added to it for peace. They had been hijacked before for antitoxin, and after a moment they accepted her rationale for the silver-slug-loaded shotgun coming through the door. Besides, what else could they do? She was a military-lab-made member of the Shadow Wolf Clan and didn't own an aura with a silver lining, so whatever she said would have to be taken at face value.

The thought gave her pause as she walked forward with

Silver Hawk, Doc bringing up her rear. That meant she was inscrutable to even Hunter . . . deep. She was scaring herself and shook the inappropriate thought as she leaped up on the stage and helped Doc up with a hard pull.

"My suggestion is that they take him out on a gurney to get the meds in him while not in this spell hot zone." Sasha looked around at the men assembled. "He'll need fluids—an IV hookup, maybe even oxygen—and he could even go into cardiac arrest, so the back of the ambulance, where they have a defibrillator and all the necessary elements of a crash cart, is the safest place for him. Once he stabilizes, we can transfer him to a room at Dugan's old B&B . . . Without nurse Margaret there at Tulane, it could be risky to have him where humans could screw up his treatment—or be in harm's way if something goes haywire."

"If he dies, you die," Seung Kwon said, staring at Sasha.

"How many times have I told you that if you address her out of order, it will be your ass, beta!" Huge canines ripped though Hunter's gums, his wolf seconds from emerging.

Sasha raised the shotgun and fired it toward the ceiling. "Safe haven!"

The Werewolves surrounding Shogun hesitated. Hunter walked off the adrenaline rush, pacing. Silver Hawk's lips circled into a snarl while Doc balled his fist at his sides, ready to fight to his death.

"Two things, Seung Kwon—one, you are delaying a healing and you *know* Shadow Wolves are natural healers. Two, I have told you that there's a bad spell affecting everyone. Look around." She leveled the shotgun toward his chest. "You are talking a lot of trash in front of a really off-the-chain alpha male about his mate, going up against a military-trained alpha she-Shadow, standing in front of our clan elder, who has kicked more demon-infected Werewolf ass in his lifetime than you can imagine, and who is just ready for a shape-shift. Plus, Doc ain't no slouch. So, do not let the spell make you that foolish, because if you lunge, we will take you and your men down, hard and permanently. The only thing that has saved your stubborn, arrogant ass thus far is the fact that we're trying like crazy to save your man, who, if you would listen, also happens to be Hunter's brother. Now back off!"

The door opened, causing everyone's attention to train on the new potential threat. Woods and Fisher stood in the arc of waning sunlight, bearing M-16s.

"What the lady said, motherfucker," Woods shouted, spitting on the floor.

"Which one you got a problem with, Captain?" Fisher said, brandishing a weapon as Bear Shadow and Crow Shadow blotted out the sun behind them.

"It's all good," Sasha said, turning back to Seung Kwon. "Isn't it?"

Seung Kwon begrudgingly nodded and held both hands up in front of his chest. "As the lady suggests, all is well."

"Get that man on a livery," Hunter ordered, walking away from Seung Kwon. "I want you—Bear and Crow—on their asses. Everybody stays cool while we work on my brother." He looked at Woods and Fisher, giving them a nod of respect. "Familiars, good job. Back up my men."

"Roger that," Woods said, spitting again and walking forward to take a defensive position.

Sasha glimpsed Silver Hawk from the corner of her eye and could see another haphazardly parked jeep through the window. "Woods . . . tell 'Rissa, Bradley, and Winters to get word to the local Fae—I don't want them near a firefight, if one goes down. They need to regroup back at the B&B and stay put—have them focus on research."

"Yes, sir," he called back to her with a salute.

But she turned to Hunter, catching his line of vision and holding it. "I think I should do this healing . . . Silver Hawk may get more intel and clarity behind Shadow lines, you understand?"

"I'm not leaving you here with them," Hunter said, snarling in the direction of Shogun's men. "They're unstable and could rush you."

"Me and Doc are getting into the ambulance with Shogun . . . only a medical team." She held his gaze, pleading with her eyes. Hunter was affected, and yet it was because of that that she needed to allow him to be in his full alpha glory. He had to be able to save face and still seem in control of the group.

"I don't like it." Hunter rolled his shoulders.

She went to him and embraced him, taking his mouth. "Safe haven," she murmured. "Remember?"

He stared at her for a few moments. "Safe haven," he repeated quietly after a long pause. "But what if he comes out of the transformation in battle mode or something . . . I don't want you to be vulnerable."

"Does he look like a man who can come out of a transformation ready for war, or does he look broken and in need of serious healing?" She kissed Hunter again, this time a slow and tender kiss. "I will be fine; we will be fine. Let me get this man medical attention while you purge your grandfather in the shadow lands . . . and maybe you can spirit walk as one to gather clues. We have to move—I just fired a shotgun in a commercial district. NOPD will be here soon, which will only complicate things."

It took a moment but finally Hunter nodded. He glanced around as he released his hold on her and then began barking out commands as his gaze slowly roved from his men to Shogun's.

"I want these men in your sights at all times. My mate is a practiced healer. She and Dr. Holland have been well versed in restoring botched transformations. They and only they are going to go in the ambulance with Shogun. We will all regroup back at the old Dugan B&B once we have clearance from Sasha to do so."

Hunter's gaze locked with Seung Kwon's in an open challenge that made the lesser-ranked wolf look away. "If anything happens to Sasha or her father, her familiars, or any of her humans while I am in the shadow lands with my grandfather to seek spiritual clues, I will hunt you down and slowly dismember you until even your own mothers won't recognize your remains."

"My castle is in shambles! When Sasha brings her clan here, I want everything to be perfect for her! What about my orders do you not understand?" Sir Rodney swept away the long pole strung with freshly hunted quail, sending it crashing to the floor amid his bewildered kitchen staff. "She is a Shadow Wolf! I want the finest cuts of wild game *on the hoof*—bison, venison, moose, nothing domesticated, nothing poultry, and anything you put before her must be grilled to perfection! All of her meals must be rare, just singed on the outside with the natural juices bursting forth."

He then turned to the other members of his beleaguered staff. "This castle must be face-lifted so that she only receives the greatest comfort! Goose down and silk should grace her bed; I want Faerie dust covering everything to keep her in a state of constant euphoria! Nothing can be left to chance, and if she goes wanting for anything I will hold you all personally responsible."

"As you wish, milord," his patient valet of more than a century announced with a deep bow. "Shall I prepare a comparable suite for her husband . . . or would you want me to—"

"Her husband! Her husband?" Sir Rodney shouted, making the staff lower their heads in fear. "She is not married! Where did you get a preposterous idea like that, Rupert?"

The valet watched his master begin to pace and he spoke slowly, calmly, and in an extremely patient tone. "Milord . . . according to Shadow Wolf custom and culture, they mate for life. It is a bond that is unshakable, unless there is a formal hearing and cause for the dissolution of the union. So, please forgive me for using the incorrect terminology when referring to our guests of honor. I should have said *life mate,* not husband. I shall not make the mistake again."

"See that you don't," Sir Rodney said, hurling a bowl against the open hearth.

Anxious staff members covered their heads as it shattered and then, in a rare display of angry magick, Sir Rodney made the broken pieces turn into small toads to hop away.

Rupert waited a moment, still carefully watching the unusual behavior of his normally even-tempered and benevolent master. Something was definitely wrong. The mere mention of the she-Shadow's mated status had sent the king of the Seelie Court into a vile explosion.

Small kitchen Pixies still covered their heads, lying prostrate before the king on the stone floor. Why Sir Rodney, who even without his Fae glamour was a dead ringer for the handsome human actor Clive Owen, would have to go to such extremes for any female was beyond his comprehension. From what he gathered at court in the Pixie gossip, Sir Rodney could and had already availed himself of the most attractive Fae and human females . . . So why was this one she-wolf causing such a stir? There was no plausible explanation. If he didn't know better, he'd swear his king had been bewitched—but who would be so bold as to commit an act of treason punishable by death or war?

All eyes remained on the king as he flung pots and pans and gave in to a full-blown tantrum. Over fifty Fae staff waited for his next bellowing command with bated breath. Other staff throughout the castle had been scurrying around in a full fright for more than twenty-four hours, attempting to placate their master to no avail.

But Rupert remained steadfast and as still as stone, head lowered but standing upright. Everyone glanced at him, their eyes begging him to say something as Sir Rodney's most trusted servant. Their terrified gazes sent a unified message; Rupert was the only one in their number who could diplomatically remind their lord what was at stake.

Rupert held back a disgruntled snort. Now was not the time to appear defiant; not when the king was in such a foul temper. One could end up as a gray-haired tortoise, or worse. However, one unequivocal fact remained: egregiously lusting after another man's wife—especially one who'd befriended you—was just not regal and could start an armed conflict that could last for centuries. It was simply bad form.

Worse, in Rupert's view, it was beneath the station and honor of his dear friend and master . . . Lo these many years, it was true that Sir Rodney had quite a reputation amongst the ladies, but a scoundrel he was not! One simply could not make a cuckold of an honest wolf friend by using Fae glamour and still call oneself the Seelie Court king—unheard of! Sir Rodney's sudden infatuation with the beautiful she-Shadow was simply an unhealthy diversion that had to end.

This truth made Rupert bold; until he got through to his king, he would be relentless, unafraid of the potentially hazardous consequences. Rupert glanced around, taking his cues from the other staff members and from Sir Rodney's slowly de-escalating tantrum. His winded king was spent; thus only now was it prudent to speak. The closer the time came to the soirée, the worse Sir Rodney's obsession seemed to become, so he had to act now—three short days before guests were due to arrive—lest his king make a complete fool of himself at the ball.

"Again, forgive me for my ignorance." Rupert bowed deeply, his attention split between Sir Rodney and the cowering staff. "I will be sure to extend the *utmost* of Fae hospitality to Ms. Trudeau and her life mate, Max Hunter—the head of the North American Clan of the Shadow Wolf Federation . . . along with his brother, the head of the Southeast Asian Clan of the Werewolf Federation, and any guests they bring."

Rupert stared at his master's back, sure that by using the titles of their guests in proper context Sir Rodney would slowly regain his composure enough to realize how imprudent it would be to start a war over a woman he could never hope to win. The Fae Parliament had sided with the Wolf Clans in their ousting of the Vampire Cartel, and the Fae, which had heretofore been fractured into feudal law, could ill afford to make war with two strong wolf packs, let alone their global Federations.

Sir Rodney straightened his spine, lifting his aristocratic chin, and then drew a deep breath as though wresting back his dignity. "I want every one of our guests who is also an important diplomatic ally to have the red carpet rolled out for them. No less than our best is all that I am striving for." His gaze scanned the assembled staff and then landed on Rupert as he turned to face him.

Both men stared at each other for a moment and then Sir Rodney looked away as though both ashamed and confused by his own actions. Rupert let out a quiet sigh of relief and responded with a satisfied nod. Sir Rodney had clearly gotten his message—the wolves were more than guests, they were indeed critical diplomatic allies.

"Milord . . . a word," Sir Rodney's top advisor said, entering the room and putting away his wand in his robe sleeve.

Rupert remained mute, as did the rest of the staff. Seeming disoriented, Sir Rodney nodded and walked out of anyone's earshot but his advisor's.

"Garth . . ." Sir Rodney stammered, holding both sides of his skull in his palms. "What has besieged me?"

"It is the dark magick, milord," Garth said with a frown. He extracted his wand from his sleeve, the tip of it still smoldering. "It has now begun to permeate the castle."

Moving Shogun was agonizing to watch. As his men hoisted his body up onto the gurney in a coordinated, single move, the wail Shogun released scored her mind. The sound of his body realigning once he'd been jostled was like fingernails raking a blackboard. The hair stood up on her neck and a hard shiver passed through her that made her clench her teeth. When Shogun began begging for a bullet, Sasha closed her eyes. Merciful Jesus, she couldn't watch this again, but she had to.

Seung Kwon and Dak-Ho handed Shogun down from the stage to Hunter and Bear Shadow. Shuddering, Shogun clawed at the padding and sheet as another hard transformation stretch pulled at his spine, cracking it as the remainder of his wolf tail receded. That's when the man simply broke down and wept. Sasha turned away and took in a few steadying breaths. She had no way to know he'd shift, no way to know any of this would have happened to him. Guilt put tears in her eyes, tears she could ill afford at the moment.

"Are you sure you're all right?" Hunter said, staring at her back—she could feel it.

"Yeah, I'll be fine." She didn't even look at him as she bounded off the stage and ran ahead of the gurney to open the door.

Baron Geoff Montague opened his eyes in his lair. It was almost twilight. An evil smile graced his handsome mouth as three cool-skinned beauties slept soundly, draped over his body. Rumor and gossip always kept the airwaves interesting. So, the Fae had a problem with their glamour while the wolves were hopelessly chasing their tails looking for a murderer of Phoenixes. *Très bon.* Vengeance was always a dish best served ice cold.

Doc gave Sasha a look but didn't say a word as they loaded Shogun into the back of the ambulance. She knew the questions he had—would she be okay back there alone if Shogun flipped out mid-transformation. Crow Shadow tossed her the shotgun before she closed the door. She caught it with one hand. Her eyes met Hunter's. Doc opened the cab door and lifted out a shotgun to show Hunter that he was also armed, should there be an issue. Hunter nodded. Then she slammed the door and banged on the interior wall to let Doc know they were good to go.

She prepped the needle like a pro. How many times had she had to do this for Hunter, she wondered. Her eyes met Shogun's and a quiet understanding passed between them. She placed her hand over his heart and briefly closed her eyes, sending Shadow Wolf healing into his body to help him relax. When he came to, she would dull the ache of torn muscles and ligaments, if he survived . . . but he'd been transforming for so long. Hunter had never endured something like this.

"I'm so sorry," she whispered and then plunged the needle into Shogun's arm.

Bumps on the road bounced the vehicle and he cried out in pain.

"Kill me, Sasha," he whispered through his teeth. "They gave you the gun—use it!"

She shook her head no and backed away to the far wall, now letting the tears she'd held back stream down her cheeks. She watched the first wave of restoration hit him as he arched and raked deep gashes in the metal interior wall. When his legs began to snap back into place she almost dry heaved. His wails became sobs that turned into an insistent plea to be shot until hard convulsions stole language from him.

He was flatlining; she knew the signs. His lips were blue; he was foaming at the mouth. His eyes had rolled backward revealing only white orbs. Working quickly, she grabbed a rubber-coated flashlight off the wall and jammed it between his jaws, and then made sure his airway was clear by pressing his tongue forward with her fingers before she paddled him.

The electric jolt lifted him off the gurney by a quarter inch and his instant reaction was to clamp his jaws down hard on the flashlight, severing it in half. Oh, yeah, he was back—and apparently very pissed off. One long agonized wail bore witness to his full transformation back. It happened in an instant, like a rubber band snap. Maybe it was the antitoxin mixed with the spell, but he was definitely way stronger than he should have been coming out of a hard shape-shift.

He spit out broken metal, rubber, and severed batteries, and leaped up to a crouching position in his human form. Shogun angrily wiped his face and mouth on the sheet and then flung it down on the floor.

"What *the fuck* is wrong with you, Sasha?" he growled, eyes glowing pure golden outrage.

"It was the only way," she said as calmly as possible. "If I didn't give you the meds and the jolt, you would have died."

He stood slowly, coming off the gurney nude and snarling. "That is so not what I'm talking about."

She eyed the shotgun; so did he.

"So now that I'm all better you would add insult to injury by shooting me after the fact—instead of when I needed you to?"

"No," she said, without apology in her tone, "but you are coming very close to invading my personal space, now back up!"

"Invading your personal space . . ." He shook his head, making the wild thicket of onyx hair sway from side to side. "Is that why you ran into the shadows where you knew I couldn't follow!"

"I went in there to avoid a war." She stared at him without blinking, truly understanding how affected he was by the dark spell. A hundred realities split her skull in an instant. She'd had time to get her mind together by going in and out of the shadows; Shogun had been in Ethan's bar, just like his men had, for hours.

"You went in there with him!"

Sasha kept her voice neutral. "I went in there alone. He followed me."

"And he was gone with you *for hours* . . . while you were in phase!" Shogun slammed his fist into the metal wall, denting it next to her head. "Do you think that I'm stupid?"

"Have you ever been in the shadow lands?" she asked coolly, never taking her eyes off his. "Have you ever seen the labyrinth of caverns in there?"

"No," he said in a low rumble, closing the gap between them. "Show me."

"Hunter took Silver Hawk in there on a shaman spirit walk, and its not advisable. Besides, I don't know if your physiology will handle it, just coming out of a hard transformation. You'll die."

"Why do you keep trying to save my life if all you do is torture me?" he asked in a sullen tone, the low timbre of his voice a melancholy rumble. "Where is your mercy?"

"I don't want you to die, don't want our clans to go to war, don't want to pit brother against brother, and . . . shit . . . what do you want me to say? I care about you, all right? I'm made of flesh and blood just like you are. But I'm trying my best to function with honor under some really fucked-up circumstances."

Why tears had risen in her eyes, she wasn't sure. All of a sudden she felt trapped and claustrophobic inside the tight ambulance confines. She needed air. Being this close to Shogun and all that beautiful naked skin was making it hard to breathe or make sense.

Shogun finally nodded and conceded with his intense, almond-shaped eyes. "You were gone for hours . . . I didn't know what to think." He let out a weary sigh. "I don't know what's wrong with me, either . . . my honor crumbles before you. Yes, Hunter is my brother . . . but . . ."

"Don't say it," she whispered. "Please don't say it."

"When you were gone with him for hours . . . all I could think of was that you'd given yourself to him as I lay in agony unable to change out of my wolf and leave like a man. Sasha, have you any idea what that was like?"

She couldn't answer that charge, nor was it advisable to get into the fine points about the fact that she was, after all, Hunter's life mate. Not right now, not when Shogun was like this—irrational, and making her that way, too.

"I came back to be sure you were all right . . . and you weren't." That was no lie, even if the rest of what she'd said had been a series of evasions and errors of omission.

His fingers gently traced her cheek and found her hair. "No, I wasn't all right and I'm not sure that I am now." He nuzzled her hair, breathing her in, pulling her into a deep embrace. "Sasha . . ."

The moan he released when his body molded to hers felt like a depth charge inside her womb. He took her mouth with desperate hunger, his hands splaying across her ass and the small of her back, moving against her as though already inside her, pulling at her clothes to get her out of them.

Functioning with a divided mind, she was losing her personal battle with resistance. Rational thought ebbed by the second. Primal urge replaced promises and protocols. His breathing was ragged, trapping hers and making it follow his. She held his back when she'd meant to push him away. God, he felt so good; his scent was so undeniably male. Her body was becoming pliant, moving with the ancient give-and-take rhythm of all species that right now invited disaster. The temptation to allow her palms to slide down over his sweat-slicked ass made her hold the small of his back harder. Want dampened her, began to swell her to discomfort with sudden heat. His nostrils flared as he picked up the scent of her need and groaned. She lolled her head back, almost too weak to stand.

"We can't do this," she gasped as he rained hot kisses down her throat. Her hands played over sinew-thick shoulders and caressed his biceps. "We're not in our right minds. There's a—"

Another harsh kiss blotted out her words and made her legs go wobbly. A shudder claimed him, claimed her, and brought her out of the kiss on a breathless gasp.

"Shogun, there's a spell," she breathed out when he sought her neck again, pressing a throbbing erection against her thigh. Oh, shit, safe haven, and there wasn't a shadow big enough to claim her—except for his. "We're under the influence . . . we're . . ."

"I know," he rasped, hands sliding up her back beneath her shirt. "It's taken me over since the first time I saw you—oh, God, Sasha, I've wanted you like this for so long. If it's war, so be it." His hands rounded her torso in a burning sweep that covered her breasts and made her cry out. "Can you stop this? Do you want to stop this?" He didn't give her a chance to answer as he pulled her bottom lip into his mouth.

Sasha's back slammed into the wall as Shogun pressed his body against her, his tongue tangling with hers, and she barely felt the ambulance jolt to a halt. A few seconds later the door opened and the distinctive click of a shotgun stilled Shogun's passion. She heard him snarl. Frantic, she wrapped a leg around his thigh to slow him down from an instant death lunge.

"Don't attack him if you care for me," she said quickly. "He's my dad."

CHAPTER 11

"Step away from my daughter or die where you stand," Doc said, his voice low and deadly. Rage danced in his eyes, the muscles in his arms and shoulders twitching from it.

"He's not hurting me, Doc," Sasha said quickly, not releasing Shogun, quite unsure of how either man would react.

But it only took a second of staring into Doc's eyes to see that he was under the dark magick influence. His normal cool-under-fire demeanor was shattered. That's when it hit her: Doc was 50 percent Shadow Wolf. Even if he did take after his mother's human side and couldn't shapeshift, he still had more wolf in him than even Woods and Fisher, who were familiars. His allegiance would still be with the clan alpha . . . Hunter, Silver Hawk, the North American Shadow Wolf Federation, where his father hailed from. And Doc would now be an outraged father. Holy moly . . . this was rich even for Vampires.

Eyes wild, in a fighter's stance, Doc flung Shogun's clothes onto the floor of the ambulance.

"He may not be hurting you like I thought, but this here, what I'm witnessing, is cutting me to the bone!"

"If you shoot him," Sasha said calmly, "I'll die right along with him—you don't have a clear shot." She glanced around. Thankfully, Doc had pulled over in an abandoned parking lot nowhere near Dugan's B&B.

"Take your hands off my daughter," Doc said evenly. "You won't molest her while there's breath left in my body."

Shogun nodded and lifted his hands slowly in the air. "That's not my intention, sir . . . I love her."

"You didn't ask me for her! Your brother did—respect! She brought your mangy Werewolf ass back to life—I gave you meds, and this is how you repay me? With disrespect? Trying to rape her?" Doc brought the shotgun up higher so he could stare through the sight. "I thought you were fighting her in there, heard the side of the vehicle opening up like a tin can . . . heard your transition wails . . . then heard the punch and the thump, and didn't hear her voice and got nervous."

"It's cool . . . uh, Dad," Sasha said, appealing to whatever altered reality was playing itself out in Doc's head. "He never laid a hand on me—like that."

Doc lowered the weapon. "Then if he ain't forcing you, what the hell is he doing all over you, huh?"

Shogun closed his eyes and cocked his head to the side. Sasha could feel the muscles in his abdomen coil with the need to pivot and lunge.

"There was no disrespect intended," Shogun said through his teeth. "What happened here was . . . spontaneous."

"Are you out of your damned minds?" Doc uncocked the weapon and looked from Sasha to Shogun, bewildered. "Do you have any idea what Max Hunter would . . ." Doc's words trailed off as his gaze finally settled on Sasha.

Shogun backed up carefully. "Can I turn around and collect my clothes?"

"Yeah! Put on your goddamned pants."

Sasha closed her eyes and rubbed her palms down her face. This was so not how any of this was supposed to go. Doc walked in a confused circle for a moment, took one look at Shogun's groin, and spat.

"For chrissake, Sasha! This was not supposed to be a

part of the transformation healing!" Doc walked back and forth as Shogun yanked on his linen pants and zipped them with a wince. "What father ever wants to see something like this? Jesus wept and I know why!"

"Doc," Sasha said, trying to keep the tremor of humiliation out of her voice, all the while resisting both the anger and defiance that was bubbling up within her. "It's not exactly black-and-white or cut-and-dried . . . there's other forces involved. I . . ." She let the protest die on an audible exhalation of frustration. Her body ached, and Shogun was clearly still messed up, but a catastrophe had been averted.

"Baby," Shogun murmured, responding to the rush of breath she'd just released. "You can't explain this . . . there is no vocabulary to do it justice. I will respect your father—this was indeed not the way for him to have found us . . . my apologies."

"Oh, God . . ." Sasha covered her face with her hands. She was a grown-ass woman but was acting like a teenager caught in the act. None of this made sense. "It's the damned spell, gentlemen!"

"My name is Bennit and I ain't in it," Doc said in a huff, rounding the ambulance to get back in the cab. "I didn't see nothing," he shouted and then slammed the door. "I'm not explaining anything, either. But you all best get yourselves together before Hunter gets back. Sasha, you need to ride up here with me or his ass can walk!"

Hunter clasped Silver Hawk's forearm in the age-old warrior's embrace the moment they entered the shadow lands.

"Grandfather, grow steady here. This is the only place to purge the dark magick that has affected us all."

Silver Hawk nodded and then closed his eyes and took in several deep cleansing breaths. "I was ready for war . . . Hatred that I hadn't felt in years filled my spirit. I feel unclean."

Hunter nodded. "It's like a dark soot that covers your eyes and permeates your soul . . . It makes you blind and stokes passions that the evolved spirit would normally shun."

"Let us take a walk and ask our ancestors what they can see from this side," Silver Hawk murmured, his tone deep and thoughtful. Then he lifted his chin and sniffed the air.

Hunter looked away.

"They will come at you and your brother through your weakness, whatever this dark magick may bring."

"I know, Grandfather."

"Then you are fully aware that your weakness is her."

"The ambulance should have arrived by now," Seung Kwon growled, staring at Bear Shadow.

"It will be here when it gets here," Bear Shadow snarled, then suddenly all the wolves were on their feet in the B&B lobby.

"Sasha really cares about Shogun," Clarissa said in a quiet voice. "If she can save him, she will." Clarissa whipped out her cell phone. "Before you guys go to war and anyone gets hurt, let me call her."

"Do that!" Seung said, turning a hot gaze on Clarissa.

"Watch your tone with the lady," Bear Shadow said in a low warning growl.

Clarissa punched Sasha on speed dial and breathed out a gasp of relief when the call connected. "Got a bunch of very nervous wolves standing around," she said quickly. "Status, Captain."

"We're on our way," Sasha said into the receiver.

"I want to speak to Shogun!" Seung Kwon shouted.

"You hear that?" Clarissa asked nervously.

"Roger that."

After a few moments, traffic sounds filled the receiver and then Shogun was on the phone. "Let me speak to my men."

Clarissa tossed the cell phone to Seung Kwon and the entire room watched as he walked away with it. His shoulders slumped and he nodded, then disconnected the call. Chin-Hwa and Dak-Ho exchanged nervous glances, their eyes asking the question that they didn't verbalize. Seung Kwon tossed the phone back to Clarissa.

"He said to go across the street, eat, and go have a drink—he'll be there shortly. He sounds like himself."

"Are you sure?" Chin-Hwa asked quietly, seeming completely amazed.

"It was him—no imposter?" Dak-Ho asked, rounding Seung to hold his arm.

"It was him," Seung confirmed and then looked at Bear Shadow, giving him a slight bow of respect. "We are, therefore, in your debt, as protocol warrants."

The human team let out a cheer, much to the surprise of the bewildered Werewolves.

"She did it," Clarissa said, laughing, slapping high fives with Bradley and Winters.

Bear Shadow gave Crow Shadow a look. "Does that mean we're off duty?"

"Can we really stand down . . . or do we need to wait for Hunter's word?" Woods looked around unsure, watching the Werewolves head to the bar across the street. "Maybe we could send a runner to bring back a coupla brewskis and some burgers?"

Bear Shadow's gaze hadn't left Clarissa since her voice hit a squealing octave that made him and Crow Shadow tilt their heads.

"If the lady would like something to eat . . ." Bear Shadow's gaze shimmered amber.

She smiled and then shrugged with a self-conscious giggle.

"We should maybe go with takeout, man," Crow Shadow said, his gaze flowing over her body.

"I think you both need to go take a walk," Woods said evenly, gaining a slow nod from Fisher as he hoisted the strap of his M-16 higher on his shoulder.

Bear Shadow rubbed the back of his neck and then

shook his head, making his long hair sweep his shoulders. "You are right, familiar. These quarters are confining. We will bring back beef and beer."

All eyes followed the wolves out the door and, once sure they were out of earshot, Bradley looked at Woods, arms folded.

"What the hell was that?" Bradley said, his chin lifted with indignation.

"Two guys that have more wolf in them than we do, near a rising moon, having just gone through a serious adrenaline battle rush . . . on an empty stomach . . . with a bad spell kicking their libidos' butts—and you've got a full-fledged male wolf stalk about to go down." Woods rubbed the tension out of his neck as he lowered his weapon. "One female, two male wolves—we could have had a beta male brawl in here . . . And trust me, if Bear started throwing his weight around, all of us stood to get hurt."

"So, what am I, chopped liver?" Clarissa said, sounding more hurt than indignant. "So it had to be a bad spell, the phase of the moon, a wolf dominance display, but had nothing to do with me whatsoever, or the possibility that anybody could be interested in me? I'm just 'Rissa. Resident psychic chick, bio brain, one of the guys." She looked around, tears standing in her eyes. "You all suck."

The remaining males in the room looked at one another, momentarily at a loss for words, when Clarissa walked out and hurried up the stairs.

"What'd we say?" Fisher asked, opening his arms.

"I'm not exactly sure," Woods said quietly. "But she's a sweetheart and the last thing I wanted to do was hurt her feelings."

"Beats the hell out of me," Winters said, looking in the direction that 'Rissa fled. "I've never seen her like this. You think she's on her period or something?"

Bradley shook his head. "You assholes are so blind." He let out a weary sigh and left the room, following Clarissa's path up the stairs and to her room.

He knocked on the door softly and announced himself with care.

"'Rissa, it's me, Bradley." He waited and there was no movement, but he heard her blow her nose. "They're dorks. C'mon, open the door."

"Just leave it alone, Brads, okay?" she said in a shaky voice. "I just need to be by myself."

He stood there confounded and rested his head against the door. "I can't just leave it, all right? There are some things I've needed to say for a long time, but . . . Do I have to do this talking through a door?"

After a moment, he heard the bedsprings sound and her feet hit the floor. Then he heard her walk toward the door, and the lock turn before she opened it.

"What?" she said, eyes puffed and clasping a tissue.

"Can I come in?"

"I'd rather you just insult me here, all right?"

Bradley closed his eyes but allowed his palms to rest gently on her arms. "I would never insult you, 'Rissa. I like you too much, respect you too much . . . Your mind is . . . I cannot describe."

She hung her heard and more tears fell as she released a sad chuckle. "I know, blah, blah, blah, I'm like the sister you never had, and you wanna remain friends and always be cool and . . . I get it. I *so* get it. Fat but smart 'Rissa, the team's dependable geek. It's just that for a half a second when Bear Shadow looked at me like I was steak, I really felt pretty for once in my life. Stupid spell or not, you know—what am I saying, of course you don't know." She wiped at her eyes angrily and then stared at him. "It was petty and female and I normally don't give in to that, my bad. Sorry I freaked you guys out, can I go now?"

So many things were competing to get out of his head and out of his mouth at the same time that his voice failed. She backed up and placed her hand on the doorknob.

"Wait." Bradley palmed the door to keep her from closing it. "You're beautiful to me, 'Rissa."

"Thanks," she said in a monotone voice, "I love you, too. I'll be better in the morning."

"Not like-a-sister beautiful," he said, still resting his hand against the door.

She looked up at him and he swallowed hard.

"Not like-a-sister beautiful," he repeated quietly.

Her hand fell away from the doorknob and she began to shred the tissue she was holding.

"You don't have to say that to make me feel better." She looked down at her bare feet and shrugged. "I know what I'm not."

"You are the blindest seer I've ever encountered," he said in a soft murmur. "Honestly you are."

She slowly lifted her head and stared at him, her liquid blue gaze shimmering with new tears. "Why are you messing with my head, Bradley? We're friends."

"You're right, we're friends, and I'm glad of that—but you're also the kindest person I have ever known. Clarissa McGill. You care about people, you're dedicated, honorable . . . You give 150 percent to everyone around you and you appreciate people." He looked down at his shoes. "I never wanted to make you feel uncomfortable at work . . . so I tried not to stare at that cutest dimple that peeks out on your chin when you laugh, or stare at the clearest, most beautiful pair of blue eyes I've ever seen when you get that far-off look in them. It's a fine line we guys walk, in the spirit of political correctness. I always wanted you to like me and not think of me as some lecherous jerk."

"I would never think that about you," she murmured.

He shook his head and leaned against the door frame, still not allowing his gaze to meet hers. "I know how you feel . . . what it feels like to be invisible. Woods and Fisher have that, I don't know . . . military, commando swagger that slays women in the bars from eighteen to eighty. They're like fifteen to twenty years my junior, buff . . . Even Winters has that cute technology-guy charisma going for him that makes coeds think he'll be the next Bill

Gates . . . And I'm just Bradley, the resident dark arts expert, who's over forty and—"

"Handsome," Clarissa said in a soft voice.

Bradley looked up at her and then looked away with a sad smile. "You're kind, but, in the male lineup on this team, I'm realistic, 'Rissa. Stand me beside one of those ripped Shadow Wolves and it's sad. So, I—"

"Just throw yourself into your work and try to tell yourself it doesn't matter."

He nodded. "Something like that."

"Try to tell yourself that it doesn't hurt when the members of your team get picked up on nights out for fun—one by one—and you're the only one holding down the table watching all the drinks."

"Yeah," he said, letting out a wistful sigh. "But after a while, you sort of get used to it."

"But that little voice inside never dies does it?" She let out a breath as his gaze met hers again. "The one that says, why not me . . . Am I so unattractive or such a bad person that you won't even dance with me? That even if I'm not the prettiest one in the place . . ."

"Oh, 'Rissa, haven't you noticed that I always dance with you and I'm always holding down the table with you?"

She nodded and swallowed hard. "I thought you were just being a gentleman."

"I was, but don't I get points for that, too?"

His forlorn tone and the irony of what he'd said made her smile.

"Yeah . . ."

"Did you ever stop and think that for the average guy it might be hard to come over to a table with a woman who's wedged between two very athletic hunks, an older dude that could be her husband or maybe a protective big brother, a young guy who could be a lunatic younger brother, and then freakin' storm trooper–looking males in the form of mini versions of the Hulk. I personally wouldn't ask you for the time, let alone a dance, Clarissa. Beauty has nothing to do with it; survival of the fittest does. That's basic male logic."

He was glad that she covered her mouth and laughed. It was a joyous, soul-deep sound that made him smile.

"Oh, my God, Bradley . . . I never looked at it that way!"

He folded his arms over his chest, leaning on the door frame. "Well, I'm glad we at least got that much cleared up tonight." He smiled at her and then unfolded his arms. He seemed not to know what to do with his hands for a moment, then shoved them into his pockets. "It's not a crime to be smart. Even though this is the twenty-first century, some guys get it backwards . . . but I'm not one of them. I think it's attractive . . . sexy, if you must really know. You're brilliant, Clarissa. That simply blows me away."

She glanced away again shyly. "Thank you."

An uncomfortable silence hung in the air between them.

"I don't want it to get weird now," he finally said. "I just wanted you to know that you are . . . special and that I do know what it feels like to be viewed as some sort of asexual being when I'm not."

She stared at him until he looked away again.

"I mean—that didn't come out right," he said, stammering.

"Yes, it did," she said quietly. "Who doesn't want to feel like someone is dreaming about them at night or wants them like that?"

He nodded, staring down at his loafers. "Precisely. It's easy to talk to a psychic—they always know what you mean, even when you botch it."

She smiled and touched his cheek with the tips of her fingers, making him look at her. "You didn't botch anything, and you don't have to make jokes about something so deeply personal."

"I'm not any good at this, Clarissa," he said quietly. "I'm a klutz when trying to express myself about things like this."

"How many years have we been working together without any dates, without any Monday morning stories about a fantastic weekend away with someone?"

"About five years," he said in a quiet rush and closed his eyes.

"Maybe longer than that?" she offered, moving closer to him.

He simply nodded and then swallowed hard.

"That's a long time to feel invisible."

"An eternity," he said in a low murmur, pushing a stray wisp of her hair behind her ear.

"I don't want to feel invisible anymore," she said quietly, closing the gap between them.

"Neither do I."

She leaned up and brushed his mouth with a tender kiss, and he deepened it where they stood, a tremor running through them both.

"What if this is the dark magick?" he murmured, pulling back. "I don't want you to ever regret . . . I mean tomorrow, you could feel very upset about all of this and we still have to work together."

She took up his hand and led him inside her room, closing the door with a gentle thud and locking it. "Does it matter if it's a spell or not?" she asked, standing before him and looking up.

"Clarissa . . . I . . ."

She took his mouth again and this time he deepened it with more ardor. But when he broke their kiss, breathless, she cupped his jaw in her palm. His hands were trembling as they held her shoulders and she didn't need any gift of second sight to understand the questions that beleaguered his mind.

"I won't judge you," she said in a patient whisper.

"I want to be able to look in your eyes in the morning

and still see some semblance of respect there," he said in a pained whisper as he rested his forehead against hers with his eyes shut tightly. "Right now . . . I'm not sure that will happen. I'd better go before I truly humiliate myself."

She backed him up against the door, and took his mouth hard until his hands found her hair like they meant it. The moment her breasts pressed against his chest and her pelvis molded to his, she felt his breath hitch. No matter how awkward his words, his body was anything but. His fingers were long, graceful, and magnificent against her skin. Warm maleness and gentle caring surrounded her; his embrace made her dizzy. How could she have been so blind?

Honorable protests about the next day melted against her touch as her hand slid between them and found his shaft. The hard clench of his stomach nearly doubled him over as he murmured her name. It had been so long since anyone had passionately breathed her name into her hair that she almost wept. Fumbling with his shirt buttons, she swallowed his moan, giving them permission to redress years of self-denial.

"I know it's been five years or more of celibacy . . . for both of us," she said on a ragged whisper. "You won't disappoint me, no matter how brief the first encounter. We have all night. Just love me."

CHAPTER 12

"You know, Bradley's been up there a long time, guys . . . You think 'Rissa is really upset?" Winters said, glancing toward the stairs.

"Nah," Fisher said with a wave of his hand, flipping channels on the remote. "You know those two—they probably got into some philosophical debate after she calmed down and they're up there talking."

"More to the point, what happened to the brewskis and burgers?" Woods stood and paced, staring out the window at the moon. "I'm hungry as hell and going stir-crazy."

"Mighta been a lot of orders in across the street," Winters said with a shrug, tossing Woods what was left of the chips. "We can always call in more deliveries—whatcha want? They'll be back soon."

"From the look that was on Bear Shadow's face, those guys ain't coming back," Woods said, catching the chips and shoving several into his mouth.

Fisher smiled and pounded Winters's fist, wiggling his eyebrows at Woods. "Shit, dude, from the look on *your* face, you're about ready to go AWOL, too."

Woods closed his eyes for a moment, his voice becoming completely sober. "You guys have no idea."

Winters and Fisher gave each other wide grins.

"I've gotta get out of here, seriously." Woods flung the chips onto the table and began to pace.

"Okay, okay, man, before you do anything stupid, let's get 'Rissa to call Sasha . . . Maybe she can talk her into—"

"'Rissa is getting laid! What about this don't you all get—are you deaf?" Woods wiped the sudden perspiration from his brow. "You can't ask her jack shit right now!"

"Are you *serious,* dude?" Fisher was on his feet, leaving Winters on the sofa, gaping. He tilted his head like a hunting dog and then opened his mouth. "I'll . . . just . . . be . . . damned."

"I have got to get out of here," Woods said, walking back and forth between the lobby door and the sofa. "I just need a burger, a cold one and—"

"Some options," Fisher said, slapping him five on the next pass.

"Okay, it doesn't take an hour and a half to get from Ethan's bar to here—more like fifteen minutes, tops," Winters said. "Dudes, we are seriously slipping. Where's the ambulance, anybody hearing me?"

"So do we leave or stay—go do recon in the streets or maintain base, like Captain said?" Fisher raked his hair and turned around in a circle. "This is so fucked up."

"I need to eat; I need to get out of this lobby before I lose my mind," Woods said, holding his head with both hands.

Footfalls made all three men look up. Sasha came through the door first, followed by Doc in hot pursuit.

"I don't want to talk about it—not now and not in front of my men. We've been debating it for the last half hour and I really can't go through this anymore." Sasha spun on Doc when he drew a breath to speak. "Not in front of my men. This is between me and you."

Doc nodded and then dropped his shotgun on the coffee table.

"Uh, guys, where's the patient?" Winters asked nervously.

"In the bar across the street with his lieutenants, most likely!" Sasha shouted.

"Or in the closest Louisiana Werewolf titty bar he could find!" Doc shouted back.

"You know the address—is it close by?" Fisher asked, smiling but completely serious.

"Cap, we've gotta get out of here," Woods said. "Like, now . . . We've gotta eat . . . just need a few hours."

Sasha spun on him, but the plaintive tone of his voice held so much longing and his eyes seemed to be filled with so much pain that, for a moment, she couldn't respond.

"Cap," Winters said. "These guys are seriously bouncing off the walls. I'm good with takeout—which we went through a half hour ago and polished off a six-pack—but they are really hurtin' pups. But back to the bigger question, did the patient go AWOL all patched up and normal again—or is he off the hook?"

"He's fine," Sasha said, placing both hands on her hips.

"Shogun is *not* fine," Doc shouted. "Neither are you, Captain. He's in—he's not the issue right now!" Doc wiped his palms down his face and looked from Sasha to Winters. "Sasha, I want a meeting with you, McGill, Bradley, and you, Winters, stat. This thing is getting way out of control and we need a containment strategy right away. If there's some bad juju, as you claim, causing everybody to go insane, then let's get to the bottom of it pronto, before anything else happens. What happened in the back of that ambulance was a near miss and can never happen again."

"All right, fine, you're right—how many times do I have to agree with you? But let Woods and Fisher go eat. Why should they suffer, just because I have to?" She turned around and saluted them. "Your chain has been officially popped till oh-eight-hundred. Just be careful and come back alive."

Woods didn't say a word, just saluted her with tears in his eyes and bolted for the door. Fisher almost fell over the table getting out of the front door.

"Umm, sir," Winters said carefully, standing slowly. "Uh, about that meeting. See . . . McGill and Bradley are, uh, doing some research and aren't available right now. But if you want me to go into the databases and look stuff up for you, I'll be glad to, but—"

"You have *got* to be kidding me," Doc said, closing his eyes and tilting his head. "I'm going to have some dinner and to get my mind right, after . . ." He shook his head and let out a hard breath. "I'll be back in a couple of hours. Hopefully they'll be finished *researching* by then. I'm leaving."

Sasha and Winters watched Doc huff out the door, allowing the screen to slam with a bang. Sasha tilted her head and looked up at the ceiling.

"Good for them," she said quietly. "'Bout time."

He sat with Silver Hawk in front of the fire in the shadow lands as the elderly shaman added more water to the hot rocks. Hissing steam filled the small sweat lodge, blanketing their nude bodies with thick, humid vapors that leached moisture from their pores. He watched Silver Hawk's ancient eyes through the opaque haze, waiting for the moment that the flames would tell him when to become Silver Shadow, when it would be time to chase the spirits beneath the blue-white moon.

His grandfather drew a labored breath and began a low, murmuring chant in their native tongue to call the ancestors. The heat and the sound slowly began to fuse into a low buzzing resonance inside his head. Almost as though his vision was doubling, he saw Sasha lying on the cavern floor, and then an opaque version of her stood—leaving her body on the ground—to walk off into the mist. Then one by one he saw them all . . . his spirit stood and then walked away from his body . . . Bear's, Crow's, Doc's, Ethan's—Silver Hawk opened his eyes when Shogun's father's wolf came.

Silver Hawk nodded. "Yes, even you, son."

"Grandfather, help me understand," Hunter said in a quiet rush.

His grandfather closed his eyes and put a finger to his lips. "Ssssh . . . Let them show me more." With his eyes still closed, Silver Hawk used his index finger to scratch out strange symbols in the dirt beside him. "Learn these and take them to her. This is part of the sorcery that calls spirits to make doubles and walk in the darkness. We must claim them back once they've been cleaned."

Silver Hawk opened his eyes with a start and sucked in a deep breath. "We must go back and warn the others. Tonight is just the beginning."

He couldn't stay in the back of the ambulance for a second longer. When Sasha had stopped to get out of the cab and bring him the cell phone so that he could talk to his men, he had needed to get away from her, lest he be tempted to bodily carry her with him. Whatever shred of rational thought was left made him bolt. The only reason he took the call was to avert a war. If Seung Kwon thought there was foul play, her team would have been slaughtered in retribution, and he couldn't have that on his head—not loving her the way he did.

On foot, he was free; he could feel the air caress his face, imagining it was still her. He could run hard and fast, even if in human form, to exercise his body, feel his limbs come back to life again. The exertion was necessary. Being pulled away from her body . . . her willing, supple body . . . was no less than a silver bullet in his skull. His men, no doubt, saw the insanity in his eyes as he entered Finnegan's Wake. He let them see that he was all right, and they followed him where he swore he'd never go . . . to his enemy's house—the New Orleans's Werewolves' Bayou House. It was still owned by the Buchanan Broussard family, the very clan that had tried to assassinate his brother and trick him into marrying their twisted alpha daughter. Rest both their sick souls in peace.

But there was nowhere else to go; supernaturals were in hiding, except the ones that had Vampire protection down here.

He hated himself as he entered the pulsing red lights that sent music through his veins, his men flanking him. It was a weakness to be this out of control, but if he took on a human female in this condition, under a nearly full moon, he'd possibly kill her from internal injuries. Accident or not, a human fatality would be on his head.

Smug smiles of recognition greeted him and his men—they wouldn't be attacked; they were clients tonight. Ones that would have their pockets turned out and be laughed at the next day for having to patronize this establishment after all. They would know that meant he'd lost his battle for Sasha. Everything about this carved at his pride.

Music strummed through his body, the wolf in him noting every male's position, size, and threat level. None visible could best him and his men. The stage commanded his focus as agile females made the poles slick with their sweat. Music throbbed in his groin, reminding him of Sasha. *Just end the torture.*

Yet, it was the principle of the thing; to pay for companionship at the house of one's enemy was the height of humiliation. Right now, after Sasha, he had no pride left.

"I didn't think we'd see you in these parts again, sugah," a tall, thick-thighed brown beauty said, caressing his back suggestively.

He stared at her full mouth, remembering Sasha. She flashed him a little canine to let him know he could play as rough as he wanted to, as rough as he obviously needed it right now. He slid his hand up her throat and she smiled. She bent her knee and pressed her calf to his ass, balancing on a four-inch black stiletto.

"Neither did I. How much for the entire party, to cover me and my men?"

"A thousand dollars a throw . . . since you boys have a reputation as not being overly friendly with our family.

We're still feeling some losses—Dana was my friend, and her daddy was good people." She moved her plump mound against his groin in a slow, sultry grind, holding on to his shoulders. "But when it comes to business, we don't hold a grudge here at Bayou House."

Shogun stared at the woman who'd dropped her voice to a sensual murmur. Pro or not, she was exquisite. The black velvet bustier was killer, holding up double-Ds and leaving little to the imagination. "I've never had to pay four thousand dollars for entertainment in my life." He looked up from her over-exposed cleavage and smiled at her, reaching into his pocket and withdrawing a knot. "But, under the circumstances, you drive a hard bargain."

"See, now, that's why there's that saying: Never say never, sugah."

Shogun released a sad chuckle as he watched his men summarily get picked up and led away. She folded his bills into her cleavage and ran her hand across his crotch.

"Darlin', I might have to give you a discount . . . because I can truly tell you I've *never* felt anything like this."

"They're *human,* Bear," Crow said, looking over the rim of his beer. "I don't care what Woods and Fisher can get away with—they're way more human than we are and can't even shift. I don't think it's a good idea, man."

"Why . . ."

Crow Shadow took a huge gulp of his beer. "Because what if you lose your mind and shift on them mid—"

"That won't happen," Bear said in a low rumble, studying the two women that had been flirting with them all night. "You've never been with a human female before, have you?"

"Yeah, of course," Crow Shadow said, hailing the bartender.

"You can't allow your canines to crest and their skin can't handle a rake; you'll seriously injure them," Bear said with a smile.

"Yeah, yeah, I know, man."

"Cannot hard roll a human female onto the floor from the height of a bed. You could break a bone, or snap her back . . . Gotta take your time, understand." Bear Shadow looked at Crow Shadow hard. "Dab the corners of your mouth. You're starting to slobber on yourself."

"Stop fucking with me, man," Crow Shadow said, frowning when Bear Shadow smiled. "I don't see why we can't just go find a wolf strip club, man—or find out where the real ladies are tonight?" Crow Shadow looked around the bar wistfully.

"Because," Bear Shadow said, his eyes on his target, "Buchanan's operation is a sure place to get jumped without backup . . . All the non-working ladies of interest are in hiding until the party. Now, I don't know about you, but three moons is a long time, brother."

"You ain't never lied," Crow Shadow said, pounding Bear's fist. "Which one you want, man . . . the blond or the brunette?"

"Flip a coin, heads it's the blond, and tails . . . ummph, ummph, ummph, it's the *brunette*."

"Don't howl up in here, Bear, man . . . Human females don't understand it."

"Says who?" Bear Shadow looked completely undone. "You obviously haven't been with one—you just told on yourself, because if you had you'd know that after you've gone downtown, or knocked the backboard out, I guarantee you she'll appreciate the sentiment. Some things cross all cultures."

"Just let 'er rip, a full-moon howl, just like that—and she won't call the police?"

Bear laughed. "Not if you've earned the right to release the call of the wild. That, I can't coach you on or help you with—you're on your own." Bear Shadow tossed back his Jack Daniels and set the glass down with a wince. "They're hot; sex scent is at 100 percent panty saturation point. I'm going in. Cover me."

"Man . . . how do you do that shit?" Crow Shadow murmured in awe, looking at the women who gave him and Bear Shadow a little wave.

"The blond is sure," Bear said, standing, his gaze straight ahead. "Her girlfriend is a little skittish, but they both want to run with the big dogs tonight." Bear shook his head and rubbed the nape of his neck. "So, I'm sending them another round of drinks, we're going to get these beautiful, delicate creatures whatever they want to eat, and then see if they might be willing to let a couple of big bad wolves huff and puff and blow down their houses."

"What a fabulous turn of events." Baron Montague strode through the crowd at Finnegan's Wake, careful to stay far away from the Shadow Wolves and Sasha's familiars. He subtly disappeared behind a server and took on his vapor form with several females in his misty retinue. "It seems every male that would have fought beside her is otherwise indisposed; even the Werewolves have lost their focus and have sought the pleasures of the flesh . . . And the boy, if he leaves the house, he's mine."

"They still have that barrier to us at Dugan's Bed & Breakfast?" a willowy, pale platinum blond murmured through her fangs. "Drat! Geoff, let's play with them tonight. There are two humans upstairs copulating, and the boy is on the sofa, bored, watching television. We could easily run all three of them out into the night. Sasha would come home to ashes. We could just burn it down."

"Yes, yes, can we, and then we could feed on Sasha's humans?" her flame-haired companion begged. "That would twist that bitch's gizzards with guilt when she came back to find her three cherished, defenseless humans sucked bone dry."

"The old man is also by himself—her father," another said pulling on Geoff's arm. She flung her silky black hair over her shoulders, giggling as they passed unsuspecting patrons that only noticed them as a chill. "He may have that dreaded, tainted Shadow Wolf blood in him, but we could snap his neck and leave him for dead . . . Maybe just savage him so it looks like a wolf did it."

"But all of those delicious options would involve us directly, *mes cheries*."

"Oh, poo," the blond said, nipping his neck. "You're no fun."

"That's not what you said a little while ago." He whacked her on her backside as they giggled and left by way of the open windows. "Patience is a virtue, and when you live forever, you can afford to exploit as much of that natural resource as required. Besides, Dugan's B&B is valuable real estate, love. Firebombing is so pedestrian, so yesterday."

Sasha's hair was still wet from the shower when she got behind the wheel. Sir Rodney's top advisor had called and asked her to go look again at where the bodies had been. She couldn't blame them for not wanting to be outside of the Sidhe at night, especially with their magick waning. And even though she wasn't sure what they were after, she'd gladly gone along with their request—she had needed space and had needed to get Shogun's scent off her, drop her clothes in the laundry, and get the hell out of there. Listening to Clarissa hit high notes and Bradley bottom out in bass notes was *not* how she was going to spend her night. There was an investigation to conclude, even if she was laboring under the influence of a jacked-up spell.

Doc might have been irrational, giving in to some *Father Knows Best* rerun playing in his head due to the dark magick, but he did have a point—they had to find out more information and get ahead of the spell reactions before anything else crazy happened. That would have led her back to the last place she probably should have been, even if Garth hadn't called: Ethan's Fair Lady.

Police crime-scene tape barred the entrance as she drove by. Okay, made sense; somebody heard the shotgun blast, no doubt, called in the authorities; they saw the hole in the ceiling, maybe even Fae arrows and scorched walls from Dragon blasts, and now the authorities couldn't find the owners on what should have been a bustling business night. Not good.

Sasha parked her jeep two blocks away and tucked her Glock into the back of her jeans' waistband, covering it up as best she could with her tank top. She slipped around the back of the building, avoiding the shadows, not wanting to escape into one and accidentally bump into Hunter and Silver Hawk—she was not ready for that yet. But there had to be something in that cellar that she hadn't seen before. Without any male triggers to create a diversion and in there alone, maybe she'd get to the bottom of it.

She kicked in the back door after listening to be sure there were no human authorities still snooping around, and slipped inside, her wolf night vision helping her to stay concealed in the darkness.

Hesitating for a moment, she stood at the top of the cellar steps. She could still smell the ash and added trace of human sweat. "Aw, man . . ." Sasha let out a hard breath. Humans had been down there mucking around in a supernatural crime scene. Something still drew her, pulled at her, and she crept down the steps on guard.

"Shit!" The humans had left boot prints everywhere, as well as their scent layer. Now any hope of going back to examine a fairly intact crime scene was shot.

Sasha stooped down to where the victim had been and stared at the eerie impression of the body that was left. Crouching closer, she stared at the floor and then began brushing away the slight film of remaining ash. Beneath it a strange series of new symbols became visible. They were totally different from the ones that had been on the actual Phoenix's body ash. Why had Desidera's body been lying right on top of this larger sigil, hiding it?

The images burned into her mind's eye. Sasha stood up quickly, bolted up the stairs to find Ethan's office. She needed paper and pencil, had to copy it down exactly as she found it. Yanking out drawers, she finally ran to the copier and snatched a stack of pages, swiping a pen from the desk on her way out.

But as she returned to the ashy spot, there was nothing there except unintelligible soot.

CHAPTER 13

Hunter entered the bed-and-breakfast with Silver Hawk. Both men stopped and just stared for a moment. Winters was sprawled out on the sofa amid pizza boxes, beer bottles, and a blaring TV tuned to the Sci Fi channel. They paused, tilted their heads, and then stared at each other.

"We've lost our familiars for the night," Hunter said, staring at the ceiling.

"And our dark arts specialist," Silver Hawk said calmly, with no judgment in his tone.

"Oh, hey," Winters said, rousing slowly and yawning. "Everything cool?"

"You tell me," Hunter said, growing edgy. "Where are my men?"

Winters sat forward chuckling and rubbing his eyes. "Oh, *man*. Those guys went out hours ago. As soon as the moon went up, they were out. But you can probably hear better than me," he added, hunting for a cold slice of pizza, "and the reason I'm down here drowning out the sound . . . Fisher and Woods brought back live game. And Bradley and 'Rissa are 'researching,' if you get my drift." He bit into a slice, and then made a gesture to offer Hunter and Silver Hawk a bite, which they declined. "Sometimes I wish . . . I just don't know how those guys do it. The one Woods pulled is *killer*."

"What direction did Bear Shadow and Crow Shadow go?" Hunter asked, his tone dangerous. "I gave them a direct order to protect this location!"

Silver Hawk landed a steady hand on Hunter's shoulder. "They have not had the benefit of your clarity in the shadow lands. This is not how they generally conduct themselves as your lieutenants. Be mindful of that."

"They rolled out with a blond and a brunette from across the street, left their jeep—probably going to the girls' place . . . which is a good thing—could you imagine the racket that would have been going on in here with five couples knocking boots? *Sheesh.*" Winters yawned again and stretched. "It's cool, though. When the pizza dude came, I was on the porch and saw Bear driving a really cute chick's car with Crow and her friend in the backseat all snuggled up . . . so I think your guys are doing just fine. No worries, no attacks, everything is peace, as they say. But I doubt you'll see 'em before tomorrow morning. Seems like all of New Orleans was over at Finnegan's tonight."

"Humans?" Silver Hawk said, incredulous.

Hunter briefly closed his eyes. This was bad. There were so many ways that volatile combination could go wrong that he couldn't even think about that right now.

"I dunno," Winters said with another lazy stretch. "I guess? Couldn't see that far from the porch to tell if they were human girls or not. You guys forget that I don't have all that sexy night vision and super hearing and whatever. I'm just the tech guy."

Hunter nodded and rubbed his jaw. "All right. Where are Doc, Sasha, and Shogun? Did they take him to Tulane?"

"No, didn't have to. Dude recovered, from what I heard," Winters said with a nonchalant shrug, scratching his head. "Everybody is just wacko tonight. Sasha bursts in here arguing with Doc—after she put Shogun on the phone. He, I guess, spoke to his men from the ambulance, and then they were out. But after Sasha and Doc had this 'I'm your father and you won't speak to me like that' blowup, Doc went across the street to eat and cool off; she headed for the shower and then came down five minutes later and grabbed one of the jeeps."

Silver Hawk stepped in front of Hunter and grabbed him by his shoulders. "Remember what we saw on the spirit walk. Remember that things are not always what they appear."

"Did Shogun's men say where they were going?" Hunter said, a low growl underscoring his words.

"No, they were out real fast, but Doc was having a conniption about them probably heading toward some Werewolf strip club in the bayou." Winters flopped back against the sofa. "All I wanna know is, how come I got stuck here holding down the fort? Like, I wouldn't have been discriminating about a lap dance. Seriously."

Hunter looked at Winters and then at his grandfather.

"That should make you feel better, son," Silver Hawk murmured, releasing Hunter's shoulders.

Armed to the teeth, Hunter jumped into a jeep—pump-action shotgun on the backseat in plain view. The decision to find Sasha or his brother wore on him, but the draw to hunt for Shogun won out. Right now, Shogun was the most vulnerable. He could pretty much guess what had sent his brother into the notorious brothel, as well as what had probably pissed Doc off. There was only one thing that would have broken down Shogun's pride to the point where he'd pay for companionship at a known enemy's house . . . where he'd allow his men to follow him on such a suicide mission. He just prayed that he'd make it in time.

Sasha scribbled down the symbols quickly, as best she could remember them, folded away the paper, and then shoved the paper and pen into her back jeans' pocket. Speed was her friend as she dashed up the cellar steps and exited the building, her mission singular—go to the other Phoenix's house and see if there was also a symbol beneath where Penelope's charred remains had been. It was a job she wasn't looking forward to, but somebody had to do it.

Based on what Rodney's advisors had told her and what Bradley had disclosed to the team, a theory took root in her mind as she drove. From what little she did know about Fae magick, if all the symbols were gone, had simply vanished, then it definitely had nothing to do with the human intervention—it would have to be either that someone had doubled back to erase them, or maybe the symbols faded a certain amount of time after they had the desired treacherous effect . . . Or maybe the symbols could only be seen right after an incident in broad daylight, before they simply melted into the night as a dark spell. Night covered a lot of things.

She pulled up to the double-wide trailer that she'd been to with Ethan, Margaret, and Hunter, and easily jimmied the door. The outline of the body was still there where it had been lying on the floor, curled in a fetal position. Sasha bit her lip as she looked at where the poor young Phoenix who never came back from the ashes had lain.

Moving through the small home, Sasha found a dustpan and broom, and, as reverently as possible, shifted the thin layer of ash to a neat pile, expecting to see a symbol scorched into the floor. Ethan wanted to have a proper memorial, and there just hadn't been time. Once all this was over, she'd be sure to help him do that.

Sasha stooped and scribbled down the strange absence. There were no symbols here combined in geometric figures that seemed to move on the floor as though alive as she'd seen at The Fair Lady. Why? Both girls had been killed the same way, but only one set of symbols showed up.

That stilled her. The question was, had the floor at Ethan's been previously marked by an invisible symbol, like a land mine for the victim to trip over, or was the symbol what appeared after the fact to mark the spot where the victim fell? But whatever the case, why wasn't there a large sigil here, a land mine for Penelope to trip over?

Bradley would know what to do with that key information, so would Sir Rodney. The issue was going to be explaining to Sir Rodney why it was necessary to inform her human squad . . . Damn, the Fae were so touchy.

The question about how the specific symbols she'd uncovered functioned was just one more to add to the dozens of others that twisted around one another in her brain. And how the heck did one use a freakin' symbol to kill somebody? She'd heard of chaos magick used to make someone sick, to hold on to a lover, or to give someone a serious case of bad luck—otherwise known as doing roots . . . But to actually make them char? No. That was definitely a new one. She flipped open her telephone and left a message for Sir Rodney, detailing her find. All she got was instant voice mail. She closed her eyes. He was in the Sidhe; his advisors were in deep, and so was Ethan. Her and her team, as well as Hunter and his men, plus Shogun and his family, were on the other side of the Fae fortress. *Just great.*

Sasha stood, let out a weary breath, and headed out the door.

Silver Hawk spotted his friend of many years sitting at a table alone, nursing a drink, a half-eaten plate of steak and potatoes pushed away from him. He slid into the chair in front of Xavier Holland, causing him to look up.

"It's no fun to eat alone without family, brother. I would have joined you."

Doc nodded and looked down into his glass. "I don't know what came over me . . . I flipped, as though Sasha was my teenage daughter . . . as though I had a right to tell a grown woman what to do. It was complete madness, and I knew it, and still I couldn't stop myself." Doc let out a long sigh. "I need to sit down with Sasha . . . as well as my son, Crow Shadow. There is so much for us to talk about, so many blanks in their lives to fill in—as well as in my own . . . But each of us has been holding back, afraid of even going there. It's as though we acknowledge the lineage, respect it, but have yet to come together to discuss how any of this had made us feel . . . And tonight, I went after her as though I had that right, and I don't."

Silver Hawk closed his eyes and rolled his neck. "This darkness has us all in its grip. I do not ever want to know what you saw that may have caused that argument, for I fear I already know. Then, I could not be impartial at a time when I must be."

Silver Hawk opened his eyes to stare into Doc's intense gaze. For a long while both men said nothing.

Shogun looked up into a gorgeous smiling face, but it was not the one he longed for. Her perfect brown complexion made her entire body seem as though it had been dipped in cinnamon. As she straddled him, her pendulous breasts swayed above him and her taut nipples competed with her eyes for his attention. Interesting how her nipples were the same color as her eyes, bittersweet chocolate.

Her mouth was kiss punished and full, her eyes smoldering still, and her hair was sticking up all over her head. Then he looked down and realized that huge tufts of sandy brown hair were in his hands and all over his chest and the bed.

"I'm so sorry," he said quietly, wondering how she could still be pleasant after what he'd done—money paid or not, it had to hurt like hell.

"Aw, sugah, it was just weave," she said, laughing and kissing him. "Gonna take me about three or four hours in the salon chair to get it all put back in, but it was worth losing every track."

He didn't understand. "Weave?"

She brushed the fallen hair off his chest and pulled it from between his fingers. "A girl can't tell all her secrets," she said, still smiling brightly, canines fully exposed. "But you could spring for the hairdresser . . . since four hours off the clock to get beautiful again is a real killer on the revenue."

He nodded and traced her smooth hips with his palms. "Not a problem."

She leaned down and took his mouth and then sat back, beginning to slowly move with him still lodged deep inside her. "You are so damned sexy and such a doll . . . What is wrong with that girl?"

"Excuse me?" Shogun held her hips firm, not letting her move.

"Oh, don't get all tight on me and paranoid. Of course I'd know about her . . . Ya called her name about a half dozen times and then came so hard I thought I was gonna have to call an ambulance for you, sugah. And right about now, you feel like you're ready to go like that again. Just feminine observation . . . but if thinking about her makes you act like that, I'll be her for you any night. Your time, your dime."

"This stays here," Shogun said, staring at her hard and then sitting up fast with her on his lap. He held her around the waist and spoke to her over a low growl. "You understand?"

Unfazed, she adjusted her legs to wrap around his waist as she kissed him and held him by the shoulders. "Everything that happens in here stays in here, always. House rules. I don't even know what we were talking about."

"I don't see why we had to go," Crow Shadow said in a forlorn voice as he and Bear Shadow trudged down the street. "They wanted us to stay until morning, and were even gonna make us breakfast."

"Two things," Bear Shadow said, counting off with his fingers as they walked. "Number one, these are human females, and the closer it gets to midnight, the more self-control you'll lose as your wolf makes you more aggressive . . . Gotta go before a tragedy happens."

"Okay . . . True, true," Crow Shadow said, rubbing the nape of his neck. "I can see that."

"She was already fatigued, yes?" Bear Shadow said as they crossed the street.

"Laid out," Crow Shadow said with a wide grin and then slapped Bear Shadow five.

Bear Shadow chuckled and shook his head. "That was my point."

"So, what's point two?"

"If you stay till morning, you stand the risk of getting attached."

Crow Shadow nodded. "She was real nice."

Bear Shadow nodded. "Mine was, too." He let out a long sigh. "I made the proper excuses for us both . . . There was no reason to be dishonorable and hurt their feelings, after they were so . . . *nice*."

"But, man, how the hell do you just get up out of some woman's bed and not have her get her feelings hurt? We're Shadow Wolves, we can't lie . . . like—"

"We had to get back to the base, which is no lie—it is not my fault if she interpreted that as though we are soldiers . . . which is also not a full untruth. We are warriors." He glanced at Crow Shadow from the corner of his eye and then looked straight ahead, speaking slowly and succinctly. "Warriors that have defied a *direct* order from our alpha, the commander and chief of the Shadow Wolf North American Federation, to guard the house. Hunter . . . is going to . . . *flip*."

Crow Shadow stopped walking, but Bear Shadow didn't. Crow Shadow bent over and grabbed his hair with both hands. "Oh, shit! We didn't even wait till Sasha got back safely . . . You know, to put our own eyes on her, man! Hunter is gonna—"

"Flip," Bear Shadow called out, now a half block away.

Crow Shadow jogged to catch up to him. "What were we thinking, man?"

"We weren't," Bear Shadow said flatly. "I had absolutely no blood flow to my brain, and that is definitely no lie."

"Like, when did it occur to you, man, that we were gonna get our faces ripped off?"

Bear Shadow let out a long weary breath. "Maybe after the third time I was done. Could have been the fourth."

They walked along in companionable silence for several blocks, each man caught up in his own thoughts.

"But I would have liked to have breakfast with her, man, if this was going to be my last meal," Crow Shadow said solemnly. "Southern hospitality and all."

"If you would have stayed," Bear Shadow said carefully. "You would have been on her body all night and she would have possibly wound up in ER in the morning. You didn't need to add that to the list of offenses."

"Okay, okay . . . But she was still nice."

Bear Shadow stopped walking and his abruptness made Crow Shadow skid to a halt.

"Did you use protection?" Bear Shadow folded his arms over his barrel chest.

"Huh?" Crow Shadow's eyes widened.

"Tell me you did not mate with a human female multiple times and *not* use human protection—just tell me."

"I don't know what you're talking about, man," Crow Shadow said, waving his arms as he walked in an agitated circle.

"Great Spirit, I know this is my punishment for giving in to my weaknesses," Bear Shadow said, opening his arms, closing his eyes, and turning his face to the sky in supplication.

"What the hell are you talking about, Bear! Stop yanking me around!"

Bear Shadow leveled his gaze. "Brother, brother,

brother . . . human females are on phase once a month. They can get pregnant at any time. They aren't like she-wolves that go into heat biannually."

"Shut . . . up . . ."

"You really didn't know?" Bear Shadow rubbed the tension away from his neck.

"You should have told me that shit, man!" Crow Shadow walked in a circle. "I thought those skins were just to keep humans from catching diseases from each other—and since we purge all infections and whatever, I thought I didn't need 'em . . . and she had 'em, but once it got going and the thing didn't fit . . . she basically said she didn't care and I got to howling and she was all hot and to the point of crying, like, and then . . . aw, man . . ."

"Yeah, that's generally how it goes down, little brother." Bear started walking, clearly disgusted. "They have large sizes, you know . . . Still might be uncomfortable, but beats a blank."

"And you're explaining this to me now?" Incredulous, Crow Shadow rounded Bear Shadow with a snarl. "I didn't know they had different sizes! The thing she gave me only made it a third of the way up!"

"Magnums . . . Those will get you halfway covered, at least."

"What? Like you couldn't have told me before—"

"Did you get her name?"

Crow Shadow stopped walking. "Yeah, man . . . It was Cassie . . . Casey," he called out behind Bear Shadow. "No, wait a minute. Kelsey! Man, don't you get religion on me now—after the fact!"

"Got a last name?" Bear Shadow shouted over his shoulder.

"Fuck you, man!" Crow Shadow shouted.

Bear Shadow spun on him and hollered down the street, pointing. "No, fuck you, little brother, if this human female comes up pregnant with a half Shadow Wolf and you have to go to the clan council to stand before *Silver Hawk* and Hunter *and* Sasha to explain how this happened, when this happened, and then have to decide if you are going to take ownership to bring the child into the wolf pack, with or without the mother . . . It gets very complicated. Doc's life is living proof of that! You don't even know this woman's last name or address, so you can't claim you were caught up in love. This was boys' night out! Kelsey was *not* your human woman that you wanted to get permission to make your life mate . . . and you bed her bareback? Are you crazy?"

"Okay, man, you're scaring me, all right," Crow Shadow said quietly.

"Good!"

Bear Shadow stood under a streetlight breathing hard as Crow Shadow stared up at the moon.

"Then can you do me one favor, man," he asked in a quiet voice.

"What?" Bear Shadow bellowed.

"Can you at least walk me back to their apartment so I can get her name and address off the mailbox?"

Hunter got out of the jeep with a shotgun over his shoulder. That same feral female scent was back, the one he'd noticed at both murder sites. Then again, this was a brothel, and the scent of feral female blanketed the area for miles.

Regardless, this was not the night anybody needed to fuck with him. Bouncers snarled and four took a stance as Hunter approached the front entrance.

"You gotta check your weapon at the door."

Hunter lowered it in a flash and took aim before any of them could lunge. "Consider it checked, or do I need to deposit silver?"

"What's your beef?" a burly manager said, parting the security squad at the front door. Gold tips capped his upper and lower canines, and the name Butch sparkled in gold-rimmed diamonds across his front teeth. "Everybody in here is having a good time. Put the shotgun up for safe-keeping, and we'll gladly accept your cash, too."

"I'm looking for my brother," Hunter said with a snarl, not giving up his weapon.

Butch nodded and chuckled. "That's all you had to say."

CHAPTER 14

A svelte, androgynous male came over to the baron's blackjack table, leaned in close, and whispered in his ear. His pale green silk shirt and linen pants provided a beautifully sharp contrast with his dark brown tresses that merged with the baron's as he deposited juicy gossip.

"It's starting, milord." The male companion tossed his brunet hair behind his pointed ear and allowed his graceful fingers to lightly rest on the baron's broad shoulder.

"How so?" the baron murmured, his fangs cresting in anticipation.

The baron's companion motioned to a server to bring the baron another blood goblet, reveling in the attention he was receiving from the ladies who drew in closer to hear the dirt. "Both males are at the Buchanan brothel and, let's say word has it that neither is disposed for combat with anyone but each other right now. The Buchanans will make their move soon."

The baron laughed and shook his head, accepting a fresh blood goblet as his ladies clapped and giggled. He lifted his golden chalice and gave them a slight bow from where he sat. "How perfect. So, after the brothers half kill each other, Buchanan's kith and kin can finish them off . . . as would be their right for erupting in violence in their establishment. We will not be culpable and will not have blood on our hands."

"Perhaps a future alliance, then?" The companion drew back to stare at the Vampire, drinking in Baron Montague's jewel-blue eyes with his own.

"Patience, Kiagehul," the baron crooned. "We shall see."

Sasha felt like she was about to leap right out of her skin as she drove back toward the bed-and-breakfast. Something was wrong; every nerve in her body was standing on end. Wolf distress was in the air. The scent of fear tickled the back of her synapses and raised the hair on her neck.

But she hated not knowing whether or not it was her human gut instinct or something more refined—wolf instinct, or just the heebie-jeebies from the dark spell. Moving bodies that had been charred to death didn't help. Still, something was spooking her internal radar, and that was hardly ever wrong.

Turning the corner, she brought the jeep to a screeching halt, pulling over to get out of the way of light traffic that was behind her.

"Bear? Crow?" she shouted, leaning over the seat towards them.

They stopped walking and just stared at her.

"You guys okay? You need a ride?"

"Sis, honest to God, I've never seen a better sight for sore eyes." Crow Shadow dashed toward her and hurled himself into her backseat, and then hugged her, seeming like he was too choked up to speak.

But Bear was more cautious. He looked around in all directions like a wanted man. "Uh . . . Have you seen Hunter?"

"No. You guys have any idea where he is?"

The expression on Bear's face was a cross between relief and jubilation. The man seriously looked like he was ready to break down and do the happy dance in the middle of the street.

"Mind if we escort you to him, stay on your flank, and, uh, otherwise be of service, ma'am?"

All she could do was stare at Bear Shadow for a moment. "Uh, yeah . . . That was sorta the idea. Hop in."

"We don't really have to go into details with Hunter about us all getting separated for a little while, do we, Sis?" Crow Shadow said quickly as Bear climbed into the front passenger seat. "What's a few hours amongst family?"

Sasha smiled. "How long were you guys AWOL?" She held up her hand. "Never mind, I don't wanna know and it's not important."

"You are a decent person, Captain Trudeau," Bear Shadow said with genuine affection. "Thank you."

Sasha just shook her head.

This was a setup, if ever he smelled one. Hunter bounded up the stairs above the strip club to the private rooms. His men were AWOL, Sasha was missing, and Silver Hawk was at Finnegan's trying to talk Doc down. And his brother was here—unacceptable.

He kicked the door with his boot, and held the shotgun to the ceiling, pressing his back to the wall. The door opened, and a female form filled it.

"Need to talk to Shogun," Hunter said in a low command. "Now."

"He's otherwise indisposed, sugah," the pretty but disheveled female said, giving him attitude.

"Tell my brother I need to speak to him," Hunter said with more snarl in his voice.

The door swung open and Shogun filled it, zipping his pants, eyes blazing.

"We need to talk," Hunter said, inclining his head down the hall away from the woman in the doorway.

"About what?" Shogun said, growling. "Clearly, if I'm here, you've won."

"Not about that," Hunter said quickly, and then reached around Shogun to snatch the female he'd been with. That scent was back, that scent was near—so close it had to be her. Hunter put the barrel of his shotgun to her cheek before Shogun could knock it away. "Drop it, bitch."

Shogun backed up as the female slowly extended her arm and dropped a small Lady Derringer on the floor. He stared at her and then his brother.

"Smell it. Silver loaded," Hunter muttered. "You would have died in your sleep."

"That wasn't for him, it was for you," she said with a lisp, as the barrel pressed into her cheek. "How did I know you weren't coming to fight him?"

Hunter flung the angry female Were away from them as his brother picked up her gun.

"Hunter, she's all right," Shogun said, frowning. "You're—"

A shotgun blast tore through the wall past Shogun, grazed Hunter, and gutted the angry woman that had been leaning against the door frame. She dropped in a crimson pool of her own blood, silver buckshot still smoldering in her skin where it passed through the wall into her.

Hunter was pure motion, yanking his brother by the arm as they started to run low while shotgun shells exploded over their heads the whole length of the long hallway. Hunter ran straight for the window. He and Shogun let loose a howl calling their men to safety as they crashed through the window, fell three stories, and landed in a crouch amid shattered glass.

They headed for the tree line and took cover, Hunter holding the weapon parallel to his body.

"How did you know?" Shogun asked quickly, breathing hard.

"Shadow walk," Hunter said, peeking around the tree. "Your instincts are off, senses dulled . . . There's dark magick that cannot permeate the shadow lands."

Shogun nodded. "I owe you."

"We're blood—no debt," Hunter said, glancing around the tree again. "You need to get you and your men out of here. There are false walls in here, all kinds of sewer tubing underneath here for escapes . . . passageways for assassins. I didn't come to fight with you—the shadow lands cleared my head and I hope your escort momentarily cleared yours."

War howls filled the air as Shogun nodded. "I have to get my men."

"You hear that?" Sasha said, driving faster until she was driving like a maniac.

Bear Shadow and Crow Shadow just stared at her for a second.

"Listen! It's a combined war call—Hunter and Shogun! Where are they?"

"At the Bayou House, but you can't—"

"I can't what?" Sasha's growl cut off Bear Shadow's statement. She stepped on the gas, barreling the vehicle toward the B&B. "Go inside and get Woods and Fisher's artillery while I keep the motor running! Tell Winters to let Doc and Silver Hawk know Buchanan's people have attacked our clans!"

The shadows wouldn't have him. Stunned when he made a running leap and hit a tree, Hunter sat up dazed. A knot was forming on his head, his shoulder ached, and the wind had been knocked out of him. But concussion or not, he had to get up. Feral female scent thickened the air and, combined with the impact of colliding with the tree, it made him nearly retch.

"I don't know what's wrong," he said in a low, disoriented rumble, getting up slowly from the ground. "I can't shadow jump."

Shogun stared down at his hands. "I'm not transforming, brother. My wolf won't come to me!"

"Then that means that your men are sitting ducks, if their wolves lie dormant," Hunter said, studying the building as it emptied of Buchanan's Louisiana clan in droves. "So are we."

Bear Shadow took over the wheel as Sasha leaped from the jeep and grabbed the M-16 that he tossed her.

"I'm going through the shadow lands as the advance squad. If Hunter and Shogun, along with his men, are holed up in the Buchanan den, they are definitely gonna need backup." Sasha took a running lunge toward the shadow cast by the brick building, hit the wall, and fell flat on her back, sprawled.

"Oh, shit, Sis!" Crow Shadow yelled, jumping out of the vehicle.

Bear Shadow stood up in it. "Captain Trudeau! Sasha!"

He bounded toward her, helping Crow Shadow help her up. She had a busted lip and a large knot was beginning to form on her forehead.

"Son of a bitch!" she said, spitting blood. "They've blocked us from shadow jumping now?"

Winters was on the porch in a flash with the door wide open. "Trudeau, what the fuck, sir? You okay? You look like you just ran into a brick wall."

A window on the second floor opened and Woods leaned out, nude from what she could see. "Captain, you're back? You all right? I heard yelling."

"Get Fish," Crow Shadow hollered up. "This ain't a drill, shore leave is over, soldier."

"Roger that!" Woods said, slamming the window.

"I'm gonna go get Doc," Winters said, dashing across the street and not waiting for a directive.

Bradley opened the third-floor window with a robe on. "Captain Trudeau?"

Sasha squinted and waved him off. Her head hurt like hell. But before she'd ever even known that she was a Shadow Wolf, she had been a soldier—and that was the one thing the dark spell-casters hadn't counted on. With support from Bear and Crow on each side, she pushed herself to her feet.

"Okay, gentlemen, we do this the old-fashioned way, then. Hand grenades, C-4, whatever else the boys packed for the joyride."

"I just cannot understand what type of dark magick could be at the root of this conflagration?" Sir Rodney leaned against the fortress wall and stared at his top advisor as though gut punched. "Why can't we see it? Garth, as my best man, explain why can't an expert investigator like Thompson give us solid evidence at this late date?"

"Someone who has had access to your personage, milord, could have gathered bits of your hair . . . a bit of cloth, a fingernail . . . maybe your seed . . . other personal artifacts of your being, to stir into a wicked brew. This is clearly chaos magick of the darkest sort—but who did it remains the mystery. Mayhap that is what the young Phoenix girl was so afraid of? She could have gleaned some evidence as to whom we seek? But there is a blind-spot spell levied against you directly, sire . . . and the rest of this erosion is only evidence of the significant danger we are all in."

"Do you know what ye are saying, man? Do you know the vast import of a charge like that? If Desidera—"

"I don't think she wittingly gave you up," Garth said, cutting off the king's words. "But whatever was left of you in her apartment . . ."

Sir Rodney closed his eyes with a groan.

"Aye," Garth said quietly. "This is why I do not say these things lightly or ill-advisedly. But it's the only thing that makes bloody sense. I shall not presume to lecture milord . . . but as the head of state, and having amassed so much additional power over the years . . . Well, frankly, sire, there are simply some things that you cannot involve yourself in any longer—at least not outside the safety of the castle walls."

Sir Rodney nodded. "I'm going to try something." He waved his hand along a section of the huge stone wall as he pushed off of it and then stood back.

His guards jumped back and gasped. The section of the wall disappeared.

"Reverse spell polarity," Sir Rodney said with a nod, rubbing his chin. "They have booby-trapped our intentions . . . So if I wanted to be unseen, I'd be seen by human eyes. If our Pixie dust was to make the day go by faster and with an energy lift for our guards so they stayed alert, it had the opposite effect of making them lazy and sluggish or inattentive. Same thing with the glamour we don."

"That's not something a coven could do, is it, sire?" one of the guards asked. His attention was riveted on the king, his voice a terrified murmur.

Sir Rodney shook his head. "Not alone. It would take tremendous coordination to blind me, my advisors, and our investigator, then to also erode our powers as well as diminish the protection around the fortress."

"Blimey . . . But who would be so bold?" another guard asked, still marveling at the apparent hole in the wall.

Sir Rodney stared at his elderly advisor. "I should think someone who stood to profit from the spoils of war—bleedin' daylight has already left us. I want these walls shored up, our entire village re-charmed!" He looked deeply into Garth's ancient eyes. "And lift that bloody blinder spell."

Garth nodded, summoning the other advisors with a spark from the end of his wand. "It will be so."

"But, sire," a palace guard said, jogging alongside the king as he paced away. "We also have to get word back to the others. The wolves that ran ahead don't know what we've just discovered."

Sir Rodney waved his hand and kept walking. "If we don't have a fortress, we don't have an army—no place to protect innocent men, women, and children. This is my first priority. The wolves are battle worthy, so are the

Dragons—the Mythics will hide . . . and the infantrymen and archers are trained soldiers. If they've brought their families, they will fight to the death."

"But the Brownies and Gnomes . . . the defenseless Pixies and Fairies out there. Even our cherished friends and brethren, the Light Elves . . . others like Ethan McGregor and his family, milord." The guard stopped walking, his young face bereft.

Sir Rodney squared his shoulders, walked back to him, and grabbed the young soldier by his upper arms, looking deeply into his eyes. "I know, man, and you did well to get word to Ethan to warn them at The Fair Lady. Understand that what I say isn't without deep consideration. I am not heartless; I know the risk that they are under now that they can be easily seen and have booby-trapped magick."

Sir Rodney walked away troubled and clasped his hands behind his back, closing his eyes as he spoke, his voice becoming low and impassioned as he tried to make the men around him understand.

"*I care,* but as a leader, there are tough decisions to be made. Lose an entire village and a garrison, or risk a few civilians being lost, tragic as that may be? The choice is hard but the choice is clear. Right now I need every able-bodied soldier here to make sure we are secured during the night. We have miles of border to camouflage with reverse glamour. First light, I'll send out a retinue to let the others know how to at least temporarily reverse what's been done to them. After we are snug as a bug in a rug, we'll also be investigating—because we need to know *exactly* which set of dirty spells they've used to attack us and our allies. Godspeed to anyone outside these walls tonight."

The king of the Seelie turned around and studied his men with determination burning in his eyes. "Our enemies have been trying to find our North American fortress to siege and sack for years. I'll not let that 'appen on my watch!"

CHAPTER 15

"I won't leave my men!" Shogun said, panting. He spun out of an attacker's claw rake, ran up the side of a tree, flipped down behind the beast and shot him point-blank in the skull, using the Derringer.

"You have to live to fight another day," Hunter shouted, unloading a shotgun blast over Shogun's shoulder to blow back a wolf that had gone airborne.

"I led them into this death trap—I was their alpha leader and should have known better! They trusted me!" Shogun yelled, running back to what was sheer suicide.

Hunter made a wide berth around the dead bodies, changing directions to follow his brother.

"This isn't your battle—fall back!" Shogun yelled.

"One pack, one clan!" Hunter shouted, clearing Shogun's path with gunshot blasts, reloading on the run with a howl.

Shogun and Hunter pressed their backs to a new tree line, staying downwind from the building, studying for ways to get back inside it. Hunter's jeep was unapproachable—the parking lot was crawling with Buchanan clan pack members beginning to track their human scents. Angry barks and howls from the enemy cut into the humid night air. It wouldn't be long before Shogun's men were found and torn to shreds; it wouldn't be long before they'd be overrun. Human body stamina would not outlast the Werewolf forms, and in a hard run there was no way they could outdistance their hunters.

Hunter glanced at Shogun, whose eyes remained steadfastly on the building, trying to figure out the impossible. In war, there were always difficult decisions to be made—survival was sometimes one of them. But he knew where his brother was right now; he was a tortured man with a soul that required peace. Shogun had violated a leader's sense of responsibility for the safety of his pack; to leave now would not be the way of the wolf . . . and to let his brother die alone, savaged to death by the enemy without putting up a fight, was also an unacceptable option to him.

"Go home," Shogun snarled. "Go back to the Shadow packs. Go back to her."

Hunter growled. "Make me."

A huge Werewolf crashed out of the side of the building on the floor where Shogun's men had been. Chin-Hwa and Dak-Ho bailed out behind it, nude, and two more transformed wolves followed them in an aerial lunge. Hunter got off a blast that gave the wolf on the ground pause, splattering the two in the air in a single body shot that penetrated both airborne wolves in the gut. But the shotgun blast also gave away Hunter's and Shogun's position.

Shogun's men dropped to the ground in lithe crouches and then became one with the trees in a flat-out dash, furious Weres in hot pursuit. Somehow, an injured Seung Kwon had managed to exit the building by the door on the roof. Using every martial-arts skill at his disposal, he was a human body against that of a fully transformed Werewolf bouncer. Seung Kwon was losing ground fast.

Insanity propelled Shogun forward to go after his cousin; strategy sent Hunter up a tree in a one-handed pull, shotgun in the other. A blast hit the Werewolf on the roof; a blast toward the ground gave Shogun a few more minutes to live.

"Fall back!" Hunter shouted, bringing his brother to a skidding halt.

Shogun gave him a glance and turned back as Seung Kwon climbed off the roof using a drainpipe.

Out of breath, Winters burst into Finnegan's, rushed over to Doc and Silver Hawk, and began sputtering an explanation. They didn't even let him finish as both older men jumped up from the table and headed out the door.

Huffing to catch up with those that had wolf in their DNA, Winters pumped his arms and legs as hard as he could, and then, just as he got midway across the street, house and porch in sight, something grabbed him.

Cold claws came out of the night in a lethal grip. His scream was choked by what felt like steel around his neck. He could see Silver Hawk skid to a stop in slow motion. Bradley was on the porch in a robe, waving his arms; Clarissa was screaming something he now couldn't hear as consciousness ebbed. Doc turned slowly, withdrawing a Glock from the back of his pants, raised the weapon in his direction, and fired.

Suddenly he was on the ground, hitting the asphalt with a thud. A horrible screech and the scent of burning flesh and sulfuric ash stung his nose and made his eyes water. Vomiting from the terror and the offense to his nose, Winters pushed himself up on shaky arms and legs.

"Get onto the porch!" Bradley shouted. "Vampire attack—get onto the porch! The house is invulnerable!"

An old man grabbed him with the strength of a twenty-year-old marine. Winters looked up, still disoriented, as Silver Hawk lifted him over his shoulder like a baby, while Doc covered them, spinning 360 degrees, constantly moving. They hit the porch and Bradley brandished two one-gallon jugs of holy water while Clarissa flung brick dust across the threshold, reciting Psalms.

"I only got one," Doc said, wheezing. "The other one, the redhead, got away."

* * *

"Is that how you thought you'd endear yourself to me, by flagrantly violating a directive to leave the boy for my enjoyment?" Baron Geoff Montague's eyes flashed coal black with rage as he backhanded his lover. "This is not our fight! We are not involved in this squabble, but we are vested in the outcome!"

Black blood splattered from her mouth and painted the red tresses that fell against her cheek. She backed away with fear glittering in her eyes.

"Safina and I were going to bring him to you, Geoff. We thought we were following your orders. You said, 'If the boy leaves the house, he's mine.' Our objective was only to bring him to you." She held her face and lowered her head in submission. "I swear to you . . . do not dispense with me harshly. I loved her, too."

"Tragically foolish," the baron said through his teeth. "I would have mind-stunned him, used his body, and returned him just to let the wolves know that we can get close to their humans anytime we so desire. It would have been a mild warning, but not one that would incite war. Had you been successful, that would have been grand—but you weren't successful . . . and not only did you lose my beloved Safina with all of this, now our enemies think that Vampires are involved in the greater conflict!"

For a moment, neither Hunter nor Shogun could move. Horror filled their eyes as three New Orleans Police Department cruisers careened into the parking lot. It all happened so fast that it seemed like everything was moving in slow motion.

Seung Kwon fell into Shogun's arms, bleeding. Werewolves that had been in hot pursuit turned on the new human threat. Police vehicle lights painted the air a throbbing blood red. Human voices echoed from a bullhorn. Two brave but foolish officers got out of their vehicle with shotguns raised. Hunter lifted his gun to his shoulder, trying in vain to give them a chance to escape. He pulled the trigger and it only clicked. He was out of shells; the officers were on their own.

Werewolves rushed them, taking the non-silver gun-shots into their bodies without slowing down. Seeing the huge creatures of the night under a nearly full moon made the officers hesitate, their minds paralyzed by what they could never understand.

The first officer's face was swallowed whole inside massive jaws with a scream. All that was left seconds later was the back of his skull and part of his brain as his body dropped and then twitched on the ground. The second officer was caught between two frenzied beasts and summarily severed in half.

A driver in one of the backup vehicles tried to throw his cruiser in reverse, but a huge wolf crashed through the window, dragging the driver out onto the hood to leave no more than a bloody streak. His partner never made it out of the cab. The entire top, cherry lights and all, was peeled away like it was a tin can, and he was extracted by jaws of steel, screaming. Two thick-bodied Weres rushed the third vehicle, knocking it over onto its side and then raking open the gas tank. The wolves fled as a half-transformed bouncer lifted a shotgun, aimed, and pulled the trigger, setting off a massive explosion that cooked the officers alive in their own car.

Shogun's men caught up to their position, breathing hard, dirty, naked, and bruised. They all looked in the direction of the human carnage, understanding; six human law enforcement deaths would be impossible to cover up. Humans were now involved.

But they also understood that, as tragic as it was, the brief diversion had afforded them a chance to possibly live. It went without saying—they owed the men who'd given their lives . . . the innocents who had probably shown up to a 911 call about shotgun reports in the area.

"In due time we will avenge the humans as a matter of honor," Hunter said, pulling back into the denser foliage.

Shogun nodded, half carrying his injured cousin.

But then all men stopped. It was amazingly quiet. Too quiet. Each man looked around into the nothingness of the bayou. Instinct kicked in. They were surrounded. Seung Kwon slowly pushed himself away from Shogun to take a fighter's stance. In extremely slow moves, like a subtle ballet, each man moved into position, forming a ring, bracing for an attack.

A rocket-propelled grenade hit the building; Werewolves came out of hiding with angry roars. Half of them doubled back toward the Bayou House, the other half charged at the small circle of men.

The dead shotgun butt became one with Hunter's arm as he swung it like a baseball bat to stun one attacker. Halving it, he then rammed the broken barrel through the skull of the wolf behind him. Shogun's agility was unmatched by the thick-bodied wolves that rushed him. Tree branches, tree trunks, anything that gave him leverage, kept him out of claw range as he ducked, pivoted, and lobbed throat-ripping jabs. Seung Kwon, even injured, was formidable when paired with his brethren. They worked in fluid coordination like deadly synchronized swimmers, using jagged branches to gouge out eyes and spear throats in bloody hand-to-hand combat.

An M-16 gun report ripped through the air. To Hunter, it was background white noise—he was in kill mode, adrenaline making him high. His wolf was caught inside his human, but his human had become a beast. Strength coursed through his hands; necks snapped at their will. His feet dug into the soft earth, holding his ground as he twisted a jaw into an unnatural position, then spun to land a haymaker that crushed a skull. His voice contained the sound of wolf rage; suddenly the predators had become the prey.

The building was on fire. There were still twenty-to-one odds. Hunter and Shogun exited the tree line to join the battle raging in the parking lot.

Sasha's howl made them both snap. Shogun left the

ground, leaping onto the back of a retreating Werewolf, his jaws powerful enough, even in human form, to rip off an ear. When the Werewolf went up on its hind legs with a howl and spun to disembowel him, Shogun quickly dismounted and Woods caught it in the gullet with a single hollow-point silver bullet. Fisher lobbed a grenade into a cluster of attackers, splattering the side of the burning building with ripe gore.

Bear Shadow and Crow Shadow were a killing blur at Sasha's side while Sasha ran headlong, squeezing off machine-gun rounds. Hunter's gaze locked with Sasha's for a moment. It was enough to send pure insanity through his soul.

In a headlong lunge, he went one-on-one with a massive Werewolf male. A head butt left the wolf stunned for a second with his belly exposed. That was long enough for Hunter to come away with entrails in both hands.

Sirens in the background, smoke billowing from the building inferno, the Buchanan clan in retreat as the sound of grenades and gunfire echoed in the air, and Hunter threw back his head and howled. Dead cops, a burning building, and dead Buchanan clansmen and clanswomen beginning to transform back into mangled human bodies would be inexplicable in any court of human law.

Fisher squeezed off shots, felling the last of the retreating Buchanan fighters in single shots as everyone piled back into the three available jeeps. No one had to say it; they all knew what had to be done. Before local authorities could arrive on the scene, they had to take the vehicles as far into the bayou as possible and then strip them of any VINs and tags, as well as doing a full fingerprint wipe-down, then pray for a mudhole to screw up any DNA evidence.

The sirens were getting farther and farther away, but as Hunter's fight adrenaline ebbed, his wolf did not. Shogun glanced at Hunter. The men shared a look as Sasha stared at them both.

Safe haven, Hunter murmured inside his own mind as they pushed a jeep into the black water of the swamp. *Great Spirit open up a shadow that will swallow me whole.*

Sasha's cell phone ringing made everyone stare at her. Then her face burned as both Shogun's and Hunter's eyes followed the sound to her ass. She quickly extracted the device from her back jeans' pocket, listening to Clarissa's distraught message as well as trying to judge the location of the distant sirens.

"They were attacked by Vampires," Sasha said, sending her gaze around the group of assembled warriors. "Two females went after Winters."

Angry glares met hers as Woods stepped forward.

"Is the kid all right?" Woods smoothed a palm over his scalp. "Jesus . . . tell me he's alive."

"Yeah, he made it," Sasha said quickly, landing a hand on Woods's shoulder and watching him visibly relax.

"But we don't have to put him down or anything, do we?" Fisher asked in a nervous tone. "He's . . . just a kid, man."

"He didn't get nicked . . ." Sasha looked off into the distance and then addressed the question to Clarissa. "Right, 'Rissa—Winters didn't get nicked." It was said as a statement, a hope, a prayer, not delivered as a question. The confirmation that her fears had been misplaced made her shoulders relax by two inches.

Sasha turned back to the group. "He wasn't bitten, just shaken up. The house is secure. Bradley and 'Rissa surrounded it with holy water and brick dust, and Doc and Silver Hawk held down the fort with artillery."

"Then they've gotta get out of there," Hunter said flatly. He nodded toward the sound of the sirens. "By tomorrow morning, if not tonight, this is going to be on the news—if we're lucky—as a big drug raid that ended in the loss of the lives of six NOPD officers. Any other gunfire heard in a residential or commercial area is going to be followed up with significant force. If that happens, the only way out of it will be for Sasha to go to her general and start the process of a Paranormal Containment Unit cover-up . . . which always opens Pandora's box."

Fisher let out a hard breath and rubbed the back of his sweaty neck. "The man speaks the truth. The only reason they probably haven't gotten to the B&B yet is because NOPD's forces are still seriously thin and a full show of force is being diverted to this catastrophe out here. But it won't be long."

"Hold on, 'Rissa," Sasha said. She placed the cell phone against her chest as she listened to the post-battle report and tried to think of where she could get her team to safety on the fly.

"They had drugs in the house, for sure," Seung Kwon said. "You name it, they had it, plus a white-lightning still. Best moonshine in the area, Werewolf headbanger."

Chin-Hwa nodded. "When they find the nude bodies, they'll say it was a raid . . . The officers walked in on some sort of untoward entertainment, then were attacked—there are shotgun shells littering the ground that show a firefight . . . Any animal attacks can be blamed on guard dogs that fled into the bayou . . . so humans will claim that the human officers gave their lives in the line of duty."

"They did," Dak-Ho said quietly. "And they should not have . . . This was not a human fight."

Shogun nodded and looked away, his expression pained. "No, this was not a human fight. They should not have died so that we could live."

"Humans do that all the time—I am so fucking tired of hearing about the way of the wolf! So the next time you guys start talking shit about what humans are or are not, remember that," Woods said, spitting on the ground, and motioning back toward the carnage behind them. "I've about had it with the *familiar* bullshit. You saw pure grade-A 100 percent US-military-issue soldier from me, Fish, and Sasha back there. That," he added, motioning over his shoulder with his thumb, "is what we do. It's what me and my platoon used to do . . . God rest Rod Butler's soul."

Sasha nodded. "God rest Rod Butler's soul." Then she moved toward her man, who was clearly reeling from the gunfight and the residual effects of dark magick. "But stand down, soldier," she said quietly, laying a hand on his shoulder. "The moon is high and so are emotions, and you're standing in the middle of a pack of post-battle-hyped wolves." Her eyes met Woods's. "I'm telling you because I love you like a brother," she said in an even quieter voice as the two alpha males behind them slowly began to snarl.

Woods let out a hard breath and relaxed. "It's just a crying shame what happened to those officers back there . . . One was no older than Winters. That's what fucks me up."

Hunter nodded and relaxed. "Humans are honorable. It hurts when you lose any member of your pack, or an innocent." His gaze went around the group. "No more low remarks cast against humans in our families—no aspersions made against those with more human blood than wolf in their veins. Agreed?"

"Agreed," Crow Shadow said, gaining nods all around.

"Agreed," Shogun said, staring at Hunter and then offering Woods a slight bow.

Sasha picked up the cell phone. "'Rissa . . . I don't know how, but you guys have to get out of there. Gunshots were fired, and . . . What?"

Silence surrounded Sasha, save the hum of bullfrogs and crickets. Background sirens dulled as her mind exploded. "Hold on a sec." She pressed the cell phone to her chest again and stared at Woods. "Two civilian girls are in the B&B in tears—no, *make that hysterics*—because they saw creatures they cannot explain, are *waaaay* freaked out, and saw Doc unload a silver, hallowed-earth-packed hollow-tip to explode one . . . Oh, did I mention that Bradley and Doc had to duct-tape them to a chair for their own safety so they wouldn't run out screaming into the streets to get bitten? Wanna talk to me, soldier?"

"Oh, shit . . ." Woods ran his palms over his hair while Fisher began to walk in a tight circle.

"Jesus frickin' Christ," Fisher said, leaning his head back and closing his eyes. "I forgot about the girls!"

"Yo, Cap, we just jumped up, went into battle mode, you know . . . hit the steps locked and loaded . . . hit the jeep, ready to roll . . . Holy shit!" Woods paced back and forth.

"Clarissa," Sasha said calmly. "Ask Doc if he has some Valium on hand." She waited a beat. "You're sure?" Sasha shook her head and looked at Woods and Fisher as the rest of the men swallowed smirks. "Doc doesn't happen to have any meds on him."

"What about in the ambulance, Sasha?" Hunter offered in an amused tone.

For a second she just looked at him and then let out a long breath. She turned her attention to the cell phone again. "Much as I hate to do this to a person . . . maybe if they can get to the ambulance, find something in there to knock them out without hurting them . . . Drive the ambulance to the hospital and bring them in as maybe having gotten something spiked in their drink at the bar . . . When they wake up in the morning, it can all be played off as a bad dream. I don't know if we can get to you soon enough to provide you with a security escort, though . . . That's the only thing. We're pinned down in the swamp."

Sasha let her breath out hard again. "I know drugging them is bogus and manipulative and screwed up—but it's either that or have those poor women mentally jacked up for life. Also, if you guys go to the hospital, which, with all the local heat on things now, puts you out of suspicion's eye . . . It also puts you guys somewhere the Vamps aren't likely to go after you again tonight; at least you'll be somewhere kinda safe.

"I know, I know, we'll be there as soon as we can," Sasha said in a weary tone as Clarissa's voice became shrill. "Call in our markers at Tulane with Doctors Williams,

Lutz, and Sanders from before. At least they're cool and know the supernatural drill. And when those girls wake up—tell Doc to be there with Silver Hawk as the older men who found them and helped them get to the hospital *unmolested*," she added, giving Woods and Fisher the evil eye, "with you, Bradley, and Winters. Maybe they'll wake up like Dorothy in *The Wizard of Oz*."

Woods let out a hard sigh as Sasha ended the call. "Sounds like a plan, Cap . . . Only one question, though—how do we get out of the bayou?"

CHAPTER 16

Woods was right. There was still enough of the Buchanan Broussard clan that had retreated into the swamps to make an ambush a deadly possibility. If Vampires were on the offensive, then out here away from the eyes of human authority, they were sitting ducks. Her hope was that the Vamp killed back at the B&B had backed them off long enough for them to think twice about going after her human team, especially if NOPD was on the way.

The one thing she was sure of was that, after their exposure and involvement with the death of a human general, the Vamps would want to stay concealed from human military types right about now. Vampires were many things, but openly foolish wasn't one of them.

And despite how badly the situation rankled her nerves, now was certainly not the time to get into it with Fisher and Woods about why they'd brought civilian females back to what was essentially base. Half of her was truly pissed off, the other half glad her men had been at the B&B and not AWOL at some chick's apartment somewhere. They had been there when needed, they had responded immediately to the call to arms, so she really couldn't dress them down about that. Nobody was on top of their game.

Shogun couldn't even meet her gaze now. As the rush of battle ebbed, understanding gained a foothold in her brain, along with a very irrational spike of jealousy that made her cry out *safe haven* in her soul.

Hunter lifted his head, breaking the silence. "Bloodhounds."

"This is the South, six cops are dead; I'd expect no less," Sasha said.

The order to move out was given with a nod. They all took a wolf's pace in a hard jog, heading deeper into the bayou. Every now and then Sasha circled back to be sure her men with the least wolf in them could keep pace—she refused to leave Fisher and Woods . . . She'd go to prison with them, if it came to that, but leave them? Never. They seemed to know that as they pushed themselves to the edge of their mostly human endurance.

"You go ahead," Shogun said, dropping back. "I can throw off the dogs—I'll split the scent trail."

Hunter stopped and turned. "We stay together."

"We stay together," Sasha said, giving Woods and Fisher a chance to stop and gasp in deep breaths. "Shogun, I know how the human military and Homeland Security systems work over here. You're a foreign national. You'll be pinned as a drug dealer who triggered the violence by bringing in opiates from Asia with your men . . . and will disappear into a CIA interrogation black site."

"Under the circumstances, would that be so bad an option?" he said quietly, staring into her eyes.

She looked away. "Unacceptable."

"But honorable."

Hunter threw a punch that felled a tree and began circling. "Don't go there, brother."

Confusion tore through the ranks for a moment, but a hail of silver-tipped arrows made everyone jump back. Weapons raised with hair-trigger reflexes.

"Hold your fire!" a heavily accented voice called out from above.

All eyes quickly scanned the tree limbs above.

"Friend, not foe!"

"It's Fae archers," Sasha called out. "Hold your fire!"

Silver Hawk moved with the speed of a wolf as Doc ran behind him, covering him with a nine-millimeter. But once the inside of the ambulance had been cleared of a potential Vampire ambush, Doc ravaged the medicine supply for anesthesia while Silver Hawk covered him with the weapon.

Everybody worked quickly, racing against the clock, racing against sirens. Clarissa was in another room in the B&B on the telephone with Tulane's physicians explaining the predicament, while Winters and Bradley spoke to the terrified women in calm tones. Their whimpers were heartrending as the men covered their eyes with strips of sheets, blindfolding them while trying to reassure them that they wouldn't be raped, wouldn't be killed.

But their struggles against their bindings and screams that had to be muffled told everyone in the house that they didn't believe a word that had been said. They were close to passing out on their own without the meds, believing they were going to die.

"We heard the explosion, first off," a tall Fae archer said, jumping down from the trees with a half-dozen armed men. "We thought the Buchanan still had finally given up the ghost—they pushed 'er like crazy pumping out rotgut, so that didn't surprise us. Nor did a couple of shotgun blasts. No offense, but the wolves often get rowdy and they have to bounce males who get too familiar with the ladies without paying the goin' price."

"But when we heard machine-gun fire," another said, "Sir Rodney sent an advance guard to be sure there wasn't an attack headed toward the fortress. I don't know if your men made you aware after they left off the McGregors, but our entire camp was laid bare."

"Exposed to the brick," the lead archer said. "Took all evening to reverse the bleedin' magick, and it's still waverin' in and out, not wholly stable. Sir Rodney said we could tell you that much, even though Fae business is usually a strictly confidential affair."

Hunter cocked his head to the side and turned on Bear Shadow and Crow Shadow so quickly that Crow bumped into a tree. "You left an Elf family in the swamp with their fortress exposed and did not communicate that information to me or Sasha!"

Silence crackled between the trees, Sasha's voice a low, calm murmur. "Safe haven . . . These men, like you and I, are under the influence."

Hunter rolled his shoulders and walked away from his men to keep from savaging them.

"You lads and the lady kicked up quite a fuss in the glen," the Fae captain said nervously, trying to divert the potential wolf fight. "Mayhap we might take all concerned back to Sir Rodney who can discuss the particulars we know about the dark magick."

It had taken a bit of maneuvering, but Doc spoke medicalese and Dr. Williams well understood the issues. The two civilian women were admitted and placed under heavy observation in ICU, just as a precaution—should they wake up screaming.

Silver Hawk held the small table rapt within the cafeteria as he explained what he saw on his spirit walk with Hunter.

"Can you draw the symbols you saw for me?" Bradley asked, his gaze intense as he pushed a napkin and a pen toward the elderly shaman.

Silver Hawk nodded and accepted the paper to begin re-creating what he'd seen.

"The use of sigils—symbols—is the cornerstone of chaos magick," Bradley said, closely studying the symbols as Silver Hawk committed them to paper.

"I would see a marking," Silver Hawk said, "and then the person—one of us . . . And a shadow self of the person would walk out of their body."

"Doppelgangers?" Bradley said, leaning forward quickly and speaking in a rushed, horrified whisper. "They've attached a dark sigil to the etheric or energy double of the person's spirit, and thus can send all kinds of malintent into that essence to twist the behavior or even rob the person of their natural gifts and talents. It is an insidious spell, but a complex, brilliant, diabolical process."

"It is theft," Silver Hawk said, his eyes burning with wolf outrage, even though his voice remained calm. "To rob a Shadow Wolf of his ability to enter the shadows is no less than severing a limb."

"To rob a person of his or her ability to reason," Doc said, looking around the table, "is no less than that."

"These symbols," Bradley said, studying the series of napkins that Silver Hawk pushed toward him, "are combinations. They're set up like bind Runes, with several spells linked together to harm one person." He let out an exasperated breath and then picked up the one associated with Hunter. "This takes away natural gifts—which is the same for Sasha . . . Look at the symbols Silver Hawk drew on her napkin."

Using his finger he traced the geometric shape. "Their natural gifts would be the ability to call their wolf selves or to merge into the shadows. But look at the one that is similar for Shogun and Hunter . . . in fact, for all of the younger male wolves. Not only have they been blocked from properly calling their wolves, which was why Shogun's shapeshift was botched earlier today as the spell took root, but there's something even worse layered on top of that."

Bradley sat back, his expression tight with repressed fury. "This is such bullshit . . . They are betting that the males will tear each other to shreds. Look at this!" he said, slapping his hand on the table and causing a mild stir in the otherwise quiet hospital cafeteria.

"Fill us in, dude. I might as well be looking at hieroglyphics or Greek," Winters said in a quiet rush. He glanced around and waited until the few late night visitors having coffee went back to their own conversations. "And keep your voice down, man."

"Bradley, whatever it is, we'll get to the bottom of it," Clarissa said, rubbing his back.

"But they're out there with weapons, all together," he said, his voice fracturing with rage and worry. He took a deep breath and composed himself. "This symbol is sexual in nature," he said, his eyes holding an apology in them as he stared at Doc and then Silver Hawk. "It increases libido in all the younger wolves; plus, follow this line," he added, tracing the symbol with his finger. "This one spikes jealousy and rage right over the top of it. I can go to any one of the grimoires and pull these sigils and I bet I'll get an exact match on what they mean; I'm 99 percent sure."

"This explains so much," Doc said, rubbing his hands down his face with a weary sigh.

Silver Hawk nodded and closed his eyes. "I have sent prayers to the Great Spirit to guide our children in the way of unity."

"I'm also praying for peace," Bradley said quietly. He returned his attention to the napkins. "Go to Sasha's . . . Her libido is being tampered with, too. But rather than jealousy or rage layered next to it, hers is entwined with indecision. Do I need to say more? Both Federation alphas are out there with machine guns and grenades!"

Clarissa whipped out her cell phone and began clicking photos and texting. "Screw the bad guys—we have technology."

Sir Rodney met them at the castle gates just as Sasha's cell phone started buzzing. Two valets rushed out, offering Shogun's men clothes. Oddly, Sir Rodney greeted her with more than his normal Gaelic smile . . . He opened his arms and pulled her into an embrace.

"We were so worried," he said, breathing into her hair.

Sasha pulled back, hoping that both alphas would take it as emotional relief and nothing more. "Thank you," she said. "Were it not for your men, we'd have been left stranded in hostile territory."

"We're in your debt," Hunter said, eyeing Sir Rodney.

"As are we," Shogun said with a little extra bass in his voice.

"My human squad is at Tulane . . . I have to take this call," she said and used the cell phone call to break the tension. But within seconds her shriek drew everyone in close. "Oh, shit! Look at this!"

Waving the cell phone, she showed Sir Rodney the pics that were transmitted, along with the text message—and then showed it to Hunter and Shogun. She dug in her pocket as though bees were in it and stinging her. She held out the crumpled pieces of paper for Sir Rodney to inspect.

"Sigils of darkness," Sir Rodney said and spat. "But these are different than the ones we saw on Desidera and Penelope like Ethan had described, only maybe worse. Where did you find them?"

"They were under Desi's body," Sasha said. "I couldn't capture the symbols exactly . . . They were in some foreign hieroglyphics that I couldn't remember enough of to reproduce. But these were geometric shapes that vanished when the ashes were pushed aside."

"Beneath the bodies?" Sir Rodney whispered, clearly revolted.

Rupert nodded. "Chaos magick is afoot, milord."

"Our clan elder, a shaman, went on a spirit walk and discovered how they went after each person's spirit with doppelgangers . . . That's how they got the spell fused with each person's etheric body," Sasha said, spinning around and talking to the others in the group. "Each person's weakness, they've exploited; each person's natural gift or defense mechanism, they've tainted. That's why we can't go into the shadows or call our wolf."

"This is important information, milord," Rupert said, wringing his hands. "But we need to know how they've black-charmed an entire fortress and castle . . . or even Ethan McGregor's bar."

"They've blocked ye from the shadows, lassie?" Sir Rodney said, clearly appalled, and only focused on what Sasha had said.

"We were in a firefight back there, ambushed by the Buchanan clan, and could not use the shadows or call our wolf." Hunter received nods of assent from his men, but Sir Rodney frowned.

"What, for the love of God, would send you into that low-life brothel—tell me it was for the moonshine, man!" Sir Rodney walked back and forth for a moment. "I don't understand. It was a clear ambush, or am I daft?"

Every man found a point on the castle wall to stare at, but no one spoke.

"I was following a scent," Hunter said carefully. "The same feral trace that I picked up at the scene of the first crime, then at the young woman's trailer."

"That's no doubt why Shogun went there, too," Sasha said, trying to help Shogun save face.

"Vampires and some type of Were scent?" Sir Rodney said, his gaze narrowing. "How so? Can you be sure?"

"Vampires attacked Winters, the youngest, most vulnerable member of my human team, when he was running across the street to get help. Bradley had the old Dugan B&B fortified against Vampire attacks, since that's where my team was making base camp. But they showed their hand by going after the kid . . . just like they'd gone after him before. Doc incinerated one of them, but the other got away."

"Good for your da . . . I'll have to remember he's a man of action and a solid shot." Sir Rodney smiled a smile that wasn't wholly appropriate for the occasion. "Why don't we go inside, eat, have some ale, and then figure out an anti-charm, shall we?"

* * *

"We only promised you access to them in a vulnerable state," Kiagehul sneered, showing his pointed demon-like teeth and standing quickly. "You come into my hidden bayou coven battered, snarling, and reeking of canine sweat and then assail me with charges of reneging on a deal? I am offended! You knew what you were supposed to get out of this bargain. The trade was fair—I was to remove the wolves as a threat; you were to receive, in exchange, the revenge you seek against them. End of discussion."

"The Bayou House is no more!" one Werewolf yelled, pounding his fist against his palm. "Our still, obliterated; our working girls, dead."

"Butch is dead," another argued, growling. "We demand recompense."

A low growl filled the throat of Buchanan's injured nephew. "This was not the outcome we paid for in the spell . . . Something went wrong and you need to pay for it!"

Several Unseelie Gnome bouncers circled the small group of Werewolves, causing a mild stir amongst the cauldrons. Kiagehul moved in closer to the disgruntled Werewolves only after the show of force was in place.

"Nothing went wrong with my spell," he said, his eyes narrowing as his glamour faded. "Dark mist can show them the chain of events; we will use the war board and go back in time.

"Escort these disgruntled clients to my private chambers. Let us review the facts before we damage our delicate treaty or someone loses their head."

Kiagehul nodded to his bouncers as he spun on his heels in an elegant turn and strode forward, his head held high with an aristocratic sniff of disdain while pulling on his midnight-blue sorcerer's robe. Although haughty, he kept a cautious eye on the distance the Werewolves were from the security guards.

Opening his private chamber with a flourish, Kiagehul

waved his hand at the available Louis XVI settees, Queen Anne chairs, and the lushly embroidered sofa, but the Werewolves declined. Suits of armor guarded the windows and an array of weaponry hung on the walls. The Werewolves glanced around, snarled, and remained standing. Kiagehul nodded as the bouncers parted and closed the door.

"Suit yourselves," Kiagehul said, going over to a walk-in black granite fireplace. "Let us trace the past . . . We always place a trace on the black magick spells and dark deals we do or subcontract out, just for instances of buyer's remorse like this."

He waved his hand and an eerie black and blue fire roared up from nothing in an instant, the living flames licking the edges of the mantel until the black wax candles on it melted, popped, and sizzled.

Kiagehul smiled. "Give me a moment to tune to the right channel." He waved his hand with a bored sigh. "The Bayou House, earlier this evening. Start when one of the wolves under our influence entered."

The Werewolf retinue moved forward, their eyes fixed on the blaze.

"How do we know this isn't more of your dark magick to trick us?" the leader said.

"You don't," Kiagehul said through his teeth. "But this is the only record of the events any of us has . . . You can go back to your broken pack and corroborate it with any eyewitnesses that are left."

He snapped his fingers and the inside of the Bayou House appeared. All wolves fell silent.

"Seems the alpha leader of the Southeast Asian Werewolf Clan entered disoriented and in quite a state," Kiagehul said with a smile. "His men are completely distracted, true?"

"True." Buchanan's nephew rubbed his neck and paced down the line of Werewolves that were in attendance. "Is that what you saw when he got there?"

"Yeah, boss. Definitely," one wolf henchman confirmed.

"And they each got picked off one by one, separated," Kiagehul said, watching events play out. "The alpha is *gone* . . . totally consumed by need. The girl is pretty, for a Were," he said, not caring that the snipe drew growls. "And, from the looks of things, quite talented."

Kiagehul chuckled when two of the wolves swallowed hard while watching the carnal act unfold across the flames. "But in the interest of time, because it does appear the man has prowess, let us fast-forward to where things began to go wrong."

"Yeah, let's do that!" the Buchanan clan leader said in a low rumble, gaining sharp barks from his men.

A snap of Kiagehul's fingers and the images shifted. "You let the second alpha in . . . making the assumption that he came in with a weapon drawn to kill the first alpha?"

"Yes, but your magick backfired!"

Kiagehul held up his hand and then slowly strolled in front of the flames with his hands now gracefully clasped behind his back. "To assume makes an ass out of you and me." He let out a breath and snapped his fingers. "Before you call foul and blame my subcontractor for wrongdoing, let's be clear about the facts. You let Hunter go upstairs. He went to the door. The prostitute was supposed to kill Shogun in his sleep, if the Shadow Wolf didn't find him first. Her weapon of choice was to be a Lady Derringer, point-blank range, aimed at his skull when he did what all men do when they finish—went to sleep. Her out would have been that he got insanely aggressive, threatened her life, and it was a matter of self-defense . . . A rogue Were alpha male that had already had infection issues well-documented by the UCE."

"Right—but he didn't go to sleep before Hunter came," another Werewolf argued. "Our man went up in the false wall and waited. Once Hunter blew Shogun away, we were gonna do Hunter . . . Then we'd be able to say that we did what we had to do, we stopped a murderer. No blood on our hands at the United Council of Entities, if it went to an investigation."

Kiagehul nervously cleared his throat and glanced at his security guards. "Yes," he added, coolly recovering. "But your man rushed the process—didn't allow the two big dogs to be in the same space long enough to fight."

"Look at your own recounting, man!" Buchanan's nephew shouted, pointing at the flames. "Hunter was warning his brother of a setup! He was trying to get him out of there, told him to bring his men out, pronto! Our man heard that bullshit while hidden in the wall—we have better hearing as wolves, just like we can smell a deal gone bad!"

"And you rushed your hand, blowing away your own prostitute in a botched hit that snapped his men out of their euphoria and sent them to war against you instead of each other! That was not my doing!" Kiagehul paced away from the fireplace and flung open the door. "This meeting is adjourned."

The four battle-ragged Werewolves transformed and went airborne. Bulky Gnomes carrying silver-bladed battle-axes rushed them. Kiagehul ended the dispute by extracting his wand and blowing out the heart of the leader in a black lightning bolt from the tip of his ancient instrument. The three other Werewolves backed off. In an instant Kiagehul spun, directing his wand toward the standing coats of armor to send silver-tipped lances into the Werewolves in a rapid-power fling.

Blood and gore coated his floor and his hands. His henchmen snarled through glistening Gnome smiles. Kiagehul wiped his sweaty hands down his robe and flung it off, to once again stand in his pristine, moss-green shirt.

"Your spell failed in part . . . They were right," a disembodied voice murmured in a lethal tone from the shadows. "Hunter did not go to war with his brother over the female . . . And this is why I said wait. I cautioned patience, because, as your subcontractor, I know wolf behavior . . . But I also wanted to see if what I had paid dearly for in this collaboration would be delivered flawlessly."

"We will redouble our efforts . . . I don't understand why Hunter had restraint. What could have interfered with his loss of reason?" Kiagehul said, backing up until his spine hit the frame of the mantel.

"I don't care what the cause was for the failure . . . I am due a young body along with immortality as payment for my contribution, just as the Buchanan Broussard clan was due their revenge. I am concerned that my needs may not be met, even after I have so dutifully assisted you."

"Everything that you desire will be taken care of. If you'd like, you may have Sasha Trudeau's."

"You make grand bargains and grand plans . . . but so far, I have only seen botched attempts." A long sigh hissed out, circling Kiagehul and making him follow the sound. "It was my mark that felled the two Phoenixes . . . my agility that entered the garden with a dark spell. Tell me, what have you done that has borne fruit?"

For a moment there was silence and then an icy sound that echoed as though someone had spat. "The Buchanan clan could have been a valuable ally in this region. It was therefore a waste of blood, and I told you how we students of *The Art of War* detest the waste of blood. Make sure, the next time we are forced to spill such a precious resource, it won't be your own."

CHAPTER 17

As they moved through the outer gates and into Sir Rodney's Fae encampment, Sasha was struck by the eerie silence. Before, the evening air had been filled with merriment, the quaint village streets lined with squabbling vendors hawking their wares. Not tonight. It was as though someone had rolled up the sidewalks. Not a soul, save Gnome patrols and Fae archers, was out. Even the air seemed different. There was no iridescent shimmer to it. The trees were a dull, normal green, not the vibrant neon colors that one would expect to see in a Crayola crayon box.

Neat little houses had the shades and shutters tightly drawn. Their footfalls echoed as they crossed the town square and continued up a steep hill toward the castle. Huge Griffin Dragons circled the towers, their ominous shapes casting dark shadows under the pale moonlight. Fatigue and pure disheartenment made Sasha's shoulders slump. This wasn't what anyone wanted—to live in fear.

Sasha glanced at Sir Rodney, identifying with the sadness in his forlorn expression. Complete dejection was etched across his handsome face and his normally merry eyes were clouded by weariness. Albeit his back was straight and his head held high, he squared his shoulders like a man carrying the weight of the world on them. The Midsummer's Night Fae Ball was most likely ruined. Lives were at stake, lives had been lost . . . and all for what? Greed? Power?

Unicorn-riding guards parted as their small, discouraged entourage of weary soldiers approached. Even the second drawbridge seemed to be tired as its pulleys creaked and groaned, dropping the massive wood plank with a thud.

No one spoke. Sir Rodney simply used hand signals to wave alert guards out of the way. The quiet, though weighed with tension, was a blessing. It gave her a chance to think. Then again, thinking only set her nerves on edge . . . There would sure be hell to pay in the human community. There were bad guys to catch, twisted Weres to bring to justice . . . and some Vampire lairs to open to daylight—starting with the baron's, on principle.

"Milord," a gaunt servant said, bowing deeply upon Sir Rodney's entrance into the castle courtyard. "We are pleased that you have arrived safely and recovered all of your guests."

Sir Rodney nodded. "Rupert . . . These good people have been to hell and back. Some may even require medical attention." He turned to Shogun's men and then looked at Shogun.

"We are fine," Seung Kwon said quickly, showing off his healing gashes. "If we eat, we'll be restored by morning."

Woods nodded. "Same here. That and some good, old-fashioned shut-eye."

"Rest, perhaps even before food," Bear Shadow said. His voice was a low rumble and his breaths dragged in and out of his chest as though he could sleep where he stood.

"Then allow these men to relax and recover," Sir Rodney said, as more staff rushed over to accommodate his guests. "Food will be delivered to your rooms, baths drawn, fresh clothing provided . . . anything you require. That you have to be sheltered here against external adversaries is a complete travesty."

The ire in Sir Rodney's voice clipped his tone as he

began walking forward again. "I need to speak with the three clan leaders, and will accommodate them equally once we're done . . . but we must develop a strategy for the morrow."

No one protested about being shut out of the leadership meeting. Hell, if she could have gone straight to her room and fallen across goose down with a steak on the way and a little bit of Faery dust sprinkled over her to take away the battle aches that she was starting to feel, yeah, she would have preferred that option. Apparently both clan male alphas felt the same way. She noted that Hunter and Shogun seemed relieved that their men were being cared for and didn't begrudge them a break in the action. She just wished that she could have gotten the rest of the team behind the walls of Forte Shannon of Inverness under Sir Rodney's hospitality. Tomorrow that would be job one.

The group split up at the huge marble staircase that spilled down into the grand foyer. Betas were headed up to private rooms with attentive staff while she, Hunter, and Shogun followed Sir Rodney past live coats of armor, expressionless palace guards, and strange three-dimensional portraits and tapestries that looked as though you could fall right into them.

Two exquisitely chiseled guards opened the doors to a large anteroom when Sir Rodney stopped before it. He didn't turn around, didn't explain, just kept walking and assumed they'd follow him.

Two-story cathedral windows covered in stained glass greeted them. The meadow scenes they contained were so serene and bucolic that it nearly drew her to touch them. Sir Rodney's footfalls echoed across the wide stone floor and Sasha peered up at the vaulted ceiling that seemed to go on forever.

Flags hung from the rafters and wall torches spit and smoldered as they passed. In the center of the room was a huge, round wooden table with strange markings on it, and standing in a row with tablets poised were bald-headed little Gnomes in monastic brown and forest-green velvet robes. Some had wiry tufts of hair in spots. Others had what she could only liken to age spots on their heads. There were five in all.

Each one wrinkled his little hooked nose when studying them and the tips of their long, pointed ears turned ever so slightly as though tuning in to something invisible the way one would expect that a giant TV antenna might. But they all had wide, inquisitive eyes that were so clear it seemed as though one could just see forever in their depths.

"Please, have a seat," Sir Rodney said, as they approached the table. "The last time you were here, you never sat . . . never neared the round table . . . This meeting should be different."

Not accustomed to chivalry at this level, she was slightly surprised when Sir Rodney didn't move, but her chair came away from the table on its own. It wasn't until she was seated that the other chairs deemed it was appropriate for them to slide away.

"This was left over from the days of old," Sir Rodney said with a smile, looking at Sasha. "I wouldn't have been surprised if Merlin charmed it this way himself."

His smile was infectious and she couldn't help the one he brought out on her face. The fact that Hunter and Shogun were slightly bristled but also contrite quietly amused her.

"You weren't properly introduced before. These gentlemen are my top advisors," Sir Rodney announced proudly. "Please show them the sigils you discovered at the death sites, as well as what was sent to you on the human contraption, otherwise known as a cell phone."

Sasha dug in her pocket as the dire-looking advisors gathered around, inserting themselves between each seated person so they could get a better view.

After a moment, what appeared to be the eldest advisor spoke, pointing at each set of symbols. "These are different than the ones found on the young ladies' bodies, milord.

These be progressive spells, milord. Look at the three moons on each and how they ascend to the top of the sigil . . . how they gradually become fuller. Thus the magick darkens each night, becomes stronger and harder to cure. If it is not broken before the last night, there will be no cure."

"This is why we need those who be not Fae," another, gaunter advisor said, glancing around the table and pointing a bony finger at Sasha, Hunter, and Shogun. "The cure is one we cannot carry—and whoever did this was banking on our Fae secrecy . . . that we would not, in pride, reach out for help beyond our own in matters strictly Fae. The ones who did this were very shrewd, indeed."

"Cold steel must cross the magick ring that holds each sigil," the lead advisor said. "St. John's wort with witchwood—the rowan, and enclosed with bundled bay leaf. That would break the spells set upon this castle and the places Ethan McGregor's people be."

"I don't understand," Sasha said, looking around. "How can we carry something to a place when we don't even know where it is?"

The eldest advisor rubbed his chin and smiled a snaggletoothed grin. "Ah! To put a spell on a place as large as this fort, one must have the power of three." He walked around the table and produced a small wand from inside his sleeve and doodled glittering gold spirals in the air as he spoke. "For a time-sensitive, progressive spell, one that relies on the sigils knowing when the light has cast and passed into moonbeams, it must be able to be exposed to the passage of time." He spun around and clapped his hands. "It will be in the uppermost floors, hidden in the eaves, not in the basement where daylight never passes. The first death happened in the cellar as a ruse or mayhap to stop a young woman from telling the king all that she knew—something that would incriminate the spell-caster. But the source . . . aye, lassie, is in the eaves!"

"The power of three locations," a third, thick-bodied advisor said, furrowing his already deeply wrinkled brow.

"Dugan's Bed & Breakfast . . . Finnegan's Wake . . . and Ethan's Fair Lady. The name of Forte Shannon of Inverness inscribed on the dark magick within the homes of members of the royal house is part of the root cause of this castle's failed glamour."

"Once the property changed hands, it became Ethan's . . . Thus all who slept there as his family," the lead advisor said, pointing his wand at Sasha, "helped the spell along."

"All who ate there," another said, "helped the spell along."

"And they put a progressive agency into it," the leader said. "That is what has hurt the Seelie Fae."

"Aye," the thin advisor muttered. "There are too many of us to do individual sigils for, but they went after the house of Sir Rodney."

"But what about what my grandfather and I saw," Hunter said, folding his arms over his chest. "We saw opaque spirit selves get up from the bodies of each of us, wearing symbols on each. It went after the wolf leadership and Sasha's familiars, even her father, as well as my lieutenants."

"Doppelganger attachments!" the leader said, looking around the room. "Insidious magick, the worst of its kind!" He walked away from the table and thrust his wand up his sleeve.

The four other advisors shook their heads as though Hunter had just said he had inoperable cancer.

"Whatever it is, these are the symbols that Hunter's grandfather saw," Sasha said as calmly as possibly, letting them see the stored cell phone pics again.

"Well, man, tell us, is it possible to get this attack off our allies?" Sir Rodney said, standing and beginning to pace. "There must be something to do for this?"

"First things first," the lead advisor said slowly. "They are wolves. They can track. If they go back to the three establishments and go to the top floors—the attic, the eaves, somewhere remote that isn't used—where no one who wasn't looking for something would go . . . they will be able to cancel the spell against the castle . . . which will remove the deleterious effects on all Seelie Fae that hail from Forte Shannon. They can lay the cold iron with the necessary herbs that we cannot touch. From there, we will have our glamour back and can send out search-and-destroy parties to aid them. Without proof positive, we cannot raid Unseelie Sidhe mounds or go after Goblins, digger Gnomes, Dwarfs, or Gremlins . . . Any of these could have been agents in delivering bits of hair, personal effects, the things necessary to make a bond to each victim's etheric body."

"To attack Sylphs," another said and then clarified when Sasha frowned. "Air elementals, milady—we must be strong. Air elementals work in the etheric realms. When we attempt to remove the sigils from the etheric body doubles or the property they've been attached to, they will fight with all their might."

"Our job is to first break the spell on the fortress, and then all Seelie Fae will be whole and can in turn help us," Shogun said, glancing around. "That we can do—but what is witchwood . . . or rowan?"

"Our Wood Sprites can show you in the morning. But they cannot touch it. The plant is highly toxic to us," Sir Rodney said. "Once you collect it, you must go out of the encampment. It is a toxin for us—you have to take it to the three locations, and then return to us with it washed off of your hands and free of your clothing."

"How long do we have?" Hunter said, leaning forward on the table on his elbows.

"You have already lost three moons. You only have one more. Then the final moon in the sigils is the night of the Midsummer Night's Ball . . . The stroke of midnight is also when the magick becomes strongest and next to impossible to break." The lead advisor looked around and his gaze settled on Sasha. "You have a question. It is in your eyes."

"Yeah . . ." she said, losing patience. "Let me get this

straight. We hit the streets tomorrow, try to keep this on the down low from human authorities that will be crawling all over these joints that we have to go back into without the aid of shadow-jumping stealth . . . and we have to do this by tomorrow *before* sunset so the Seelie can come out and ransack wherever to find *our* sigils—the thing that's making *us* weak and vulnerable. Did I get that right?"

Five small heads nodded in unison.

"Okay," Sasha said, ruffling her hair up off her neck in frustration. "But all the while, we're getting crazier and crazier—and now we're finally thinking this is magick that could possibly only be delivered by the Unseelie."

No one said a word. It was suddenly so quiet in the large meeting room that Sasha stood to keep from screaming.

"And these sigils of ours could be anywhere in the world," she said flatly.

Again five heads nodded in unison.

"And we're pretty sure that Vampires are involved, like we just found out tonight that the Buchanans were lying in wait for us, so these sigils could be on any of the above-mentioned estates—which are heavily fortified." Sasha walked around the perimeter of the table slowly as though hunting something in the center of it. "There has to be another way to break the Unseelie spell against specific individuals. I get it that you can unbind a group that was bound as a group more simply . . . but someone went after us on a very personal level."

"They did, indeed, lassie," the lead advisor said quietly. "There is a way . . . but . . ."

"Why us?" Sasha looked around the room. "If it's the Unseelie, why us—the Wolf Federations? We're not involved!"

"I'm afraid you are," the lead advisor said calmly. "If you are our strongest allies, the ones who united our fractured Parliaments, then, sadly . . ."

"The friend of my enemy is my enemy," Shogun said flatly.

"Yes," Advisor Garth said with a weary sigh.

"That is some Vampire bullshit, if ever I've heard it," Sasha said.

"With a weakened Louisiana Werewolf clan seeking vengeance and willing to aid in the confrontation," Hunter said, closing his eyes and massaging his temples. "How do we fix this, reverse the dark spell?"

"We haven't gone into direct conflict with Queen Blatand of Hecate since the Penicuik Wars that split apart the Midlothian Council," the second advisor said in a distraught murmur.

"If her attack came from the core of her power base, then we would have to capture and behead her top advisors to still this Unseelie magick, and even if we knew they were guilty as sin—it's much easier to locate the actual sigils and undo the black spell than to capture and unglamour members of that powerful group to behead them. By rights, there should be a trial . . . and evidence presented, she will argue . . . and then if they are found guilty, the treason charge could be levied and their magick bled away from them. But that is their game. There isn't time for a trial."

"And it sounds like there also isn't time for us to find the locations of all these sigils that are tainting our etheric selves," Hunter said in a low, growling tone.

"Under the circumstances," Shogun said, rubbing the nape of his neck, "it seems a lot easier to go to war than to try to find a needle in a haystack."

Sir Rodney stretched tension out of his back as he walked around the room. "What did the property investigation show? Who might have been angry that their inheritance went to McGregor?"

"A name came up from our property search as you requested . . . Kiagehul would have stood to gain much, milord," the senior advisor said quietly.

"Kiagehul? Cousin of Enoksen and Elder Futhark?" Sir Rodney stopped pacing, closed his eyes, and shook his head. "Enoksen and Elder Futhark are her top advisors . . .

Even if we go after his magick by just finding that little weasel, it will incline her to war once she listens to them."

"Has anyone seen this man—do we know how to spot him?"

"No, milord," the eldest advisor said. "His identity is shrouded . . . but we have our investigators working on this as we speak."

"Then war it is," Sasha said. "We cannot have two major Wolf Federations go down, along with innocent humans on my squad and the Seelie nations in the Americas, because some little bastard got greedy and thought he could get away with murder because the Vampires and some rogue wolves had his back. The queen will have to get over it."

Sir Rodney just stared at Sasha for a moment.

"The queen doesn't get over anything, milady," the lead advisor warned.

"How well do you know the queen and her capabilities?" Hunter asked, turning his attention to Sir Rodney.

"Do you know this enemy well?" Shogun asked, growing impatient. "We could capture this Kiagehul and interrogate him in a way that would make him understand the need to cooperate."

"A manhunt could take who knows how long . . . Plus he could be holed up in Vampire turf or in hiding. If Unseelie magick is behind all this, we send a message to the queen to tell her to call her man back. If she isn't an accomplice to it, and doesn't want to start a war, she will. If she's too arrogant or is somehow involved, then we do this thing." Sasha walked back and forth, feeling trapped. "But Sir Rodney is right, guys. We have to lift the spell off the Seelie Fae and this fortress so we have a strong offensive, plus a solid fallback position. We've gotta get the rest of our team behind these walls tomorrow."

"Then let's get back to the question that Shogun and I asked, because it is important to know the enemy before deploying a tactic that could backfire." Hunter leaned on the table, looking across it at Sir Rodney. "Do you know this queen well enough to negotiate with her?"

Everyone that had been seated around the table was now on their feet.

"Yes, I know her bleedin' well enough—*and* am all too familiar with the full extent of her wrath, which is how I wound up in the Americas and not in the Bonnie Isles," Sir Rodney said, rubbing his palms down his face. "She's me ex-wife. A show of force is the only thing she bloody well understands."

CHAPTER 18

"Rupert, please show the lady to her room," Sir Rodney said as casually as possible, eyeing both male wolves. When Hunter cocked his head to the side, Sir Rodney kept his tone even and calm. "We have all been under an inordinate amount of strain. The morrow brings a major campaign. We cannot afford to have anything rip our alliance to shreds. A good night's sleep would serve us all well."

"Safe haven," Sasha said quietly after a moment. She stared at Hunter until his hardened gaze lost some of its resistance. "Good night." She nodded at both Hunter and Shogun, in the proper order, and then bid Sir Rodney good night. Her eyes said thank you as she turned to follow Rupert down the long corridor that led to an entirely separate wing of the castle. The Seelie Fae were such diplomats; it was a shame that their peaceful way of life was probably going to devolve into an all-out war.

For now, though, her being in her own suite alone was the only way, the only thing that made sense. Who knew when irrational possessiveness would return, and none of them could afford that level of drama right now. At the moment, she was so exhausted, if she didn't lie down, she would fall down—and if any male, wolf or not, tried to put his hands on her, she'd definitely have to kill him where he stood. More to the point, she needed every ounce of brainpower to noodle the problem of what to do about the individual spells that could make them all self-destruct.

Rupert stopped in front of a massive door, bowed, and then stepped before her to open it in a grand, sweeping gesture. "If it please milady?" he asked in an ebullient tone, his eyes expectant.

"Wow . . ." Sasha murmured. She didn't move, just gaped for a moment as she took it all in.

Everything was white on white on white and twinkling with Faerie dust sparkles. Tall white candles sputtered with iridescent flames, and a perfect wash of blue-white moonlight spilled across the bed and floor. A series of thick white alpaca rugs dotted the polished stone floor. It seemed as though, for all that was lost in the rest of the castle and village in terms of bewitching, nothing was spared on making her room spectacular.

There was no getting used to Fae surprises, no matter how much she tried. As silly as it was, for a moment she felt like a princess, and almost looked down to see if her mud-crusted boots had somehow turned into glass slippers. Now, as she stared at what lay before her, she felt too dirty to even walk into the pristine space Rupert offered. The wolf life pretty much followed natural law, but the Fae had a way of turning even the most basic of life's accoutrements into a wonderland.

An ornate, four-poster bed was positioned against the far wall, draped in gossamer sheers. White satin pillows littered a thick duvet. Behind an opaque screen that was partially open, she could see the edge of a white porcelain claw-footed tub. Her gaze quickly took in the antique white vanity loaded with every conceivable potion and lotion a woman could dream of, down to a sterling comb-and-brush set.

Sprays of white roses in delicately etched crystal vases were everywhere—on the vanity, on the bedside tables, on the dining area table, and two bookended the fireplace mantel.

Lush white-on-white satin overstuffed chairs and a

love seat were scattered about. An antique white armoire stood against the wall flanking the bed. Closer to what seemed like the outer, less personal space of the grand suite was a table set for two, complete with a silver-domed tray and slim, elegant silver chalices.

"I literally don't know what to say." Sasha turned to Rupert, who seemed pleased by her admission. Yet, with the obvious strain on castle resources, a twinge of guilt and worry niggled her.

"Shall I draw the lady a bath?"

How could she say no? Sasha hesitated and then looked down at her clothes for a second.

"The closet is full, milady." Rupert waved his arm, not entering her room and keeping a dignified distance from her. "Everything here has been attuned to your total comfort. Just ask and it is so. Your soiled clothes and boots can be left in the white hamper by the armoire and within an hour you can retrieve them folded and laundered, your boots polished, as though new."

Sasha looked over her shoulder quickly as she heard the sound of bathwater filling the tub. She could only imagine how her guys were taking all of this. Woods and Fisher probably had tears of joy in their eyes. She just hoped the alphas weren't affronted by this extraordinary display of Fae male prowess. Wolves did the strong sexy thing; the Fae did the smooth sexy magick thing—but regardless of species, a male display was a male display, peacock-plume spread or rhino head butt, it was what it was.

"There are fresh towels in the bath laid out for your use, milady." Rupert stood aside further to encourage her to enter the room. "In the closet is a variety of choices, from ball gowns to more casual options. And when you desire a meal, just state your choice out loud, then lift the lid off the silver platter, and your meal shall be served. If the selection should not please you, simply cover it up and it will be immediately removed. You may observe the same process when you have finished dining."

"This is really, really, *really*... over the top, and deeply appreciated... but the expense of all these resources on me..."

"Is what Sir Rodney *expressly* demanded," Rupert said with a worried smile.

Sasha monitored the slight strain in his voice and the troubled look in his eyes. "Then please tell him thank you. Let him know that I was simply blown away."

"You heard Doc," Clarissa said, rubbing Bradley's shoulders, standing behind him as he hunched over a computer keyboard. "Sasha told you no less. That's your fifth cup of coffee and you have to get a couple hours' rest."

He didn't look up from his task of typing and furiously scribbling notes as he responded to her. "There has to be a way to call the doppelgangers to us... And if we create a charm that is made of iron, rowan..."

"You're scaring me," Clarissa murmured, hugging him from behind. "Sasha said to stay put. Silver Hawk can't even get back into the shadow lands now, anyway. Come on, let's get out of Dr. Williams's office and go get some shut-eye in the residents' lounge with everybody else."

He nodded, quickly acknowledging her hug with a fast peck on her cheek. "The shadow lands aren't blocked to all Shadow Wolves, just to the ones who've been targeted—the leadership. I've been studying the sigils," he said, finally looking up at her. "Their wolves might have been blocked in a blanket spell against the leaders and their top lieutenants, the very clansmen that would be accompanying them to the Fae ball. But to shut down all the shadow lands would be too much of a drain on their dark resources, and they'd have to have had a power-of-three location spell that was time-sensitive to the light."

Bradley pushed away from the desk and stood, talking as he walked about, thinking out loud. "'Rissa.... What if Bear and Crow put on the alpha amulets that would allow them to enter the shadow lands with cold iron and rowan and whatever else I can come up with to break the stranglehold this curse has on our etheric doubles?"

"But what if they get lost in there . . . They aren't alphas that can go in alone."

"What if they had a seer?" he asked quietly, staring at her with an unblinking gaze.

"I can't go through the shadow lands; no human physiology can."

"I would never put you in harm's way," he murmured, seeming hurt that she thought he would. "But an astral projection of your mind to their minds, your unfettered consciousness, could guide them as well as help them lure the misguided etheric bodies to them. All they would have to do would be to pierce the sigils that were fused to them, and the doppelgangers would be freed of the impediment. Then you bring them out of there as quickly as possible." Bradley ran his fingers through his hair. "On the outside, you'd have me, Silver Hawk, and Doc to anchor you in the power of three on this side."

"I could do that," Clarissa said, gaining confidence as the concept sank in. "In fact, I could fuse my consciousness with Silver Hawk's before I went in as a guide with Bear and Crow. His wisdom in there would be invaluable."

He smiled and let out a deep breath. "Yes! I love it when it begins to come together—finding the solution. At least part of it. I'll start working on how they bewitched the Fae fortress after a few hours of shut-eye . . . Yeah, you're right, I am tired, but the coffee is kicking my behind. Tomorrow we have to get to the occult shops to get iron bullets, handcuffs, iron rods, and to see of they have a stock of rowan and herbs." When she didn't comment, smile, or blink, his enthusiasm ebbed. "What?"

"Your mind," she said softly, going to him, "is so beautiful that I am at a loss for words."

Sasha watched her clothes and boots drop into the hamper and disappear. Standing naked and dirty in the middle of the floor, there was nothing to do but take a bath. Common sense told her that the light-headed feeling of peacefulness was nothing more than faux Fae euphoria. But knowing that all was well and her guys were safe, she didn't fight it. A hot tub filled with rose petals and sweetly scented bubbles was calling her name.

She crossed the room and slipped behind the privacy screen, testing the water temperature with her hands. Perfect. What else had she expected? Sasha giggled and then splashed her face with a little of the water, then released a light moan. Even the water was bewitched. The scent of roses and something she couldn't define, but was heavenly, filled her nose. Her skin drank in the ultra-soft wetness . . . the water didn't feel like water. It was as though any harsh minerals and iron had been removed from it . . .

Then she laughed out loud. "Of course! No iron in the limestone, blimey! This is a Fae house, what were ye thinkin', lassie?"

Sasha pirouetted, laughing, and grabbed a huge, fluffy white towel and sank her face into it. The moment she did, it felt like each strand of terry was massaging her skin as though they were teeny, tiny starfish cilia. The floral scent was so divine it made her heady. Weaving slightly, she abandoned the towel on a white cushioned bench and stepped into the water. Tendrils of pleasure rushed up her legs, drawing her entire body down into the endless bath.

It felt so good that she couldn't even grip the sides of the tub to keep from drowning. She just began to slide and kept on sliding until she was fully submerged, hair and all. Then the supernatural buoyancy of the water pushed her to the surface again so she could breathe.

"Oh, my, God . . ." Sasha came up and this time held on, albeit with her eyes closed. "You guys sure know how to treat a lady, yes, siree." Her muscles were so relaxed that she could barely extend her arm to reach for the soap, and when she did a creamy confection filled her palms and made them tingle. "Dude . . . stop," she said, laughing, but applying the buttery-smooth lather to her body.

A quiet moan escaped her as she lathered her hair, and every ache from hitting a brick wall and fighting rogue Werewolves vanished under her fingertips. Every cut and bruise on her healed and sealed. Her spine felt like every disc in it had been replaced by jelly. She could barely sit up long enough to rinse. But the bed was calling her name and hunger was clawing at her.

She dunked under the water again, marveling at how the bath was a tub on the outside, but the moment she submerged it looked like a vast, fresh-water Caribbean sea. She stretched out her arms and legs, swam a few feet, and then came back to the light portal that was the obvious surface where she could get out.

"How freaking cool is that!" she shouted, tickled by the discovery and looking down to the bottomless tub. Then, testing it, she stood, amazed that there was an invisible floor that held her weight. "Way cool. How did you guys do that?" She stomped around in the tub for a few moments. "I can walk on water! Crazy!"

Totally revived, she held on to the side of the tub and propelled herself out of it in a swift vault. Her wolf was raging, wanting to run under the moonlight, but she thought better of it, half-Fae euphoria high or not.

When she wrapped herself in the thick, newly warmed towel, she moaned. The bench might as well have been spa-hot rocks that heated it to a luxurious temperature, massaging and sloughing her skin with tiny fingers as she snuggled down into it.

Had a robe not appeared on a hook she'd never noticed, she would have taken the towel with her to bed. It never got wet, just renewed itself with dry warmth. She looked at the fluffy white robe and let out a sated breath. "If you're charmed, just stick a fork in me because I'll be done."

It took several minutes to release the towel. But unexpected warm air blanketed her instead of the normal knifing cold air that would be in her bathroom. Yeah . . . The Fae were the best when they rolled out the red carpet. No wonder the Vampires hated them so much. Plus their guys could come out during the day and were just as handsome.

"Haters," Sasha said, giggling and holding a conversation between the self inside her head and the self outside her head. "Man . . . this is some really strong euphoria . . . whew!" She pulled on the robe, closed the sash and then gasped, sitting down on the bench hard with a thud.

Loving sensuality poured over her skin, caressing her as though it were applying body oil. Peacefulness and desire became one. But when she felt her nipples tighten and her body begin to get moist, she stood and quickly headed to the armoire.

Basic common sense told her to find something else to sleep in. If she fell asleep in the charmed robe, she was going to start a wolf war with her howl.

Sasha flung open the armoire doors, practically frantic, and began hunting. But sheer, lace gowns, obscenely indecent lingerie, and white silk sheaths glistened back at her, clearly charmed. The other options weren't much better. There was an elaborate ball gown that stole her focus for a moment, and she pulled it out to hold it up against her as she stared into the full-length mirror attached to the door.

It was a glimmering blend of moss greens and woodland earth tones splashed across a sheer overlay with a forest-green silk sheath. The arms were bare, cut in a scoop to reveal her shoulders, but the front came up at the neck and was collared by exquisite genuine emerald beadwork. She turned sideways and pulled out the train and noticed that it was backless. But sheer panels fanned out on the floor—the gown was so beautiful that she gently returned it to the white padded hanger with reverence. A pair of silver-heeled, amber- and emerald-crusted shoes sat twinkling on the crystal rack beside a small emerald-encrusted purse. A white, velvet case revealed teardrop emerald and amber earrings.

"Oh, Sir Rodney . . . you shouldn't have." The note inside read, *Happy birthday, love.* She quickly closed the case and put it back, deeply conflicted, as she gently shut the armoire door.

Food. She needed to eat, clear her head, and stay focused. It didn't matter that she'd brought a really inexpensive little black dress from Target to go with a pair of basic black pumps to wear for her birthday. She had never been a fashionista and black seemed to work with everything—but damn. If she wore that to the ball, she'd be vastly underdressed. But if she wore what Sir Rodney had left for her . . .

Sasha slapped her cheeks. She had to stop thinking about irrelevant things! "Steak, rare, with string beans—not too mushy, cooked but still crunchy . . . And, uh, new potatoes and a really, really cold beer would be nice," she called out, testing Rupert's instructions.

Within seconds the smell of broiled meat filled the room.

"Gotta love the Fae," she murmured, pacing to the table.

A chair moved itself out for her to take a seat. Sasha just shook her head and plopped down. What the platter revealed made her close her eyes and say a little prayer. Gratitude filled every fiber of her being as she took up her fork and knife to find that there was no need for a steak knife. It was free-range bison, marinated to perfection and so tender that all she had to do was gently press the side of her fork into it and the meat cut. "Damn . . ."

It was impossible not to wolf down her meal, and the cold beer that she'd asked for made her stop with the first sip and close her eyes, holding the chalice in midair. "Oh, man . . ."

Bread baked to Dwarf perfection with honey butter made her lose her manners as she sopped up the juice on her plate and moaned with every bite. Until she had started eating, she hadn't realized how starved she'd been. The vegetables were grilled to perfection, the potatoes so sweet and tender they melted like the bread on her tongue. Every bite of her steak made her close her eyes and moan out loud. By the time she covered the platter with the silver dome and polished off her second chalice of ale, she could barely keep her eyes open.

But it was amazing what a bath and full belly could do to a she-wolf's mind. Relaxation brought clarity. Sasha sat up slowly. They didn't have to do a frontal assault on a powerful Unseelie queen that would put the Fae at war. Queen Blatand of Hecate, for all her possibly unsavory qualities, most likely was unaware of the goings-on of the lower members of her court. Woman to woman and leader to leader, Sasha had to admit that she'd be equally pissed off if someone attacked her base just because Bear Shadow or Woods did something stupid.

Sasha stared at the moonlight. If something like that happened, the first instinct would be a defensive strike—then, and only then, would there be conversations about who'd shot John . . . And then the bottom line would be where was the respect? Why didn't your nation come to our nation and lodge the complaint? There was no warning shot fired over the bow and you've attacked us? Nah . . . the Wolf Clans wouldn't go for that, either, so why would a powerful Unseelie queen?

There had to be a way of forcing her hand, diplomatically, into outing the members of her own court that were involved in wrongdoing. And those guys were most likely here, not overseas wherever she resided.

An angry smile tugged at Sasha's cheek. If they were with Vampires, an attack had already been launched against her people at Dugan's old B&B . . . which meant that they had technically gone after Winters on Fae land. The Seelie Fae owned Dugan's old spot, as well as the bar that Winters was running from. Winters was a clearly unarmed human that was resident in a Fae hostel, thus a guest, and therefore, by UCE law, the Vampires had launched an unprovoked attack on both the Fae and a member of the Shadow Wolf Clan's protected membership. Beautiful. Baron Montague was gonna spit out his eyeteeth over this!

"Yeah . . ." Sasha said, thinking out loud. They could burn Vampire lairs in daylight looking, supposedly, for the female—the redhead—by law. And, knowing the Vampires, they would out the Unseelie spell-caster that had cost them so much prime real estate. Once they had the little son of a bitch in custody, they'd turn the screws on him . . . Wouldn't take much; Shadow Wolves could always smell a lie. An emergency UCE trial could be called by the second night, and the Unseelie queen would be barred from retaliation. "Damn, Sir Rodney . . . I wish you didn't have to wait for the morning to get this," she murmured.

A light knock on her door startled her and yanked her focus away from the window. Flustered, she got up and went to the door, tucking her wet hair up into a loose twist. For a few seconds she just stared.

"May I come in?" Sir Rodney asked, his expression so serious that her body stood aside without consulting her brain.

He was freshly bathed, smelled divine, and wore only a long forest-green silk robe.

"Umm . . . I think I misspoke," Sasha said, quickly closing the door behind him.

"You said you didn't want to wait until morning," he murmured, coming closer to her until her back hit the door. "Sasha . . . I . . ." His words fell away as his fingers trembled against her cheek.

"You've bewitched the room," she said quietly. "No fair."

He shook his head. "It is I who has been bespelled since the beginning."

"Oh, Lord." She closed her eyes and dropped her head into her hands.

"No need for formal titles between lovers," he said in a thickly sensual murmur.

"No, no," she said quickly, pointing up. "I was talking about that one."

He chuckled and stepped back an inch with a good-natured smile. "Even the Fae don't tangle with the Ultimate . . . So what caused you to send up a prayer? Am I that much of a disappointment?"

"No," she said quickly, placing her palm on his chest. "It's not that . . . I did want you to come here, but because I want us to figure out a way to avoid an all-out Fae war . . . Your people cannot endure that; the humans cannot endure that. There must be a way."

He stared at her, the humor fading from his incredible jewel-blue eyes, desire replacing it. He took up her hand, deeply kissing the center of her palm, and allowed it to fall away from his. When she hugged herself he touched her cheek, studying the facets of her face as though she were a priceless gem.

"Sasha, you are not only beautiful, radiantly so . . . but your heart is that of pure gold. Not fool's gold, but pure gold; do you understand the difference, love? If you don't, let me assure you that we Fae are well aware . . . and you are what lies at the end of a rainbow."

She swallowed hard as his eyes left hers to slowly survey her body so intensely that it sent shivers down her spine. She couldn't answer, much less move. The sexual energy that radiated off him was complete devastation.

"There is honor and integrity, the likes of which would knock the wind from any man standing. I have been felled by you, Sasha . . . And yet, it is this same integrity that frustrates the bloody hell out of me as we speak. You consider yourself mated, a married woman."

The last part of Sir Rodney's statement came out more like a wistful question. Her brain struggled to find the right gear to make her mouth work, stalling out like a bad transmission, slipping, not catching.

"Uh, yeah," she finally sputtered out. "That's a problem."

"Are you sure?" Sir Rodney said in a low, baritone murmur, stepping closer. "It doesn't have to be."

His hands found her wet hair, as his mouth sought hers. Warm male body fused with her stomach and thighs and breasts in a hot, blanketing wash. As he intensified the kiss, a channel of heat filled her mouth, traveled down her esophagus, to implode in her stomach and course heat throughout her belly until it overtook her womb.

"We have to—"

Another ardent kiss stopped her protest, but as he went for the sash of her robe, she grabbed the ends of it and pulled hard.

"Wait a minute, wait a minute," she said, gasping.

"My apologies," he gasped, heaving in large gulps of air.

"I'm not offended," she said, staring up into his pained eyes. "Just . . ."

"Conflicted."

She nodded, and suddenly he became blurry as she nodded even harder. What the hell was wrong with her!

"Oh, lassie . . . I'm sorry. I didn't mean to make you cry . . . didn't mean to offend to such a degree."

She waved her hand and bit her lip, totally freaked out that something like this could make a war veteran shed tears. It was ludicrous.

"It's not you . . . Just look at all you've done." She nodded toward the table, pointing out the bath, and then caught a sob as she pointed to the closet with a shaky hand. "I've never in all my life been given . . ." Sasha snatched back her hand and then folded her arms. She had to get her mind to jump back into her skull. It had definitely fled the room somewhere between the bath, the dinner, and the kiss.

"That was given from the heart, no strings attached. Take it all or leave it all, I just wanted you to know you are cared for."

She bit her bottom lip harder, but the tears flowed

regardless. "My men . . . you took them in; all my people . . . Hunter, Shogun, are ready to go to war—shit."

"I would lose an entire garrison for you, Sasha," he said quietly.

"No! I don't want you to do that—and stop being so damned wonderfully chivalrous." She slipped around him, jamming her hands into her robe pockets to keep from hugging him. "That, I admit, is my weak spot—you found it, and you're dancing a Fae jig on it—now cut it out." She wiped her face with her robe sleeves and stared at him, glad to see a lopsided smile overtake his handsome face. That was easier to endure than that intense, sexy, Gaelic stare of his.

"I see we're both smitten by the same set of principles, then."

"I refuse to answer that charge," she said with a half smile and a sniff.

"But I would go to war for you and empty out a fortress for you, and you know what I'm saying is the truth."

Again they stared at each other for a moment. Her she-Shadow senses confirmed that this man, not unlike Hunter or Shogun, was also no liar.

"I want minimal casualties; in fact, none for your people, or mine."

"Do you not think that is part of why I love you so?" He swallowed hard, clearly still aroused, but transfixed where he stood.

She would not look down at his silk robe so she kept her gaze fastened to his face. "I had a plan that jumped into my head that I think might work . . . after we lift the spell on your fortress in the morning."

"So ye would ignore my statement, then, as a form of avoidance?" He smiled a sad smile. "And I thought the wolves had superior hearing."

"I heard you," she said quietly. "And it made my stomach do flip-flops." She bit her lip again, frightened by her own honesty. It was as though everything she'd meant to keep inside her mind was leaping out of her mouth like frogs!

She looked at the door and then at Sir Rodney.

"The wolves are resting," Sir Rodney murmured.

"There are two factions under your roof . . . and your guards; anything that were to happen that's not on the up-and-up could break down alliances, trusts, friendships . . . and that is part of the dark magick plan."

"Spoken like a true woman of diplomacy," he said with a wistful sigh.

"And . . . and . . . the gown and jewelry are beautiful, Sir Rodney, but—"

"Now, that would offend me if you returned it," he said with an easy smile. "And just Rodney . . . please . . . The sir title is much too formal between us, don't you think?"

"But it's—"

"A gift," he said gently, his gaze matching his tone. "And where I come from, in Fae culture, a gift from our people to someone not of our kind is the height of respect."

She more than respected this man, she liked him, and maybe a little more. Maybe something that she wasn't ready to investigate. He gave her body a once-over with longing, and tightened the sash on his silk robe with a sigh. Her eyes betrayed her and looked where she knew she shouldn't have . . . and the sight of his bouncing arousal only ignited hers, but she didn't move or flinch. Soldier mode took over as she lifted her chin and watched him walk to the door. But, God . . . He had a fantastic ass.

"Good night," she said, wishing it had come out curtly. But it didn't. It came out as a gentle caress of words that made him turn and stop to linger by the door.

"Thank you for everything," she said more quietly when he didn't move.

"Thank you for leaving a man hope," he said without a smile. "The one who finally wins your heart will indeed be a lucky man." He hesitated again, his eyes filled with yearning but also with dignified acceptance. "Sweet dreams, love," he murmured and then blew her a kiss that she felt on her cheek. "I will respect a lady's wishes and will not attempt to start a war amongst suitors tonight. You may rest easy knowing I am a man of my word." Then, just like that, acceptance seemed to win out, and he turned away, opened the door, and left her all alone.

He'd walked out with his head held high and with the carriage of a true king. The moment the door clicked shut behind him her shoulders dropped from relief.

Pacing across the room, she snatched off the bewitched robe, letting it fall wherever, threw back the duvet, and climbed into the bed in the buff. Just a few hours of shut-eye was all she asked for. But as her body sank into the softness and her head hit the pillows, Sasha let out a weary groan. Silk sheets slid against her as rose petals rained down on her from the sheers. The damned thing was no doubt bewitched for all-night lovemaking, and the longer her head rested on the pillows, the more erotic thoughts accosted her brain.

Sasha closed her eyes with a plea in her voice. "C'mon, Rodney, give me a break."

CHAPTER 19

At dawn, Rupert knocked gently on her door and announced that breakfast would be served for all in the round table hall. She dragged herself out of bed, answering the valet with a croak, but anything was better than tossing and turning in the sheets for another hour.

As promised, the hamper produced her clothes—and given the sexy leather outfits deemed casual clothes in the closet, she gladly chose the old standbys. But the second she reached for her cell phone and checked it, she groaned. Fae cleaning magick had wiped out the freaking memory—all her phone numbers, all her pics, everything!

She made quick work of washing up and going through a boot-camp-fast morning routine. Armed guards awaited her as she exited, providing a welcomed security escort to the round table hall.

Hunter was already seated with Shogun, one man slumped over a steaming cup of coffee, the other over hot green tea. They both looked up at the same time, eyes weary and five o'clock shadow covering their jawlines. It seemed as though nobody had gotten anything but fitful sleep, from where she was standing. Sir Rodney didn't look much better as he slowly stood for her, his actions encouraging the others to get to their feet. But the rest of the men looked refreshed and well rested. Oh, yeah, this male-lust spell was definitely getting worse by the night.

"Good morning," Sasha said, feeling surly.

Rupert lifted a glass pitcher of freshly squeezed orange juice. "For the lady?" he said, seeming so nervous that the pitcher shook in his grip.

"Please," she said, taking a seat. She lifted the silver dome that was covering her plate, and steak and eggs and hash browns were on it. She lowered her nose and took in a deep inhale, closing her eyes. "Mmmmm . . . Thank you."

Food. Good food; fantastic food. She was beginning to feel better already—that is, until she opened her eyes and noticed that two alpha male wolves were staring down her throat. She set down the silver tray cover very carefully; there was so much tension in the air that she could practically see it arc as she lifted her knife and fork. The moment she took a bite of steak, Hunter licked his bottom lip. Shogun slowly closed his eyes and Sir Rodney picked up his mug of coffee with trembling hands. The other guys held their forks in midair, bodies tense, bracing for sudden battle.

"I have a theory," she said quickly, slurping her juice. Her quick, jerky motions overlaid by nervous chatter seemed to temporarily snap the three male contenders out of their dazes.

"Coffee, milady?" Rupert said, rushing to her side, appearing to understand her strategy to keep distractions going.

"Yes, plenty, with—"

"Cream and sugar?" he sputtered, and then spun toward a far door. "Kitchen! Cream and sugar for the lady." Rupert was so undone that he splashed coffee on the white linen cloth that covered his sleeve.

"Have you gone daft, man?" Sir Rodney asked in a low, warning tone, setting down his coffee slowly. "Is this how you present yourself before—"

"It's fine, it's fine," Sasha said quickly. "He was just

rushing to get it for me fast because I'm so not good in the morning without joe—bad habit since who knows when . . . But I haven't had my coffee yet. Thank you, Rupert; sorry about your spill. So, it looks like we're in for another bright and sunny day." She was babbling and couldn't seem to stop herself. The only option was to take a hurried sip of her coffee without any of the additions Rupert had called for, but that made her burn her tongue. "Oh, boy, that's hot—but that's a good thing."

"You seem undone," Hunter said slowly, his voice a sensual rumble. "Baby, how did you sleep?"

Oh, shit, he was going for the verbal possessive! She had to get these guys fed and out hunting so they could kill something or blow something up, fast.

"Good, good, was really very comfortable. I take it everybody slept well—we have a lot on the agenda today."

Elves ran forward with cream and sugar, deposited the items beside her, and then dashed off, taking cover.

"No, we *all* didn't," Shogun said in an intense murmur, taking a long sip from his tea as his gaze connected with hers for a moment and held it. "But we do have much to accomplish today."

Sasha took several mouthfuls of eggs and promptly began coughing. Three males stood quickly to rush over, but she held a napkin to her face with one hand while waving them off with the other.

"I'm okay—just was so hungry that I was wolfing down my food too fast."

"Live game? Name it," Hunter said with a low growl. "If this isn't doing the job, I'll bring it back still twitching."

"She has to survive to eat it," Shogun said, throwing back his chair and coming dangerously close to Sasha so that he could pat her on the back.

"I'm okay, I'm okay," she said, coughing harder.

"Put your hand on her and you'll lose the arm," Hunter said, squaring off with Shogun.

Her men were on their feet; Shogun's men were up and in battle stances. Bear Shadow and Crow Shadow were up and snarling. Fae guards whipped silver-tipped arrows from their quivers, lifted bows in a flash, and drew. Sir Rodney spun on his serving staff that was huddled by the door and flung his mug on the stone floor with a crash. "What were my demands? Everything was to be prepared to her approval!"

"Guys! Save it for the enemy!" Sasha shouted, finally catching her breath and holding out both hands.

Times like these made her want to pull her hair out by the roots, but at least war in the round table hall had been averted. All potential combatants stood in the long corridor outside the grand foyer, breathing hard but slowly regaining their composure.

"I'll send you through the tapestries; there, you'll meet the Wood Sprites, who can guide you to the plants you need to collect."

Sir Rodney looked around the group. "They are shy, nervous creatures by nature. If you guys go alpha wolf on them, don't expect 'em to help you. They love sugar," he added, dropping several cubes into Sasha's palm. "Put these in your hip pocket. Once they've shown you the rowan, they'll guide you to the way out. From that point on, and as long as you're carrying rowan or iron, we'll have to stay at a distance. But your men will cover you, along with our aerial tree archers, to the edge of the bayou, where our Brownies 'ave borrowed a human vehicle."

Sasha tossed Sir Rodney her cell phone. "All the numbers got accidentally wiped out—but when this rings, it means we've finished the job and are on phase two—blowing up Vampire lairs."

He looked at the cell phone with appreciation. "I have to get used to using these things more than our missives. It still amazes me how, without magick, this little device can truly help the humans talk to each other over great distances. It's just a shame they aren't impervious to Vampire hijacking, but it's not bad for a human development."

She smiled. "It's their attempt at magick, but not nearly as elegant as the Fae's."

Her words seemed to please him as he tucked the unit into his breast pocket. "But she won't work in the castle."

Sasha shook her head no. "You'll have to post a guard just outside the glamour zone. Seems that human technology doesn't work in any of the distorted dimensions. My cell always goes dead in the shadow lands, too."

"I like the part about where we start blowing up lairs, Cap," Fisher said, getting antsy.

"I like the plan," Woods added, checking his weapon. "Sure wish I had more shells, though. Ammo got real low back at Buchanan's."

"That's an easy request, man," Sir Rodney said with a twinkle in his eyes.

Fisher nodded. "We'll be on the other side of the walls, locked and loaded."

"As will we," Bear Shadow said, bumping his fist with Crow Shadow.

"You men are on train yard detail," Shogun said, looking at Seung Kwon. "Once you collect enough iron, stay hidden and make your way back to the three positions."

"That's the primary thing—that each of you stays out of sight until one of us arrives with the rowan and other ingredients we gather. Then we must gain entry to the properties and find the dark altars." Hunter's gaze traveled around the assembled group. "We may only get one shot at this, so let's get it right."

"I've been calling up Sasha's phone," Bradley said, closing his in frustration. "I've left her countless voice mails, but I don't know where she or the team is."

"The last time we made contact," Doc said calmly, "they were on their way in to the Fae fortress. Our gadgets don't work in there."

"When the time is right, we will be able to communicate our plan," Silver Hawk said in a wise, peaceful tone. "Clarissa and I do not sense danger at present."

"I really don't," Clarissa assured him.

Winters looked around the group with a shrug. "Dude, so let's just chill and go get that iron gear you were talking about."

It was the eeriest sensation, feeling her body sucked into a small pinpoint of light. One moment, Sir Rodney had a fistful of dust in his palm, blowing it in their direction, with them all standing in the hallway—the next moment, she became smaller and smaller until she could actually see each line of thread in the huge wall hanging so closely that it became impossible to see the entire pasture scene. Everything became larger-than-life and blurry, distorted by the extreme shift in size. Then, as though a cyclone had swept her up screaming, she felt lighter than a dust particle, whirling in between the fabric threads to land on her butt on a green, green hillside.

Hunter and Shogun were dazed and sprawled out beside her.

"Remind me never to jack with the Fae," she said in an awed murmur.

Even though they'd never admit it, she could tell the guys beside her were a little more than shaken. There was newfound respect for Sir Rodney's capabilities.

Hunter jumped to his feet in a move that Shogun matched. Both male wolves scanned the terrain cautiously, canines beginning to crest.

"If I were a Wood Sprite," Sasha said, pushing herself off the ground. "I wouldn't show myself to you guys, either." She walked off from them a bit, growing weary of the display of testosterone, and called out gently. "We're here as friends, not foes, on behalf of Sir Rodney Clerk of Penicuik . . . you know, the guy who runs Forte Shannon of Inverness, current king of Seelie Court and Clerk Castle?"

Sasha's shoulders sagged as they waited, and then she finally sat down hard on the grass—using hand motions to get Shogun and Hunter to also sit down. To a small Wood Sprite, king's orders or not, she imagined it might take a bit of courage to lead several scary wolves deeper into the forest. That had to be the antithesis of all things they were taught according to the Faerie tales.

"Friend, not foe," Hunter shouted, losing patience.

Sasha cocked her head to the side and placed a hand on her hip. "That tone had foe all in it. Wanna try again—this time losing the growl?"

"It was a long night," Hunter said, staring at her.

"Friend," Shogun said in a low, sensual rumble, the edges of his eyes beginning to blaze wolf. "Definitely not foe."

Hunter turned and tilted his head. But before things got ugly, a small face peered out of the bushes right next to Shogun, giving Hunter a start. It took a moment before Shogun realized what had made Hunter back off. All Sasha could do was laugh.

"Well, hello," she said in a chipper voice, trying without much success to swallow away a smile.

The Sprite waved and then ducked its head back into the bushes.

"You big guys back up," Sasha said, going to the shrub where the tiny creature had appeared.

Hunter loped off, with Shogun following, and stopped several feet away. Sasha bent down and glanced over her shoulder, but shook her head as Hunter turned away from her, rubbing the nape of his neck. Shogun had paced away to lean against a tree, facing away from her with his eyes closed. Men.

She returned her focus to the frightened Sprite, trying to coax it out with a sugar cube. Holding it on the flat of her palm the way one would feed a horse, she slowly moved her hand closer to the bush, just inside it, so the Sprite could make off with the sugar cube without being seen.

The sensation of it grazing her hand and snatching the cube away tickled and she laughed. Apparently, it responded to happy tones of voice, and it peeked its small face out with a cheerful smile, licking the cube that it held between both hands.

"Ah . . ." Sasha crooned, "so that's it. You heard me giggling before and came out."

The Sprite squeaked a happy sound and licked the cube, then released what sounded like a contented bee buzz. That only made Sasha laugh more. "You are *sooo* adorable," she said, going down on her hands and knees.

It had a small face tinged light green with wide brown eyes and the longest lashes she'd ever seen. Its soft brown hair was swept up in an updo of wild hazel-toned ringlets. Pretty autumn-hued leaves covered its body in a makeshift dress, laced with vines, and its tiny toenails were each painted a different fall color.

"Aw . . . just look at you," Sasha said as though doting over a cute toddler. She pulled out another sugar cube, offering it just to bring the small creature closer to get a better look.

But another tiny face popped out from behind a leaf and made her squeal in surprise. Both Sprites giggled as the second one, brown faced and with green hair, stretched out his arms for the sugar cube Sasha had promised.

"There's enough for both of you. You guys are *soooo* awesome. I didn't know what to expect, honestly." She laughed and gave up the sugar, watching the second Sprite thoroughly enjoy it while swinging his legs as he straddled a small branch. "You don't have to be afraid . . . You can have more if you want it."

Yes! She'd made contact. Now was the delicate balancing act of getting the two edgy males behind her not to make any sudden moves while she asked for something deadly. She turned to glance over her shoulder to give them the eye to be cool, and then could only shake her head.

Hunter was leaning against a tree, one arm fully extended, back turned to her, taking in very slow breaths. A deep V of sweat stained his t-shirt. Shogun had claws dug into the bark where he remained, motionless, head back, eyes closed. They were so not going to be much help.

"Listen," Sasha said, keeping her voice gentle and happy. "Sir Rodney needs us to find a really bad plant and to take as much of it out of the forest as possible . . . that way it won't be over here to hurt you . . . And he sent a couple of big, bad wolves to do that—because they're real strong and can carry a lot. They can also protect you, if we have to go somewhere scary to find it."

The Sprites stopped licking their sugar and seemed like they were about to flee. "Would we have been able to get royal castle sugar if we were trying to trick you? Look at the stamp in it. This came from the king himself."

With raised eyebrows of suspicion, the Sprites slowly turned the cubes over and then relaxed when they saw the royal coat of arms indented into the sugar cubes. But they then cast a questioning look at the two male wolves struggling to breathe by the tree line.

"Yeah, I know," Sasha muttered. "I'm not that keen about going into the woods alone with those guys, either."

CHAPTER 20

Sasha's voice had sliced through Hunter's groin so brutally that he'd broken out in a cold sweat. After needing her all night, the near-full moon staining his suite in madness blue . . . tossing and turning, nearly mating with the sheets, to hear her voice low and cooing . . . the words she said sending twisted translations through his head, her backside perfectly accented by her jeans, and then she'd gone down on all fours?

There wasn't enough "safe haven" in the entire world. He had to walk it off. The fact that Shogun did, too, was forming a growl inside his chest. She was radiant at breakfast, the smell of her she-Shadow and rose petals and whatever she'd bathed in. Great Spirit help him; do not let him kill his brother in these woods.

"You guys ready?"

Both he and Shogun spun at Sasha's voice. Were they ready? Did the sun rise in the east and set in the fucking west?

"We've gotta go get the rowan," she said firmly, hands going to her hips. "If you scare these Sprites, I swear to . . ."

"We're ready," Shogun said, releasing a long breath.

Hunter nodded.

"You're showing canines, gentlemen. The wee folk don't like it—it makes 'em nervous."

Hunter rubbed the nape of his neck and walked away for a bit. Shogun rolled his shoulders and walked away in the opposite direction.

"Anytime you're ready," Sasha said, folding her arms.

Hunter and Shogun both turned slowly to stare at her.

"You're going to have to use a better choice of words." He nodded to the bush as she opened her mouth and then closed it. "Let's get out of here."

Winters came out of the occult shop digging in the bags. "This stuff is kinky, dude. Like, who really uses this stuff? Iron collars, cuffs, stakes, damn . . . If I didn't know better, I'd swear you and 'Rissa—"

Both Clarissa and Bradley spun on Winters, Bradley grabbing him by the back of the shirt.

"My bad!" Winters said, struggling to get free.

"Not in front of Doc and Silver Hawk," Bradley said, making the threesome come to an abrupt halt on the sidewalk.

Winters held up both hands, banging a bag against his chest by accident. "See no evil, hear no evil, speak no evil."

"Good," Bradley said, releasing his shirt. "Because from what you just saw in there, Clarissa and I are the last people in the world you want to have a grudge against you."

Arms loaded down with branches and red berries, they trudged to where the nervous Sprites had pointed. A small, crystal-clear brook zigzagged before them, and it seemed so cool and inviting that she wanted to stop and take a sip from it, but couldn't risk losing her toxic armload in the Fae water supply.

"Crossing running water is another way to break

spells," Sasha said, looking at Shogun and Hunter. Their faces were slicked with sweat, pure wolf in their eyes, and she could tell that they were nearly deaf to what she was telling them.

"All right," she said, peeved. "On three, we jump the brook—keep those branches out of it so we don't cause an ecological disaster out here. Where we land, your guess is as good as mine." That's all the time she had before Hunter rushed her.

She crashed through bramble and hit the ground with a thud. Hunter flattened her, crushing leaves and berries into her back. Shogun somersaulted out of the bushes, crouched, and released a warning growl.

Gun clicks and warning arrows helped all three alphas return to the present and clear their minds. Both males jumped back, eyeing each other, with Sasha between them. She pushed up slowly, the wind having been knocked out of her, looked at Hunter, and snarled.

"You rushed me? Have you lost it?" Sasha brushed twigs out of her hair, not caring if she sounded out of control or not. Right now she was.

"We cannot stay in the presence of rowan fumes," a Fae archer said, pulling back.

"We've got 'em covered," Woods said, helping Sasha up. "You cool, Captain?"

"Never better," she said, scowling at Hunter as she stood and brushed herself off.

"It was the woods. I'm sorry," Hunter muttered, brushing off his clothes. He gave Sasha an apologetic glance, humiliation resonating in his tone, and then looked away. "Had a flashback to the Uncompahgre. Won't happen again."

"You *rushed* the lady?" Shogun said, now snarling.

"Don't judge me when you have no point of reference!" Hunter shouted, pointing at Shogun.

"You think not?" Shogun shouted back.

"What?" Hunter tilted his head as though he hadn't heard correctly and walked toward Shogun with murder in his eyes.

"Yo, Max," Crow Shadow called out. "Don't go there, man."

"Hunter—reason . . . Safe haven!" Bear Shadow said and then looked at Sasha, openly confused that the words she'd given them to use in an emergency were falling on deaf ears.

She could feel the lunge coming the way old bones forecasted rain. Yanking a nine-millimeter out of Woods's waistband, she fired a warning shot into the air.

"First man to go airborne dies where he lands. Enough of this bullshit! We've got work to do!"

It had to be the longest twenty minutes in the world for Sasha, sitting in the back of a panel-body truck, enduring bayou heat, no air-conditioning, wedged between two very edgy alphas and two very nervous betas. However, that was the best arrangement, given that they were traveling through *Deliverance* country and six cops had died the night before. It made the most sense to put Woods and Fisher up front and to keep the more colorful cast of characters concealed in the back.

But the tight confines did give Bear Shadow and Crow Shadow a chance to tell them all about Bradley's brilliant plan. Woods had gotten the cell phone call the moment they cleared the castle walls; Fisher's phone was lighting up, too. Sasha leaned her head back against the warm, metal interior of the truck and dug into her jeans' pocket.

"Here, Crow. Take my amulet. You be safe in there with Bear and 'Rissa. But if anybody can get you there and back safely, it's Silver Hawk."

Her brother accepted the amber and silver amulet and held it in his fist for a moment, staring at her before looping it over his head. "I'll do you proud, Sasha."

Bear Shadow lowered his head as Hunter looped the

alpha-male leader amulet over his head, something that had been in the clan for generations. "I will do my best to be worthy of this honor."

"Just come back alive, brother. That's all we ask of both of you," Hunter said in a somber tone.

They traveled a long way in relative silence, but then everyone froze when the truck slowed down.

"Roadblock," Fisher said, turning quickly to call over the backseat. "Pull that tarp up. State troopers."

"Wanna open up?" a trooper said, leaning into Woods's window.

"USMC, sir . . . headed to Fort Polk, NAS. Got ID that says so—and got artillery back there that's Homeland Security issued. Don't want civvies that are out here in this line gawking to see it, sir. I'm not trying to be an ass or to make your job any harder, much respect. But those are my direct orders; that's why I'm traveling in a camouflaged vehicle. If you've got a problem—like I said, those are my orders. My commanding officer is General Westford and I can give you a direct line to his office."

Damn, Woods was awesome. The tone of voice he used didn't waver. He sounded like he had the right to be where he was, doing what he was doing. So now it was a game of chicken between him and the trooper. Sasha waited. Nervous anticipation and heat covered her body with perspiration. Male pheromones coated her sinuses and the back of her tongue with their scent. She closed her eyes as a trickle of sweat rolled down her spine, between her shoulder blades. Two bangs on the side of the truck almost made her jump.

"You boys keep doing what you're doin'," the trooper said. "Wasn't for you, wouldn't be no hope. Jus' wish I knew what newfangled weapons y'all had up your sleeves."

"Biohazards," Woods said. "It's living organisms . . . Wicked shit when it's let loose on the bad guys."

"Now *that's* what I'm talking about!" the trooper said,

and slapped the side of the van again. "You boys go on ahead and you get those terrorists! We'll be working on whoever went after some of our local boys, but the fight's all the same. We all wear the colors, all wear a uniform."

"Same war, different day—good luck and sorry about the loss of your men," Woods said, rolling the truck forward.

"Sorry about the loss of yours, son," the trooper called out. "Hey, Joe, escort this military vehicle around that line of traffic! Get 'em to the front of the line."

Just like that, they were free. After a while, Fisher gave them the all-clear to come out from under the tarp.

"Same pack," Woods called over his shoulder. "I guess humans have loyalties and bonds, too."

When they reached The Fair Lady, Woods slowed the vehicle and Fisher opened the door. Hunter got out and did recon with one of Shogun's lieutenants, who were hidden in the shadows. Sasha watched with her heart in her mouth as Hunter took Ethan's establishment, which was crawling with cops. Rather than the direct approach, she saw Hunter and Chin-Hwa go into the adjacent building and come out on the roof. NOPD would be in the cellar, maybe going through the office records, as well as combing through the alley and the first floor, spending hours trying to figure out what looked like some type of dark ritual that ended in a possible shoot-out. All she could do was pray that Hunter and Chin-Hwa could find their target to lay the iron and witchwood bundles, and then get out.

Shogun took Finnegan's Wake, which was the lesser evil of the two bars. It was still functioning, and Seelie Fae knew the deal. Sir Rodney's guys had told them to give Shogun and Dak-Ho full access, even if NOPD was hanging around and asking questions. But when they went in with rowan, herbs, and iron bundles in duffel bags, Shogun and Dak-Ho cleared the joint. She had to remember to ask

Sir Rodney's advisors how to go in after the spell had been broken to remove the hazmat from the attics, or the establishments would be virtually worthless to the Seelie Fae.

"You ready to go in, Cap?" Woods asked, turning around in his seat.

"Ready as I'll ever be," she said, grabbing her duffel bag, checking that the coast was clear, and jumping down when Fisher opened the door. "You guys come back from the shadow lands in one piece," she said to Bear Shadow and Crow Shadow, wishing like hell that she could have gone in their stead.

But there was no time to dwell on that now. Seung Kwon was waiting for her in the alley alongside the building, behind the Dumpster. Their eyes met and he gave her the sign that the coast was clear. The B&B was apparently locked up tight and hadn't shown any signs of unusual activity. They must have assumed the shots fired came from the bar across the street, which was why NOPD had been in and out of this joint.

Good—at least something was going right. A lot of things were, actually, when she thought about it. And then reality smacked her upside the head—that couldn't be a good sign.

Sasha watched the van pull off with a sinking feeling in her gut. What if Hunter got apprehended? What if Shogun got caught? There were no Fae in the building now to staff the establishment, leaving only oblivious human workers there, who had been told that the men in the attic were exterminators going in to look for rats and squirrels in the eaves . . . what a crock. And what if Bear Shadow and Crow Shadow ran into a serious problem in the shadow lands . . . or Clarissa's soul got hijacked by dark forces while it was an astral projection. Sasha rubbed her palms down her face.

"Are you all right, Captain Trudeau?" Seung Kwon's voice held a new level of respect, one that came from people who'd valiantly fought side-by-side.

"I'm good," Sasha said. "It's just the heat out here and the damned mosquitoes the size of quarters."

He nodded and looked up at the building. "We can break in through the back door."

She dug into her jeans' pocket. "I was staying here, remember? How about we go right in the front like we're a couple, using a key?"

Sir Rodney stared down at the cell phone. "They are done so fast? Have hit all three installations already?"

"It's been ringing off the bleedin' hook, milord. Almost as soon as I went to stand guard outside to wait," a tall archer said, handing him the device. "I do not know how to work it, but she was clear that we should wait till it sounded, and then we'd start the Vampire raids."

With no air-conditioning on and all the windows locked up tightly, the house was stifling. Drawn shades didn't help; all they did was make the place seem like a death trap. Checking for intruders as they managed the stairs, their wolf instincts keen, Sasha and Seung Kwon climbed until they hit the top floor. Both pairs of eyes scanned the ceiling and stopped on the pull-down stairs to the crawl space.

"You pull," Sasha said, removing the nine-millimeter from her waistband. "I'll point and click."

Seung nodded and leaped up, yanking the short cord that brought down the steps. Silence greeted them. Seung took the stairs in a crouch, brandishing iron railroad ties as he went up each step. Sasha moved forward and hiked the duffel bag up higher on her shoulder. It was amazingly quiet—too quiet.

They peered around the half-story space, disappointed that there was nothing there but dust and a few boxes.

"Maybe it is just not in this building," Seung Kwon said, glancing around.

"Yeah, maybe not," Sasha said, and then dropped her duffel bag on the floor. But as she did so and the dust moved in a plume, she remembered the ashes. "Get your iron ready," she said, quickly going inside her duffel bag and yanking out rowan branches.

"What are you doing?"

"Sweeping the floor." Sasha stooped and began walking backward toward the only natural light source, a tiny attic window that faced the street and Finnegan's Wake. The moment the rowan touched a certain spot along the wood planks, the floor spit and sizzled. "Bingo, drop the iron, man!"

She left the rowan where the floor reacted and jumped back as Seung Kwon dropped a railroad tie over it. Immediately, the floor began to glow red in an ever-widening circle as the rowan branches burst into flames. Sasha skirted the inferno and backed up toward the pull-down stairs, mesmerized as the symbol bubbled up like crude oil and began to heat the iron until it became iron ore.

"Go, go, go!" she shouted as the heat fanned out, the eaves caught flame, and suddenly, blue-white entities fled out of the symbol's center, bearing what looked suspiciously like demon teeth.

The creatures shut the crawl space stairs, tangled in her hair, and clawed at her and Seung Kwon's faces. It was impossible to get a shot off while they were dragging him closer to the lava-like inferno, savaging him as he yelled and fought them.

Sasha picked up the duffel bag, noting that they stayed away from it and had flung it to the far side of the room by the strap. She snatched out more rowan as she elbowed the vicious little creatures off her back. The moment she held it in her fist with a gun in the other, they fled to focus their full torment on Seung Kwon.

"Catch!" she hollered. "They can't stand it!"

He grabbed a branch of rowan laden with berries, and when it touched three of the little beasties, they exploded into green guck. Sasha went to work on the trapdoor, trying to escape the flames. But the inferno was dying down.

She and Seung Kwon stared at each other. The trapdoor fell open. The floor sealed back up. The railroad ties and rowan that covered the circle were gone. All that was left were a few berries that sparked and popped on the floor, then disappeared.

"I think we need to go across the street and make sure Shogun and your pack brothers are all right."

CHAPTER 21

"It has to be up here," Hunter said, pointing at the window. "It's the only source of light."

Chin-Hwa glanced around nervously, hanging close to the roof hatch they'd been able to open. He kept one hand on the ladder steps leading out, constantly glancing toward the crawl space's drop-down entrance. "The authorities might have heard us—we have been back and forth here dozens of times, but nothing is to be seen . . . The Fae were wrong."

"Look around, man!" Hunter said through his teeth, keeping his voice low. "There must be something!"

In frustration, Chin-Hwa flung down the branches he'd been holding, releasing berries that rolled across the floor. As soon as several hit the edges of the sunlight-bathed spot on the wood, it popped and sizzled and the symbol they sought instantly became visible.

"Milord? We are to mount an offensive without confirmation?" The captain of the guards stared at Sir Rodney for a moment. "But, sir, our magick's not returned as promised yet."

"Were this not the time for immediate action I would have you court-martialed for questioning my command!"

Sir Rodney's troops lowered their confused gazes.

"I will not have her left out there stranded! If she sent the signal through her own device, then that is good enough for me!" Sir Rodney held the cell phone out to his men as he walked down his garrison's line, armed to the teeth. "If I had been outside the fortress walls, I would have received the call meself. She showed me how to hear her voice in the air with it! How to push the button to stop the chime and to let her speak to me clear as a bell. That much I know how to do, but I do not need to hear her voice to know that she needs my sword! Are we not men without our magick? Do we not know how to destroy this foul beast called Vampire?"

A lackluster aye returned to him from his troops.

"Then the way we would for the Lady of the Lake, for Sasha Trudeau we ride!"

Chin-Hwa came out onto the roof with angry flames licking up behind him; Hunter dropped three stories down into the middle of a police investigation, covered in air-elemental scratches. Before anyone could react, the top of the building blew. Guns were drawn; people on the scene shouted and scrambled against the perceived threat as Hunter ran zigzag through the police like an NFL quarterback.

A hot-wired SUV skidded to a sideways stop as police cruisers got thrown into service amid the distinctive pop of gunfire. Hunter jumped into the SUV as it careened off. The sound of helicopter blades beating the air made Chin-Hwa panic and bail off the roof, wolf style. He hit the ground on all fours, looked around for a second to find an opening, and sprinted.

Sirens blared, and Sasha leaned over with Shogun driving. Seung Kwon opened one door; Dak-Ho opened the other. Chin-Hwa came to a skidding halt out of a back alley, pursued by breathless foot-patrol officers.

"Get in!" Sasha shouted.

The car was still moving and Chin-Hwa had to run to

catch up to it. A bullet caught Hunter in the upper arm as the vehicle slowed and he yanked Chin-Hwa inside. Both doors slammed shut. Shogun peeled rubber as Hunter held the wound, swerving through traffic, nearly colliding with parked cars and pedestrians.

"Did it get the bone?" Sasha leaned over the seat but everyone ducked down as NOPD shot out the back window.

"Passed through the muscle but hurts like a bitch." Hunter leaned his head back against the seat, grimacing as the vehicle lurched and pitched.

"If you can hang on till we get somewhere, I can heal it."

"First we've gotta live," Shogun said, bouncing over a curb and taking a hairpin turn.

"We'll never outrun the chopper," Sasha said as Shogun maneuvered into a back street and came barreling out of the other end of it, taking half a storefront with him.

Hunter cried out as Shogun slammed on the brakes hard and bounced over the pavement and a median to head in the opposite direction, causing traffic to screech to a halt in four directions.

"We have to get off the street before we kill somebody. I need a phone—take us inside a building, any building, where there're no people on the first floor, then everybody scatter." Sasha turned, repeatedly glancing back at Hunter.

"We'll be trapped, sitting ducks!" Seung Kwon shouted.

"You trusted me back there at Dugan's old place just now, right?" she shouted over the seat as the SUV almost rolled over. "Shogun found the symbol in his building, too, right?"

"I trust the lady," Shogun said, turning hard into a building and taking out the entire front bay of an auto body shop.

Pedestrians scattered, metal slammed against metal, but she and all the others in their vehicle were up and out as airbags burst forward.

Hunter slapped a shotgun out of a foolish owner's hands. "Where's the phone? That's all we came for; insurance should cover the rest."

"Come out with your hands in the air!"

The unmistakable blare of a police bullhorn made everybody freeze for a moment. Hunter, Shogun, and his men stared at Sasha as she dialed the telephone.

"How's the arm?" Shogun muttered.

Hunter didn't immediately answer, just wrapped the bleeding wound with duct tape. "It'll heal."

"We have the place surrounded! Let the hostages in the store go!"

"Hey, Sir Rodney?" Sasha said quickly. "How's your Fae magick working right about now?"

"We've gotta go," Woods said to Fisher. He looked at Doc and then Silver Hawk. "It's going down. You all have got to cover Bear Shadow, Crow Shadow, and 'Rissa in there. We can't do anything but provide security out here, if maybe something tries to come out of the shadows on you guys, anyway." He tossed Doc a nine-millimeter. "Saw that you know how to use one of these."

"That I do."

"Good," Woods said, looking at Bradley. "You take care of our girl." Woods gave Clarissa a brief hug.

"Armed with iron, rowan, and brick dust, as well as a few little things that are a special blend of my own."

"Good man." Woods bumped Bradley's fist.

"Did she say what she wanted us to bring?" Fisher started hunting through the cache of weapons hidden at Tulane from the last battle.

"Everything and the kitchen sink."

"They don't see us?" Shogun whispered, walking past police officers that had their weapons drawn.

"Nope," Sasha said quietly and quickly, hurrying the group along.

The frightened Fae civilian that was called out of hiding kept his eyes squeezed shut for a second and then dashed ahead of them. "Hurry, hurry, please hurry . . . We just got our magick back and I'm only here because of Sir Rodney's insistence. I'm an innocent bystander—we're not even from New Orleans! This was not how we had intended to spend the day before the ball!"

"Sir, I know you're upset," Sasha said calmly, glancing around. "But if we could impose on you for one more favor or two . . . We need that van over there turned into a military vehicle, if you can . . . and anything you need to use as material—like wheel lugs—to transform into AK-47s or M-16s, whichever is easiest, and silver shells for them. Maybe you can use the steel tire irons for the on-the-fly alchemy? But we need weapons, a vehicle, and a way out, stat. Appreciate your help."

Sasha went to the side of the van, marveling at how the police continued to shout through the bullhorn as the SWAT unit arrived. Shogun caught the Elf under his tiny arms before he fainted.

"We're a peaceful people," the Elf said, gulping. "Do I have to make guns?"

"I will be your eyes," Silver Hawk said as he sat across the table from Clarissa, with Doc and Bradley by her side. He looked up at Bear Shadow and Crow Shadow and waited for them to nod.

"I will be your ears," Clarissa murmured, looking at both men.

"Listen for our voices and only our voices to direct you . . . or that of the Great Spirit," Silver Hawk said quietly. "I will call the positive ancestors. I will call the shaman guides. I will ask the Great Spirit for your protection. You must free our people from the shackles of this curse!"

Sir Rodney dropped down from the tree line with a smile as soon as Sasha's vehicle came into the long drive.

"I knew you wanted us to be here," he said with a wide smile, vindicated, and glancing at his astonished men.

"Thank you," Sasha said, jumping down from the armored jeep and coming up to Sir Rodney with a wide smile. "Seems I've been saying that to you a lot, lately. Your man in town outfitted us beautifully . . . but we wouldn't have gotten out of there if it weren't for a traditional Fae glamour. Although I think your constituent was so upset that he may need medical attention—that or a good therapist. We stressed the poor man, and we apologize for that."

"Men, listen up—you 'eard what the lady said." Sir Rodney beamed and glanced around at his troops. "There would be no more Seelie Fae glamour 'ad these brave wolves not gone in and undone a foul curse on the House of Clerk."

He waited until the cheers and whistles died down and then turned to Sasha. "We thank *you* . . . The least we could do was provide you some military fatigues, a wee bit of munitions, and a chance to escape . . . Standard bibbidi-bobbidi-boo; easy charms, milady. The stuff of Faerie tales and Dragon lore." His men laughed as he took a deep bow, seeming much revived now that his magic was back to full strength outside his castle walls. However, when he looked at Hunter, his smile faded. "This man has been shot."

"Bullet passed through my arm, didn't knick bone. Twenty-four hours and a session with a good healer, and I'll be fine," Hunter said, studying the plantation-style mansion. "Trees to the east are good cover. We have to decide how to take the property—there will definitely be security forces present. Humans to prevent daylight incursions. Maybe even some wolves from the Buchanan Broussard camp—so let's not get overconfident. It ain't over till it's over . . . Never underestimate Vampires."

"True. And Vamps are like sharks," Shogun said. "You know that, brother. You're bleeding and you can't merge into the shadows . . . This isn't like going up against humans; in a pitch-black lair they move faster than—"

"I know. I understand the risks. But we go in there full force, one clan, allies." Hunter's gaze slowly surveyed the group until he received nods of agreement.

He motioned with his chin toward the large, antebellum mansion. "Quite a beaut . . . I'd say forty, fifty rooms to sack, and who knows what they've got under the ground?"

Fisher lifted a shoulder cannon and smiled. "We could do it the quick, just-add-water way and be home before dark to have a brew."

"I like the way this man thinks," Sir Rodney said with a smile.

"Before we blow the roof off the sucker," Sasha said, staring at the mansion, "we need to know if there are any innocents in there."

"Anybody in there is not innocent," Sir Rodney said. "But if it'll make you feel better, we do stealth very, very well."

Baron Montague opened his eyes and sat up slowly in the dark chambers beneath the house. "We have guests," he said calmly as two female Vampires gathered in closer to him yawning. "I smell blood." He looked up at the vaulted ceiling in the concrete cavern. "Blood tainted by silver," he said snarling. "Guards!"

A huge blast rocked the house. Small crumbles of concrete rained down on the bed as he jumped up and dressed in a flash. All above him he could hear battle raging. He shut his eyes and his entire estate came into view. The manor was an inferno above—that would draw humans!

"Fools! There will be blood for this transgression!"

"Give them Kiagehul!" one of his lovers screeched. "The little bastard has caused us nothing but trouble—we are not involved in this . . . There are Fae out there fighting alongside both wolf clans!"

The baron slapped her in frustration, but fear for her life made her hiss and challenge him. "You may not like to hear my words but you cannot deny the truth."

Her sister screeched and drew to her side. "Listen to her, Geoff—they will find the vault and open this sanctuary in broad daylight, damn you! Give them the fucking little troll, or whatever he is! Let the Unseelie queen be outraged that they took the law into their own hands and beheaded him! This is not our battle."

"Oh, but there will be hell to pay for an unprovoked attack without proof!" the baron snarled between his fangs. "A botched attack on their human boy does not *begin* to redress this offense . . . We lost one of our own—according to law, that is enough of a fine for going after the little miscreant . . . And now they've laid siege to my lair in an unauthorized attack?"

"Feel the walls," the other sister said in a hiss. "They are practically glowing. How long do you think it will take for the house to burn down to ash and for them to find us huddled in a corner, screaming for them not to open this tomb!" She stood up on the bed and then levitated toward him. *"Give them the betrayer!"*

The baron sent a black charge toward her, but she and her sister deflected it with a snarl.

The eldest sister circled him like a hissing cat. "You do not have enough energy to hold them off from this lair, keep it cool enough in here that we not suffer, and fight us—now choose!"

Priceless antiques were going up in flames. Machine-gun reports rang out and echoed in his mind's eye. His best human security forces were slaughtered . . . his bouncers in upper-floor lairs had been sentenced to instant death by daylight. The baron turned away from her, closed his eyes, and sent a hard, flashing image of Kiagehul's hidden coven to Sir Rodney.

"Fall back!" Sir Rodney shouted.

Sasha looked at Hunter as he jerked back a silver-shell-loaded AK-47. Shogun caught up to them, dusting dead Vampire embers off his fatigues.

"Woods, Fisher!" Sasha hunted for her men in the billowing smoke, but let out a hard breath of relief when one last grenade blew and she saw them jogging from the far side of the building as it collapsed.

Sir Rodney used two fingers to point toward the woods, and then closed his eyes and grabbed his forehead. "I can see him," he said, wincing. "The Vampire gave him up, put the image in me bleedin' 'ead! But we will have hell to pay . . . The Vampires were not involved, only spectators in the larger game. I can sense it in me magick; it's deep in the marrow of me bones!"

"Oh . . . shit . . ." Sasha stood numb for a second. "The retaliation is going to be a bitch."

"I'll say." Woods spat on the ground.

"Who would ever have believed that Vampires were innocent?" Shogun dragged his fingers through his hair and began to walk in a circle.

Hunter ran over, grabbed Sir Rodney's temples, grimacing as his right arm shook from the pain. "We're healers . . . by nature," he said, breathing hard. "I'll take the pain; he's stabbing the image into your mind, enraged . . . but the information is invaluable."

"Your arm," Sasha said. "Let me do the extraction."

Hunter just stared at her but didn't stop. She nodded and backed off. It was an intimate process; if there were other thoughts, they could complicate matters.

"Just get it outta me bleedin' head! For the love of all things holy . . . it was duplicity in its highest form!"

Sir Rodney slumped as two of his best men held him in Hunter's grasp. After a few moments, Sir Rodney's body relaxed and Hunter's eyes rolled into the back of his head. When he came out of the daze, he was snarling and his eyes were pure wolf. He dropped Sir Rodney in the arms of his men, pivoted, and took off into the glen. Shogun and Sasha were right behind him with a retinue of archers swiftly navigating the trees.

Helicopters were not far in the distance. Fire-engine

and police sirens were closing in. But Hunter had the trail in his mind. He picked up the scent on the back of his palate; if he could have called his wolf, he would have been four paws on the ground and one with the wind.

When Hunter found him, Kiagehul was barricaded in a mansion that instantly faded to nothing more than a quickly drawn black magick circle. The onslaught of now strong Seelie Fae tracking magick had left his target exposed. Hunter skidded to a stop, and the frightened Unseelie brandished a dark charm and a wand, following Hunter's every move.

"Stay back, wolf!" Kiagehul shouted, fear stripping his glamour.

"Your head is mine," Hunter said, taking short lunges to terrorize the evil being that had wreaked so much havoc.

"If you touch me, you will be cursed for a hundred generations!"

"Don't touch him, Hunter!" Sasha shouted.

But Shogun left her side to begin circling with Hunter.

"MacDougall?" Sir Rodney said, pushing past the wolves. "Me own damned bodyguard—me best man? What is this madness?"

"Kennan *Kiagehul* MacDougall! Did you even know my Unseelie name, Kiagehul?" the Unseelie shouted, holding his wand out before him. "Disinherited! Abused in your Seelie Court because of who my father was . . . Never in line for what was rightfully mine—well this time I decided to take it!"

"Treason!" Sir Rodney shouted, his fingertip sparking as he pointed hard at Kiagehul. "You were my most trusted, because of who your mother was to my court!"

"As though my father's Unseelie line never mattered?" Kiagehul said, his eyes narrowed with hatred. "Had the Fae wars waxed differently, I would have been in line to rule."

"But they didn't . . . and I gave you a high post nonetheless—for *your Seelie mother*!" Sir Rodney shouted, veins of rage now standing in his neck and at his temples. "You take up your fate and lack of inheritance with your coldhearted queen, not me! She was the one who passed you over because of your father's ineptitude in battle. I gave you asylum!"

"Dead man walking," Hunter said, snarling.

"It's like watching a foxhunt when the quarry is finally at bay, eh Kiagehul, you rat bastard?" an archer shouted from the trees, and then spit out the twig he'd been chewing on. "Only I'd like to see these dogs of war leave nothing of your stinkin' carcass to bring home."

"Did your queen know?" Sir Rodney paced along the perimeter of the black magick circle. "Out with it!"

"My queen will benefit greatly from your fall," Kiagehul sneered.

Woods and Fisher finally caught up to the group, but all the Fae backed up as Kiagehul began to scream.

"Thrash him with the rowan branches to strip him of his power," Sasha ordered. "Then cross his pentagram with the iron, gentlemen, and make sure you put a piece in his pocket so there's no chance he'll get away. This SOB is going to court tonight."

Bear Shadow stood in the mist beside his pack brother, nerves taut, gaze sweeping. Crow Shadow held the implements to break the curse; his job was to walk point and call the spirits. But something was wrong as he called Hunter's name. Only strange silence came back . . . Then he saw it. Hunter's wolf with red glowing eyes, a demon version of his courageous alpha.

The beast lunged so quickly that he didn't have time in his human form to evade it. It was not pure mist but was dense, had weight, its jaws savaging his skin, tearing his flesh. Crow leaped in and tried to stab it with an iron stake, but it grabbed his arm between massive jaws, almost snapping bone, but Bear had climbed on the beast's back to force it to turn its attention away from Crow.

There was no time to see with Silver Hawk's eyes or listen to Clarissa's shrieks. Crow Shadow gored the beast as it reared on its hind legs, standing Hunter's wolf height of seven feet tall. Iron plunged through the beast, exploding it to cinders. Bear Shadow hurled a handful of rowan berries over Crow Shadow's shoulder, screaming for him to get down as Sasha's wolf charged out of the nothingness.

But that only burned away her fur, leaving a scorched demon wolf skull with glowing red eyes and a mangled, bloody coat. She stalked both men, circling them and waiting for Silver Hawk to enter as a demonic version of his Silver Shadow self.

"Something's gone wrong!" Bear Shadow shouted out loud. "They're not etheric doubles, they're demons!"

Crow Shadow backed up with him as both warriors took a stand, surrounded.

"Pull them out!" Clarissa shouted, breaking the trance. "Something's happened, Bradley."

Doc shook Silver Hawk as he slumped forward on the table. Bradley jumped up from the table with Winters and dashed to the computer.

"The spell's been changed, reinforced somehow. The one who cast it had to have been tipped off!" Bradley began searching through screens.

"They won't last that long," Clarissa shouted. "They've got one demon down; call Sasha's cell! See if you can get through to Hunter to go in there and get his men out!"

Sir Rodney handed Sasha the cell phone as his retinue of soldiers blended into the trees. "It's for you," he said, puzzled. He nodded as she accepted the unit and pressed it to her ear.

"What?" Sasha grabbed Hunter's uninjured arm as the retreat came to a full stop.

"I don't mean ta rush the lady," one of the archers said,

"but we've got to get this bag of rot back to the dungeons and us out of the humans' way, posthaste . . . And problem is we need a wolf to carry 'im through the forest, due to his iron-clad condition."

"Hunter's men are trapped in the shadow lands," Sasha said quickly, relating the drastic events. "They're up against my dark shadow self and Silver Shadow's evil etheric, as well as Shogun's, all alone . . . And who even knows how formidable the others will be?"

"It'll take me a half hour to forty minutes to go back, assuming I'm not stopped," Hunter said, beginning to pace.

"They'll be dead by then," Kiagehul called out, laughing a hysterical laugh of the criminally insane.

Sasha went to Hunter. "No. You were the first etheric double they put down. You go in there, focus on killing mine, and call me—I will hear you in my soul. Then let me go in there and fight with you to kill the rest. Your arm, baby," she said, gently touching the edge of the tape. "Trust me to be by your side . . . Call me in there with you and don't you dare die on my watch."

She didn't care if she'd just made an open declaration, a clear choice with witnesses all around, and didn't care if Shogun or Sir Rodney was offended. She didn't want to hurt them, but it was what it was. Something was lifting, breaking up like the congestion of a bad cold . . . The haze was gone. Hunter stared at her for a moment, his inner vision clear for the first time in days—she could feel it inside her like she knew her name, and that private knowing anchored her.

Hunter nodded. "I will call you as soon as the shadows are yours again."

"Hunter," Woods said, tossing him a semiautomatic. "This might not work, but it's worth a try. Silver bullets might kill demons, who knows? At least they could slow 'em down."

"FYI, Winters and Bradley brought back iron bullets,

handcuffs, a bunch of shit from the occult shop," Fisher said, outright worry thick in his tone. "If you're jumping shadows, thought you'd like to know."

She watched Hunter take a running leap into the shadow of a huge weeping willow tree and enter it. She closed her eyes, suddenly realizing how precious a gift she'd had and how it had been robbed by a foul hobgoblin of a creature.

Sasha walked over to Kiagehul and backhanded him. "If he dies, I'm going to make you *eat* rowan berries for lunch, I promise you!"

CHAPTER 22

Running, pure velocity, pain shooting through his arm, hair lifting off his shoulders, the hunt had Hunter in its jaws. He sailed over the rock-hewn cavern, his focus on the battle so the shadow lands would bring him directly to it. But it took a moment for his mind to sync up with what his eyes witnessed.

Sasha . . . his beautiful, silver-coated mate, was hideously transformed. Her face was mangled and half burned away; his men were huddled back-to-back and brandishing rowan and iron pikes to keep her away while she tried to rush them. His grandfather was a massive wolf, a maggot-ridden demon transfiguration of his former regal shadow self. Bear Shadow and Crow Shadow were even forced to fight themselves, as copies of their wolves were snarling, hideous beasts.

He lifted his weapon and fired. The demons turned on him. Silver had no effect. Without rowan or iron, he was an instant target. His men called out to him, shouting no. As the beasts lunged, Bear Shadow threw him an iron railroad stake, hurling rowan berries behind them like shrapnel.

Sasha's chest sailed over him as he crouched down low, came up, and took her heart.

"Your arm!" Crow Shadow shouted. "Don't let their contagion get into your wound!"

"Clarissa speaks from the other side. Silver Hawk sees here now, brother!" Bear Shadow shouted, dashing in with more supplies to take part in the battle.

With a quick pivot, Hunter spared his arm from his grandfather's jaws, driving the stake into his temple. The beast howled as it exploded, sending embers and ash everywhere.

Seconds mattered, in the beat of a heart two more Shadow Wolves joined the fray. Hunter turned just long enough to see the regal Silver Shadow leap off the ground to collide with Bear Shadow's demon wolf. Hunter was on the felled pair as they struggled on the ground, goring the demon in the throat as his grandfather sprang into action to chase Crow Shadow's demon form. Crow Shadow didn't hesitate. The moment his demon wolf lunged, he stabbed it in the chest. Both man and demon fell backward, leaving Crow Shadow beneath burning ash.

Silver Hawk pulled the younger man up with a hard yank, having shifted back into his human form. All men spun as screaming banshee-like demon forms of Doc, Winters, Woods, Fisher, Bradley, and Clarissa came running at them. The human beasts ran fast, moving in limb-distorted ways, with savage jaws, hollowed-out eyes, and hooked claws. The Shadow pack made a circle facing outward, stakes and rowan in hands. Then a voice made them glance over their shoulders for a second.

"Get down!"

Four men hit the ground; rapid machine-gun fire obliterated demon bodies. Green guck splattered everywhere, exploding into black slime. Then it became quiet, eerily so. The Shadow pack lifted their heads. Sasha stood wide-legged, breathing hard, holding an M-16 that had been loaded with iron shells.

"I got the call—not the cell phone variety," she said, catching her breath. "I heard you in my soul, but thought I should make a pit stop to go get some of that ammo Winters and Bradley brought home from the occult shop."

Hunter flipped himself up and pulled his grandfather up beside him. "Thank you," he said quietly, beginning to weave.

"We need to get this man out of here. He's lost a lot of blood, and with the demon doors opened around him . . ." Bear Shadow said.

Hunter looked at Bear Shadow. "I'm good."

Crow Shadow and Silver Hawk caught him before he hit the ground.

Cartel Elderman Vlad opened his eyes, receiving Baron Montague's telepathic transmission. His fangs lowered slowly as outrage caused his hands to tremble with fury.

"I don't know who to be more vexed with!" he shouted into the darkness of his lair, also transmitting the message as a searing telepathic barb. "You would risk sending our nation to war during this precarious time of rebuilding in New Orleans—and for *what,* to toy with one of the wolves' humans? Vengeance over a small taxation matter against your blood club? That is hardly worth the exposure to human authorities!"

"It was for much more than that, Elder Vlad," Baron Montague shot back. "I had been monitoring the progression of Unseelie Fae dark magick, whereby, if they had been successful, we would have had a rare opportunity to break the Wolf Clan Federations that united against us, as well as break the back of the very fragile and newly united Seelie Fae Parliament, along with those third-world groups like the Mythics, The Order of the Dragon, and the others that sided with the wolves. My goal, sir, was to simply monitor the situation as the Unseelie magick weakened those allied forces, got them squabbling and at war amongst themselves, and thus . . . in time, we would have been in a position to be restored as a single voting bloc at the United Council of Entities. There was a larger objective than a mere blood club and a couple of casinos. However, we are not culpable for any of this, beyond the attack on the boy—to which I lost a lover . . . This illegal retribution was beyond the pale, and now they owe us for the offense."

Deadly silence lay in wait between them. Baron Geoff Montague remained stone still. An infraction of this magnitude could cost him his life.

"Fix this," Elder Vlad finally murmured. "You are a valuable member of our society and the Cartel . . . I would hate to have to witness your untimely demise. Make sure that it is clear, in court, that your hands were clean, so that none of this causes backlash on our Cartel."

"It shall be addressed immediately upon sunset." Baron Montague closed his eyes and released an inaudible breath of relief. "All that is necessary is the UCE trial and—"

"I don't think so," Elder Vlad said with a hiss in his tone.

"Sir? Pardon?"

"Several issues are at hand . . . Have you not been monitoring the human airwaves—their news reports—while in your lair?"

For a moment, Baron Montague couldn't respond. "Uh, sir, I was battling for our lives using all available energy to keep my crypt concealed and to quell the inferno of the mansion and—"

"Well, let me give you a news update," Elder Vlad said with a hiss. "The humans think there is Mexican drug cartel activity erupting in the area, since the establishment of Buchanan Broussard burned to the ground . . . and they found machine-gun casings, dead bodies, and drugs littering the property. Then, earlier this afternoon, smoke was seen billowing from Dugan's Bed & Breakfast and Finnegan's Wake, and there was an actual police shoot-out followed by an unsuccessful attempt to apprehend what the humans believe to be a vanload of drug terrorists that firebombed Ethan's Fair Lady. However, like at the other establishments, the fire was immediately brought under control with minimal damage."

The baron said nothing as the ancient Vampire drew a wheezing breath and continued his energy-sapping rant from his hidden crypt three parishes away.

"All of that would have been fine, except that there was a fire at your estate that left human bodies, shell casings, rocket-propelled grenade blasts, et cetera, et cetera, et cetera. That cannot be dark-glamoured away by your Unseelie friends. *That* cannot be removed from the collective consciousness of the entire American public. *That* is already in news archives!" the elderly Vampire shouted.

Elder Vlad didn't allow Baron Montague to draw a breath to interject. His voice became punctuated by warning hisses as his rage spun out of control.

"*That* is a highly visible debacle that literally leads to your front door, which means it has led to our front door! It could possibly open us up to human investigation into all establishments, like our casinos, bars, restaurants, *waste management contracts,* oil companies, our military mercenary and security firms abroad, everything that is linked to you—which is *way* too much at risk. Do you realize that if the stupid humans believe that this is all a part of Mexican drug cartels moving into the southern region, crossing the border, with their economy in shambles and an aggressive new administration, they could nationalize a significant part of what we own? The war started at Buchanan Broussard's wolf house—his lineage is from Texas—that's been all over the news, including the mysterious disappearance of him and his daughter only months ago. The humans have made a leap in thinking—and it all circles back to us!"

"I will fix this, sir . . . You have my word."

Elder Vlad drew a shaky breath. "You might want to ensure that you do before the trial."

"Yes, Your Eminence." Baron Montague sat up and then stood. "They must have clear evidence that we were involved, and they don't."

He bent and held his head as Elder Vlad sent a black

lightning strike through his mind. Tears of black blood leaked out of his eyes as the ancient, stronger entity exploded in a fit of rage.

"You do not know how you could be implicated, simply by *monitoring* the situation, as you say. How many times do you have to see with your own eyes, Sasha Trudeau was human, and US-military trained! She wouldn't allow the wolves to simply rip your liaison to shreds and to decapitate him to reverse his spells. They *captured* him in iron and rowan bondage! They are not so foolish as to go to war directly with Cerridwen!"

"Queen Cerridwen Blatand of Hecate is coming to trial *here*?"

"If this doesn't go right," Elder Vlad said very quietly, "I will rip your heart out myself with my own bare hands when I see you. As I said earlier, fix this."

"What do you mean *they went dark*?" General Westford shouted into the cell phone. His short, blond hair was spiked with nervous sweat and his ruddy face had bloomed to near crimson as his voice exploded into the receiver. "I want to know what the hell is going on in New Orleans, Doctor. Has Sasha Trudeau flipped near her twenty-fifth birthday like the others did? Is the virus in her system under control or what? Is she stable? Do we need to send a Special Forces squad to put her down?"

"No, she's fine and doing what she's been trained to do in Delta Force, Special Ops Command. She's in full control of all her faculties and is advancing the cause of the PCU."

"But how can that be when there are bodies all over creation?" the general shouted. "This is supposed to be a covert operation. I'm getting calls from the Joint Chiefs; everybody needs answers and I haven't got any to give them!"

"The entire reason PCU came back into this region after having left it not so long ago is that Captain Trudeau rightfully suspected a resurgence of evil-entity activity that could threaten the human population here." Xavier Holland dragged his fingers through his gray hair, speaking in deferential tones while pacing away from the séance still in progress. "She went undercover with her known sources, and at present, I don't know exactly where she and her team—"

"Find her! How dark could they be if a state trooper said what sounds like two of her men came through a roadblock carrying what our boys said were biohazards! Holland, this bullshit came right to my door! The Paranormal Containment Unit is supposed to do just that—*contain the threat,* not have it spill out into the city streets of New Orleans in broad daylight in car chases and gunfights! This isn't the Wild Wild West."

"Sir, I assure you that—"

"State police called for us to send in backup, if we could, because they think we're about to go to war with the Mexican drug cartel on our borders. They're about to contact the White House, do you read me?" General Westford let out a hard breath. "Local law enforcement said one of our USMC guys told them that he was under my authority to transport biohazardous weaponry through the region on some secret mission. After the roof of the bar in the French Quarter blew up and a plantation in the high-rent district burned, they remembered that and called me, Holland! They wanted to be sure no viral threat was released in the explosions and are asking if they need to evacuate the area!"

Xavier Holland cringed, closed his eyes, and rubbed his temples. "Sir, we will fix this."

"You'd better, because NOPD lost six good men in a firefight in the bayou—and from the way it sounds from what was left of them, it could have only been Werewolves involved! Tell me it wasn't Werewolves and we can end this call right now."

"Sir, we will have more intel and a full report when Captain Trudeau returns, but I hesitate to speculate—"

"Stop yanking my chain, Holland! Was it Werewolves or not that savaged those poor boys in the bayou?"

"We're pretty sure it was that phylum of supernatural that attacked those innocent officers, which is why Captain Trudeau went to extreme measures to apprehend the perpetrators of—"

"Jesus H. Christ in heaven, man, I've got local authorities with credible witnesses saying that they saw men jump off a fucking three-story building to land in the street like ninjas—and they were with a woman. A gray-eyed woman who sounded too suspiciously close to Captain Sasha Trudeau. Then they vanished. How is that going dark? That travesty happened in broad daylight, Holland! People on public transportation saw it, a news chopper got part of it! Later they recovered *a military vehicle* at the burned-out Montague mansion! Rocket-propelled grenades, military-issue C-4, M-16 rounds. I want answers!"

"The mansion was owned by a leading Vampire Cartel suspect, sir."

Dead silence met Doc Holland's response.

"What am I gonna tell the new president when he calls?" the general said, his voice now weary and subdued. Fear made his question sound like more of a plea than a direct demand for answers. It was clear that the man was struggling for comprehension as his world turned upside down. "The Vampires have *a cartel*? I thought it was just one or two . . . like . . . like Dracula or something. I thought that was who was working with a couple of infected Werewolves . . ."

"No, sir, there are covens of Vampires . . . nests all over the world, just like there are federations of Werewolf clans—some friendly, some hostile. That's what our captain went in to root out."

"But PCU is only a handful of soldiers and some special

subject matter experts." The general's voice had lost all its bluster and sounded like that of a bewildered child.

"Yes, sir," Doc said, looking back at Clarissa, concerned about her worsening condition. "This is why we're hamstrung."

"We need more resources," the general said quietly. "This wasn't a few isolated incidents. With our small staff, how long will we be able to keep this from the general population? I need a full line item in the budget, to hell with bank bailouts. This is a cabinet-level conversation . . . We might need a new cabinet-level post, for all I know. I might really have to take this to our commander-in-chief after all, Xavier."

"True, sir. But, our new president is progressive and forward thinking; he understands new technology . . . science . . . research . . . We might have to just tell him the truth and hope he's willing to more than just diplomatically reach across the aisle, but to embrace the new supernatural reality, too."

"When Trudeau returns, I want a meeting, stat."

The call abruptly disconnected in Doc's ear—that issue he'd have to deal with later. Hunter fell through a shadow with Bear Shadow and Crow Shadow holding him up. Sasha was right behind them with Silver Hawk bringing up the rear. The older man swept his clothes off the floor and began dressing as though it were the most natural thing in the world. Right now Silver Hawk seemed fully recovered, but Clarissa clearly wasn't. And Hunter was semiconscious.

"That man needs blood," Sasha said between bursts of breath, pointing to Hunter as they laid him on the table. "It's a gunshot wound and overexertion—I can heal him, but Clarissa doesn't look good. Bear and Crow are all right. Woods and Fisher took the POW in with Shogun and his men; Seelie prison until trial later tonight."

"Let me work with her," Silver Hawk said, going to

Clarissa to stroke her hair. "The young one has been under psychic attack."

"How are her vitals?" Doc asked Bradley.

Bradley shook his head. "Silver Hawk came out of the trance and went into the shadows whole; she didn't come out at all. She's still under deep and her breathing isn't right."

"Get her on a table," Doc said, as he grabbed a blood pressure cuff off the desk and yanked a stethoscope out of the drawer.

Sasha was at Hunter's side, but her focus was divided. "Can we get Dr. Williams in here to assist with a transfusion, maybe get a saline drip to get some more fluids back into Hunter's body?"

Winters and Bradley lifted Clarissa's limp body and Silver Hawk came over to place his hands on either side of her head. As soon as she was situated, Winters was on the phone getting a support team of medical personnel in that had worked with PCU during battle conditions before, including Dr. Williams.

"In the shadow lands," Silver Hawk said quietly, causing everyone to look at him, "there is a thin veil between that safe passage and demon doors. This is why alpha warriors wear the protective amulets that always guide them into the right passageways within the shadows, lest they accidentally fall through the wrong portal into ultimate darkness. The caster of the dark magick ripped the veil, which should never be, and got through to the shadow lands. I saw pure evil in us attacking our men."

Bradley stroked Clarissa's hair away from her clammy forehead. "They had to have used spells from the *Pseudomonarchia Daemonum* to call demons to attach to the sigils they'd already attached to everyone's etheric bodies . . . Madame Cottrell said there was a backlash. I should have known . . ."

"We were prepared for the backlash," Hunter murmured

drowsily. "Sylphs . . . air elementals, attacked us at the attic sites. We were ready enough."

"Lie back and rest," Sasha said, slowly removing the duct tape from his arm. "That little bastard, Kiagehul, reinforced the spell when we lay siege to the baron's lair. He knew we were coming for him, so he was trying to make it near impossible for us to break our bondage. You couldn't have known about that, Bradley. It was all going down in real time."

"Regardless . . . now she's caught in a dark consciousness trap," Bradley said, his voice strained.

Doc listened to her heart, checked her vitals, and removed the blood pressure cuff. "Her blood pressure is rising at the same time as her pulse is erratic."

Bradley kissed her forehead. "My concern is that she could have a heart attack or a stroke . . . or that if her mind has been attacked, an embolism could be forming on her brain." He looked up at Silver Hawk and Doc, his eyes pleading. "When demons attack the human physical body, they manifest illnesses that mask what it really is. Help her . . . please."

"My Shadow Wolf healing is for natural injuries—like the one Hunter has sustained. The physical body is relatively easy to fix, because it dwells in the realm of the natural and the body will fight to help you help it. But a spiritual injury . . ." he said, allowing his words to trail off with a weary sigh. "This requires prayer and the intervention of the Great Spirit. I can only try."

"Then please try," Bradley said, his voice quavering.

"I think we need to move her to a room, get her connected to monitors while Silver Hawk works," Doc said as Dr. Williams entered the room with support personnel. "Silver Hawk and I will stay with her, and if her physical levels drop, we can do everything in our combined power to keep her heart beating and her breathing . . . especially if vital organs begin to suffer."

"That young woman sounds like she needs a CAT scan

and an MRI, then to be located in ICU," Dr. Williams said, looking around, confused.

"She does, but your staff is going to have to allow the shaman to be with her at all times, as well as me and her teammate, Bradley." Doc exchanged a look with Dr. Williams that said, remember—we've been through something like this before at Tulane together.

Dr. Williams nodded. "What about this patient?" he said, referring to Hunter and then frowning. "Tell me that's not duct tape over a gunshot wound!"

"Okay, so I won't tell you that," Hunter said, sounding worn out. "But that's all they had at the auto body shop's front counter at the time."

"A bed, a drip, a transfusion from me, a steak, and a few hours of shut-eye, and this man is good," Sasha said calmly. "But if you can spare a private room, that may reduce the strain on your PR Department."

Dr. Williams walked to the door. "Consider it done in the name of homeland security for active military personnel . . . But anything beyond that, I don't wanna know."

CHAPTER 23

"I'm sorry about Clarissa," Hunter said, looking across to Sasha's bed from his. A double IV drip hung above his; one ruby-hued and filled with Sasha's blood, the other clear, to restore potassium and other vital fluids and minerals he'd lost.

"Yeah, me, too," she said in a distant murmur. "I feel so helpless just lying here."

"Believe me," he said, locking his gaze with hers, "I know that feeling well. But the doctor said for you to just give it forty-five minutes so you don't overexert yourself and pass out—which could be very bad, depending on where that is."

"I know, I know." She looked down. "How's the arm?"

"Better after your healing."

She smiled a sad smile and tried to make a joke. "Beats duct tape, I guess."

There was nothing to say to her that would change the facts. He watched Sasha slip back into her own morose thoughts, helpless to fix the condition that had plunged her there. One of her team members was critically injured. There was no way to make that be all right. Even retribution was a hollow win, when the only thing she wanted was for that person to be okay. He understood that, had lived through crises of this type himself.

He just wished he could have done for Sasha's spirit what she'd just done to his arm, place his hands over the site of the injury . . . her heart . . . and allow the heat to transfer from his palms into that delicate organ . . . siphoning out pain, knitting back torn tissue and muscle. Closing up the hole left in it from the damage, until all that remained was a superficial scar. If he had the power to heal the mind and spirit like that, he would. But even Silver Hawk, the wisest shaman of the clan, acknowledged such limitations.

Hunter let out a long sigh that he hadn't meant to release. Sasha looked at him.

"You okay?" she asked, eyes worried.

"No," he said quietly. "I'm not, because you're not. Clarissa is a decent soul. This never should have happened to her."

"I know," Sasha said, leaning up on one elbow. "This kicks my ass that some little . . . hobgoblin thing could cause so much pain to so many people." She swung her legs over the side of the bed and hugged herself. "Bradley will just positively fold if something happens to her . . . and the rest of us . . ."

"Sasha . . . what if . . ." Hunter's voice trailed off as he stared out toward the window, sitting up.

"Talk to me." Sasha came and sat on the edge of his bed.

"There are three of us—three strong alphas. Me, you, Silver Hawk. Just like the attics required three sets of bad symbols to be placed in order to affect an entire fortress, what if three powerful prayers said in the shadow lands, where the terror for Clarissa became real, were said in a shaman's white-light circle of truth?"

Sasha was on her feet. He reached to yank out his IVs and she held his arm. "Bring it with you; we need you strong."

"The Vampires have told you what?" Queen Blatand shouted, swishing her ice-blue satin gown out of her way as she paced from her ornate ice throne to her visioning table.

Small icicles chimed against the diamonds and pearls that crusted her train, and her clear, ice stiletto heels made a harsh sound against the opaque ice floor. Her servants bowed obsequiously, fearing the queen's notable wrath. Her fingertips were pale blue beneath her alabaster skin, threatening an icy jolt at any moment. She set the palest of blue eyes on the clear, lake-like surface of the table and spread her fingertips against it, summoning quick, spider-vein cracks to form as the table misted over. When she wiped her hand across it, the table instantly cleared so that she could begin to see events unfolding.

Angry but unsure of the politics, she smoothed a chilly palm over the back of her platinum French twist and pursed her thin blue lips.

"They are calling for a trial," Elder Futhark said. "Kiagehul is up on capital charges, which is an affront to the entire Unseelie nation."

"They have not summarily executed him, as is their right if your cousin committed the first act of war against the Seelie king. They seem to be employing due process. Therefore, as much as I despise Rodney, law is law, and I see no reason to expend precious resources on what appears to be a very personal matter of magickal transgression."

"He is in bondage, my queen," Enoksen implored. "Held in Sir Rodney's dungeon with iron and rowan."

"That does seem to be cruel and unusual punishment," she said carefully, appraising her top two advisors. "But what have the Vampires to do with all this?" She waved her hand about, causing it to briefly snow in the chamber.

Gremlins and Goblins hid behind the huge icy stalactites and stalagmites hanging from the endless vaulted ceiling and thrusting up through the chamber's permafrost floor. Burly digger Gnomes stayed hidden in the shadows and squinted against the northern lights that dappled the upper air, also waiting on the queen's advisors' response.

"You are slow to answer," she said in a threatening tone, "which gives me pause." She smiled a wicked grin. "Many an avalanche has been caused by the untimely drop of a misplaced pebble."

"Kiagehul was retained by them to keep them updated on their enemy's movements, and the Vampires were wrongfully attacked," Elder Futhark said quietly, and then glanced at Enoksen.

"For personal gain or for the gain of my Unseelie empire was he so employed?" she asked coolly, her breath coming out as a white mist. She narrowed her pale blue gaze.

"I'm sure he was doing so to annex power to the Unseelie Court," Elder Futhark said quickly.

"How so?" she asked in a sudden, stormy burst, waving her arms and causing swirls of mini snow squalls to spin around the room.

"The Seelie have banded together with the Werewolf and Shadow Wolf Federations," Enoksen said, bowing. "The trilateral alliance is an enemy of the Vampires, and also a threat to the Unseelie . . . as they guard and honor humans."

Queen Blatand became very still, as though suddenly flash frozen. Then, without warning, she became animated again. "That would make Rodney extremely formidable."

"Yes, my queen," Elder Futhark added quickly. "Hence, when our cousin saw a way to ally with the Vampire Cartel by simply sharing information, finally having something that they might find of value . . . something that he could negotiate with, he seized upon the opportunity. The only small bit of remuneration he asked was for the rightful return of his Seelie-nationalized property . . . the old Dugan Bed & Breakfast and Finnegan's Wake, the drinking establishment."

"Seems a fair price for such intense labor," she said, beginning to walk while thinking out loud. She tapped a cold, blue finger to her lips. "Such an alliance with the undead ones could have far-reaching value . . . whereas Sir Rodney's newfound friendships could be catastrophic to our quality of life."

"Yes, yes, my queen. This is why we must go to the UCE trial to urge that Kiagehul be remanded to our custody—it is far less harsh to be banished from the Americas, versus being beheaded."

"So, after all these years of straddling the fence and working for Sir Rodney, the prodigal son wanted to return home to me. Interesting. I wonder what gifts he'd meant to bring?" She nodded as she strode back to her elaborate, ice-sculpture throne and sat. "I do need to stay more connected with the goings-on at the UCE; I just hate to travel to New Orleans in the summer."

"We don't know if this will work," Sasha said quietly, holding Silver Hawk's and Hunter's hands as they stood around Clarissa's bed. "But if we can go into the shadow lands as one, we might have a chance."

"This man still has an IV attached to his arm," Dr. Williams said, glancing at Doc for support.

"We put it on a walking pole," Hunter said. "It's either that or it comes out. Time is essential—we need to go in and reinforce her before the sun sets."

"Anything that you can do," Bradley said, clasping Clarissa's hand. He gave Sasha a pleading look and then handed her a small, white, linen charm bag on a long, white satin cord. "It's got an iron slug in there, a copper penny, rowan, bay leaf, brick dust, a four-leaf clover, St. John's wort, a St. Anthony medal, myrrh, frankincense, sea salt . . ." he said as his voice cracked and tears rolled down his cheeks. "With a lock of her hair and . . . and . . ."

"You keep this on her, Bradley," Sasha said, slipping her hands out of Hunter's and Silver Hawk's. "We have the amber and silver amulets from the clan." Sasha gently looped the charm bag over Clarissa's head and kissed her forehead. "You put so much love into that charm, Bradley, that it belongs right over her heart."

Silver Hawk nodded and the confirmation from the older shaman seemed to help Bradley's confidence. Bradley wiped his face with the back of one sleeve, never letting go of Clarissa's hand.

"The power of prayer always triumphs over the power of evil spells," Silver Hawk said, landing a time-weathered, supportive hand on Bradley's shoulder. "You continue to pray with all your might . . . you, Doc, and Winters, a strong pack bond of three—while we go into the darkness to bring her soul back to wholeness."

"We have to go," Hunter said, looking at the waning sun.

Sasha and Silver Hawk nodded, stepping into the nearest shadow with him.

"Sir Rodney! Sir Rodney! Lower the drawbridge!" A breathless Fae archer held his prancing chestnut Unicorn tightly as the beast reared and the drawbridge came down with a thud.

"A cold front just blew in to New Orleans," the guard said, not waiting for the normal protocols. "We must send reinforcements to the area to brace for a possible onslaught! We have Seelie civilians . . . humans . . . there could even be ice storms in June—we don't know what all could occur, but our people must be evacuated immediately."

Woods and Fisher ran up to the front gate with Shogun and his men.

"Just like we helped you get the prisoner down to the dungeon, we'll help you get him to UCE trial and will assist with the evac efforts," Woods said, staring at Sir Rodney. "We've got your back out there in the streets of New Orleans, too. Sasha wouldn't have it any other way. Plus, if humans are involved, we're involved."

"We owe you," Shogun said. "This battle is not yours to fight alone."

A nod of acceptance was all that was needed. Sir Rodney

turned to his guards and prepared them for war. "Full garrison alert," Sir Rodney shouted. "I want all civilian Seelie behind these walls before sundown. As we've expected, there will be vicious Vampire retaliation for the accidental lair destruction, if they've gone so far as to call me ex-wife."

Hunter and Sasha sat quietly inside the full-moon circle that Silver Hawk had drawn on the ground of the shadow lands, listening to the low, resonating prayer chants of their clan shaman. The insistent wail of his voice and the rhythmic thud of the finger drum he used soon merged with their heartbeats and breaths until it was all one and the same. Then his sad, native chant ceased and he closed his eyes.

"We ask permission to speak with Clarissa's higher spirit," Silver Hawk murmured. "Let her come into the healing circle that is guarded by those of the light."

Sasha fought not to gasp as Clarissa's battered soul drifted into the center of the circle. Her eyes had been put out and her ears were bleeding. It seemed like her spirit was struggling to breathe as she scrabbled at her throat. But there was no way Sasha could stop herself from reacting in horror as Clarissa opened her mouth and her tongue was missing.

"Oh, baby . . ." Sasha said, covering her mouth and rocking. She finally allowed her hands to fall away. "'Rissa, who did this to you?" she whispered.

The spirit slowly lowered herself to the ground, and scratched out the letter *K* into the dirt.

"It was a specific hit," Hunter said toward his grandfather.

Silver Hawk nodded. "Kiagehul went after the weakest target . . . She was psychically open in here; the others were not, save me, but he could not attack around my Shadow Wolf's silver aura. But the human woman was vulnerable . . . and he knew that that would hurt us all."

"He was going after Bradley," Sasha said through her

teeth and almost went to Clarissa when her body started thrashing about in unnatural ways on the ground.

Sasha turned away as Silver Hawk and Hunter gripped her hands tightly. Clarissa's head spun upside down as her limbs cracked backward, making her twist into a human, crab-walking monstrosity that peered at them through vacant, black holes.

"Yes," Silver Hawk said in a tight voice, controlling his rage. "The backlash was sent against the one who figured out how to break the evil spell—that would have been Bradley . . . and the best way to shatter him would be to sacrifice her."

"Seal her in the protective circle, Grandfather," Hunter said with a snarl. "I know one way to break this spell is to behead the little bastard that cast it."

"We have laid down light-prayer sealants to keep her from being drawn into demon doors or being lost as a wraith in the shadow lands," Silver Hawk reported in a sad tone. "We called for the ancient spirit healers of all time and higher realms to come into the circle to stand with her and to heal her of this nightmare condition."

"We surrounded the circle with brick dust, sea salt, holy water, you name it," Sasha said, touching Bradley's arm. "This way nothing else can attack her, and it buys us a little time to figure out how we can undo this really bad thing that's happened to her."

"Not much time, though, I'm afraid," Doc said, glancing around the group. "Her MRI and her CAT scan came back with lesions forming in her brain, her eyes, her throat, and her lungs. There's a black mass also forming around her heart . . . It's like hematomas and embolisms are just ripping this girl apart from the inside." Doc let out a long breath of anguish. "The closer it gets to sunset, the worse her vitals become . . . We may have to move her onto a respirator soon and even begin dialysis. Her toxin levels are off the charts and her kidneys aren't doing their job."

Bradley held his head in his hands as Winters hugged himself and rocked in a chair across the room. Bear Shadow and Crow Shadow just hung their heads, thoroughly dejected.

"I should have never, ever, ever have suggested that she go into that level of darkness . . . I intellectually understood this stuff . . . but never had direct combat contact with it. I was always your researcher—the man with his stupid nose in dusty books. I put her on the front line, let the one person who truly believed in me down," Bradley said, looking up at everyone with bloodshot eyes. "I promised to keep her safe, and I didn't."

"You did everything you could," Sasha said, encircling Bradley with her arms and hugging him hard from behind. "You saved an entire team and the Seelie Fae nation . . . Now let us go to the UCE and see what help we can get for her, all right?" She walked around Bradley and held on to his upper arms, squatting down to face him. "We are not going to just roll over and allow her to die. I promise you, that is not the way of the wolf."

"No, it definitely is not," Hunter said, landing a strong hand on Bradley's shoulder. "We will bring your mate back to wholeness." His open, wolf gaze held no guile as the two men stared at each other. "I saw my Sasha, my grandfather, and my men all demon corrupted . . . I know the pain of witnessing such a tragedy. You have given me my family back . . . I will fight to the death to restore yours."

A nurse came through the door and hailed Doc, making everyone look toward her. "Sir, there's a Lieutenant Woods on the phone who says it's an emergency and that he needs to speak to a Captain Trudeau."

Doc headed to the door with Sasha and Hunter. "My cell was off in the ICU . . . pray to God nothing else terrible has happened. The general already wants a meeting with the White House, specifically the president."

Sasha gave Doc a look but didn't comment. She couldn't even begin to process that issue right now.

"Bear, Crow, you stay with Silver Hawk to guard the patient. Three strong Shadows . . . Doc will be here with a man who knows the dark arts and one who is adept in human technology." Hunter followed Sasha out of the door, his instincts twitching as they dashed down the hall to Dr. Williams's office.

By the time Sasha got to the telephone, she was out of breath. "Yo, Woods, talk to me."

"Major evac going down," Woods said. "Unseelie Fae spotted in the area; Vampires are pissed—as we knew they would be. We've got to get a prisoner to court under hostile circumstances, but also have to get Seelie civvies behind garrison walls before sundown. We're in position down in the French Quarter as we speak."

"Roger that," Sasha said, circling the desk as she spoke. "Have any humans been attacked since that last attempt on Winters?"

"That's a negative, Captain."

"All right, hold your position. We'll meet you down there. But that's a tightrope walk in that area, because the blood clubs share turf and will be opening up within the hour."

"Affirmative. That's why we're moving like greased lightning, Cap. We're at Aurelia's Ale Alley down on Bourbon; it's an underground little Fae pub, and that's where we've been able to get the word out. Most of these folks already know the way to Sir Rodney's camp and are gone, but for the slower-moving ones or the seriously frightened, we need to give them an escort."

"Are Sir Rodney's troops in the area already?" Sasha rubbed the nape of her neck, her eyes on Hunter and Doc.

"Affirmative."

CHAPTER 24

It was great to be able to shadow jump again and get where she needed to go without delay or discovery. She held the returned amulet in her fist and said a quiet prayer of thanks as she jogged alongside Hunter and emerged in the pub. Nervous Fae archers were milling about. Woods and Fisher stood the moment they saw her.

"Damn, you guys are a sight for sore eyes," she said, just having killed their demon spirits with rapid machine-gun fire.

"Missed you, too, Cap," Woods said in a confused but good-natured tone. "How's everybody back at Tulane?"

Hunter shook his head as Fisher stepped closer.

"What happened?" Fisher glanced around their small group.

"Clarissa is in critical condition," she said in a tight voice. "I need to talk to Sir Rodney's advisors to see how to break the dark spell."

"Son of a bitch," Fisher said, spitting out the wad of gum he'd been chewing. "I knew we should have smoked that little weasel the moment we saw him—right between the eyes."

Hunter nodded as Sasha rubbed Fisher's shoulder. "Have you seen Shogun? It's getting dark; there's trouble brewing . . . The hair is standing up on my neck."

"He's cool. He's on patrol outside with his men," Woods said. "He's—"

A huge crash shattered the plate-glass window, as a body fell through it. Everyone stopped, ducked, and took cover as patrons screamed and ran. Tables overturned, and patrons bailed over the bar. Wolf howls rent the air. Sasha and Hunter were a blur.

The body was human; she could smell the blood as she passed it. Sulfur hung thick in the air, but oddly it wasn't a typical Vampire signature. Whatever it was had used a human as bait, trying to draw the wolves out since they would never be able to find them behind Sir Rodney's fortress walls. Cowards! This would only add to the heat from the NOPD.

Sirens immediately sounded; the local law enforcement agencies were on high alert. Sasha ran like the wind, her hair lifting off her shoulders as she and Hunter closed in on the scent. Fae archers were on lampposts and telephone wires, fleet-footed agility keeping them aloft as they went after their invisible prey.

Hunter ducked out of the way of a fireball that hit a tavern and set it ablaze. In an instant he was inside the inferno, ushering out humans that would have been trapped. Then a Fae archer turned to put out the fire and paid for the service to mankind with his life. A blue ice bolt came out of nowhere and speared the gallant archer in the chest.

Seelie archers yelled a war cry; arrows were cast down; wands came out; the battle had clearly changed to Fae against Fae.

Innocent people were in harm's way; Sasha and Hunter turned from the battle, doubling back to help civilians out of burning cars and collapsing buildings. Collateral damage was mounting and there was seemingly no way to stop it.

White lightning and colorful sparks streaked the sky, hit rooftops like fireworks, and turned eaves into tinder. New Orleans was burning. Sheets of ice covered rooftops, making it difficult for Seelie Fae archers to stay aloft. But they zapped the roofs dry, put out flames, and went in hot pursuit of the aggressors.

On the ground, wolves become a single pack, following the undead scent. A blue-lipped Fae crashed to the ground right at Sasha's feet, stopping traffic as he clutched his narrow chest, holding on to an arrow lodged in it. But something invisible and deadly whirred past her that had an animal scent that she'd never encountered.

Human pedestrians gaped and screamed; one woman got blown off the corner by a swirling gust of snow as Unseelie fighters raged past her. Hail came down like bullets, crashing through windows, damaging roofs, and bringing downtown traffic to a complete standstill.

Police vehicles couldn't get through. SWAT choppers beat overhead. Three Unseelie warriors materialized in the middle of the street; Shogun leaped, becoming wolf before the viewing public to collide midair and rip out a throat.

Humans shrieked, not knowing which way to run first. Cars drove into buildings, disoriented drivers slammed into other motorists. A blue Gnome dropped down behind Sasha and she spun, kicked him in the face, and sent him into Hunter's powerful grip.

Machine-gun reports echoed in the distance. Aurelia's had to be under siege, and that meant her men were, along with all others in the establishment. Her men would be trapped. Police helicopters took stationary positions so that the NOPD could take aim at the only thing they could, wolves attacking what they clearly thought were people on the ground, not realizing the wolves were savaging Unseelies.

Assault rifles squeezed off rounds. Shogun and his men dodged bullets by seeking the alleys. Then suddenly the choppers' blades ceased whirling; ice covered them, the outer skin of the choppers froze over, and men plummeted to the ground.

The results were horrific; the explosion catastrophic.

They had to get the fight out of the city limits. Law enforcement vehicles were everywhere and they were sitting ducks.

"Let Kiagehul go!" a female Unseelie screeched as she materialized for a second and pointed at Sasha. "Your humans die if he dies. Fair exchange is no robbery!"

Sasha and Hunter looked at each other. Vamps were obviously in this now, after the lair bust earlier in the day.

"The blood clubs!" Sasha shouted. Dodging traffic, she mounted a roof through a shadow and grabbed a Fae archer's arm. "They want the prisoner and are using humans as hostages. Fall back and take it to the blood clubs. That ought to get the Vampires to force the Unseelie to come to court and bring a cease-fire. Since they want to play hardball, let's do the same damned thing!"

Hunter ran ahead of the pack as Sasha doubled back for her men.

"Listen to me, Woods," she said, ducking down behind a Dumpster in back of the building. "I want you and Fisher out of this hot zone now!"

"But—"

"No buts," she said, eyeing him and Fisher hard. "You've done your part. I want you to guard 'Rissa and Doc. This is gonna get uglier before it gets better, and you hear all those sirens out there? NOPD and all types of authorities are gonna be crawling all over this place . . . Westford already got a call from state police."

"Oh, shit," Woods said, leaning back against the building.

"Yeah, oh, shit. That's why I want you guys to have plausible deniability, if this doesn't end up right."

"But we're not big on leaving your ass out in a firestorm, Cap," Fisher said.

"I love you guys, too—but right now, cover your asses and make sure the rest of the team at Tulane doesn't come under attack. Use the iron shells and the rowan as well as silver. Vamps and Unseelie could be working as a unit . . . plus there's something else out there that I can't see."

She didn't have time to argue with them, it was a direct order. Fall back. "Where's the grenade launcher?"

Fisher and Woods gave her wide smiles.

"In the van we came in, across the street," Fisher said, seeming much improved.

Sasha was in and out. The Dumpsters cast a shadow; there was nothing but shadows inside the van. Full metal jacket—she was locked and loaded. So the Vampires wanted to allow their Unseelie buddies to use innocent humans as hostages, huh? She came out of the darkness in front of the baron's Blood Oasis, aimed, and fired.

"Kill another innocent on my watch and it's your ass! I, Sasha Trudeau, declare war!"

She slid into another shadow, but not before she saw Shogun in her peripheral vision. He and his men were decimating fleeing Vampires that came out of the inferno like rats jumping off a sinking ship.

Insanity had her in its grip; she walked in the front door of the baron's casino, a semiautomatic in each hand, hit anything with fangs point-blank, and was out. Wolves came in right behind her, savaging anything that dared to move.

Overturning crypts, she sent a message that the next time it would be daylight. She, Hunter, and Shogun came together at the edge of the swamp with Fae archers. Sir Rodney's men had captured eight Unseelie and one Vampire.

"Dead or alive?" Sir Rodney asked his men.

"Dead," his captain of the guards said, taking Sasha's gun out of her hand and pulling the trigger hard twice toward the Vampire prisoner's head. His men let go as embers exploded. "In the morning, we torch all their graves."

"Truce!" a disembodied voice called out. "This is a matter for the courts to decide!"

"Good, you bloody bastards!" Sir Rodney shouted. "Court is in less than an hour!"

* * *

This was a very different session than she'd attended before. This time there were no neutral parties. Order of the Dragon security forces were clearly vexed with the Vampires and Unseelie; Fae archers had hair-trigger tempers, having just lost a man. Wolves were united, except for the very small minority faction that still had allegiances to the Buchanan clan. Mythics and Flame of the Phoenix members were so traumatized by the carnage that even they wanted blood. Then there were the Vampires—who were flanked by the Unseelie Fae.

Yeah, this time was wild. Sasha looked around at the tense groups waiting for the UCE's pillared hall to rise out of the swamp and for the emergency session to be called to order. Everything was out of control. She had no way to know how many innocent human and Fae civilians had been hurt or killed as collateral damage. If something went wrong here, there was no neutral party to intervene and to restore order. It was as though all of the superpowers in the region had their fingers on the nuclear buttons, and everyone was so riled up that they really didn't give a damn if they left a smoking black hole—even if they'd go up with it. The entire issue of principle seemed to be the core of the debate. Screw the greater good, the helpless, and the meek. The entities coming into this hall wanted a pound of flesh.

The blind, old crone that always presided over the trials came out with her bewitched ledger and pen, which looked more like a wand than a writing instrument. She set the book of records in the air aloft and flung the pen at it so that the pen hovered above the book.

"There is no stenographer, save the book. It records only that which is truth. The normal recorder is too traumatized to attend . . . She is of the Mer—a Siren crier of the deep—and even she will not be party to this travesty."

The crone's voice sounded like fingernails on a blackboard and all the wolves in attendance cringed until she was done speaking. She pointed to the gavel and it immediately stood on its handle and spun around, wildly shrieking.

"All rise . . . Court is in session! The book shall be the judge, the record cannot be altered!"

The large, dusty tome that appeared as though it were covered with ancient black serpent skin creaked open with a thud in the air, flipped several of its moldy pages to a clean page, and then waited as the pen poised itself above it.

"We have a very serious complaint," the crone murmured. "A capital offense that could and has caused war to break out even in front of humans." She turned toward the back of the court and pointed with a gnarled, arthritic finger. "Bring in the prisoner!"

Wolves howled and Shogun and his men escorted the slight figure down the aisle bound in iron and reeking of rowan. Fae drew back and covered their noses and mouths with cloths and forest leaves, but their eyes hardened and their jeers rang out as a sickly-looking Kiagehul passed their grandstands. A growl crawled up Sasha's and Hunter's throats; this was the man who had nearly wiped out their entire family. Vampires curled their lips, showing fangs, insulted by the open hostility exhibited by the Seelie in court.

But the aisle suddenly became ice slicked as a frigid blast dropped the temperature by forty degrees and caused frost to cover the boxes and chairs. Sir Rodney turned from where he sat with Sasha and Hunter in the front box on the right and all eyes followed his as Queen Blatand of Hecate strode down the aisle.

This new threat absorbed Sasha's complete focus for a moment. The queen had the most fragile features she had ever seen. If she weren't so evil, one might have called her beautiful. She had large, amazingly clear, pale blue eyes. Her eyebrows were a perfect arch of platinum hair that nearly matched her skin as though she were albino. Set against her huge, questioning eyes was a delicate dusting of white lashes. She had a tiny button nose and a cherub's mouth, interestingly hued a deep blue that caused such a contrast against her skin that Sasha had to stare. Her small breasts were the perfect teacup size, pushed up in an elegant, old-world, beaded gown, her entire tiny torso and wasp waist held firmly by unforgiving corset stays.

Icicle earrings sparkled in her ears; seed pearls, diamonds, and bits of blue ice crusted her ice-blue gown. In her delicate hands she carried an ice wand and a large fan made of packed snow that had a pattern of snowflakes. But it totally blew Sasha's mind to see her strut down the center aisle in ice stilettos, eyes locked in hatred with Sir Rodney's.

"Clearly you did not believe that I would allow you to put a member of my court to death without the proper trial and formalities to be sure that action would be sanctioned." She gave Sir Rodney the evil eye and then promptly slid into the Vampire booth, taking the baron's arm.

"I might have known that you would be in bed with that cold-blooded Vampire bastard," Sir Rodney spat. "Ice water also runs in your veins, so I'm not a bit surprised by the alliance."

The queen fanned herself as the Vampires hissed, remaining cool. "Always hotheaded, my summer prince," she said in a deceitfully sensual tone. "It is uncomfortably warm in this swamp of a location you've exiled yourself to . . . therefore, I do not take your unchivalrous welcome as an affront. It must be the heat that has you so cross and unmannerly."

"Welcome to New Orleans, Your Majesty," the baron crooned, his eyes black with rage as he looked over at the Seelie bench. "Although this has at times devolved into what amounts to a kangaroo court, today our objective is justice for your captured national who is being held hostage—as well as for my wrongfully attacked lair and establishment."

"Held hostage?" a Fae archer shouted from the back. "The bastard killed me brother!"

"Order, order!" the gavel yelled, whacking itself on the empty judge's bench.

"My top advisors tell me that when the Seelie Fae archer died, my court member was in iron chains," the queen said coolly.

"Metaphorically speaking," Sir Rodney argued. "Your man was in custody at the time, true, but he is at the root of all of this."

The queen turned to the Vampire box, and looked at them and then the Unseelie who were seated behind them, her gaze falling on her top advisors. "Surely a man shan't be put to death for metaphors?"

Loud jeers rang out from both sides of the aisle and it took several minutes for the gavel to regain order.

"Let us have the first complaint," the crone screeched, making the pen above the pages quiver.

"We do this with blood oaths," Sir Rodney demanded.

"I object on the grounds that there is no presiding judge or neutral party, thus any testimony that is inadvertently twisted could endanger the life of the witness called," the baron sniffed. "It is *the law.*" His black gaze raked the courtroom. "Testimony is taken, then corroborated with blood seals *after* all testifying parties are safe within their respective fortified encampments or in some sort of protective custody—unless there are neutral peacekeeping forces present . . . which, if you have a look around, there are not."

"Objection sustained," the gavel called out and flailed itself against the bench with a loud whack.

"You always have an angle, don't you, Vampire. Well, tonight, one night before Midsummer—the height of our Fae power—your luck has run out!" Sir Rodney stepped forward, recounting the series of events as the pen wrote furiously. "We have evidence," he said, concluding. "The human girl who now lies injured in the human hospital—Tulane—took cell phone photos . . . and we have eyewitnesses who went to the three attics, and were attacked. Only, this time, they all lived to tell about it, so you do not have the shroud of death making the evidence impossible to fathom."

"Step forward," the crone said, curling her finger toward Sasha, Hunter, and Shogun. "Speak. One at a time."

"You saw for yourselves what has been reported in the human news," Sasha said, looking around the court. "Normally we cannot produce evidence, because magick fades or Vampire stealth cannot show up on any device that captures an image. But a fire that burns like the one captured on the news, you all know to be from Unseelie spells reacting with a backlash. Each spell had a dead man's switch in it so that it would be hard as hell to defuse without blowing yourself up . . . And that's what happened to one of my human teammates. She saved our lives, but hers is hanging in the balance. If nothing else comes out of this trial, I hope that someone with the specialty of unwinding bad magick will help us help Clarissa."

Murmurs of discontent filled the courtroom, but Hunter stepped forward and that brought curious silence.

"As Shadow Wolves," Hunter said, "we cannot lie. Lies are caught in our aura and trapped by the silver in it . . . The scent of burning sterling gives us away. So, I am no liar when I tell you what we encountered in the shadow lands . . . and how my family was barred entry to our natural right, and stripped of our gift to travel free and unfettered, by evil spells cast by the Unseelie named Kiagehul—aka Kennan MacDougall, when in Seelie Court."

"Dual identities, leading a double life," Sasha snarled from the sidelines.

The court grandstands were rapt, so quiet that only the sound of inhales and exhalations could be heard as Hunter gave a full accounting of all they'd endured. Shogun stepped up next and told the heartrending tale of brother being turned against brother, editing out some of the more personal issues. He described the firefight that took place at the Buchanan Bayou House and ended his argument with a challenge.

"Anyone that has the capacity for crystal-ball magick,

or is a seer of the past, can go in and slowly replay the events that took place that night," Shogun said, folding his arms over his chest. "My brother came in and pulled me and my men out of an ambush—one that was orchestrated by the Vampires through the agency of the one named Kiagehul! The Buchanans attacked, but Vampires and Kiagehul were behind it!"

Wolves turned toward the Vampire side of the courtroom and growled. Vampires hissed as the Fae erupted again.

"The Buchanan Werewolf clan must be exiled for siding with Vampires!" the North American alpha Werewolf leader shouted from the back.

Pandemonium broke out as stronger wolves leaped over the box rails and took the sparse remaining members of the Buchanan Broussard pack into custody. Once the snarling outlaws were secured, the commotion died down.

"We demand a full and fair trial of our own," a beta said between his teeth, but quieted when he got punched in the face by the big alpha.

"Bet on it," the alpha snarled and then returned his focus to the court proceedings at hand. "Let the lady tell the story."

"But the worst of all offenses," Sasha said, striding up to the Vampire box, staring past Elder Vlad and taking on Baron Geoff Montague in a bold eye-to-eye challenge, "were the human deaths. You brought this to the streets and outside of the supernatural community, where the beef should have stayed, you rat bastard!"

Order of the Dragon bouncers tried to gently nudge Sasha back to her side of the room, but fury had a stranglehold on her and Hunter was over the edge of the box, challenging the security guard, who backed down.

"You are dangerously close to a breach of court procedure, young lady," Elder Vlad said in a menacing tone. "State your case from *inside your box*."

"Fuck you!" Sasha shouted and pointed at the ancient Vampire.

Gasps cut through the courtroom from the Vampire box.

"Touch her, black bolt her," Hunter said in a rumble, "and there will be blood. Lots of it. Wolves can sniff out lairs and we'll open everybody's up if *anything* untoward happens to my mate."

"You all killed innocent people back there, human and Fae alike!" Sasha said, her voice trembling with rage. "That matters!"

Baron Geoff was on his feet. "You are out of order, and after the blood you let at my estate and at my establishments, *how dare* you disrespect our leadership! Since when is a human life more valuable or sacred than one of ours? We did not retaliate tonight until we had to fend off your attack at the Blood Oasis—the same as when you wrongfully breached my lair!"

"That's a lie," Sasha said, pointing at the baron with a hard snap. "There were Vampires in the conflict!"

"Anticipating a hostile affront to our peaceful way of life!" the baron spat.

"Tonight, you involved innocent people who didn't have anything to do with it," Sasha shouted. "Pedestrians, parents, who knows—people's sons and daughters who were just out to shop, or eat, or go to work, or go grab a beer, and they're dead! *That* you will pay for, no matter what! This isn't over, Baron, not by a long shot. This goes beyond what the rules are at the UCE, this is an issue of human justice!"

"Oh, to be sure this is not over, *bitch*," the baron said evenly as his gaze narrowed.

"What?" Hunter shouted, lunging, but was caught by Shogun and two of his men.

"And are we not getting away from the true point, which is always the Vampire diversionary tactic?" Sir Rodney called out. "You, Baron Geoff Montague, commissioned a member of the Unseelie Court, one Kiagehul, to report on the progress of black magick spells he cast against my castle—thereby partially financing this treason against the Seelie, which is aiding and abetting a person committing known treason, thus making you an accomplice, and therefore inadvertently declaring war on the House of Clerk and all members of the Seelie Court that fall under my protection . . . including the Wolf Federations, thus specifically declaring war with the Southeast Asian Werewolf Clan and the North American Shadow Wolf Clan . . . By harming their members, the human population, you have by extension also declared war against members of the US military!"

"Monitoring the activities of one's enemies is not the same as an attack!" the baron shouted, looking around. "I admit, we have been watching you and will continue to do so for this very reason . . . but we had no hand in the dark magick. That is provable—we have ways to draw a confession from the prisoner that are time-tested."

"I don't care what you say. On the way to court, you tried to bait us out of the protection of Forte Shannon of Inverness so that we would release the Unseelie prisoner, and you ambushed our evacuation attempts. We knew you'd try something, so we had to be sure that innocent Seelie were out of harm's way—we just didn't think you'd stoop so low as to butcher innocent humans and throw them through Aurelia's Ale Alley's front window as bait," Sasha shouted, veins of outrage standing in her neck. "Humans, Seelie, wolves, human authorities, everyone got caught in the crossfire!"

"That is a lie!" the baron shouted, walking over to the book. "Strike me, draw the blood and you will see that this time, she-wolf, you have erred and it will cost you dearly."

He produced his wrist and the pen struck it, causing thick, black blood to ooze from the slashed vein. When his testimony took, the court erupted again and the crone ran forward waving her hands, shouting over the gavel. Sasha and Hunter glanced at each other and then toward Sir Rodney and Shogun. This was not good. The baron gave Sasha a smug nod and returned to his box.

"Enough, enough—there are so many capital offenses here that we must call the accused! Bring the prisoner up," the crone yelled as the gavel banged on the bench.

"We don't have to sit for this out-of-order travesty of indignities and injustice! I demand recompense now!" Baron Montague shouted, still standing.

"Sit," Elder Vlad said evenly.

Baron Montague sat slowly and smoothed down his lapels, but it was palpable that his nerves were drawn tight by the ancient Vampire's words. He shared a look with Queen Blatand as Kiagehul was roughly brought to the front witness box by very disgruntled wolves. They shoved him into the seat and the book and pen swished closer to him to take his testimony.

"How do ye plead?" the crone screeched.

"Not guilty by reason of insanity!" Kiagehul called out.

The court erupted and, after many attempts by the frazzled gavel, the audience finally settled down.

"Speak," the crone said, and then walked away shaking her head.

"I was influenced by very strong forces," Kiagehul said, beginning to weep. "My queen, I wanted to do it for you . . . It wasn't for the money."

Sasha laughed a cold, hard laugh as she walked back to her box with Hunter. "The little bastard just threw you under the bus, Baron."

"That is an outright lie!" the baron said, standing and pointing to Kiagehul. "He came to *me* and offered me a chance to build an alliance, for a price. He wanted the lands and establishments that should have come to him under normal inheritance law—but that had been nationalized by Sir Rodney . . . Dugan's properties!" The baron regained his composure and then looked at Elder Vlad. "He then said that he would show me the extent of his capabilities in a way that would utterly shock and surprise me . . . I of course had no knowledge of how far he would go; my goal was to one day meet the queen of the Unseelie Court to see if there was some common ground. But there is a third party—again, I was simply a monitor of activities, not a direct participant!"

"She is formidable; the Vampire speaks the truth," Kiagehul called out in a shrill voice. "My queen, save me; I've been duped! She has not come for me."

"I bet the baron did business with this unnamed third party," Hunter said with a snarl.

"No . . ." Baron Montague said, smiling, his eyes glittering with rage. "You will have to make blood restitution before it is all said and done, wolf."

"Care to put some more blood on the line?" Sasha said, turning her wrist up so that the magick pen could open a vein. "Once your black blood hits the pages of your testimony this time, even money says they'll torch, Baron."

"This hypocrisy and twisting of words and intent," the baron said calmly, "is all a fraud."

Queen Blatand narrowed her gaze on the baron and then on Elder Vlad. "Am I to understand that I have been brought all the way here from Iceland to learn that my court member is an outright liar?" She tsked. "Elder Vlad . . . what do you think it will do for détente if, after this man is beheaded, I find out that his argument had merit? Might that cause an unusual, albeit strained, alliance between my court and the Seelie like days of old? If any Fae finds they've been duped by another species, we, too, are known for our unrelenting grudges . . . We do have that in common with the Vampires."

Elder Vlad stood and left the box. "I should not like to see us have a falling-out and create an unnatural power-base shift that is so thoroughly one-sided, dear queen. Balance is always the way to ensure no one group becomes unmanageable."

"Cerridwen!" Sir Rodney called out as the queen left the box to walk with Elder Vlad. "I may have been many things, made many missteps, and our views and politics may have clashed, but I have never, ever, attacked you unprovoked."

She stopped her retreat and something close to warmth filled her eyes. She cocked her pretty head to the side and wrinkled her smooth brow in disbelief. "Nor have I ever attacked you unprovoked, Rodney . . . What would make you even say such a thing? I had no hand in this."

"Those were not your warriors, then, that fought against my men in the heart of New Orleans?" Sir Rodney held her gaze as the queen shook her head no.

"There was a force out there, animal in scent," Sasha said quietly, glancing around the court. "Feral female."

"Disembodied?" the queen said, looking at Kiagehul. "That is very dark magick, my dear . . . Whomever did you get to give up her body to increase your powers? That is never allowed without my express consent, for obvious reasons."

The queen walked forward as the entire court silently watched, turned over her delicate wrist, and allowed the pen to strike her flawless skin. A slow, cool blue ooze slid from the small gash and the pen dipped itself in it and then signed the page of her entry. All waited and the book never even smoldered.

"Then how do you account for these men?" Sir Rodney said with less force in his tone.

His guards dragged in seven Unseelie fighters and she looked at them with disdain.

"Our courts are large. These men are anonymous to me. With profit from a source willing to pay mercenaries, I am sure they could have been bribed to carry out the vile acts the intemperate young she-wolf spoke of this evening." She looked at her advisors. "Or there could be those who wanted to assure the release of Kiagehul, whether it was the right thing to do or not." She returned her focus to Sir Rodney. "We should only war about things that are a matter between us, not others."

"Then, if I put them to death for treason, milady," Sir Rodney shouted, "you will not take that as an act of aggression against the Unseelie?"

"No," she said calmly. "Some things we can discuss privately. I admit that I miss our warm chats . . . when there was a slight frost to the spring air . . . We found a way to compromise at times." She looked Sir Rodney up and down and then turned away.

Sir Rodney turned toward his guards and lifted his chin. "Take them to the dungeons—in the morning there will be a firing squad."

The courtroom remained rapt as the queen put away her wand and took Elder Vlad's arm, sending a thin coating of icicles over his robes.

"But what about me?" Kiagehul shrieked, bitter tears now wetting his face.

The queen stopped walking, but did not turn to face him. "Who did you disembody, Kiagehul?"

"Lady Jung Suk," Kiagehul whimpered.

"My aunt?" Shogun shouted, leaping out of his box and menacing the prisoner. "How? Why?"

Sasha shared a look with Hunter. Now the feral scent added up.

"I met her in the icy regions," Kiagehul sobbed. "She wanted what I wanted—respect! A Snow Leopard's strength, with shape-shifting ability . . . She was old, strong, and wiser than even the Vampires."

"We smelled her at the site of both murders," Sasha said in disbelief, her gaze going to Shogun.

Hunter nodded. "And at the Bayou House . . . She was stalking you."

"The sigils on the bodies that we couldn't identify . . ." Sir Rodney said, horrified.

"Ancient Chinese calligraphy, put there by a very old sorceress," Shogun said between his teeth, almost lunging toward Kiagehul as he spat out the words.

"She carved them into those women as a disembodied

spirit . . . Heresy!" Sir Rodney looked around the court. "Do ye hear this, all of you? A man blinds me within my own castle, having access to everything personal, even my advisors, my investigator, while all the while plotting treason and committing multiple felonies!"

"I had cause!" Kiagehul shouted back. "I got rid of that meddlesome Phoenix, who'd eavesdropped on Vampire gossip; got rid of her friend, too." Wild-eyed, he looked at Baron Montague, pointing at him. "Had you not been gossiping, she would not have heard about the dark magick—so you killed her, not me! It was so easy for my Leopard sorceress to go to her, unseen, as pure spirit, and claw the foreign sigil that would make her flame right into her creamy flesh." He released a pleased sigh and then returned his attention to Sir Rodney. "Milord, you should have seen them burn. It was beautiful. Almost as beautiful as executing Ethan's bartender."

"The man is mad," Shogun said, stepping back. "I have never seen a viler creature in my life."

"Put the sick bastard out of his misery," Hunter muttered. "I don't need to hear any more."

Kiagehul blinked furiously, beginning to laugh in madness, his mind breaking under the pressure and the toxic effect of the rowan. "My Leopard taught me things of pleasure from ancient texts that I had never known . . . and had access to your father's hair—which holds your combined DNA . . . And it was so easy to pilfer those items from the rest who'd stayed in my cousin's establishment," he added, glancing at both Shogun and Hunter. "With bits of this and bits of that, it was so easy to deliver personalized spells against all of you . . . just like it was so easy to stay one step ahead of you, one step ahead of the bungling idiot, Thompson. A blinder spell, a blocker spell, so easy when lain within the same castle where you live."

Hunter and Shogun shared a look as the deadly silent court gave Kiagehul its full attention.

"My love knew your weaknesses from your sister, Lei,

before she died, Shogun. Lady Jung Suk, as you recall, was shunned by your self-righteous lineage. Don't pretend to be shocked. She told me the whole story of how, just because her own Snow Leopard father never stuck around to legitimize her lineage in the clan, leaving your grandmother temporarily disgraced until the baby could be sent back to the mountains as a stillbirth and an acceptable royal marriage could be arranged, your people acted as though Lady Jung Suk didn't exist. They called her a stillbirth, but she is very much alive. Southeast Asian Were politics are always complex, I suppose . . . but please do not act as if you are a sudden stranger to political expediency and mitigating scandals."

"We will find her and bring her to justice, too," Shogun said, his voice containing a low, threatening promise. "She was given a lineage allowance—but that was obviously not enough for the twisted and ambitious evil thing she's become."

"She, like me, was a hybrid," Kiagehul said with a satisfied smile, "a being caught between worlds, and she knew what it was to live in shunned duality—it was easy to trick Sir Rodney; he, like Shogun, is arrogant. Who would suspect Kennan MacDougall, the faithful, the overlooked, on errands to do the king's bidding? I was a step ahead of you at every turn, because, as your investigation progressed, I received full reports and knew how best to hide, and when to increase my magick to turn up the maddening heat. Even Sir Rodney's top advisors were blind to the malcontent within your own court! It was no different than Shogun's blindness, thinking he could shun his aunt, thinking there'd be no consequences, sharing nothing but the crumbs from his table with her . . . She is perfect . . ."

Kiagehul's gaze roved over the stunned courtroom before it returned to his queen's rigid back. "I, alone, would have broken Sir Rodney's court, as well as the Wolf Federations. My Lady Jung Suk would have had her body restored into whatever nubile young one she chose—perhaps

Sasha Trudeau's . . . Yes, yes, I would have accomplished that for her, once it was all complete . . . And I would have been able to support her, since I would have been wealthier than my wildest dreams—Vampires would have owed us, my queen. Had this unfortunate turn of events not occurred, I would have also had revenge on the baron for killing my family member . . . Dugan."

Rubbing his hands together with insane glee, Kiagehul turned to the Vampire box, mocking Elder Vlad. "I would have set Baron Geoff Montague up to take the fall—his arrogance also made him blind enough to discount me . . . What Vampire would think that a small Unseelie, low in the court, would craft such a plan to hang him out to dry? I was almost successful, that counts for something—I still got his lair breached, ha! The she-Shadow still firebombed his Oasis!"

Kiagehul laughed a shrill, mad laugh and stared at the shocked baron. "You think that Vampires are the only ones to carry a grudge? We, the Unseelie, are remarkably known to redress an offense!" Kiagehul wiped his oily face. "What say you, Queen? Do you see my plan, how it could have helped your empire, as well as built one for me? It was all so perfect, had the wolves not been involved. Who knew Sir Rodney, *a monarch,* would break with Fae secrecy—he is the heretic, the blasphemer of our culture, not me!"

Queen Blatand turned and blew Kiagehul a kiss that immediately formed blades of ice in the air. The second she lowered her hand, the blades took off after him like heat-seeking missiles, severing his head from his shoulders. She looked at her advisors with the coldest blue eyes Sasha had ever seen.

"Sometimes, in the interest of alliances, there are sacrifices." The queen turned to Elder Vlad and lifted her chin. "All of this jockeying for position was done without my express knowledge or consent, therefore I sacrifice the fool from my court. Outright war is costly."

"Indeed," Elder Vlad murmured, instantly sending a black lightning bolt toward a stunned Baron Montague to fry his black heart inside his chest cavity. "A new alliance, Your Majesty, requires that both parties put in equal weight. Consider the Vampire Cartel's portion . . . several pounds of worthless, resource-squandering flesh. I am glad that we are of the same accord."

"Good . . . We will hunt down this disembodied Snow Leopard together then, to clean up this unfortunate mess." The queen smiled as the Elder Vampire gave her a gentlemanly nod.

No one moved or spoke for several minutes as the new alliance was clearly forged. Sasha looked at Hunter, then Shogun, her gaze finally locking with Sir Rodney's. This wasn't over by a long shot. Sasha shivered, feeling the chill in her bones left in the icy queen's wake.

If anything, the Unseelie forging a power bloc with the Vampires—and both having lost face as well as key men—was going to mean they could all expect revenge to be served ice cold. That fact was as plain as day and written all over Sir Rodney's worried face.

"I know," Hunter murmured and squeezed her hand. "I'm bracing for winter."

Finally, the gavel came out of hiding and timidly tapped on the bench.

"Court adjourned."

Clarissa sat up with a gasp and began choking. Hospital staff immediately rushed to help Doc begin removing tubes from her throat while the rest of the team held Bradley up as he sobbed into the folds of her sheets.

"The general wants to have a meeting, ASAP," Doc said with a smile.

"Yeah, I know . . . This was really, really bad."

Sasha sprawled out in a chair in the lounge. The whole team was gathered around, except Bradley and Clarissa.

Doc had insisted on them running a battery of tests and another series of CAT scans and MRIs before she could go home; Bradley wasn't leaving her side for a minute.

But at one in the morning, Sasha was so tired that she could barely lift her head and was glad that Hunter's quiet, solid presence remained just behind her. All the Shadows were in the room; she didn't even have to open her eyes to feel them.

"But, since you're still dark," Doc said with a sigh, throwing up his hands and smiling. "And since tomorrow is your birthday, as well as the Seelie Fae ball . . . and under diplomatic circumstances, you really are supposed to take a team deep undercover to be sure all threats are secured . . ."

"Yes!" Winters whispered, and squeezed his eyes shut.

Sasha opened her eyes and glanced around at the expectant faces in the lounge. "Doc," she said in a quiet, hopeful voice. "Are you serious?"

"What's the general going to do, fire me?" Her secret father laughed and shook his head. "Then he'd have to hire me back as a supernatural consultant making ten times what I make now for the Feds . . . And, anyway, the real meeting isn't until next week."

Sasha leaned forward and hugged Doc. "What real meeting?"

"The one on Air Force One. Seems our new Commander-in-Chief is thoroughly fascinated by the concept of anything new—and they've even got a defibrillator on board for the general."

EPILOGUE

There had been a solemn memorial to bury the slain Phoenixes and a full Fae wake and service for the soldiers that had fallen, and now the Sidhe was simply taking the wakes to the next level by celebrating the lives of those lost by making the Midsummer Night's Ball an extension of it all.

This time, her suite was muted shades of forest green . . . And it had one lovely addition: Hunter. She smiled as he stood in front of the armoire on the opposite side of the room, with only a towel casually slung low around his hips, deciding.

"I've never worn a tuxedo in my life." Hunter peered into it and held out the shirt. "C'mon, Sasha . . . French cuffs?"

"You don't have to if you don't want to," she said, going over to the other armoire. "Just close the closet door, think about what you want, say it, and then reopen the door."

"I cannot get used to a bewitched suite," he said, dragging his fingers through his damp hair.

"Betcha it has some serious advantages . . . But get dressed," she said, laughing as he looked at her over his shoulder. "Later, later; it would be too tacky not to go downstairs for a few hours."

She turned back to the armoire to extract the little black dress she'd brought, and the only thing that was there was the gorgeous ensemble that had been there before. She let out a short huff of annoyance and then opened the white velvet box. But the note it contained made her smile.

This time I'm not under a dark spell and this gift is not for you, it's for my friend, Hunter. You will look ravishing and I hope he takes full advantage of you tonight. Enjoy, my darling, and thank you for giving me my castle back and not making me go to war with my ex-wife.

Your friend and comrade in arms,

Sir Rodney.

Please accept my humble gift in the spirit of the Fae alliance.

She now understood why the ice queen had melted, even if for a moment; Sir Rodney was a living doll. She took her fashion loot behind a dressing screen, laughing as she felt her hair twist up into a bun and delicate brushes dust her face. "Oh, Sir Rodney," she whispered, "you guys sure do bibbidi-bobbidi-boo the best."

"What's that, baby?" Hunter said from across the room.

"Nothing," she called out, laughing. "Have you decided what you're wearing yet?"

"No . . . Working on it. I don't do fancy affairs; you know I'm a beef and beer kind of guy, Sa . . ." Hunter's words trailed off as she stepped out from behind the screen. ". . . sha."

"You like it?" She turned around and then beamed at him. She couldn't help it, it was such a contrast with the normal her.

"You look . . . wow," he said, at an obvious loss for words. "I'll put on the tux."

"You don't have to."

"No, seriously. I'll put on the tux."

The grand ballroom made her heady as she looked around. Despite the tensions and sad losses in the Seelie Court, people seemed to have come to bury the dead through celebration. Food and drink of all kinds were so plentiful that there was simply too much to choose from. Her guys were having the time of their lives, and it warmed her heart to see Clarissa all dolled up and in Bradley's arms, dancing a waltz as though a thousand other beings weren't in the same room with them. Those two had found that magical place all on their own.

Shogun had challenged Hunter to shots, and as she watched, the brothers laughed and talked to each other, while three very beautiful she-Werewolves openly vied for Shogun's attention.

"May I fill your champagne glass, milady?" Rupert said with a humble smile.

"Thank you so much," Sasha said, allowing him to pour. "In fact, thank you for everything."

He bowed. "No, you are our guest of honor, thank you. It is nice to have the castle back and put to right with everybody's head on straight . . . Well, except for those who've committed treason, but we shan't discuss such nasty business on gorgeous Midsummer Night."

She smiled and lifted her glass to him, but his change of focus over her shoulder made her turn.

"Might I redeem my former bad behavior by asking a lady for a dance?" Sir Rodney bowed, but then stepped back a little. "Unless that would be out of line and your life mate would take issue? I would not ever want to jeopardize such a firm alliance, nor make you feel uncomfortable"

"I don't even know what you're talking about," Sasha murmured, handing Rupert her glass. "I would love to dance, and my life mate is having the time of his life."

"Good," Sir Rodney said, leading her out onto the dance floor, but holding her with a little space between their bodies. "Thank you for coming back to my castle for the ball. I thought I might have chased you off for good."

"I'm harder to scare off than that," she said, chuckling.

But as his face grew serious she began to worry.

"Thank you for wearing the dress and the shoes," Sir Rodney said quietly, moving her around the dance floor and never missing a beat. "Happy birthday."

"You really, really—"

"Ssssh . . . It's all right. The enchantment that we were all under wasn't wholly evil . . . it worked with what was always there. Hunter is a lucky man. Shogun and I are old enough and wise enough to remain friends and philosophical about some things . . . but do know that you are completely bewitching."

They danced on for a bit in silence and then he looked down as the song almost ended. "I do hope that the truth doesn't make you sad." He smiled at her and inclined his head. "I am Fae . . . Shogun is a Werewolf, the room is bedazzled—we gentlemen shall recover."

She laughed and shook her head.

"Enjoy your mate, Sasha. We all want what you two have . . . someone loyal and kind in our corner."

He let her go with a gallant bow and was off to find a pretty damsel that was available. She stood where he'd left her for a long time and then suddenly she had the urge to find Hunter.

It wasn't just a "huh, I wonder where he is" urge. It was something akin to panic that made her quicken her steps and dash across the ballroom floor. She found him joking around with Woods, Winters, and Fisher, and their newfound dates, talking about how Bear and Crow had abandoned him in the game of shots with Shogun and his men.

"Hey," Hunter said, obviously feeling no pain. "I was wondering where you were."

Sasha laughed and put her arm around his waist. "You won the bet with Shogun, I take it?"

Hunter threw his head back and howled, gaining howls and laughter from his men and all the other wolves in the ballroom. Fae gave him jaunty thumbs-up as he pulled her onto the dance floor.

"You having fun?" She stared up into his face and touched his jaw.

"The most fun I've had in a long time," he said quietly and then kissed her.

She hadn't expected it, wasn't prepared for it, but was glad that he did it.

"We're always working," he said as he broke the kiss. "After what just went down in New Orleans, who knows when we'll get to do this again . . . especially after you meet the president."

"That's why I'm glad you came . . . why we got to do this."

She snuggled in close to him, breathing in his fantastic scent, not caring that it was laced with whatever Fae shots he'd done. She didn't care if a tux was foreign to him—he looked damned good in it. Didn't care if he was a man of few words and didn't possess the eloquence of some of his rivals. He was hers and she was his.

"With all this insanity going on," he said after a moment, nuzzling her hair, "I never got to get you a birthday present. I had it made . . . but never got to go back and get it. I know that sounds lame, but you know I am no liar. Baby, I'm sorry . . . Happy birthday anyway. I'll make it up to you."

"I know you are no liar," she said, cupping his cheek and looking up into his eyes. "This, right now, you being alive and laughing and dancing the night away with me, is the best birthday present in the world."

"There were a lot of times I didn't think either one of us would make it . . . I feel like Bradley did at the hospital all the time. I just never tell you how broken I would be if you never came out of the shadows."

She brushed his mouth with the pad of her thumb and inclined her head. "There's a really big bank of shadows over there by the pillars. Wanna get out of here and really celebrate my birthday?"

A slow half smile tugged at his cheek as he spun her around and danced her into the nothingness.

Read on for an excerpt from the next book by

L. A. BANKS

NEVER CRY WEREWOLF

Coming soon from St. Martin's Paperbacks

Hunter stalked away from Sasha and punched the wall, taking out a huge chunk of plaster with his fist. “This is bullshit, Sasha—complete bullshit!”

“Yeah, tell me about it,” she said. She knew her apartment was being monitored. “Care to discuss this somewhere else?”

She opened the coat closet door and said, “After you.”

Hunter shook his head. “Ladies first.”

Sasha stepped into the shadows within, and two seconds after they’d entered the Shadow Lands, “I cannot believe it! And the pure tragedy of it all is that you told me one day this would happen,” she shouted, walking a hot path back and forth in the misty cavern. That arrogant sonofabitch colonel they replaced me with—he’s going to get an entire squad slaughtered, not to mention however many innocent civvies in the streets of New Orleans!”

Sasha whirled on Hunter and folded her arms over her chest, breathing hard. “Go ahead. Say it. You told me so. Said that I couldn’t live a double life—being a part of a Shadow Wolf pack and being a part of the human military. Just go ahead and get it out once and for all.”

“First of all, I’m not the enemy.” Hunter looked at her, his eyes blazing. “I have no interest in saying those things to you, Sasha,” he added in a low tone. “My only interest is with those who have injured you. Give me their names—starting with the colonel."

Sasha quickly realized that her mate had gone into hunt and protect mode. She held out her arms in front of her. "Whoa, whoa, whoa—I was just metaphorically talking about ripping out the guy's throat."

"And you know I don't deal in metaphors, Sasha," Hunter said in a low rumble. "Give me the bastard's name, and I guarantee you he won't ever disrespect the alpha mate of the North American Shadow Wolf Clan again."

Perverse gratification flitted through her spirit for a moment, before logic overruled it. "Thank you," she said, more calmly, now not nearly as enraged as she'd been. "But I can't let you do that."

Hunter cocked his head to the side as though he'd heard her wrong. "Let?"

Sasha rubbed the nape of her neck and then released a hard sigh. "You know what I meant." She looked up at him. "I'm not the enemy."

"To be sure," Hunter said, beginning to pace. "Nor am I about to stand by and allow your territory to be challenged! That is a matter of principle. What gives them the right to take your position?"

"You understand hierarchy and rank, Hunter," she said flatly. "That part is the same in both the wolf world and in the human military world." Her true statement caused him to walk away from her, but she pressed on, feeling more defeated as she spoke. "They have much higher rank than I do and replaced me with someone *they* could trust, since I'm a hybrid . . . a being with one foot in the human world and one in the wolf world." She blew out a weary sigh. "I'm probably not even defined as a human being. I wonder if I even have the same civil rights as the average citizen . . . and as long as I'm in uniform, most of that shit doesn't apply anyway."

Hunter turned to look at her and pointed out toward the mist. "I don't care about their stupid, short-sighted laws—*you exist*, therefore you are a being with inalienable rights.

They summoned you down into the bowels of their military base, which to me is no different than one of our clan dens, and then set upon you like a ravenous pack! Then they placed you under the command of a full-blooded human who knows nothing of our ways or those of the paranormal community's! They have done what they have always done—broken a treaty, a covenant that would keep the peace between the nations . . . and, yes, Sasha, this is like having a human diplomat that was well-liked and well-respected get replaced by a fool. You do realize that if the humans do a pre-emptive strike on the paranormal community, this is undoubtedly going to be war?"

"I know," she said quietly and then closed her eyes as she let out a slow breath.

"This time, they will not be able to just exterminate what they find. Genocide will not be allowed."

"I know," she repeated, now staring at him.

"As Alpha clan leaders, we have to make the packs aware of the situation, as well as alert our allies."

Sasha just nodded, too weary at the prospect of what this could all mean to even speak.

"I'll alert my grandfather. Silver Hawk can carry the message throughout the region. I can also contact my brother, Shogun. However, we should both speak directly to Sir Rodney."

"I can't leave the area, remember," Sasha said flatly, and then turned to begin to walk deeper into the mist.

"Then where are you going?" Hunter jogged to catch up to her.

"To the bar to throw back a fifth of Jack Daniels with my very dejected squad."

Hunter grabbed Sasha's arm and stayed her leave. "I've never seen you like this," he said quietly.

"Like what?" she said, blowing out a hard breath and blinking back tears.

"So angry that you've lost your drive to fight. You're letting them win."

"Maybe you haven't noticed, but they *have* won, Hunter." She released a sad chuckle and then looked away from him. "I've been put out of my human pack, okay? One botched mission and they turned on me."

"It wasn't a botched mission," he said, not letting go of her arm and forcing her to look at him with his voice. "It wasn't," he added more gently.

"But that doesn't matter, now does it?"

"Yes, it does." Hunter's gaze searched her face. "It matters to the countless paranormal nationals that got saved. The humans aren't the only ones that exist. Sasha . . . you are a head of state."

"In a secret world," she said more quietly than intended. "An unrecognized, secret world—but to them, I'm just a grunt."

"Never, ever say that in front of me again," he said in a low, firm murmur. "You are not a word I refuse to dignify by repeating. You are not a lab mistake. You are a North American Clan alpha she-Shadow." Hunter lifted his chin and cupped her cheek with his palm. "You are majestic, Sasha Trudeau. You are a warrior and it is time for the wolf within to decide which pack she wants to belong to—theirs or ours . . . but that is always going to be your decision. I will wait, no matter what."

Deep conflict tore at her insides. The time was fast approaching when she would have to decide if she was going to fulfill her duties or leave it all behind and go AWOL. And if she did . . . the hunter would become the hunted.

Experience the dark pleasures and animal passions of

CRIMSON MOON

The acclaimed series from *New York Times* bestselling author

L.A. BANKS

BAD BLOOD
ISBN: 978-0-312-94911-2

BITE THE BULLET
ISBN: 978-0-312-94912-9

UNDEAD ON ARRIVAL
ISBN: 978-0-312-94913-6

Available from St. Martin's Paperbacks

Don't miss the Vampire Huntress Legend™ Novels
from *New York Times* Bestselling Author

L. A. BANKS

MINION
ISBN: 978-0-312-98701-5

THE AWAKENING
ISBN: 978-0-312-98702-2

THE HUNTED
ISBN: 978-0-312-93772-0

THE BITTEN
ISBN: 978-0-312-99509-6

THE FORBIDDEN
ISBN: 978-0-312-94002-7

THE DAMNED
ISBN: 978-0-312-93443-9

THE FORSAKEN
ISBN: 978-0-312-94860-3

THE WICKED
ISBN: 978-0-312-94606-7

THE CURSED
ISBN: 978-0-312-94772-9

THE DARKNESS
ISBN: 978-0-312-94914-3

THE SHADOWS
ISBN: 978-0-312-94915-0

THE THIRTEENTH
ISBN: 978-0-312-36876-0

Available from St. Martin's Paperbacks

BAN Banks, L. A.

Cursed to death.

Lgw